Puddin' for Breakfast

Mary,
Thank you.
Enjoy the read —
I enjoyed writing it.
Smiles,
Jo Anne

Puddin' for Breakfast

Joanne Bunyak

This is a work of fiction. All names, characters, places and incidents are fictitious figments of the author's imagination, or are used fictitiously. Any resemblance to any actual events, names, places or persons, living or dead, is entirely coincidental.

US Library of Congress Copyright © 2009 by Joanne Bunyak under the title *Puddin' for Breakfast*

Registration Number: TXu1-585-415

All rights reserved by the author. No part of this book may be produced or transmitted in any form, or by any means, without the written agreement of the copyright owner.

ISBN: Hardcover   978-1-4363-9581-6
          Softcover   978-1-4363-9580-9

This book was printed in the United States of America.

To order additional copies of this book, contact:
Xlibris Corporation
1-888-795-4274
www.Xlibris.com
Orders@Xlibris.com
57073

CONTENTS

One Bright Morning 9
J 11
Anna's Dream 15
The Wedding Gift 21
Breakfast Pudding Recipe 31
Timmy 32
That Damned House 33
Simpler Times 41
What a Memory! 51
A Nickel 53
Shoes from a Catalog 56
Pet 62
Full October Moon 63
We're Goin' on a Picnic 70
One Special Christmas 73
The Watermelon Dress 81
Jake 84
Holy What? 85
Fishing from The Raft 98
Soft Bunnies 106
Happy Mother's Day! 110
The Feed Man 112
That Hurts 119
Junk Yards And Treasure Hunts 123
A Day of Giving Thanks 126
Cindy 137
What's Insulin? 138
Puddin' For Breakfast 148
The Last Trip 158
Junior 164
A Summer To Remember 165

Goin' Fishin'	179
What's Next, Jake	183
Polly	194
Cry, Baby, Cry	195
He's Coming Back	206
Sleeping in the Hay	220
Easter Morning Coming Down	233
Finally A Freshman	241
A Quick Date	250
One Week Was Enough	260
Good Deeds	268
A Priestly Visit	273
So, You Want A Job!	281
Driving Blondie	294
Adela	299
You're Goin' Where?	300
A Wedding or a War	319
Time Flys	339
Where Does the Time Go	352
Just Let Me Walk	360
Bud	370

A photograph of the author in her watermelon dress, which sparked the idea for this novel.

ONE BRIGHT MORNING

After 48 years together, they stood in the warmth of the sunlight.
She unthinkingly gazed at him, and he at her.
He saw her hair as glistening gold . . . sun kissed.
She saw his hair as shimmering silver . . . moon emblazoned.
Her eyes also glistened . . . ever green . . . much like on their first Christmas morn.
His eyes were a grayed hazel . . . holding memories of the past . . . youthful sunlit days.
Her cheeks remained soft and rosy . . . another memory . . . a wedding day long ago.
She studied his handsome weathered face. It still held an inner strength unlike any.
Her frail hand reached for that strength that his hands still possessed . . . he reached to her in kind.
They smiled softly at one another . . . a smile that had endeared pleasures, and endured pain, over so many years.
Slowly, one lonely tear trickled down onto the pinkness of her cheek.
She lowered her head, whispering so quietly that he almost missed the anguished words,
"We've become so old!"
He gently returned a whisper, "No, my sweetheart, we're not old . . . we've just taken the time to be loved.

J

This story's about J.
She's the core of this book.
Her young life, one big pustule,
read on, take a look!

She was christened Johanna,
then nicknamed Joni or J.
Her Dad called her Clementine,
the name that would stay.

She grew up in the midst of confusion;
coming from a dysfunctional family, at best.
Her education sought grace and salvation,
while her nursing skills found the world a test.

Don't think her complacent,
just the opposite is true.
Down to earth is her motto.
Individualism, also, will do.

Some early role models,
must have been just and kind
to reach beyond the borders
of an innocent's mind.

She saw what she saw
and heard what she heard.
Hope after hope
flew away like a bird.

She did have an angel,
a guardian, dear.
One who held her hand tightly
and kept her ever so near.

When her Baba left this earth,
she said, "I won't be too far away.
I'll gently watch over you, and
I won't let you stray."

"Do good with your life.
It will be better than here
in this damned old house,
where you'll never find cheer."

"I'll help you find happiness,
I know that I can.
When you know Heaven on earth,
it will be with one special man."

"Your soul mate, he'll be.
He'll love you forever.
Josef was my true love,
may you inherit my treasure."

J will attempt to tell
a secret tale or two.
Heaven and earth know
that they're long overdue.

Trials along the way? She's had quite a few.
Pains and troubles? There have been too many.
Love and joys? She's enjoyed one helluva lot.
Regrets in her life? There's almost been not any.

Deigned a strong inquisitive character,
Her life's lessons were always driven hard.
Scars may have been kept tucked deeply,
though she never drew the lucky high card.

She escaped the grandma's curse,
when she left that *damned old house*.
Who knows, she may return to visit one day,
in the spirit form of a nosey old mouse.

She was the first of her family
to receive a college degree.
She became a registered nurse,
learning quickly, nothing in life came free.

As a compassionate nurse
for more than 30 years,
she earned the reputation
as an intuitive consoler of tears.

She loved her nursing jobs,
seeking perfection in many ways.
Her many patients became her many friends,
and it is them for whom she now prays.

Someday she'll reach her final reward,
when she meets St. Peter at the Golden Gate.
She'll prance through quite fiercely, for it's known
that she's paid the earthly commission rate.

She'll drift her way up through the clouds
where God will be heard to say,
"I don't think I'm ready for this inquisitive one . . .
not now, no how, no way!"

Today though, she writes her thoughts and memories.
She shuffles her words around once, at times twice more.
She lets her feelings rise to the heavens,
finally allowing her spirit to soar!

She thinks about reincarnation,
and wonders aloud at times.
"Anna and Josef, J and Ben.
Chance meetings or soul-mate mimes?"

ANNA'S DREAM

Anna shifted her body slowly so she wouldn't awaken Josef, although it had been Josef who'd awakened Anna with a soft moan and his throbbing manhood pressed against her backside. Willingly, Anna turned to face him, but in those brief seconds his hardness had dwindled to a stump and he had begun to snore again. Josef was nearing fifty and his health was precarious these days. Although Anna knew she was no spring chicken, she often longed for the old days when she and Josef would rollick freely on the fresh summer's hay in the barn loft, or make love on the dewy grass under the balmy spring stars. She remembered how often they had lain together on the cold kitchen floor boards near the warmth of the winter's blazing coal stove after the children had gone to bed. He may have turned old, but Anna felt youthful and still had the cravings of a hot blooded Gypsy tramp. She had learned that it didn't pay to dwell on her memories, so she forced herself to concentrate on the moment and she quickly realized that this moment had cooled considerably in more ways than one.

The air had become frosty cold in their small bedroom and it only took a brief second for her to realize that she needed to go downstairs to get the fire blazing again. Although the log cabin had been shingled over, it was still poorly insulated and the dampness seeped through the crevices causing a mustiness to linger in the air. The large gaps between the logs allowed the heat to escape through the tar paper, at times quicker than the flames could spit out the warmth from the lowly kitchen coal stove.

It was just past midnight, but Anna knew that she needed to go shovel some more coal onto the stove's hot ashes. It seemed to Anna that the bituminous coal must have burned away quicker than she'd anticipated. She knew the soft coal had a tendency to burn much faster than the hard anthracite. She should have thought of that before climbing the stairs for the night. She thought that she'd banked the coal chunks before going to bed, but then again, maybe she'd forgotten. She had gone to her bedroom feeling exhausted after working all day in the unusually cold weather to prepare the vegetable garden for early spring planting, as well as doing her usual daily housework and cooking for her family of seven.

After a few minutes, Anna built up enough courage to slink out from under the warmth of their padena, a feather-filled quilt made with pieces of blue-striped ticking material. Her feet slowly made their deliberate descent to the icy-cold floor. She reached out in the dark to feel for the candle stub she'd left on the wooden crate that was her current nightstand. Finding the candle, her fingers then grappled for the box of wooden matches lying next to it. Striking one match, Anna was able to bring a flame to the candle wick and sparingly shed enough light onto the bedside flooring to find her shoes. Slipping her warm toes into her cold shabby leather shoes, she shuddered before finding the old and tattered woolen shawl she had left hanging on the bed post. Wrapping the thin coverlet around her shoulders, she aimed her shivering body toward the staircase.

Stepping through to the short hallway, she looked in on her five children. They were all sleeping soundly. Their thin, narrow mattresses were aligned side by side in the tiny room that served as the children's one and only bedroom. Jack, the eldest, was snoring. Anna watched as Mihal, her youngest son, reached across to nudge him. "Stop your snortin', Jack. You're gonna wake everybody up," he whispered to his brother.

Glancing up at the intrusive candle light, Mihal quickly arose from his bed and asked, "What's wrong, Ma? Why are you up? It must be late."

"Yes, Son, it is late. Get back under your covers. Hurry, before your blankets cool," Anna said.

Her whole body gave a quiver when she had begun to speak. Her breath gave off steam just as Mihal's had when he had spoken into the cold night air.

"I'm going downstairs to stoke the fire and put on some more coal. It's so cold up here, even with that register opened the air feels like it could freeze off our noses," Anna said, as she pointed to the curlicue metal grate on the youngster's bedroom floor, which had been purposely positioned directly above the kitchen stove to circumvent the rising heat into the children's bedroom. That one registered opening was the sole source of heat to the upstairs two bedrooms. Anna knew that they'd need a larger stove installed before the next winter set in. Josef's deteriorating health would demand it.

"I'll go, Mom," Mihal said. "You go back to bed and I'll take care of the stove," he uttered through chattering teeth. "Give me your shawl. It's mighty damn cold in here."

Wrapping the woolen rag around his shoulders, Mihal took the burning candle from his mother and gingerly began stepping down onto the rough wooden stairs. Mihal had learned early on that it was necessary to step softly and squarely onto the uneven planks. Experience had taught him to comprehend the severity of a puncture wound. He was well aware that his thin socks wouldn't stop a stubborn splinter from bending upward to penetrate the soles of his feet. With every step, Mihal judged his steps cautiously. Mihal had already had a go-round with a rotten wood shaving and so he reminded his feet not to repeat the performance as he maneuvered the stairs.

Snuggled warmly next to Josef, Anna fell asleep listening to the banging noises Mihal made while tending to the kitchen stove's fire. Her last thought before dozing off to a sound slumber was of the pride she felt toward her maturing, good-natured children. They all were hard workers. None of them complained about their hardships. None of them bore any malice toward their parents for pulling them out of the one-roomed Gunther Elementary School to find work in the mine or the clothing factory. They all seemed to understand the necessity of their employment. Anna had described how their father was gravely ill with the miner's lung disease. She told them that he probably wouldn't live much longer if he had to continue working in the cold dampness of the coal mines. The mine's company doctor had explained that Josef needed outside work in the sunshine if he was to have any chance of extending his lifetime. The family comprehended their father's ill-fated diagnosis and unselfishly responded to the medical man's knowledgeable suggestions. Anna had only to make the requests to her children and they were amendable.

As Anna dozed soundly, she dreamt of Mihal, the youngest of the children. He was the only child born to her and Josef. Now thirteen years old, he was six feet tall and brawny. His hair was thick auburn and wavy. His face was God-like, as though chiseled by a gifted sculptor. With Greek-like features, his high cheekbones exaggerated the deep-set grey eyes. A cleft chin set him distinctly apart from his siblings, but mirrored Josef's facial features. He had a smile that lit up a room. All he had to do was beam his large pearly teeth and girls in any setting swooned. Anna's lady friends told her "Mihal had charisma", but Anna only asked herself in wonderment, "What the Hell is charisma?"

Anna had often wondered what was to become of Mihal and his handsome appearance once he was old enough to appreciate the effect it had on women. She had noticed his head turned when attractive women entered a room, especially blondes. Mihal was taller than Josef and far more impressive. Anna was just grateful that he was such a decent boy. He was considerate, yet humble. Everyone, it seemed, took an instant liking to her charming Mihal. Yet Anna knew the time would soon arrive when her Mihal would discover the joys that would unfold as he matured and began courting the women who he now only admired from across a room.

In addition to Mihal, Anna and Josef had three other boys and one girl to contend with. They were a good looking bunch, but homely when compared to their Mihal. Anna never did reveal to Josef who the fathers of the other four children were. Anna justified her illicit deeds in her own gratified moral conscience. She was putting food on the table and managing their farming lifestyle, all while keeping the overhead cabin roof from caving in on the lot of them, Anna was satisfied with her rationalizations. It was a delicate balance, but it was a norm for their depressed era. Despite her actions, in her heart Anna remained faithful to Josef and that was all that mattered to the two of them. A compassionate Anna couldn't stand by as Josef worked long, hard hours in the coal mines. She knew his paycheck was barely enough to keep the property taxes and his doctor bills paid. She buried her pride and did what she'd always done to keep her family afloat.

Anna realized that her husband had to have suspected something was amiss, because no two of their five kids bore any direct similarity to one another. Anna explained away the different skin shades, the mixture of hair colors and their short stocky statures by comparing them to her European relatives. Josef seemed accepting and amendable to her reasonable explanations. Mihal, though, had an undeniably remarkable resemblance to her Josef. There were no doubts there. He was definitely Joseph's off-spring, and he was Josef's absolute concept of a good son. One true son was enough for Josef. He could live with the rest.

As Anna slept, her dream lingered. She seemed to be standing on the sidelines and watching as Mihal danced smoothly to polka music with a tall and slim blonde Polish beauty who had wavey hair that hung to her waist. She smiled sweetly when she looked at Mihal but sneered when his back was turned, and it was then that her face became that of a jackal's. There were children, all sizes and ages, dancing to the quick-stepping music mimicking Mihal and the blonde. There was another man in Anna's dream. He was a tall, sandy-haired, blue-eyed stranger who kept cutting in on Mihal and the blonde as they danced. Mihal would gallantly step aside, then go to a darkened corner and weep.

Anna was trembling violently when Joseph shook her awake. "What's wrong with you, my love?" Josef asked with a lilt of concern in his voice.

"I've had a bad dream, about our Mihal. I haven't had any dreams for years. The last time I dreamt about anyone, it was my mother. Don't you remember when a few weeks later we got word that she had died? This is a foretelling that our Mihal is in for a storm when he gets of age. He will never find true contentment with the woman he chooses as his wife. You will see, Josef. You will see."

Anna, the fortune-telling gypsy, had resurfaced. Her talents had lay doemant since coming to America, but now she realized that the foreshadowing compelled an urgent obligation to her son. "I saw him crying out in anguish. He was calling out to me. He couldn't understand what he'd done to deserve the shame or the pain a bastard son had brought upon him."

Anna's emotions seethed, as she dreaded awaiting the wretched events she'd seen in her tormented dream.

"Get me my ring, Josef. I want to look into the ruby and see what agony our child will endure. I want to prepare myself for his desperations, for there will come a day when he will need me. I feel certain of that."

Anna continued her cosmic reading, predicting bits and pieces of the life to come for her Mihal.

"He will be given two bastard children, a boy and a girl. From an evil beginning, the boy will cause him misery, but the girl will bring him joy with her unconditional love. For better or for worse, Josef, our son will have to live out his life as the Gods have professed."

Anna had spoken to her husband while still in a hazed trance. What her watchful eye had seen in the gemstone frightened her. There was nothing she could do now about the future plans of the Heavens. She could only stand by and wait and watch for opportune moments to come to her son's aid. In the years to come, she remained vigilant to monitor the Polish woman's deceit. Then, and only then, would Anna call upon her ancestors to help her place the ultimate curse on the witch whom Mihal would one day marry. The blonde woman would never escape the Gypsy woman's curse. That was the one sure bit of soothsayer knowledge Anna held in her heart. Her soul knew that curse was etched in The Great Beyond. When the blonde woman committed those wrongs against Mihal, Anna would be ready. The blonde one would live to regret her maliciousness. That too had been seen in the core of the ruby ring.

"Go back to sleep, Josef," Anna whispered, as she wrapped her arm gently across her husband's back and nestled her body into the curve of his back.

"Sleep away into the morning. You don't have to rise early. It's Saturday. I'll help you rake the hay from in the fields. We'll get the children to help and the work will be done in no time at all. Forget about my dream for today. We'll come to terms with my predictions when they come due. Go back to sleep my honechko, my dear one," she cooed.

The endearment fell on sleeping ears. Josef was already snoring contentedly. He knew Anna had envisioned Mihal's tortuous future, but for the moment all was as it should be.

THE WEDDING GIFT

"What do you mean you don't want to live with us in our house on Lemon Lane?" Mihal asked his future bride, Blondie.

"It's a pig sty," she answered sullenly, "and besides, your folks still live there!"

"What do you want me to do? Throw them out on their ear?" Mihal asked.

"This is their house! They're givin' it to us for a wedding present, but they're still gonna live here with us," he insisted.

Anticipating a sympathetic response, he continued, "My dad is sick with cancer and the coal miner's black lung disease from working in the dank coal pits. My mother takes care of him and everything else in that house. It's the only life she's known since her husband joined her here in America."

"Yeah, yeah, I know," Blondie sassed. "I've heard it all before. She's raised five kids in that house and all of you grew up just fine! There are only four rooms, a pantry, and a cellar. How she managed is a wonder! Where'd she make all that moonshine? Where did she hide it? Better yet, what'd she do with all the money she got from sellin' it?"

Blondie's harsh questions pounded like a sledge hammer in the closeness of the small kitchen. Determined to persuade Mihal to go out on his own and find a house for just the two of them, she persisted. "We don't need a big house. Let's just find somethin' of our own," she pleaded.

"I don't want to face your mother every mornin' after making love all night! Can't you see my point?" she wailed as tears streamed down her cheeks.

"Oh! I can see your point, but it's not gonna make me change my mind. I don't have tons of money stashed in a shoe box somewhere, and neither do you. Where will we get the money to buy any kind of a house? Answer me that," Mihal shouted.

"Whatever little money my mother got for sellin' her hooch, she earned. She took a lot of chances. She's lucky she didn't get caught by the local cops and thrown in jail! And another thing, she used her money wisely to buy this land and house for herself and her family. With the left over money, she bought houses as weddin' gifts for my three brothers and my sister, Maryanne," Mihal responded with an air of pride for his mother's diligent accomplishments.

"She didn't squander her money, but her finances have run out and so has her spirit! I'm the one left to look after my parents. It's my place to take care of them now that they're old. That's the custom and that's how it's gonna be! Can't you try to understand?" He had stood his ground, determined to convince Blondie with his instinctive reasoning.

Blondie confronted defiantly. Mihal was put on notice that there was nothing lacking in Blondie's fiery spirit. "Sure, it's easy for you. You know your parents' customs and habits. They know how it is to live in this shack of a house. I'm not so sure I want to learn this life of such ignorance."

Sobbing, she continued, "Just because you think you have me over a barrel knowin' I'm pregnant doesn't mean I can't still leave you here to rot! Our weddin' hasn't even been planned yet. I'll be damned if I'm gonna put up with this kind of crap all my life!"

A frightened Mihal stood staring wide-eyed at his tall, slim, blonde beauty. "I can't believe you'd threaten to walk out on me! You know I don't have much to offer you, but I do love you. I will love our child. It doesn't matter if you're pregnant, as you call it. We can make a good life, you'll see!" he said. Drawing her close and kissing her passionately, Mihal was successful at temporarily diffusing the intensity of the moment. He never doubted his charm. It always worked with the ladies.

Just as the honeycomb becomes molten in the hot July sun, so too did Blondie melt. She blended right into his arms. He knew that would happen. She couldn't resist him. He knew that, too. He knew exactly how to woo his woman. His impressively chiseled face had won him favors with women for quite a few years before he found Blondie, but this was the woman he wanted for his own. He had fallen for her at first glance. "She sure was a beauty!" It was a phrase he'd repeat many times throughout the course of their fifty-six year marriage.

Being of Ukrainian and Hungarian gypsy heritage, Mihal had been called handsome and charismatic, but this was the one moment when he had to reach deep within his soul and call upon that charm. Blondie conceded. She couldn't resist this statuesque man with the face of a Greek God. He was going to be her husband. She knew she had made all of her girlfriends envious. She had cast her line and had been the one who caught the one man they were all trying to snag! *I got him, hook, line and sinker* was a thought she'd arrogantly embrace during the months of their courtship.

Any disagreements about the housing situation were put on hold. Wedding preparations were placed in the fore-front, and all relatives' purse strings were loosened to give the love birds a gala July 18, 1931 celebration. It only took a week to coordinate a church ceremony to be held by a Polish priest in a Polish church. An impromptu Polish reception held at Blondie's parental home took even less time to organize.

Money was scarce, jobs were at a premium, and getting by was a struggle in these tough times. Deciding to borrow her cousin's wedding gown and veil, Blondie's enthusiasm heightened. The borrowed outfit was as good as new. It had only been worn once. The white silk dress was ankle length with an empire-waist and long pointed sleeves. It just needed a stitch here and a tuck there to fit the lanky young woman perfectly. A veil of white Chantilly lace would be held in place by a braided crown of waxen pearly teardrops. She would carry a bouquet of large pink crepe paper roses, handmade by her girlfriends. Her slightly worn shoes were bought in a small, local second-hand shop at the lowly cost of fifteen cents! Her long white-cotton stockings cost a nickel! With her bridal outfit complete, the only thing missing was a shiny gold wedding band which Mihal would present to her during the tedious Catholic ceremony.

Blondie used a portion of her sewing factory wages to buy Mihal his wedding ring. Little did she realize that he would wear it only on their wedding day and then once again in his casket. "I don't need some ring to tell me I'm married to you, Blondie. A ring is for the woman to remember who her man is," he told her when they finally bedded down for a bliss-filled honeymoon night.

With limited change in his pockets, Mihal was concerned about where his money would be spent. So he wore the same dark blue vested suit he'd worn a year ago when he was best man at his brother's wedding. Not having a single pair of socks without holes, he did have to spend ten cents for a pair of black silk stockings bought at the five and dime store in the neighboring town. His shoes were also leftovers from George's wedding. Mihal's feet had grown in the past year, unlike his bank account. There was nothing to be done about the almost new shoes except to experience the day with his toes curled under. His pal, John, suggested, "Shoot the tips off the shoes," but not a one of his pals were courageous or idiot enough to fetch the shotgun!

It wasn't until Mihal had drunk a few beers during the reception that he got the notion to take the shoes off. If nothing else, it made for a good laugh as he kicked them under a chair and teased, "Oh, what the hell! What's a weddin' if the groom can't dance in his stockin' feet and kick up a little sawdust with his bride?"

And kick up a bit of dust they did. As newlyweds, they danced well into the night, not skipping a beat to the jovial Polish and Slovak tunes being played by drunkards on old world instruments. Finding themselves fatigued, they eventually gave in to slumber and dozed quietly as they sat cock-eyed on a couple of rickety-wooden kitchen chairs. Awakened by exuberant laughter in the wee hours of the morning, Blondie's mother's shrill cackle chased them off to an upstairs bedroom. "Shoo, you two! Go find yourselves someplace to sleep on this your wedding night!"

Some guests were still dancing to the polka music being played on an old-world concertina by the bride's father. He was accompanied by a beer-sodden fiddle player who had a problem standing, let alone trying to mark time with the music. The one, two, three tempo held the musical notes in the air until the dancer's frenzied feet hit the floor. Wide smiles on the guests cheerful faces radiated pure and simple enjoyment for those caught up in the rapture of dancing at a festive occasion in an economically depressed era.

Some lingering guests were trying their best to drink dry the rotund kegs of beer, while others ate from the remaining vestiges of ethnic foods laden on the large platters that were strewn about the kitchen and dining room. Wafting aromas of cabbages, breads, cakes, ham and kielbasa lingered throughout the house. The pungent aromas convinced all persons attending this gala that the bride's parents had, without a doubt, provided a joyous feast for these newlyweds.

At three o'clock in the early morning, Mihal and Blondie stumbled up the stairs. They blushed as they overheard giggles and snickers from their friends. "We know where you're goin', and what you're gonna do. You're goin' to your bedroom and you're gonna screw!"

The lively partiers had locked arms and laughed boisterously as they swayed to the beat of the rhythmic tune they were singing to the dreamy-eyed newlyweds.

The shy couple ignored the cajoling and pretended to be oblivious to the crude remarks. "Let them say what they want. We're married now," Mihal whispered, as he gently pulled his bride closer to his heated body and began caressing her breasts.

"Let's go do what they think we're gonna do. How about it, Blondie? Let's go have us a real weddin' night. Tonight you are my virgin," Mihal cooed.

Blondie was as eager and ready as any hot-blooded bride would ever be as she climbed the staircase. She felt quite secure snuggled in her handsome husband's embrace.

The festivities had begun on Saturday the 18th. When the visiting relatives first arrived they were greeted as revered guests. A week later, on Saturday the 25th, the tune changed from merry praises to vile insults. The "God damned parasites" were being shoved out of the front door to the uncomplimentary undertones of Polish cursing calling them "freeloaders".

"What the Hell were those jackasses waitin' around for, another weddin'?" The bride's father asked. His generous attitude had rapidly deteriorated.

Even the worst of the ethnic curses was heard coming from the bride's mother, "Dog's blood to the devils. May they return to Hell!"

Blondie's parents were perhaps as happy to be rid of the loitering idiot guests as they were to be finally rid of their nineteen year old spinster daughter. Three of Blondie's younger sisters had married long ago and had already delivered healthy chubby babies for the grandparents to bounce merrily on their knees. Blondie had some catching up to do, and do she did. It would seem that it didn't take long at all before she had babies crawling all around *that damned house.*

The newlyweds would move in with Mihal's parents the day after their wedding, but agreed to save their pennies for a home of their own. They quickly learned pennies were hard to save in a household where Mihal was the only breadwinner. The two women didn't have any income. Mihal's mother was too old and frail to be of much use for any substantial workload. Blondie was younger, but soon found herself suffering a pregnancy that awakened her every morning with bouts of dry heaves and nausea. Her condition was also complicated by a fatiguing flare-up of her chronic iron-deficiency anemia.

Added to the household mix was Mihal's sickly father. He spent his days dozing quietly in an overstuffed chair and his nights moaning on his straw-mattress bed. He did little other than sip broth when he felt hungry, or get out of his bed to use the slop jar when he needed to facilitate his toileting needs. It was only a matter of time before he'd be out of the equation.

There was only one paycheck coming into the house and that was Mihal's $15 every Friday. This meager sum came from hard labor in a coal tunnel-mine where Mihal worked ten to twelve hours, five days a week.

As time marched on, so did Mihal. It seemed he met himself coming and going on the roadway leading to and from the Koxis coal mines. *I must have been crazy to get myself strapped with a family. Why didn't I enjoy my freedom when I had it* his thoughts lamented. He forced his daily steps forward. He had no choice and he knew it.

I should have listened to my Dad about this hot-tempered Polack. He said I'd be sorry if I married a pushy spoiled woman. She gets whinier every day. I did this to myself and now I'll pay for it. Oh, God, how I'll pay for it! Mihal had plenty of time to think while he hiked the miles to and from the coal mine.

His thoughts did not cheer him at all, especially when he had to listen to his wife's whimpering. Mihal learned quickly how Blondie could whine! Oh, could she ever whine!

"When are we gonna get our own house? When?"

"We've been here six months already, and there's still no money in our coffers."

"This baby will be here before you know it, and we'll still be here in this shack!"

"I have to listen to your mother's crap everyday! I don't know how much more of it I can stand!"

"Where are we gonna put this baby, in a dresser drawer? There's not enough room for us, let alone an added baby!"

"Your mother is drivin' me crazy with her slovenly ways. What other woman do you know who doesn't wear underpants, and who pisses standin' up anywhere she gets the urge?"

"And what other husband brings his paycheck home to his mother, not his wife? Tell me, Mihal! Tell me where she spends your money! I never see any of it! Then try to tell me how we're supposed to save for a God damned place of our own!"

Mihal began resenting her selfish attitude, her relentless ranting and her unnerving raving. He was doing his best under the circumstances. Turning to his friends for a little peace of mind, the weekends became an outlet to avoid arguments with Blondie. He resumed his previous roaming habits. His motorbike was pulled out of the storage garage. He began taking long rides into the countryside with his single buddies. Riding a motor bike was something Blondie couldn't do because of her pregnancy. He was actually glad about that! For a few hours each weekend he was able to ride with the breeze on his face and to think clearly. He relished this short-lived freedom.

These outings didn't last long, however. About a month to be exact! Once the baby arrived, Blondie quickly realized she was no longer encumbered by the pregnancy. She now insisted on riding with Mihal every time he'd take the motor bike out with his cronies. One ride on the old putt, putt, putting cycle and the clattering from Blondie began.

"Where do you think you're goin' and who said you're goin' without me?"

"Who said we're goin' to the Deerfield Fair?"

"I thought we were goin' home to Anscola to visit my folks."

"I can feel every wrinkle on the road. I feel as if I'm ready to fall off every time you hit a bump!"

"Why'd you ever buy this thing, anyway? It's a death trap!"

"Did you think you'd have your freedom forever? You better think again, Mister!"

On and on her complaints rode along with them and it took only a few weeks before Mihal realized what needed to happen.

The bike was sold. A bank account was opened. "Okay, Blondie, we're savin' for a house now! Satisfied?" a glum and resentful Mihal asked.

With her back turned to him, Blondie smiled wryly thinking *I can't wait to get out of this dump and away from his stinkin' mother, the bitch.* Then turning and facing her husband, she smiled demurely to him. "Thank you, Mihal. I knew you wouldn't let me down."

Her heart and her mind were racing though. Blondie was thinking again. She seemed to always be pondering her situation. She wanted to speak her piece, but she was reluctant to tell him that he had better not let her down or by damned he'd pay. She kept her thoughts crammed inside her brain. At times, her thoughts were so tightly bound that she thought her head would burst. She was intelligent and she remained sane enough to conceive *I've got him by the balls now that we've got this tiny baby girl to worry about. He's crazy for her.*

Right there and then, Blondie made a pledge to herself. *If he doesn't straighten out and start actin' like a husband, I'll take this kid and head back to Mom and my own little Anscola town myself! That will make him wise up real quick. I'm certain of that.*

Mihal had no choice. He knew his wife was clever and had him pegged as a soft mark. That little girl was visibly the apple of his eye, but before Petronella was six months old Blondie revealed to him that there was another apple growing on the tree! When that second apple fell from the womb, Mihal had a son, Mihal Jr. Now it really was time for Mihal to settle down and become the man of the house, even if *that damned houses* still belonged to his parents.

Blondie didn't have time enough to whine and complain anymore. Not with two toddlers constantly demanding her attention. She still pined for her own home. She didn't know it yet, but before too many years had passed, she'd have a peck of apple-cheeked babies under her care and four other babies planted six feet under. She eventually resigned herself to her station in Gunther and acknowledged to her lady-friends, "I'm now as stuck as horse's hooves in spring mud."

For the rest of her earthly days, Blondie regretted not having moved into a home of her own on her wedding day instead of into *this damned house* in this damned cow town.

The in-laws home remained just a house to Blondie. She refused to make any effort to conjeal Anna's attempts at comraderie. Blondie viewed Anna's attempts at conversations as raw and irritating gnawing. Many years ago, Blondie had decided to never accept Mihal's mother as her equal. "There's no castle big enough for two queens," was Blondie's rationalization of her escalating rudeness to her mother-in-law.

Mihal's father died one cold snowy January night. He simply fell asleep and then forgot to open his eyes in the morning. His wake was held in *that damned house*. The small parlor room was cleared of all its furniture. The casket remained on a catafalque at the one parlor wall without doors or windows. Baskets of flowers could be placed around the base without the danger of someone tripping over them.

Neighbors and co-workers gathered and mingled with the family. Light conversing flowed easily.

"He looks good for what he's been through."

"He had such a struggle to come to America."

"The poor guy really suffered with sickness these past few years."

"Thank God Mihal took such good care of him and his wife," was one comment overheard by Blondie as she poured coffee and served up the donations of cakes and cookies that had been brought to the house by the neighbors.

Mihal my ass she thought. "I'm the one workin' like a dog around here and takin' care of the house. Who do they suppose is doin' all the washin' and cookin' for the bitch and all these kids? Who do they think emptied his slop jar?" she mumbled to herself, hoping no one could overhear her loathing as she bustled around the confines of the kitchen.

She was beginning to hate *this damned house*, these bogus mourners, the gardening, the barn work and especially these rambunctious piss ant kids. She couldn't wait for the youngsters to get old enough to help with all of the work that needed to be done daily. "I'm gettin' pretty sick and tired of it all," she whispered to herself quite frequently.

Mihal thanked God daily that they were able to supply themselves with garden vegetables and tree fruits. Initially, one cow provided enough daily milk for the four of them, but soon it became necessary to have a few more milking cows. Although more cows meant more work for Blondie, the milk provided the heavy top cream to churn, which in turn gave them fresh butter and buttermilk several times a week. Meat was served on Sundays only, in the form of a roasted homegrown chicken or a vegetable beef-bone soup and noodles meal. Weekday meals were sparse vegetables or noodle dishes, but they sufficed. They had to. That's all there was to feed the growing family.

Blondie became adept at many skills. Canning fresh foods for winter use, boiling fruits and berries into jellies became her specialty. Baking dough into breads, pastries and Polish dishes rapidly became family necessities. Thankfully Blondie had learned cooking and baking from her own mother. Her talents became her own salvation.

Blondie's mother had acquired her skills from chefs and cooks while growing up in a large family in Warsaw. The Polish family had been wealthy and influential before coming to America. Their financial status dwindled quickly, however, after Blondie's father became ill and died from dropsy soon after arriving in Pennsylvania. Poverty soon followed, then a fire destroyed their homestead forcing Blondie, her siblings and their mother to be scattered among neighbors and friends until Blondie's mother remarried a gentle widower. Together they combined two families and survived the hardships that confronted the people during the depression of the 30's. Through hard work and diligence, they prospered. Life had indeed handed these immigrants dandelions and they surely learned how to convert the weeds into salads and wines!

Blondie learned to secretly be proud of her resourcefulness, just as her own mother had demonstrated. Bitterly referring to Mihal's mother, Blondie would confide her feelings to her neighbor friends. "The bitch can't boil a decent pot of water, but I can cook. I'm the one who puts the food on the table every day. This might be her house, but it's my kitchen," she'd tell them.

Because of her childhood diagnosis of anemia, Blondie was allowed certain privileges while growing up. As a youthful weakling, she wasn't permitted to help with any heavy manual labor or barnyard chores. Instead, she did light household chores and prepared meals. She didn't mind those duties. As a matter of fact, she appreciated having a chronic illness and used this platform to her advantage. She manipulated her station in the home. Her siblings often complained, "Blondie gets away with everything, just 'cause she's anemic." Most of the siblings had no idea what anemic meant. They were sure it just meant she got preferential treatment by their mother.

Blondie couldn't have cared less what they thought. "You're eatin' good, aren't you?" she'd blast back, "so, just shut up and enjoy your meal."

While growing up, farming was the last skill at which Blondie wanted to become knowledgeable, but that was a large part of her day after she married. Nor did she want charge of a large brood of children, but that became a definite reality also. Occasionally she'd glance at herself in a mirror. She still fancied herself a young and pretty woman. While Mihal worked long hours in the mines, and slept away his nights, Blondie found the way and the means to share her empty moments and her hungry lust with someone who made her heart sing and her hormones roar. She lived every waking moment longing for her Ed's arms. In her heart she knew she had enough kids and animals to satisfy the Gods, but the Gods weren't through with her yet. Not by a long shot!

On one early July morning in 1942, Blondie's cow, Bessie, gave birth to a healthy brown and white spotted bull calf. The next morning Blondie, at age 33, would give birth again in *that damned house* to another girl; her tenth pregnancy and her seventh daughter, so far. They would nickname this one "J". Her birth name would be Johanna. It would be in honor of Josef and Anna. The combined name would be at Mihal's urging, but it would only serve as another reason for Blondie's anger to rage. She had wanted the girl's name to be Edwina. Instead, she'd be reminded of her mother-in-law every minute of every day for the rest of her life and not Ed, the man she called "my true love".

Blondie had desperately hoped for a boy. She had so wanted a boy to replace her Timmy. During her eighteen years of growing and living in the house at #11 Lemon Lane, J would be told many times, "I wish you'd have died and my Timmy had lived. He was a big beautiful baby not a monkey face like you."

Through the years, tears would rain down Blondie's cheeks each time she described Timmy's untimely passing. "Too bad pneumonia got him when he was only six months old. He would have been the best of all you kids, I just know it!"

Often Blondie would be heard to utter, "My boys are the best things in my life. They'll always be my favorites."

"Younse girls are all nothin' but whores," Blondie would say to her daughters at the slightest irritation. It usually didn't take much annoyance to provoke this volatile response from her.

Until J was fourteen years old, she had no idea what the word "whore" meant. She had hoped and assumed the word was a complement until a kind friend assured her that it definitely was not.

BREAKFAST PUDDING RECIPE

¾ cup cornstarch
1-1/3 cup sugar dash or 2 of salt
2 cups cold milk
6 cups scalded milk
4 teaspoons vanilla

(Chocolate variation:
Add 1-1/3 cups cocoa
Increase sugar to 2 cups)
Mix dry ingredients with cold milk.
Gradually add hot milk and cook until bubbling, then add vanilla.
Cool to lukewarm, if the kids will let it set in the pot that long.
# of servings: enough to feed a dozen kids and their makers!

TIMMY

Timmy, I didn't know you.
You were six months old when you died.
I'd be reminded of you when I got called a whore.
Told I should have been the one who died, I cried.
You lay forever in a cold grave
and in your mother's warm heart,
but according to her loyal prayers
you two were never far apart.

So, if you can hear me,
know that we all cared
for a brother we could have loved
and a life we should have shared.
Rest in peace, baby Timmy.
Know your life was not a ruse.
Your mother adored your sweetness
and never did let anyone fill your shoes.

THAT DAMNED HOUSE

"I put a curse on this house. It will be damned for your children and your children's children. You will never again be at peace here. The Gods will see to that, as a favor to me," the gypsy woman shouted to Blondie.

"I gave this house to you and my son as a wedding gift. You have turned it into a whorehouse. I know your dirty secrets . . . yours and that feed man's. I sold my body and soul to make this log cabin grow into a home for my family. Why must you show such disrespect? Those two innocent children will pay for your folly," she said, pointing to the boy and girl standing in the kitchen doorway.

"At every turn, Blondie, your wrath is upon the girl, but not the boy. Is that because he looks so much like your lover? Huh? What, you can't answer me? My Mihal will learn the truth before I die. I promise you that!"

With her tirade completed, the old woman turned to J, the girl she called her granddaughter, and said, "I will protect you from this heathen of a mother. I make you that promise, child."

Stunned by her mother-in-law's outburst, Blondie attempted some semblance of a retort, but the old lady, with the kid in tow, was already leaving through the warped wooden kitchen door. They were holding hands and headed for a walk somewhere, anywhere, away from *that damned house.*

Blondie tried calling out to the old woman, "You're nothing more than an old witch, you stupid bitch! They should burn your ass at the stake."

The old woman tauntingly cackled loud enough for her daughter-in-law to hear. "This witch will watch you burn in Hell. You'll see," Anna shouted back to Mihal's wife.

Anna slowed her angry steps so that J could keep up. The petite girl took tiny steps, as the backs of her legs were still stinging from her mother's whipping with the pliant willow switch. The youngster still didn't know what she had done to deserve such a beating, but that was the case many times.

The grandmother was so right about Blondie not needing an excuse to give J a beating. Blondie's flaring Polish temper was reason enough to reach for the switch and lash out at J, no matter who or what was the cause of her anger.

Skinny and fearful, J became the frequent recipient of her mother's lashings. J feared her mother with just cause, but she wouldn't show emotion during these beatings. J's refusal to cry only irritated her mother, who would then beat her even harder. J's fear resulted in a strong disdain toward her mother. Hatred grew out of that same just cause.

As grandmother and granddaughter strolled through Mihal's wooded acreage that particular day, J would be calmed by her grandmother's soothing rhythmical voice repeating her fanciful stories about coming to America. Anna would relive her story, but only as she would see it in her own memory, or so she thought. The little one walking beside her would remember the words in her own imagination as well, and repeat them someday to her own grandchildren.

As they walked, they sang softly. It was a short sing-song verse the Hungarian grandmother, Baba, had taught the children.

Honechko, dueschekko Sweet one, Dear one,
Ejas doh coschela? Are you going to church?
Veda ya na ejam, Boh. For sure I'm not going, God.
Ya bulla scheddha. I was there yesterday.

"You will grow up and leave this place. Life will be kind to you." Baba told J. The old woman had stepped into her fortune teller role at that moment, and began foretelling the girl's future. The singing calmed the attentive girl's trembling body. The coming story would sooth her quietly sobbing soul.

"Josef was so surprised when he came to me here in America," Anna began her story.

"I told him about the house I was able to buy for us. I knew the small log cabin wasn't much to look at, but it was all I could afford."

"I convinced him to believe that the evil deeds I had done were necessary for my survival. While I was waiting for him to come to America, I learned that making wine was my best way to make money. Selling it to the locals was easy, but I had to watch out for the constable. Somebody was always squealing on me. I hid the bottles of hooch behind the kitchen wall boards. No one ever found them, no matter how much they searched."

Speaking in halting broken English, mixed with her native Hungarian Finno-Ugric dialect, Anna said she was slowly able to explain to Josef about her life during her early two years without him. It had been a weary period since that fateful day when they had parted and said their loving goodbyes.

Attempting to embellish her story in a way that the child could understand, she continued talking. "I stood with my parents on the gray wooden platform of the Budapest railroad station dreaming of the day we would be reunited. Josef had vowed to follow me and my sisters to America, just as soon as the fates graced him with money for ship fare. I came to America with only one old, worn satchel. Inside was a shabby, dirty-wool coat, one black dress and a pair of well-traveled street shoes. My money was pinned to my petticoat for safe keeping. Nobody could be trusted. I knew that better than anyone."

When Anna had first met Josef Youstek, she found him to be a disgruntled and unemployed Ukrainian roaming the city streets of Budapest. Just to stay alive, he would beg for any menial job to earn a few coins or a meager meal. Anna had been kind to him. She was attracted to the handsome and interesting character, and so she persuaded him to travel with her family of Magyar gypsies. "Come on a journey with us. We'll teach you how to enjoy the rich man's scraps," she urged him.

Anna's gypsy family was an independent group. Loosely applied, they were gypsies, tramps and thieves who were able to travel freely about to enjoy their unorthodox lifestyle. Earning an honest living was the farthest thing from their happy-go-lucky minds. They willingly engaged in socially unacceptable practices to maintain their daily existence as a free-spirited bunch of rogues. They had their own ways of gainfully acquiring their needs. Their favorite method was working a crowd.

Attracting a group of townspeople allowed the shifty gypsies to cunningly steal money or jewels from the trusting peasants or unsuspecting rich. A few high-spirited family troubadours from their gypsy group would play lively music on the hurdy-gurdy organ and sing their playful tunes, slyly enticing the meandering persons to gather 'round. The slippery-fingered members of the clan would mingle with the crowd easily blending in with the distracted onlookers. Working in pairs, the gypsy thieves quickly reversed many jingling pockets into silent ones. By simply nudging or bumping into a bystander, a couple of attractive gypsies could often make enough pocket-change to buy food for a few days. Or, with a slightly exposed cleavage, the coquette of the pair would accidentally stumble on a pebble and then catch her fall by grasping onto her target's arm. She would then smile suggestively, while seductively hugging the unsuspecting victim, and only then would she apologize. "I'm sorry, I am so clumsy," she would swoon in a sultry voice. Meanwhile, the other of the pair practiced his expertise at pocket-picking and escaped with the plundered loot.

Fortune telling was another means of bringing some money into the clan's fold. This was Anna Negrej's specialty. Palm reading, tea leaves, a crystal ball or her ruby ring were all called upon to reveal the future. At times, she would use simple predictions. Adept at her craft, she cleverly convinced the addle-brained and the astute of her accuracy. By Anna's own admission, manipulation of the patron's own spoken words was the real key to her successful prophetic readings. Anna became highly skilled at her craft. Wearing a bright dress and a woven shawl to barely cover her almond skinned shoulders, she'd exude an air of confidence. "I can promise happiness will follow you and you're beloved, if you will only believe in each other," became a rehearsed sentiment. A few token coins became a hasty payment from an unsuspecting, but grateful, peasant. Ignorance bestowed many rewards to a crafty Gypsy.

Of course, as a patient but curious child with a diligent mind, J was fascinated to hear Anna spin her fable. "When I was a young girl," Anna would say, "I was a beauty. I had curves in all the right places. When I held my head high like an aristocrat, I could show off my long black curly hair. I had learned to spin a smooth tale to women who were as naive as eager children wanting to hear of romantic prospects in their lives, especially if they were told a tall, dark and handsome man was soon to enter into their future. They'd believe my fortune telling as if it were a Gospel from the Bible. After allowing a sneak peek at a voluptuous cleavage, the old and fat rich man could easily be lured into an alley with promises of entertaining gypsy pleasures. There the naïve man could rapidly be convinced to stay pleased, and to stay alive, by giving up their purse at gunpoint. That scenario only bought trouble though, and that meant the family would have to move again to stay ahead of the local constables. The stolen money would be spent loosely by the group and soon we'd be hungry again."

At this point in her story, Anna usually took the time to shake her head in wonderment. She'd laugh in a delicate stifled manner. "What a life we had in the Old Country," she'd say, as if in disbelief of the colorful chapters in her own fairytale.

"Hunger was our constant companion," she would explain of their nomadic group.

Anna would detail that most of the food was plucked from happenstance gardens found during their endless travels. Guard duty and pilfering fruit, vegetables or poultry became Josef's jobs of distinction. Though he was a man of short musculature stature, he seemed to fear nothing or no one. Anna admired him for his easy acceptance into her generally skeptical group of rogues.

The family quickly learned to rely on his pillaging. Sneaking into a vegetable patch or a chicken coop, Josef's unerring agility proved an asset to the band of gypsies. Spreading his coat out on the ground as a blanket, he was able to wrap and carry large quantities of food in a knapsack fashion. His provisions were the main ingredients for meals of soups or roasts. Preparing cooked foods in large caldrons over open fires became a familiar sight. The transported aromas of fresh vegetables or meats stewing were enough to gather the drifting gypsies into singing and dancing clusters while the meal was being readied for their dining pleasures.

"It was music to make the heart sing like the chirping nightingale and the feet to dance with the westerly winds," she'd explain. "We were as free as the four winds."

Anna explained that there were many joyful noises around their campfires. At times their jubilant chattering was so loud that it attracted other wayfaring strangers who were seeking a handout. Always vigilant for wardens, thieves or poachers, they became their own sentry. During their travels, they were asssured of surviving as a band of troubadours by guarding their own possessions.

Anna would continue her story by describing that it wouldn't take long for the townspeople to discover that a carousing band of gypsies was in their area. This knowledge would begin a quick search for the unwelcome intruders. The idle group of crafty drifters would escape by rapidly gathering their belongings and abandoning their campsite. Traveling about was easier when they had horse-drawn carts, but they mostly walked from place to place dragging their belongings on makeshift litters and pulling their prized hurdy-gurdy.

In blustery weather they would bundle themselves in their warmest woolens, or pull thick robes around their bodies for protection. "When it was cold and snowy, we'd look for a barn or shed where we'd spend the night huddled together. In warmer weather, we slept under the stars."

Anna explained how on hot summer days only bare essentials were tolerated and worn. This was the way Anna learned of comfort and expedience in doing without underclothes, much to the delight of the men she later seduced for the price of a home for her Josef.

Josef had banded with Anna's family in Budapest and traveled freely with them through Hungary and Romania. The young couple soon realized that confined lodgings only encouraged a seduction that couldn't be ignored. Anna and Josef found themselves in love, or more accurately "in heat", as Anna would later describe the courtship to her grandchildren, "We became like animals chasing and sniffing after each other."

During story-telling around her favorite setting, an evening bonfire, Anna would include spicy details of her nomadic life in *the old country* to keep the children interested in her fables. At times, she even dressed in her few remaining ornate old-world garments. Singing her native songs, she'd reverently dance the steps of a true gypsy around and around the blazing fire. Long into the starry night she reminisced until only golden embers glowed amidst the ashes.

She detailed an aimless lifestyle. It was an existence that left Anna and Josef yearning for security and riches. While roaming throughout Europe, they had heard many exciting stories about life in America. Tales were handed down from someone who knew someone, who knew still someone else who had gone to the great country.

"There's gold in the rivers."

"The rich throw money to the poor in the streets."

"There are plenty of jobs in the factories."

"If you work hard, you get good pay every week."

"You can even become the boss in some businesses."

"Food is everywhere. It's yours for the asking."

To Anna and Josef, these were as good as first hand accounts of life over there in the new and great frontier. They were smart enough to know that if they didn't take a chance while they were young, they'd never have the courage to leave once they started their own family. They weren't sure what adventures awaited them in America, but they felt it had to be better than the nomadic ways they were living in Budapest. They wouldn't learn, until many years after they had both arrived in Pennsylvania, just which hardships were eager to greet the ignorant foreigners.

By and by, it was hastily decided that Josef and Anna would have a wedding in a small Greek Orthodox Church near Budapest. It was shortly after that ceremony when Anna and her sisters sadly left for America. Knowing only too well that they would never see their aging parents again, at least not in this lifetime, they bid their sad adieus. Hoarding the family's meager savings, the frightened sisters traveled by cargo ship to Canada. The young women encountered many strangers and countless indescribable frightening mishaps as they then journeyed by train to find welcome refuge at a distant cousin's home in central Pennsylvania. There Anna would await Josef's arrival. Exactly when that would happen was anyone's guess. Anna knew she could be patient.

Eventually, Josef did arrive on her doorstep. One foggy April morning nearly two years later, he knocked on the heavy wooden door of a brown shingled house Anna called home. Although Josef had missed Anna's passionate companionship, he had remained true to their dream. He had bravely faced the fear that loomed over the peoples of Europe. As unnerving as the plague of earlier years, the unsettling issues between the Allies and the central Powers of Europe had begun to unfold.

A war was imminent. Any fool could see that. Josef's only wish was to safely leave Hungary before the battles began. Looking toward the Heavens, Joseph often thought *I can see the dark clouds forming overhead. I must get away from here and go to my Anna.*

He worked endlessly and ate sparingly while pinching every coin worth saving for the trip to be reunited with his bride. "I have to get out of here before the world explodes into a war. That's my only chance for a future with my Anna," he would repeatedly tell himself anytime doubt overcame him.

Anna had been patient, but she hadn't been unproductive. In anticipation of Josef's arrival, Anna grew increasingly eager to reveal her enterprising accomplishments to him. Josef had no way of knowing what surprises Anna held in store, but indeed it would only take a fleeting moment for him to stare in wonder at what awaited him.

Even in the early morning light of springtime, it became quite evident that Josef's Anna had grown larger. *She's fatter,* he thought. The picture in his head didn't match the one standing before him. She was still beautiful, but he paused to ponder *why is she now so fat?*

What the Hell? A billowing question arose in his mind. He wanted to draw her near, to inhale the lilac fragrance she was wearing, to just feel her warmth and to know that he had arrived safely to her side. He attempted to wrap his arms around her waist, but they didn't fit anymore. "What is going on? What has happened to her?" he asked himself.

"Josef, my love, is this really you?" she asked. "It has been two years. Let me look at you. Yes, yes, it is you. I can't believe you are here, but now that you have arrived I can finally have this baby. I've been waiting so long for you to be with me at that moment."

"A baby," a dumbfounded Josef paused before asking, "and you've been waiting all this time to give birth?"

How can that be? Josef's thoughts bounced around in his skull. Before he allowed her to answer, he realized that his wife had been unfaithful to him. A heat began to rise in his chest, but then he quickly remembered the many times he, himself, had been unfaithful with Anna's girlfriends back in Hungary. *I am a hypocrite. I am scum,* he thought. How could he expect her to remain pure and chaste when he hadn't?

"Hush, my Anna, I am here now, and you can have our baby."

He allowed her the deception. He would act the buffoon and let her keep her pride. He would raise the child as his own. He would be the child's father. No one else would be permitted to stake that claim. He and his Anna were together again. He was a very happy man. The next time he reached to hug her, everything meshed. "Ah! Love is great!" he whispered to his wife.

It was then Josef lifted his eyes to look around at the kitchen he had just entered. "Is this our house? You did this for us? How? How is this possible?"

Her answers took hours to tell, but it was his turn to be patient. He would listen to her tales of making wine out of dandelions, elderberries, blackberries, grapes, cherries or anything else that could be fermented in a jar. She would disclose to him how she had cleverly hidden the bottles of brew behind the kitchen wainscoting, so that not even the local police could detect the cleverly aligned boards. She even admitted selling herself for money to make late payments on the house loan to avoid losing all that she had worked for. She had done all of it for their future. Through quiet sobs, she murmured softly, "In my heart I have been faithful to you, Josef, in my heart."

She described eating beans and bread for weeks on end, just to pay off that same loan. The house and two hundred acres of flowering meadows were theirs. Anna's cheeks flushed and her eyes glistened as she asked her lover the question she had anticipated so frequently. "Aren't you proud of me, Josef?"

He could only smile and nod, "Yes, Anna, I am very proud of you."

Josef held her body close to his as he gently stroked her beautiful face. He watched her drift into a peaceful slumber just as the sunrise peeked through their cracked bedroom window. He had no way of knowing, but this was Anna's first restful sleep in two years

The grandmother's many words are echoes from the past, bouncing between two mountains; one explains truth, while the other describes fiction. Just as the grandchildren had to decide which was which, so can this storyteller and her readers. Anyone with a vivid imagination will not find it difficult to distinguish the truth between the two.

SIMPLER TIMES

In the late 1940's and early 1950's life was a post-war period of ease and opportunity. Depression days of the 30's were not forgotten, but they were challenged.

In a small Pennsylvania coal mining village named Gunther, life may have been simpler, but it wasn't easier for a burg that blossomed after WWII, thanks to the coal mining industry.

Earning a living and enduring a hardship went hand in hand. A penny was never overlooked, no matter where it was found A cup of coffee, a glass of homemade wine or a loaf of fresh bread were all respected for the labor that went into their making. When a glass of homemade root beer was poured, none was wasted; that was a treat and a half! When, or where, the next meal or drink came from was always in question for many of the impoverished families in this small coal mining town.

Everything, it seemed, could be used for something! Not much was discarded. The simplest item could be made useful. A matchstick attached to an empty thread spool by a rubber band became a makeshift toy tractor. This simple contraption could keep a child playing contentedly in a dirt pile for hours. Try and make his happen today. Kids would laugh their parents off of the planet.

A print flour sack could be recycled to make a bolero with a matching skirt for a teenaged girl. The sack's white fluffy flour helped create sweet-smelling, mouth-watering yeast breads, cinnamon rolls, apple dumplings, lemon meringue pies, raisin-filled cookies, crumb or fruit cakes. That one sentence alone should be enough to make one drool with envy at a bygone era.

Ethnic foods prevailed in the homes of this small town. Pierogi and halushki were two examples of low cost Polish dinner dishes that pleased the palates and filled the bellies at #11 Lemon Lane. Many dishes of other ethnicities began in the flour sack and took all day to prepare, unlike today's twenty minute quickie-meals. Fifty pounds of bleached flour was always stretched to the limit by the homemakers of this era. Even accidentally spilled flour was swept into a can, and when mixed with a little water made glue for a kite or a magazine photo collage. Paper dolls wearing catalog dresses could, and did, keep a girl creatively busy for hours. "Waste not, want not" was a frequently applied phrase in those days.

Hand-me-down clothing was as common to the farm family as it was to the coal miner's. It was charity at its finest. It didn't matter who the garments came from, as long as they could be repaired or were usable. New dresses or coats were purchased by city slickers, who in turn passed their outgrown clothing on to country bumpkins, often begrudgingly. When the urbanites made their annual summer vacation trek to visit their poor rural cousins, the city parents would comment in voices resonant enough for kids and adults alike to hear, "Don't forget, if it wasn't for us these poor kids would be running around bare naked!"

Once, and only once, one of the youngsters was brave enough to add, "Brother, can I get an Amen to that!" That one comment was comical enough to lower the in-house tension with an outburst of much needed laughter.

Any new (and the term is used loosely) clothing found in a rural closet was usually homemade. Dress or coat patterns were hand-drawn on a piece of butcher's wrapping paper. With the used paper smoothed out on the floor, a child would lie down on the paper and then the mother would accurately trace the body measurements with a flat pencil. Material for the homemade clothing came from remnants of old clothing, which had previously been tossed into a rag bag of used garments from some other city slickers' kids. At #11 Lemon Lane, Blondie's resourcefulness at sewing amazed her neighbors, her sisters, and mostly her husband. He eventually caught on to her cunning ways, though. Whatever Blondie saved by creating garments for the kids, she could spend on something for herself.

After an outfit was completely sewn, the remaining scraps were cut into narrow strips, rolled into large balls and sent to a carpet maker to weave colorful floor coverings on a large carpet loom. It was quite fashionable to have these rag rugs concealing most of the fern patterned linoleum that all houses of that era seemed to have. That so-called expensive linoleum had to be protected by any means available and these housewives certainly had their own set schedules for doing just that!

On Saturdays, the freshly scrubbed and dried linoleum flooring would be covered with Friday's laundered loomed rugs. The rag rugs would then be covered with yesterday's newspapers. This routine kept all aspects of the flooring clean for Sunday mornings, when the paper was rolled into balls and became kindling for the kitchen coal stove or cellar furnace. "Waste not, want not!" Remember? The people of this era lived by that motto.

For the hard working Gunther wives, words such as eclectic or coordinate didn't yet exist. The post-war woman's idea of style was matching the linoleum color to the patterned wallpaper. That was it! Period! No consultations with a decorator were necessary! Stripping wallpaper was an unknown task in that era. A fresh strip of wall paper was adhered to the previous wall covering with boiled laundry-starch paste. Argo starch, what a commodity! It was glue, doily stiffener, or laundry starch. It was also used as a wake up call for the husband who found his underwear starched. He knew he was in the dog house for some misdeed and had better arrive home from work the next afternoon with a box of chocolate covered cherries in hand.

More often than not, those many coats of wallpaper were the only source of insulation in a room, and thus came the reference to paper-thin walls. The woman of the house got to choose, and hang, this modern marvel! She was her own interior decorator. Every room had its own designated pattern; ferns and feathers in the dining or living room, floral patterns in the bedrooms, and red cherries or strawberries in the kitchen. Blondie's farm house was no different than the neighbors' homes. No two rooms were alike. They were all a surprise when the dangling string on the centered ceiling light bulb was pulled.

After many hours of speculation and deliberation by the little lady, whatever pages remained in the mail-order wallpaper catalog became a novelty for the kids. The book would be a source of entertainment to make valentines or paper doll dresses. Childish squabbling over a certain patterned page often required refereeing by a parent. "Stop this arguin' right now, or nobody gets nothin'! Do you want the switch to come off the hook?" Disagreement ended!

During the holiday seasons, other thick mail-order catalogs called *wish books* would arrive. Countless hours were spent poring over the many, many items that would never find their way into these paltry post-war homes.

That didn't seem to stop the children from dreaming though, especially at the Christmas season. Dolls, trains, footballs! Dresses, sweaters, shoes! *What kind of people could afford such things,* the children at #11 Lemon Lane would wonder.

They knew it wasn't them, or most of their friends and neighbors, but they clung to their dreams. Once the dreaming was done and the holiday long gone, the discarded wish books served greater purposes. The shiny colored pages were torn out and saved to wrap sandwiches that were placed in school lunch boxes. The pages that remained were placed in the outhouse for use as toilet paper. The men had a standing joke about the black inked sheets. "That's a poor man's butt tattoo," they'd laugh. The larger the catalog when it arrived, the happier the mother when she placed it into the outdoor *shit house*.

Outhouse locations were usually changed twice a year, always keeping attuned to the summer and Christmas catalog disposals. A new large hole would be dug and the old seasoned house moved over it. The dirt from the new hole was then carted to the old human waste pit to fill the *shit hole*. To be a part of the youthful outhouse crew meant punishment had been delivered for some serious infraction! These were not happy workers, not by any stretch of the imagination.

Chores meant that free child labor was available in this pre-appliance era. Laundry was agitated in a wringer washer, which was kept out on the back porch for easy drainage into a flower bed. Somehow, the dirtiest water served to impress God's given earth and encouraged the largest blooms. The only thing automatic about this handy-dandy appliance was the mother's impeccable sense of timing to an established routine that was shared with all other females in the household. The laundry was done every Monday whether the heavens sent rain, snow, sleet or sunshine. The whites were washed first, then the colored items, and finally the coal miner's clothes.

This system led to the laundry water gradually becoming dirtier. Each load went through a wringer to squeeze out the soapy water, before dropping each item into a square galvanized tub of clean cold rinse water. The final step in the process was to reverse the wringer and crank the rinsed garments through it again. Then, and only then, did the drying process begin. A flag waving summer breeze served as the fabric softener for the garments clipped to a wire clothesline. Winter freezes brought stiff long johns into the kitchen where they'd stand at attention until the coal stove's warmth encouraged them to surrender into a sopping heap onto the linoleum floor.

Wooden bushel baskets entered the Monday laundry picture and were taught how to multi-task. In the morning, they carried clean laundry to be clipped to the lines for drying, but in the afternoon they could be seen carrying garden vegetables or orchard fruits for meals and preserving.

Then Tuesday arrived; the designated ironing day. Clothes that were hung out to dry on Monday were sprinkled from a pop bottle filled with water and dampened on Tuesday to iron. There didn't seem to be much logic to this system, but every housewife followed the Tuesday commandment.

Thank God for the modern-day electric iron and a collapsible ironing-board. Would the lady of the house have survived without them?

Appliances were at a premium. Only a handful of women owned an electric vacuum cleaner, the rest were proud owners of brooms. Husbands joked that their wife's broom served two purposes; sweeping floors or short flights on premenstrual nights. A string mop was used by the lazy woman, the others got down on their hands and knees to scrub their floors. A manual bottle capper forced tops onto bottles of home made beverages, such as cider, root beer, beer, wine and at times, even ketchup. Shoes were repaired in the home by using an upright iron shoe form and short shoe tacks making footwear last forever. "Oh, good God no, not more hand me down shoes," the children would wail as they realized they were the recipients of the scuffed and out-dated monstrosities.

Today's food-mixer, food processor or blender was in that day a strong arm on a healthy housewife. An egg beater was a fork, held by a female of any age. Pre-sifted flour meant the all purpose flour went through the mesh wire of a hand spun cylinder, a useful tool to encourage an antsy kid's involvement with baking activities.

Ice cream was hand cranked at home on a winter's day using ice blocks from the frog pond to pack the core container into the outer wooden keg. For some unknown reason, there were always at least five extra kids sitting in anticipation at the kitchen table on those days. Whose kids they were was not always known. Dining out meant taking your sandwich and sitting under the apple tree to eat. Getting bakery bread meant taking a short walk into the kitchen and pulling a fresh loaf out of the oven.

Entertainment was from a radio show, static included at no extra charge. An adult's ticket to a picture show cost a nickel. For a kid, going to see a movie at the local theatre was a special dress up occasion. This rarity was not taken lightly. Mihal loved going to the local movie shows and went every chance he got, accompanied by Blondie . . . or not.

Live music concerts were held by any, or all, capable family members or their friends. An inherited musical instrument prompted spontaneous singing and dancing on the front porch after the day's work was done, and not until then. Many dusky evenings were greeted by melodic strains of a hopping polka or a bopping jitterbug that were accompanied by Mihal keeping tempo with two kitchen spoons. Often he was interrupted by a resentful Blondie's nagging. "Mihal, don't you have some kind of job to keep you busy? You're just botherin' the young people. You should be ashamed of yourself, buttin' in where you're not wanted."

Mihal would just smile coyly and continue tapping his feet to the beat of the bouncy tune, while clickity, click, clicking those two old silver tablespoons, or twing-twanging along on his juice harp. "That's what you think, Blondie. I'm havin' some fun and so are they. You should try it sometime," he'd answer.

The only response Mihal would receive was a cold stare from two big blue Polish eyes, followed by Blondie's backside sashaying through the warped screen door. "I have work to do Mihal, not play. Those dancin' feet of yours aren't gonna bake tomorrow's bread now, are they?"

Blondie had her own methods of stifling Mihal's grating tongue, and she didn't hesitate to do what she felt was necessary to keep him in his place. "He only thinks he's the boss around here," she'd tell her friends.

It didn't matter how fatigued the man of the house was, the wife seemed to frequently find some task that needed attention before he could call it a day. It seems time hasn't changed that tradition. Only a few of the residents in those bygone days could afford to have a real repairman, otherwise it was fix as needed fixin' by the resident handyman.

Occasionally the little woman of the house would get in on the action. For instance, installing a Congo wall was a greatly desired kitchen addition of the '50's. Well, now that was another story! Congo walls were for the poor household. It was a thin linoleum in a two toned squared pattern that was designed to resemble a rich man's ceramic tile. It was glued onto the wooden wainscoting which had been a home improvement remnant of the '30's. Congo walls! What pride and joy they brought to the handy housewife. Every Pennsylvania farmer's wife wanted them in the early 50's. Most wives became quite adept at doing the job themselves, or it usually didn't get done! What Blondie wanted, Blondie got, so Blondie became adept and surprised her husband with gray and maroon kitchen Congo walls. "I thought I'd walked into somebody else's kitchen," Mihal laughed heartily when telling this astonishing tidbit to his buddies.

Farming was either a dream or a nightmare for the mining families during these years. To the large family, it was an absolute necessity. Success, at times, depended on family size and the many moods of God and Mother Nature. If a garden was planted, there was reasonable assurance of fresh fruits and vegetables during the summer months, and a promise of canned foodstuff in mason jars for the winter season. Canning was an all day process. This was a lesson in fragrances and aromas. This was matriculation and graduation at its finest when the mouth-watering treasures were enjoyed long after their seasons were spent.

Some young ladies thought preserving these delights was a deliberate design to hold reign over the female offspring of a household. These gals would hear from their mothers, "How will you take care of your own family if you don't learn these things now?" or "You'll go outside to play when all of this (the beets, the pickles, the berries, the peaches, the pears, the beans, the tomatoes or the corn . . . and on and on and on) is blanched and jarred!"

As the queen of #11 Lemon Lane, Blondie reigned loud and clear!

During berry-picking seasons, mothers would hasten, "There's no dancin' for you until we get the wax lids poured onto all the jelly jars. You don't work, you won't eat!"

Blondie never did let the kids forget that she was the mother and the champion of all hasteners.

Today's children will never comprehend the bonding and the merriment that often accompanied household chores. The singing, the harmonizing, the acting performances and the comedic timing could very well have possibly spawned the last generation's greatest entertainers. The best audiences and the best critics were usually found right there in those somber homes.

Today's children disregard a parent's advising wisdom as old fashioned. They roll their eyes and mumble "Yadda, yadda, yadda!" before going their own merry way. Yesterday's child would never have dared to be sassy or disrespectful to a parent dispensing guidance. *Children should be seen and not heard* was the thought and the rule back then. Blondie's kids thought she was the originator of that eleventh commandment.

A mother's talent and knowledge was passed from one generation to another. The art form of safe food preservation fell into that category. No available food escaped the chef's expertise. Even a staple such as cabbage didn't escape a razor-edged cutting board where leafy heads were shaved into shreds. The cabbage shards would be layered with freshly picked apples to make sauerkraut and pickled apples for winter enjoyment. This tangy taste on the palate rekindled a memory of summer sunshine bright enough to light any cold, dark winter evening.

Mothers were known to ask their daughters, "If I don't teach you how to be a dandy wife, just who will?" Mother and daughter already knew the answer. Keeping their offspring busy was as much a mother's chore as was teaching those useful skills. Where better to learn than within the family's own culinary arts center, aka the kitchen?

The bigger the family, the more fresh and preserved food was required. The more food needed, the bigger the garden! The larger the garden, the more weeds to be pulled and the more soil to be tilled! Gardening was only a small portion of the farm work. Ask any farmer, they'll tell you. On second thought, don't ask. A farmer will be only too happy to take a break from his workday to talk. He could keep you engrossed in conversation for hours!

There were always animals to be attended. Cows and bulls, pigs, horses, chickens, turkeys . . . all played a role in the food chain. All needed fodder. Summer meadows of wild grasses and winter barn hay fed some. Grains and slop fed others. Cows needed milked. Manure needed shoveling and then hauled away to the big pile to ferment for next year's fertilizer. Grasses needed planted, then cut, raked and pitched with a large tossing fork into the hayloft for winter animal banquets. Barn floors required daily rinsing to deter bacterial growth. All of this required long hours of manual labor. That's where a large family and shared chores became the solution to farm life equations. Yesteryear's farm evolved to foster today's co-op enterprise.

The mining and farming families knew that without everyone's energy the close-knit community itself would be hard pressed for luck to survive. What affected one family touched all, and they weren't ashamed to share their joys or their sorrows.

Most farmers in this small village were also employed full-time at other jobs in nearby towns. The majority of men in Gunther worked in the Koxis coal mines, although some of the others were more fortunate. The post-office in this tiny village employed a husband and wife team, affording them a clean leisurely life. The one and only grocery store was privately owned by the so-called rich people, the Helmsleys. "Cash, not credit" was their motto. That was clearly pointed out to the customers by the large hand printed signs on the entry door, on the cash register, on the shelves of canned goods, on the ice cream cooler lid, and even embroidered on the aprons of the owners. No second guessing about the Golden Rule in this place.

At the far end of town, there was a small confectionary store serving two purposes. Candy, ice cream or soda were sold by the Andrews brothers as treats for the kids in the front half of the building, while the back-half held two pool tables and a large circular card table. That back-half was specifically deigned as the men's room for weekend poker rounds or billiard competitions. Coming home late from that back-room wreaked havoc for many men, young or old! Some men were too thick-headed to learn a lesson, while still others didn't seem to care. Just how much trouble could a male get into playing poker or pool? You could be certain there was always a female around to enlighten her man's poor judgement.

Myopic reflection is good for the soul. Though not always totally accurate, reminders of the simpler life will bring a smile to those who lived through those hard-working, yet peaceful, post-war days.

Home was a valued commodity.

Family was something to be cherished.

Parents were the backbone of the home.

Children were seen, but not heard.

Marriage was a sacrament; an honorable vow.

Divorce meant failure and shame. Those who dared divorce were ostrasized.

Commitments were made to be kept.

A handshake was a binding contract.

Weak marriages were not admissions of insufficiencies; their problems were simply swept *under the rug* or kept behind closed doors.

Parental pride was expressed affection and encouragement, not arrogance.

Some children were disappointments, but only their family knew why.

It was a proven fact that every large family had one bad apple in the barrel.

Shame was something brought on by oneself, but with maturity learned responsibility was cautiously honed.

Teachers were respected, and placed in the same category as parents, pastors and policemen.

Small towns attested to self-worth by displaying street signs on macadam roads.

Neighbors resolved their differences with mutual respect for one another.

Community members shared their excess produce without any exchange of currency.

Another pregnancy in a large Catholic family meant another row of potatoes added to the garden.

Whatever was placed on the dinner plate was eaten. Homemade bread sopped up the last of the brown-flour gravy.

"There are children starving in China," was a daily reminder of the wealth in the U.S.

Baptisms, weddings and wakes were celebrated in the homes where joys and sorrows alike were shared by those who truly cared.

Friends were trusted and reliable.

Genuine smiles bloomed easier.

Amicable greetings were the norm.

Religion was a revered theology, not a political tirade or a comedy routine preached from the pulpit.

Soldiers and patriotism were custodians to honorable parades of courage.

The American flag was saluted, not trampled and burned.

Before the first note was heard, everyone stood for our National Anthem. Everyone present palmed their heart and sang the words along with the music.

Freedom was valued and appreciated.

Love of God and country was esteemed.

It may have been a simple life compared to today's standards, but it wasn't taken for granted. It wasn't then, and shouldn't be now!

Amen to that!

WHAT A MEMORY!

"Stand up straight," the grown-up voice is saying. "You got shit all over you."

"Me cold, Mum," the little voice replies, as she looks at her naked self in the crackled and aging rectangular mirror that hides a medicine chest. She knows the pink, sweet-tasting belly-ache medicine is hiding behind that mirror and she wishes her Mum would give her some right away.

The little voice knows her name is J. She knows that she's had a belly-ache for quite a while and that she'd awakened to a slippery, shitty bed. The girl does know what shit is. She's heard that word explained many times before by her Mum.

"See mamoona. That's you. See the *monkey face* in the mirror," the grown-up mother's voice says, "that's you, a monkey face." Using a scratchy rag, the mother's yellow-rubber gloved hands roughly scrub the dried yellow diarrhea slime from the girl's torso. With quick motions, the mother repeatedly rinses the soiled cloth in the same chilled water the girl is standing in. The water is a cloudy yellow color now, not clear as it was to begin with.

"Me cold," the little voice rings out again, this time barely audible through her chattering teeth.

"Shut up! Do you think I like playin' in your shit? From now on you go to the potty like a big girl. Do you hear me?"

The harsh voice is right up against the little girl's ear, so she can't miss hearing what her mother is saying.

"Yes, me go potty," she answers softly. Shivering with fright and chill almost uncontrollably, the girl is pretty sure she knows what's coming next.

Sure enough, she's lifted out of the cold porcelin sink she's been standing in. Soaking wet and naked, she's told to stand where she's been placed on the floor. She's handed a pair of underpants and an undershirt to hold.

"Bend over. You know what you're gonna get now, don't you? You're no dummy, not you, but you're not smart enough not to shit in your bed," her mother hisses.

With undergarments in hand, the still naked little girl with the welted rear end and stinging legs is barely able to climb the stairs to her smelly bedroom where she carefully dons her undergarments first, then her yesterday's soiled socks, her wrinkled slacks and her berry-stained shirt. Too weak to climb back down the stairs, she curls up in a corner on the cold, fern-patterned linoleum floor and covers herself with her older sister's pink chenille bathrobe that had been draped on the corner of a nearby bed.

"Joni, what's wrong with you child?" the old grandmother asks, but she can smell what's wrong and she can guess what punishment the girl must have already endured. She's certain of it when she attempts to turn the girl over and the little one whimpers in pain.

"Mihal, get in here," the old woman calls to her son. "You have a sick and beaten child in here."

Moments pass and the girl still hasn't shed a tear. She won't give in, although she does timidly sip the warm golden broth the trembling old woman gently feeds her from a large silver spoon.

A NICKEL

The little girl was three years old, that's what her dad had said when J asked, "How old me am?"

"You're supposed to say, "How old am I?" Mihal corrected the toddler's grammar.

"You're three years old now. Hold up three fingers, like this," he'd instructed by folding down her thumb and pinky finger.

"That's it, Joni. You got it the very first time. You're gonna be a smart girl, aren't you?" Mihal had asked the skinny freckled child with the long stringy-blonde hair.

Within that same evening, she had mastered counting to twenty. Using pennies, Mihal had sat and taught her how to count the copper coins in bunches of five. Mihal grew sleepy long before the ambitious girl did. She relinquished her counting lesson, but only after her dad promised he'd finish teaching her the very next day.

The father went to bed thinking *she won't remember any of this in the mornin'*.

J went to bed repeating the numbers she just been taught, and thinking *I'm gonna learn them all tomorrow.*

Early the next morning, Mihal was awakened by a tiny cold nose giving him a bunny hug. "What the heck?" Mihal started, but the three year old stood at his bedside jingling her small tan muslin tobacco pouch of pennies in front of his face. She was raring and ready for more counting. "Let's go. You a sleepyhead, Daddy," she chimed cheerfully.

"That's gonna have to wait for awhile, kid. I have to go to a funeral this mornin'. Old Man Kitchner is getting' buried. You ain't never been to a funeral, have you?" Mihal asked the little freckle-faced girl who stood at his bedside pleading with those great big green eyes.

"What's funeral?" she innocently asked.

"Well, it's when someone's body dies and their spirit goes to live with God in Heaven. They don't have any more worries in Heaven," he tried to explain minimally.

"Oh, okay," the girl said, also minimally.

"I want ta go with you. Then we can count more pennies."

Mihal's mind sniggered. *Oh, to be young and innocent again without grownup problems, but it's too late for you now, Mihal. Get up and get yourself movin'.*

"Okay kid, go get dressed. Tell your Ma you're goin' with me this mornin'. She'll be happy to have a mornin' with one less kid yappin' at her."

"Look, Dad," J shouted as she ran after her dad who was walking through the front gate toward his car. Holding up a child's church collection envelope, she explained, "Ma put nickel in here. Ma says that like five pennies. This go in church basket at funeral," the youngster explained to Mihal.

Tucking the envelope into her coat pocket, she jabbered away about her coat that once belonged to her older sister, Polly. "This my red coat now. My collar called velvet. My dress red plaid and my shoes black. My shoes too big. See, they flop up and down. My stockings too big, too."

She demonstrated by stomping her feet and watching as the long white stretched hose fell down around her ankles. This set the girl into a fit of giggles and Mihal followed suit. "That's a real trick, Joni. Do it again," Mihal requested with a wide grin.

Yanking the hose up around her thighs, the little girl did as she was told and the stockings were once again down around her ankles. Spontaneously, they were both bent over in laughter.

The funeral Mass was lengthy and J took advantage of Mihal's lap by snuggling close and resting her head against his chest. It didn't take but a few minutes for Joni to fall into rhythm with Mihal's breathing. Once the pattern was established, she drifted off in slumber. Mihal sat through the entire service and gazed at his little angel's face. Occasionally she smiled while dozing peacefully. When J smiled, Mihal did too.

He found himself explaining later to an angered wife, "So she missed the Mass. She's got a whole lifetime ahead of her filled with Masses of all kinds. I've watched you sleep through a few of those sermons myself, so don't be such a hypocrite," he defensively countered.

"Did she throw her envelope in the basket?" Blondie cuttingly questioned.

"There are no collections at a funeral Mass. Did a good Catholic girl like you forget that fact, Blondie?" Mihal mockingly teased.

"So, where's the nickel then?" Blondie wanted to know.

"It's in our bellies. We stopped and had us an ice cream cone; strawberry for her and chocolate for me. Maybe we shoulda brought you one, huh?" he kidded with a smirk on his lips and a twinkle in his eyes.

"And you know what? While we ate our ice cream cones, she learned how to count to one hundred. Let her show you how she does it. She caught on so fast, I couldn't believe it myself. All the people in the store were watchin' and laughin'. We had a good time. Too bad you missed it. It was a lot of fun, Blondie," Mihal excitedly relayed the tale.

"J," Blondie called, "get over here, and bring your bag of pennies."

Thinking she was going to demonstrate her newly acquired knowledge, J excitedly toddled over to her mother, the penny bag jingle-jangling away as she ran. "Comin'," she responded in a tiny girl's voice.

"Give me that damn bag. That's worth a dollar and that's one dollar you don't need," her mother said.

With one felt swoop of Blondie's talon, the bag was transferred from the girl to her mother. The claw-like hand that now held the bag made a complete turn away from the little girl and walked off toward *that damned house*.

It took about half of a second for Mihal to reach a standing position from where he'd been resting on his haunches at an eyeball level with the little girl. With a few slinking steps he quickly caught up to Blondie. The little girl couldn't hear what was said, but Mihal returned with the tan muslin sack. "Here you go, kid. I believe this is yours. You hide it when you go upstairs to change your clothes, okay?"

The bag stayed hidden for a short while behind a torn piece of wallpaper in a closet nook, but like everything else of any value in *that damned house* it eventually disappeared. It was only mentioned at opportune moments when Blondie wanted to verbally inflict anguish or insult.

It's strange what a three year old can remember, isn't it?

It's even stranger what a three year old can't forget.

SHOES FROM A CATALOG

Morning after morning, the four year old girl sat quietly and flipped through the pages of the latest spring-summer catalog. Colorful pictures, alternating with black and white pages, were scrutinized closely by those huge green eyes. She had her sights set on a pair of white eyelet sling-backed sandals. Nothing short of nothing was going to stand in the way of her asking if she could get those for her Easter shoes.

Each of the children had been told by their Dad, "You'll all get new shoes for Easter this year. You'll have to take care of them," he admonished.

"They'll be your summer shoes, too. Look through this catalog and pick out the pair you want," he suggested to the youngsters.

Getting something new was a rarity for these children, not to mention that they were being permitted to make the selection themselves. Each of the five children took his or her time making their selections. This was, after all, a major decision for each of them.

Petronella, the eldest and the practical one, selected a pair of saddle shoes.

Polly, the pretty and popular one, chose mid-heeled black pumps for "dressing up and dancing".

Adela, everybody's friend, picked brown penny-loafers, "They'll go with anything," she said.

Junior and Jake decided to order cordovan laced oxfords because their mother said so.

As an independent four year old, J had her heart set on the pretty white sandals. She had an idea brewing in that pea-sized brain of hers, and that was that.

Their father sat with them to write out the order. His wife had refused to help, but she was able to verbally blast, "That should be a catalog order for me, not shoes for them brats."

"You kids have to be patient with me," Mihal said. "My writin' isn't all that good, but we'll get 'er done."

Mihal's jovial voice conveyed excitement to all the kids sitting around the wooden kitchen table, so "Get 'er done," they did.

"We had a good month at the mine, so we'll use the extra money to get you kids some new shoes," the proud father explained during their chit-chatting, "but you all know you're gonna have to be patient. It's gonna take a few weeks for them to come through the mail. I don't want to hear any complainin' or whinin'. Okay?"

Five heads bobbed a resounding *okay*!

While the excited children were gathered at the table, their mother stomped around the kitchen, irrationally banging and slamming pots. Begrudging all of the labor involved with her supper preparations, Blondie's temper flared, "I should be gettin' that extra money. I'm the one doin' all the work around here. I'm the banker in this house! I should be able to spend that extra money any way I see fit, and I wouldn't waste hard-earned dollars on new shoes for these ungrateful piss ant kids. Well, they better keep those damn shoes shined or they'll find them thrown into the furnace. Are you listenin' to me, Mihal?" Blondie bellowed, demanding his immediate attention.

Her anger only succeeded in putting a damper on the merry evening. Their father didn't voice his thoughts at that moment. He just remained quietly attentive to the task at hand. Becoming more aware of the all too frequent raving episodes from his wife, he whispered to her, "We'll talk about this when the kids go to bed," but he received only a glaring side-glance from his wife indicating that as far as she was concerned the subject was closed.

Later, the children listened to their parent's festering argument through their Baba's bedroom floor grate. The floral iron grate allowed heated air to rise from the kitchen to the grandmother's upstairs bedroom, but it also was the ideal place to sit and eavesdrop on the adults' kitchen conversations or disagreements.

"Why did you have to say those things in front of the kids?" the gentle man asked.

"For once they have somethin' to look forward to, like other kids. You got new shoes and a new dress last month. Not a one of those kids griped about that. I haven't gotten new shoes for at least three years now, but do you hear me grievin'? So for once, just keep your mouth shut!" Mihal snapped, determined to demonstrate his strong disagreement with Blondie.

Blondie was eager for an argument, though. "Don't you think for one second that you can tell me when any of these kids need somethin'. Listen, you son of a bitch, I run this house, not you or that mother of yours. Don't you forget that."

"The girls can wear the shoes or clothes my sisters send them. If those things are good enough for my sisters' girls, they're good enough for your pissy girls, Mihal. The boys are always gonna need new shoes or clothes. Boys are just naturally rougher on their clothes. You don't see them gettin' many things given to them. Besides, you're always sidin' with your girls. You're always spoilin' them," Blondie continued her stubborn haranguing.

Mihal interrupted, "And you're always makin' excuses for those pet boys of yours. You'd let them get away with murder if you could. Keep quiet now, and I mean it!" he shouted.

He addled up to his wife, and grabbed her shoulders in his large paw-like hands. Gripping tightly, he softly hissed, "Those kids need to get to sleep, but you're loud rat trappin' is bound to keep them awake. It's time for you to shut your mouth, Blondie."

Mihal shoved Blondie backward, but she stumbled and fell onto a kitchen chair just as Mihal raised his closed hand to her face and added, "You'd better get to bed before I stifle that mouth of yours with my fist."

"I'm not keeping quiet for you or anybody, you bastard! Do you hear me?" she interjected, stretching her neck to watch him strutting up the stairs to turn in for the night.

Four a.m. would come soon enough, and then he'd be off again to another day at the coal mine. His body ached with fatigue. Coal mining all day long, five or six days a week, and then farming on the weekends made him a tired man. Arguing only exhausted him further. Besides, he didn't want to lose his patience. He wanted to harbor the good feeling that he'd done something special for his kids. They were the soft spot in his heart. He smiled as he laid his head on the bed pillow. He knew that he'd sleep well this night.

Several weeks did pass before a large brown box arrived at the post office. The eldest child was entrusted with the correct C.O.D. funds, and sent off to retrieve the package. Raymond, the postmaster, realized the box was entirely too cumbersome for Pet to carry home. He was kind enough to drive her and her treasure home. "What did you get from the catalog?" he asked out of a friendly curiosity.

Pet was so excited that she blurted out, "All of us kids got new shoes for Easter. We can't believe it! We never had our very own new shoes before!"

"Well, that is something special," the man responded softly.

Her vivid excitement was so very contagious. Raymond wished that he and his wife had a child of their own to experience an innocent's happiness, and he told Pet just that as he drove to #11 Lemon Lane, "If I had a daughter, I'd keep her as happy as you are right now."

"Oh! I'm happy alright," Pet said, "but you just wait until you see the rest of the kids when we get to our house."

"She's here!" the kids were shouting repeatedly as Pet and the postman pulled up to the gate at #11 Lemon Lane.

Screams of "Oh, boy! Hip, hip, hooray!" filled the warm spring air.

The postman grinned as he listened to the eager shouts that were so very audible inside his tightly closed car. There were as many whoops and hollers coming from the children as there were kicks in a rodeo! Smiles were on every young face. Giggles echoed from child to child. They didn't know if their excitement could be contained as they waited for their father to return home from his job at the coal mine. It had been an early agreement with their dad to wait and share the opening of any shoe boxes once they had arrived. The notion and the ordering had been his doing, and it only seemed fair that he should participate in the excitement of the moment.

It was dusk when someone spotted Mihal's coal-blackened shape walking into view at the crest of Lemon Lane. The kids knew that was their dad coming home from the coal mines. They spotted the glow of his carbide lamp flickering atop his mining helmet.

"Hurry, Dad, they're here. The shoes are here!" shouted the little ones.

He slowly raised his arm in a wave, "I'm coming. Be patient. Somebody get me a glass of water. I'm thirsty," he answered knowing very well that he was stalling to make the most of the long-awaited moment.

"Let me go wash my face and hands," Mihal teased. His white smile looked as bright as a circus clown's on his coal-dusted face. The "No, no, no," children's responses tore holes in the balmy April evening.

The kids were too excited to postpone the opening task any longer. The zip, zip, ripping of the tape from the outer box made J jump up and down in anticipation. Finally, her new shoes were here. Opening the small cardboard shoe box, J saw her new sandals. Immediately, she tried them on her little dirty feet. The shoes were beautiful and they fit! The other kids tried on their footgear and, miraculously, they fit perfectly. There was even a little growing room in them for the summer months ahead. What a wonderful day!

Every kid slept until sunrise with their new treasures tucked tightly in their folded arms. What a glorious night!

Early the next morning, while everyone was still asleep, J crept out of her bed. Still in her pajamas, she slid her feet into a pair of sloppy, red, rain-boots and slipped out through the back door. She headed for the newly plowed farm acreage. With a small digging trowel in her right hand and her new shoes tucked under her left arm, she began her journey trudging through the morning mist. If anyone had witnessed the happy little munchkin trotting down the pathway they'd have thought her a dwarf off to the diamond mines.

Helping her Dad several days ago, J had dropped corn kernels and pumpkin seeds into the small holes readied for spring planting. He had explained to her, "We put the little seeds into the ground, cover them over with soil, then wait for them to grow. We have to be patient until the plants get big enough to give off their new growth. The corn stalks will get taller than me," he explained.

"The cornstalks will get baby cobs on them, and then before too long we'll have big ears of corn to eat. The pumpkin seeds will grow vines along the ground. Tiny pumpkins will start to grow out of the yellow flowers. Do you understand?" Mihal asked the scrawny girl.

She may have been a little girl, but she was as bright as the sunshine coming over the horizon. She knew her shoes were the smallest of all that had come from that catalog. *They are seeds,* she thought.

So, she planted them out in the middle of fifty acres. She dug a hole, carefully placed the shoes into it, and patted the soil over her seeds the way her father had shown her.

She could be patient! She'd wait for her shoe plant to grow and blossom. She wondered if it would be a stalk or a vine. She hoped the flowers would be pink, or maybe purple. She slogged her way back to the farm house, all the while sloshing a trail through the muddy furrows. With each step she thought about how long it would be before something would germinate.

In her youthful mind, the little girl thought in little girl words, *I hope my shoe plant won't take as long to grow as the pumpkins or the corn.*

She felt so proud of herself, but she wasn't quite sure how she'd convey that feeling to her parents. She just knew she felt fuzzy and warm all over. She had been very brave doing her gardening chore all alone at the crack of dawn.

When J re-entered the house, her inquisitive mother asked, "Where have you been so early this mornin'? Why are your boots all covered with mud?"

"I planted some seeds!" she promptly announced. "I planted my shoe seeds, so I can grow more of them," the gratified girl answered.

"You did what?" screeched Blondie.

"Where? You show me right now where you planted those shoes! Do you know what you did? I oughta' whip your butt right now. I told your Dad he was crazy for lettin' you kids get your way," she ranted.

Grabbing the girl's upper arm, Blondie practically dragged J all the way to the plowed expanse. J's short legs couldn't keep up with her mother's long strides. She had to run most of the way to avoid falling into the muddy furrows.

"You better find those shoes or you'll be goin' barefoot this Easter, Missy!" her mother harped.

Well, she didn't go barefoot for the holiday or for the summer. She wore her older sister's scuffed hand-me-down gray utility shoes. The other kids shamelessly called them "clodhoppers".

They laughed and made jokes about J's new Easter shoes. They even sang as they played at jumping a rope:

"Hey, J!

Fifty acres, that's a lot.

Garden grown shoes, not store bought!"

She didn't care. She knew once her plant began to grow, it wouldn't be long before she'd have plenty of new sandals to call her own, *and then who would be laughing* she wondered.

She had been defiant, but now she needed to be content and to be confident. She would wait for her shoe plant to grow. Somewhere out in those unyielding fifty acres that were searched thoroughly that morning by her mother, J knew her shoe seeds were a beginning. She just knew everyone would recognize the shoe plant once it sprouted. It would be easy to spot. It would be unusual and way different than any new stem they'd ever seen.

J promised herself that she would be patient!

She would just wait . . . and wait . . . and wait . . . and wait . . . and wait . . .

PET

Petronella, Petronella,
in life's verden pastures
did you find sweet vanilla,
while growing your own asters?

Cooking and cleaning,
always chores to do.
Pet, the perfectionist,
no one did anything as good as you.

Pet, you planted flowers,
grew veggies, too.
You lovingly nurtured
those who loved you.

Baking, cooking and canning,
crocheting brought you local fame.
You took life's lessons by the horns
and learned to plow through life's game.

I'm sure there were times,
When you were barely getting by.
It wasn't a lack of courage,
for there wasn't a day you didn't try.

Cautious and frugal,
you measured life by the penny.
Went to your grave,
loved and favored by many.

FULL OCTOBER MOON

The air was crisp for a late October 22nd afternoon. There was cool air from the slight breeze that was blowing in the warm sunshine. The girls had been told to weed and rake all of the flower beds. This was something new! Usually the flowers were allowed to go to seed, before autumn winds blanketed them with a layer of protective leaves for the cold months ahead. *Just what is going on? We never left the beds this way before,* they all wondered.

All questioned the directive, except Petronella. She easily surmised, *I know exactly what's going on here.*

Petronella had been nicknamed Pet by her dad. She was the eldest of all the children. She thought of herself as third in command, but only when she needed to be, of course! She was seventeen, a senior in high school and a dreamer. For as long as she could remember, she had fantasized about attending beauty school.

Pet had saved every penny she had ever earned or received since deciding on a beautician's career. Her money was always placed in the same old tin can and hidden in her underwear drawer. Occasionally counted, the total sum gradually increased to a tad over two hundred dollars. During high school, she had been promised by her parents that a cosmetology education would be given to her after graduation, but last Tuesday she had been informed otherwise by her sharp-tongued mother,

"There's no money for you to go to any kind of school. We'll be lucky if we have enough money to buy coal for furnace heat this winter. Your Dad got laid off from the mines again. Who knows how long it'll be before the coal mines open again and the miners get called back to work."

Rubbing her large tympanic belly, Blondie scornfully added, "Further more young lady, this next baby is comin' any day now, and there's no money in the bank account to pay the doctor when he gets here."

Pet felt an emotional excitement knowing that in the spring she'd be able to surprise her parents with her tin can stash. It had been such a long time that she'd been saving and hoping for her future. She could just imagine what a wonderful day was ahead. Pet had studied so hard to be an A student. That was an absolute necessity to be readily accepted into the Altoona School of Cosmetology. *Well,* she thought, *their worries will go right down the drain when they see that I've saved most of my tuition money all by myself.*

Pet remembered her mother's outburst last Tuesday, but it was now a week later and Pet did indeed know what was happening. She'd seen and heard it all before. From an upstairs bedroom window Blondie could be heard barking out orders as though she had just returned from a soldier's boot camp.

"Mihal, bring in the copper laundry boiler, set it on the kitchen stove, and fill it with water from the faucet."

"Stoke up the coal and make sure the fire's burnin' strong in the kitchen stove. With a birthin' comin' we're gonna need a lot of hot water for clean-up."

"Send one of the bigger kids to get Big Annie. She'll know how to reach Doc Williams," Blondie didn't hesitate to bellow laboriously between contractions.

"Tell Pet to take the rest of the kids outside to clean up the leaves and the flower beds. That'll keep them out of the way. Pet knows what's happenin'." Blondie's shrieking didn't cease until another contraction seized her gut.

It was only a matter of minutes before Big Annie, the neighbor and self-trained midwife, arrived and started giving her orders. Booming loud and clear, she became as the colonel her position necessitated when called to a confinement. Big Annie was a tall and chunky Slovak woman. She was a jolly old soul who didn't just speak, she bellowed. Her experiences with her own children had taught her that yelling got things done quicker. Calling loudly to Pet, she began shouting to put everyone on notice that she'd arrived. "Pet, you take care of the little ones. Keep them busy outside," and then turning to Polly she said, "Polly, you go get me some clean sheets. White ones, if you can find them."

As an after thought, she turned to Blondie's husband, "Mihal, have these kids had their supper yet?"

"Yep," he answered. "Blondie just got them fed when she started with the pains."

From her experiences with previous deliveries at #11 Lemon Lane, Big Annie knew Mihal was useless in the kitchen, and that he only took up valuable space in the bedroom if he was asked to assist with the birthing. "Well, the Doc should be here anytime now," Big Annie spoke loudly, "so Mihal, you best head for the barn and take care of the animals for the night."

Big Annie knew these deliveries didn't take long, not when this was the eleventh time around for Blondie. Big Annie also knew pregnancies and deliveries didn't always go smoothly, so she was only able to relax and slacken her heavy breathing after Doc Williams reached the household when he could oversee the birthing. She would no longer be in charge then, and that suited her just fine.

Arrive he did! Doc Williams was as dependable as he was old. He arrived in his recognizable shining black '45 Ford coupe. Carrying his familiar black satchel, he began handing out lollipops to the kids who were busy raking the autumn leaves. He was a whiz with kids. He would need them to be quiet and stay out of his way. *These rascals were a rambunctious lot,* he remembered correctly from previous visits to this house. "Okay, let's get this show on the road," he said to himself as he approached the rest of the snot-nosed bunch.

His friendly thundering voice greeted all within earshot. "Hello, hello, hello! Who can tell me, where's this big emergency?"

"It's no emergency, Doc," Pet answered. "It's just another one of these," she sarcastically informed him as she pointed to a youngster already happily licking her red lollipop.

Rudely directing the doctor, an unsmiling Pet waved him on with her extended arm. "Just go on into the house. You know the way. Besides, our dad is in there with Big Annie. They can show you where to go."

Biting her tongue, Pet withheld the rest of her thought, *to Hell!*

Pet was so correct. Old Doc Williams knew the way to the upstairs bedroom where Blondie was about to deliver *another one of those.*

Blondie was trying not to hurry the excruciating contractions, although she knew there was no controlling the cramping surges. She knew that once the pains were finally stilled the delivery would be complete, thereby bringing an additional *kid* to worry about and another *mouth* to feed. Still, Blondie was only too aware of the importance of a doctor's presence during the birthing procedure. After all, her good health and post-partum recovery depended on his expertise.

Doc Williams greeted Big Annie, who was standing in the shadows waiting to take his orders. He quickly asked, "How are you, Annie? Are you ready with everything?"

Big Annie's only response was a nod of her head. She was as prepared as she'd ever be in this bedroom.

Only then did the doctor turn to speak to the expectant mother who was lying in her bed, rubbing her huge abdomen and writhing in pain.

"Hello there, Blondie," Doc gruffly greeted her with a cold stare as he proceeded to pull on a pair of brown rubber gloves.

"Done it again, huh? You and Mihal should think about quitting the baby business one of these days. Or at least you could try using some kind of protection. Haven't you two heard about rubbers? How many kids do you have now? You're not getting any younger, you know. You should think about that. Who's going to take care of all of these kids if something happens to you or Mihal?"

Doc unmercifully confronted Blondie. Firing a staccato of questions at her, he disallowed time for her to answer. He really didn't have any interest in hearing anything she had to say on this day, or any other day for that matter. Neither did a discreet Annie, who remained standing in the doorway near the second floor staircase. She was as silent as a German carrier pigeon, ready to fly away at the first opportunity to escape.

"I have a baby about ready to come into this world. You don't need to start preachin' at me now," she shouted back to the doctor.

"Do what you need to do. Just get this crap over with. I'm all sweaty, I'm all tired out and I'm ready for some rest. So Doc, just save your breath," was Blondie's answer to Doc's lecture.

She knew how many children she had delivered already. A reminder wasn't necessary. She'd be reminded in the morning, when a new cry wailed throughout the house. There would be a reminder every time she nursed the new brat or had to change its smelly diaper.

With every jolt of nauseating pain, there was a cause to shout out in anguish. Blondie reminded herself, *I'm already being tormented and the kid isn't even out of the womb yet.*

"You'd think I'd be used to these contractions, but they're unbearable when they come," she angrily informed the doctor as she let out another piercing scream in response to a renewed gripping spasm.

"The pains are comin' closer and harder," she hollered.

The disgusted doctor was long past being sympathetic to this whining heifer. He reached to his ear and turned off his hearing aide. He saw her lips moving, but he didn't care to hear what she was bellowing. *Let this loony bitch suffer a bit. Maybe she'll learn to keep her knees together for a few years* he cruelly thought as he pushed his Hippocratic Oath onto a shelf in his brain.

Little did Doc realize that he'd be long gone from this earth before Blondie stopped opening her knees for Mihal. He should have saved his breath.

The acrid screams coming from the opened upstairs bedroom window startled the kids down in the front yard. "What's goin' on up there?" their squeaking voices were demanding.

Becoming frightened, they asked a variety of questions.

"Is Old Doc hurtin' Ma?"

"What's he doing to her?"

"Can we go and find out what's happenin'?"

"Can you go, Pet?" Polly asked.

"No," Pet answered sharply.

"The doctor will be down in a little while to tell us why Ma's screaming. I was just up there listening behind the bedroom door, and I heard him say, "It's almost done. He'll be coming down soon, you'll see. It's time for all of you to get ready for bed now," Pet stated firmly.

"Polly, you go get some water heated and get the young ones cleaned up. They can take a Polish bath tonight," Pet ordered her younger sister.

A Polish bath was an understood rushed *once over* with a minimal amount of water on a washcloth that was applied sparingly to the face, hands and feet. Once that feat was accomplished, the same speedy wash would be given to the privates, tits (if one had any) and arm pits! It was more of a joke on the bath itself, but most certainly a time-saver where there was only one bathroom sink, one basin of warm water and a baseball team of dusty-faced kids.

It was only a few minutes before the doctor came out of the front door and announced, "Well, you got yourselves a new sister. Your Ma said her name is Cindy. You Ma's a mite disappointed. I guess she wanted a boy to replace her Timmy," Doc said while shaking his head in disbelief.

"You'd think she'd be grateful for the healthy kids she does get. Oh well, I can't figure her out and I'm not gonna try. I can't believe it's been eight years since that little guy died of pneumonia. I wonder if she'll ever get over that day. She seemed to get done with her mourning pretty quickly when it came to the girls she lost, but not that boy. Your dad will be down in a minute. He'll tell you when you can go see your mother and the baby. You kids be good and quiet though, because your Ma needs to rest for a while."

"We'll be quiet," responded little J," but you can go home now. Don't come back neither, or be bringin' anymore babies in that black bag of yours!

We've had enough a' them babies dropped off 'round here already. We don't have enough food to go 'round, no how."

Old Doc laughed heartily at the little girl's dissertation as he slowly turned to face Mihal. Holding out his right hand, the doctor greedily accepted the two hundred dollars in loose bills and change that was placed on his upright palm by Blondie's husband. "This is for the delivery and for our other bills. We're all square now, right?" Mihal asked the question and the old Doc nodded the affirmative with a toothy grin.

Two hundred dollars! Pet stared open-mouthed as her dad counted the money for the doctor. Mouthing the count silently in unison with her father, Pet couldn't believe what she was watching. She had counted her savings so many times herself, that very same way.

That was my cosmetology tuition money! They didn't even ask me if they could borrow it! A shocked and horrified Pet watched the transaction. An immense feeling of disgust, mixed with disappointment, caused her body to shudder. At that moment Pet truly hated her parents, their promises and their encouragement. She realized that what they had offered her were only empty words. Her aspirations of attending beauty school had just disintegrated. Her anguish fermented. She became the billowy mushroom cloud that followed an explosion. She couldn't lift her hanging head. It was just too heavy.

Pet thought about the offer from a loving, childless and elderly aunt and uncle who wanted her to come and live with them in Washington, D.C. To accept their charity was the last thing she wanted to consider. She had worked so hard to be the valedictorian at her graduation. *For what,* she wondered. She knew she wouldn't have a choice, though. They had offered and now she would have to accept. "We'll just have to find a city job fit for a country girl," they cheerfully confided to her.

"Good luck with that," Pet answered softly. Thoughts of a different graduation ceremony filled her mind. Nothing was as she had envisioned these past few years. "You can forget a graduation dress or party," she had been told by a smirking mother who also didn't hesitate to add, "there's no money for shit like that!"

Though her graduation day was still eight months away, she knew her disappointment would remain longer than she could ever imagine. Her heart ached for a dream that would never materialize.

Pet stood sullenly still at her mother's bedside that October evening. The other children became animated at the sight of the newborn. They couldn't contain their "ohs and aws" as they ogled the newly bundled cherub nestled and nursing noisily on its mother's breast as it lay cradled in the crook of their dozing mother's arm.

"She's so tiny."

"Look at her little nose."

"Look she's smiling."

The children's chirping voices grew louder, but Pet remained silent, even when she heard her father whisper to his wife, "Thank you, Blondie, for saving up the money to pay Old Doc."

To hide her tears, Pet turned and gazed out of the bedroom window. She quietly embraced the brilliance of the night as she watched a full bright October moon surrounded by a vast universe of twinkling stars. Struck with a sobering revelation, she realized *the whole world is before me. Here I am nothing more than a slave.*

For the eldest child at #11 Lemon Lane, leaving home had just become a whole lot easier.

WE'RE GOIN' ON A PICNIC

"Come on, Joni, we're goin' on a picnic. Adela and Jake are goin' too. Go help your Ma carry some stuff to the car like a good girl," Mihal called to his little helper.

"We've got fresh bread and bologna sandwiches, sweet pickles, raisin filled cookies and the Raleigh man's cherry drink," Jake told J and Adela. "I helped Ma pack the basket."

"J, you and Adela each grab a handle and carry that basket to the car. We're goin' to my old homestead to have a picnic," their mother announced.

I can show them the stone foundation that remains standin' since our home burnt down. That happened when I was just a kid. Just rememberin' the flames lickin' away at everything we owned brings on a heart ache. That was the only time I ever saw my parents cry, she recalled spontaneously. *Why is it that I've never thought of them cryin' before this moment* Blondie wondered?

Blondie often said that her memory would never let her forget the event. She'd say that her heart never truly recovered from the aftermath of misery their family endured when the children were split into groups, and then scattered to live with different farming or mining neighbors.

"Your dad needs to get some bags of coal from around the Minewiser's deserted tipple. We could use some more loose coal for baking and cooking. Let's take a walk past the ole *moud.* You remember that partial stone foundation that's still standing from the old homestead, don't you? I found an old tea cup in the grass the last time we were there. Maybe we'll find somethin' today. I have such fond memories of my childhood and livin' on our farm. Findin' some little trinket seems to ease some of my lingerin' pain."

Their mother's eyes welled with tears as she stumbled through her trembling words. Her spoken memories blew away with the stirring breeze that blew through the open car window as they drive along. She must have known the children were too young to comprehend the sorrow in her fostered tragedy. Blondie stared at the kids' faces and decided they didn't have any idea what she was feeling. *Look at those empty balloon heads. Ignorant little piss ant kids, every last one of them,* she thought.

"Jake's gonna help me get the coal, ain't you Jake?" Mihal asked the boy sitting so straight and proper in the center of the car's back seat.

"No, Jake's not gonna help you get no coal. He's gonna help me set up our picnic. Them two girls can help you hold the bags open and drag them to the car," the mother responded quickly for the boy.

"No, Blondie, the boy's gonna help me, and the girls are gonna help you. That's how it's gonna be, end of discussion," Mihal said rather sternly.

Mihal's Gypsy-gray eyes glared at the mother's Polish-blue eyes before he returned his concentrating gaze to the road ahead. He thought that he'd settled that dispute just a tad too quickly. *Bondie's got somethin' up that baggy sleeve of hers. I can just feel it in my bones,* Mihal's silent thoughts rumbled through his brain as he drove the rest of the way to the old site.

"Ma, I don't want to help Dad," Jake whispered to Blondie as they exited the car.

"I want to stay with you. Please, please, please," Jake again pleaded to his mother as they watched Mihal walk over the hill toward the abandoned coal mine.

"You just stay here with me. Don't you move an inch, do you hear me. You're not goin' anywhere. Girls, go with your dad and help him. Get now, and tell Dad that you want to help him," the mother ordered them.

"Shoo," she shouted after the girls as they headed for the grassy knoll that Mihal had just walked over.

"Dad, we're ready to help you. Ma said we want to help. Come on Adela, let's sing while we help. That will make the time go by faster," J told her older sister.

While the girls helped gather the scraps of coal chunks to fill the bags Mihal had brought along, five year old J egged her seven year old sister to begin singing her favorite song, My Darlin' Clementine. Mihal listened attentively to the tune. He decided he enjoyed the singing and became proud of their unselfish efforts. *Thank God these girls don't have that stubborn lazy attitude that Jake carries around on his shoulder,* Mihal considered.

Before long, four burlap bags of coal were loaded securely into the car's trunk and then three hungry workers were ready for some food and drink.

"Okay, Blondie, get the grub out here. We're hungry, aren't we girls?" Mihal said.

"Well, you three didn't come when we called, did they Jakey boy?" Blondie responded. "There are a couple of sandwiches left there, but you'll have to share them. Jake was a hungry little boy. He ate all the cookies. Didn't you Jakey?"

Blondie's snippets were voiced in defense of her favorite boy. "Here, share this drink. There's enough for the three of you to wet your whistle," Blondie said with a feigned giggle.

Mihal had a strange look in his eyes and a strained frown on his face, but he shared the leftovers with the girls. As he ate, he scrutinized Jake and Blondie who were packing up the basket remnants.

As they began the slow drive home, Mihal stopped the car only once, and that was at the Andrew's store. "Come on, girls," their father called to J and Adela as he approached the small confectionary store.

"Stay in the car with your Ma, Jake," he ordered. Disdain was written all over Mihal's face as he and the girls entered the doorway. That scornful appearance was gone when the three exited that same door. They were all wearing wide smiles and humming a gentle tune. Mihal glared at his wife, as he re-entered the driver's seat. His frozen stare remained, but the threesome's frozen treats were dwindling as they licked their ice cream cones.

"How's your strawberry ice cream, J? I think from now on I'll call you Clementine. You girls sang pretty good back there at the mine. How about you, Adela da bella da ball? That's your new nickname, by the way. Are you enjoyin' that chocolate bar? I can smell the creamy sweet cocoa way up here," Mihal razzed, enjoying every word that rolled off of his tongue.

"Oh and how are those cold Coca Cola's? Pretty tangy and thirst quenchin', huh?" their dad asked, taking another lick from his double-scooped, silky-chocolate ice cream.

"Well, Jakey boy," Mihal said as he turned to look at the pouting boy sandwiched between his sisters, "I'm glad you and your Ma ate so much that you couldn't possibly have been hungry. You two saved me a few pennies. Thank you for doin' that for me, and that is the end of the discussion, Blondie," he taunted sarcastically.

Driving out of the small parking space, Mihal directed a flagrant stare into Blondie's glaring eyes. A wry smile on his deliberate ice cream-coated lips was his victorious statement.

ONE SPECIAL CHRISTMAS

The true spirit of Christmas is supposed to ring loudly of peace, joy and love, with a core belief in the birth of Jesus Christ.

The family at #11 Lemon Lane tried desperately to find these expressed delicate sentiments during each Christmas season. They didn't always succeed.

Romantic and religious lyrics of holiday songs were replicated on greeting cards, whether sent or received. Radio programs broadcast music and sermons creating the stirring feelings of the Christmas holiday. Schools began each morning in December with a songfest. The teachers led with piano music that was especially chosen to highlight the festive mood. Holiday carols made the atmosphere lighter and the attitudes friendlier. Cheerful messages were everywhere, spontaneously convincing young and old alike to believe in this heartfelt feeling called *the holiday spirit*.

At one time or another, the children at #11 Lemon Lane believed it all. They bought the entire concept, temporarily at least. When they felt the spirit, they found that their hearts, their souls and their minds were filled with hope.

As usual, the real meaning of Christmas would be recited by their Baba, Mihal's mother. Her Hungarian dialect was no deterrent to her grandchildren. They were accustomed to her inarticulate English, which often sounded to ouotsiders to be more like gibberish than a form of communication. The grandchildren understood her accented depictions of Mary and Joseph's journey to a manger in Jerusalem for the safe birth of their baby, Jesus. For her own reasons, Baba didn't buy into the theory of the three wise men starting the tradition of giving Christmas gifts to children. "That idea came from some traveling salesman looking for a way to make a living. This Santa Claus business is a fairytale, too," she'd add with a marked tinge of hostility.

The suspicious woman had learned life's lessons the hard way. "Remember Judas," Baba would remind the children sitting around her. She knew which tale to doubt and which to believe. "I've lived a long difficult life. I'm no dummy. It brings me an inner peace to believe in the story of Jesus."

She often spoke of "meeting my Saviour someday," but she certainly didn't believe Blondie's church was the one true highway to Heaven or to that assemblage. She preached her own thoughts about faith and decency as a way of getting one through the Pearly Gates. Knowing what she knew about Blondie, Baba had plenty of questions about the path that led to Blondie's priest and his teachings. She felt that her daughter-in-law's roadway led to a dead end.

At Holy Trinity, the priest's holiday sermons were supposed to invigorate the congregation, thereby bringing renewed beliefs in the Catholic religion. Instead, the repetitious annual homily came across as crusty and stagnant.

Basically a religious hypocrite, Blondie would seek any excuse to avoid attending Mass. Mihal wasn't a proponent of organized religion and said so without apology. Anyone who knew him knew his true character. He was more comfortable kneeling under the bright sun and the billowing clouds which protected his family, his garden and his apple orchard. "Thank you, God! You gave us another day, another meal, another chance at life," was his idea of saying a solemn prayer. An optimistic short, sincere and concise delivery was directed to his Master's ears only.

Blondie's pessimistic prayers began, "Oh my God, if there is a God."

Her prayers ended with, "Amen. Enough said, you're dead."

Blondie had tried to get Mihal to attend Mass regularly, but she'd come to accept that her one real chance was on Christmas Eve. Not that she went any more frequently than Mihal, but she needed him to, more or less, taxi the kids on Sunday mornings. "As long as I send the kids to church every week, the neighbors will think I'm a good Catholic," was her phony, but poignant and haughty attitude when Mihal questioned her shady motives.

On the way to midnight Mass one Christmas Eve, Mihal imitated Father Joe's baritone voice while paraphrasing, "Let this Christmas bring the love of God into your hearts and into your homes. May you find peace in being charitable this blessed season. Everyone can show their holiday spirit by supporting this ministry. Now pass the basket."

The kids, who were literally piled into the backseat of the '39 Chevy, laughed boisterously at their dad's attempt at humor. Even Blondie got a kick out his comical rendition. With restrained giggles, she managed to say,

"Some devout Christian you are, Mihal. The devil's taken over your tongue tonight. What else did he take over?"

At that, Mihal's shoulders bounced as he snickered quite loudly, "Blondie, you'll just have to wait and see."

The older kids understood their parent's comments. They covered their mouths with their hands and kept their chuckling concealed in their chests. This evening's fun and frivolity with the parents was a rare occasion, but certainly one which would be remembered and treasured. The children knew tomorrow would bring another day and other postures.

Although the grandmother prominently attempted to explain a true meaning behind the Christmas story, Mihal and Blondie's kids weren't exactly buying all of her theories. As other kids the world over, these kids wanted presents from Santa. It didn't matter how simple the gifts were. "Screw Baba's idea that we don't need presents," was Jake's thought on the subject.

"We're all gonna get something, you'll see," he ascertained to the others.

"I already know what every gift in Santa's bag is and who's gonna get it."

Jake sure was his mama's boy, and he absolutely knew all the secrets that Santa's bag held.

After each year's Christmas Eve meal, Santa Claus would arrive to visit the youngsters at #11 Lemon Lane. It was a traditional event, and one not to be missed. This particular Christmas routine would prove to be no different from the past years.

While the children were kept occupied by tidying the kitchen and washing the supper dishes, Mihal was costuming himself in the Santa suit and Blondie was filling the large canvas bag with gifts for Santa's dispersing.

Holiday caroling, compliments of the kitchen dish-washing crew, could be heard meanwhile through out the house. Silent Night or Away in a Manger would be replaced by Rudolph the Red Nosed Reindeer or Jingle Bells. Often the songs would be repeated several times before the dinner dishes were a completed chore. Exuberant and excited merriment made each musical note a joyous gift from the children to *this damned house.* For this one special night, this was a happy shack.

The kids had decided Santa was an okay kind of guy. They tried not to notice that his waning suit was a shabby mess. The faded and wrinkled outfit looked to be an original. "Do you think it possibly could date back to the year of the original Santa Claus?" Baba had jokingly asked Blondie on one festive Christmas Eve. Blondie didn't appreciate the old woman's comedic attempt. Blondie didn't crack a smile, let alone give away a chuckle. "You're not funny, Bitch," Blondie mumbled under her breath as she turned her back on Mihal's mother.

Santa's three pieced garment may well have been an original, but an original of what no one would lay claim to know. Cut from an old bed sheet and pillow case, it had been pieced together using an old treadle, foot-powered sewing machine. Once sewn, it was then dunked into a vat of some type of a questionable red dye.

Despite having been kissed by a red hue in 1932, the garment had slowly generated into various shades of hot pink. The hat was the topper, though. It became a real joke for those who even got a glimpse of it. That Santa hat was definitely a different fade of pink. The conical end toted a ball of matted sheep's wool and a blackened jingle bell. It was a court jester's cap, to be sure. The mask, however, was definitely believable as an old man's face with its many crinkled cracks and crevices. Somehow, its retained rosy cheeks and smiling mouth seemed to approve the ruse.

Mihal laughed heartily every time he donned the outfit. "I wonder which of the kids will see through the facade this time. We have some smart kids, Blondie. They'll all recognize me sooner or later. We'll have to have some more kids to keep this sham going. What do you think?" Mihal joked to his problematical wife, as he melodically began to sing a double conjecture, "Santa Claus is coming tonight."

The moment of Santa's arrival was the pinnacle of an anticipatory day. The given gifts were anticlimactic. Every action leading up to Santa's arrival only served to increase the level of excitement for the children. For weeks, Blondie's cautions could be heard echoing up the staircase before reverberating down again.

"You better be good."

"Santa is coming in a few days.'

"Do you want a present or not?"

"Santa can see you, so you had better quit doing that."

It was Santa this and Santa that, so how could the kids be anything but anxious and excited?

An evergreen tree started the celebratory mood every Christmas season. A week before the big day, a beauty was cut and stolen from way back in the Terrier's evergreens and then dragged home to be propped in a bucket of sugar water. After being placed in the rarely used parlor, the tree was gaily decorated with a variety of objects.

The one and only set of electric lights was strung around the tree boughs. All of the bulbs were not always present or lit. Some years only a few bulbs brightened the branches, while other years they all sparkled brightly. Finances were well known to dictate every aspect of the season in *this damned house*.

Heirloom Polish glass ornaments, hand carried by Blondie's parents from Europe, were carefully tied onto branches with butcher's string or reused ribbons. Other trimmings, accrued from children's crafts or the local five and dime store, were hung with an equal air of importance. Wrinkled dried apples, gathered from the orchard's floor, were given painted faces then affixed to branches with colored dynamite wire. They were used as fillers to hide the bare spots of a scrawny evergreen.

Popped corn brandished the neighbor's pine trees, but popping corn was considered by Blondie to be a food. Chastising the kids who dared ask about popping and stringing a few kernels, Blondie's retort was always the same, "Food will not be wasted in this house to decorate a tree. Who's gonna eat it when it becomes stale? It will have to get thrown out with the trash."

The last decoration applied was tinsel. Thin strands of silver foil were hung individually to avoid tangles. In the children's eyes, *this freak of ugliness* called a Christmas tree was only a remnant from their mother's childhood. It was a tradition in which she forced her kids to partake.

To Blondie, who would stand a short distance away from the trimmed tree gazing bright-eyed in amazement, it was a sight to behold. Every December 24th she'd languor, "Look at that beautiful Christmas tree. It brings back so many memories of Christmas on our Osceola farm."

After the trimming was completed, she voiced her remembrance. She had closed her eyes and began speaking. "Those were the good old days, when I was a kid and didn't have a care in the world. My life was peaceful. I was so ignorant in my youth. Why did I do this to myself? Why? Why? Why? If I could only turn back the clock to what I . . . ," but she didn't complete the sentence, not with all those little frightened eyes staring up at her anguished face.

"Oh, what's the use? What's done is done and that's that," she languished.

Leaving her children to wonder what she'd have done differently, she ambled from the room to gather more trinkets for Santa's burlap bag. More meager gifts were needed than she had on hand. "I should have started collecting this junk in July," she grumbled, launching a treasure hunt to find anything that was at least half-suitable to throw in the sack.

What do they know? They're just stupid little piss-ant kids. They'll take what they get and like it, she decided.

The children expected Santa to give them each a gift. They knew better than to anticipate real presents. Other families were giving their kids candy canes and popcorn balls, bicycles, red wagons, balls, bats and mitts, store bought gloves, bracelets, hats, coats, or new dresses. The children at #11

Lemon Lane were lucky to receive pauper's presents. An orange, a couple of walnuts, maybe half of a candy cane, two sheets of stationary with mismatched envelopes, six plain buttons attached by butcher's string to a cardboard square, a pair of mittens sewn from a blanket remnant, slightly used jewelry with missing rhinestones, or a skirt made from a patterned flour sack for one of the older girls were just some of the holiday gifts that could be found in Santa's sack on any given year. These were the types of eagerly awaited presents doled out by Santa at #11 Lemon Lane.

Store bought presents were generally out of the equation for the kids in this household. There was one exception, Blondie's Jakey boy. There would be just enough loose change found to buy him a small truck, a small box of BB's, a bag of marbles or a pair of knit gloves. Jumping up and down, he could be heard shouting excitedly, "Hey everybody, look. See what Santa brought me. It's exactly what I wanted."

To the child who stood holding an orange and two walnuts, but dreaming of a pretty little doll, this somehow didn't seem fair. Stealing a couple of cookies from the pantry shelf later that night without getting caught was fair!

Pet, the eldest child, had been six years old when she figured out the true Santa Claus scenario. Taking delight in witnessing this folly since her first Christmas, Pet relished the pleasure this North Pole antic gave to her younger siblings. A few of the toddlers would squeal with excitement, others would cry with fright at the jolly old man's arrival. They all eventually grew to realize who was the "Ho, Ho, Hoing" figure in this crazy looking outfit. They would all be cautioned at one time or another by the man himself, "Don't tell the little ones. Just keep this a secret from them," he'd plead.

"There's no sense in ruining their fun, is there?" Mihal would ask.

Of course, one by one, year by year, the kids learned the reality and agreed to continue the pretense as a favor to their kind and gentle dad.

J was a bit slow to learn the truth. She was six and a half when she noticed some oddities about this Santa Claus guy. After one particular Santa visit, J quietly confided her perception to her Father as she sat next to him on their old, lumpy, quilt-covered sofa.

"Santa wears the same boots as yours, Dad. His even had the same manure on the heels that yours does right now and his hand has a scratch on the thumb, just like yours does. I think I know the secret. Am I right?"

Mihal just grinned. "You're a bright girl. It was fun while it lasted, wasn't it?"

Before J could answer, Mihal quickly asked, "Can you keep the secret?"

Smiling back at him with two missing front teeth, she slowly turned her head to the right. Saddened, she now understood that the Santa fantasy was a charade. No one noticed the knowing tears flowing down the child's cheeks as she answered her dad's question with a meager "Yep!"

That one determined affirmative word sealed the mystic of the season for her younger siblings that one particular holiday. Who knew what secret would be uncovered on the next Christmas, or the one after that.

Sixty years later, J sat silently in a Michigan church. In quietude, she was listening to the spirited choir sing reverent carols. She was attending Midnight Mass on a Christmas Eve with her own family. She was contentedly living her life hundreds of miles away from the memory of her Pennsylvania hometown.

Deep in thought about her young son's recent painful divorce, J began thanking God for blessings he had bestowed upon her and her family. Grateful to be in this elaborately decorated parish, her green eyes sparkled as she sat gazing at the twinkling evergreen trees and the brilliant-red poinsettias. She felt a profound peace while sitting between her two toddler granddaughters who had been deserted by their mother. Holding their tiny fragile hands, she felt eternally grateful that her son had acquired full custody of the little girls and that their bar-hopping mother hadn't been considered fit to assume the responsibility.

J listened attentively to the young priest's homily. He was retelling the age old Christmas fable. His soothing voice and the velvety Christian words were so unlike the memory of her Baba's dialect when she'd recited her Gypsy rendition of Christ's birth.

J sat quietly trans-fixed. In a fugue-like state, she transcended to a memory from ever so long ago. For the minutest of moments, she was a child at home again. The feeling was spiritual, but she was hypnotized by this realistic scene.

She heard her sibling's giggles. She saw Santa in his faded suit come through the old kitchen doorway. She watched as her father emerged and sat down next to her. She even felt warmth emanating from his blue plaid flannel shirt. She imagined an itch from the hand-pieced wool quilt with its vivid colors that was still covering the old lumpy sofa. She smelled the distinct pungent sharpness of her dad's chewing tobacco and saw the red coffee-can spittoon on the floor next to his high-top work boots. She noted brown manure on his boot heels and a reddened scratch on his thumb.

She smelled smoke fumes from the old kitchen coal stove that were distinctly mingled with the hovering aromas of Christmas ham and fresh bread.

Glancing into her dad's grey tear-filled eyes, she felt his calloused hand on her knee and gently placed her hand on top of his. He began to pat her left knee. He tapped three times; an ever so gentle *tap, tap, tap.*

Smiling slightly as he faced her, Mihal whispered softly, "It's alright, Joni. Everything will be alright now."

The scene was intensely graphic. It was as though she had clearly been transported back in time. She had returned to a precious moment, but then in a blink the vision was gone. In a flash, the recollection was gone. He was gone. She turned slightly, intent on hiding her face from her husband. It was then that she began to sob timidy. Slow-rolling, delicate tears fell down her cheeks.

Only J had revisited this brief, but wonderful memory.

Only she had envisioned her Dad's tears.

As some sixty years ago, no one noticed hers.

THE WATERMELON DRESS

Hesitating ever so slightly as she stepped up the weather beaten steps to the grungy back door, the skinny girl listened for any sounds from the kitchen. Thinking silence meant she could sneak into the house and up to her bedroom, she proceeded to slowly open the patched and warped wooden screen door into the kitchen. An aroma of fresh bubbling strawberry jam hung in the air. She remembered hearing the squeaking of the aged hinges, just before feeling the sharp whack to the left side of her head.

A high-pitched ringing had performed a balancing act between her ears, and she had realized that someone was bellowing, "You had better pray hard tomorrow, you sinner. You better save my soul after what you made me do!"

Was she crazy or what, the girl wondered. *Nobody can make a grownup do something like what she did that morning.*

Even at seven years old, the girl knew that! *The woman was just mean and hateful,* that's what she knew in her brain and in her heart. All of the kids knew that about her. Even her boys knew it. Her boys were the kids she favored. It didn't matter what pranks they pulled, or what mischief they conjured up, they were her favorites. Her sons sure could pull some Lulu stunts, but their mother always overlooked their nastiness. Jake smoked corn silk and caught the haystack on fire, but she just laughed saying, "Boys will be boys."

Yet, if one of the girls forgot to replace so much as a hairbrush onto the pantry shelf, they would soon learn what a sorry mistake they'd made. A girl's mistake warranted the use of a weeping willow switch to be swiftly lashed to the back of their legs. With a flick of the wrist, the pliant switch would arc through the air as deftly as a whip on a horse's ass nearing the finish line. Those swollen red welts stung for the day's duration. They were a lesson for every kid to see that's what happened if you didn't tow the line.

Maybe having so many kids made this woman so cruel, but the girl doubted it. She had decided, a long time ago that this woman was just as wicked as the gruesome witches in those children's fairytales. As a young girl, J had decided that not even a woodland fairy could convince her otherwise.

So, she's telling me to pray for her soul in church tomorrow morning the girl's thoughts continued. Jake was the one who had thrown the tiny orange colored kitten into a dirty bucket of barn water. Fear gripping her stomach, the confused girl had wondered *how am I gonna tell God that I saved that tiny critter from drowning just so she could pull it out of my dress pocket the first time it moved?*

"What do you have here?" the woman had asked as she held the kitten high above the girl's head. "I thought I'd told you not to bring animals into this house. You just can't listen, can you? I'm just gonna have to teach you a lesson, Miss Smarty Pants."

"But it was drowning," the girl had stammered. "I put it in my pocket to dry off its fur. I'll put it back with its mama right away," she had quickly continued as she slowly slid her hand into the now empty, wet pocket of her favorite dress.

The watermelon dress, stylishly patterned with colorful, pink-dotted slices and adorned with green melon buttons, was her only treasure from the closet of hand-me-downs. She so loved the comforting feeling that soft cotton dress gave to her skinny frame. With tear-filled eyes, the motionless girl hung her head as she moved her nimble fingers up and down while repeatedly counting those large green melon buttons on the dress bodice.

Shoving the girl aside, an angry twisted mouth had begun a low growl that grew into, "Oh, and noooooo you won't. You're not goin' anywhere, and neither is that cat! I told you not to bring it in here. Now I'll show you what happens when little girls don't do as they're told," the huge woman had continued her barking as she loomed over the smallness of the girl standing before her.

While grasping the kitten in the air with her left hand, the woman then used her right hand to grab onto a stove-top handle. She lifted a round iron lid off the top of the old farm's coal stove revealing a hole of reddened coals. The embers glowed and sizzled. The scene was as a blazing Hell from the mouth of the stove's belly.

The woman held the meowing kitten by the scruff of the neck. She had taken one final look straight into its startled green eyes, and then plunged the innocent kitty into the gaping illuminated hole. Forcefully she managed to replace the iron lid faster than the flames could be mashed back into the coals.

All of the lids in the world would never drown out the wailing cries of that little fur ball. After what seemed an eternity of its pitiful screams, the deafening silence set in. The quietness was shattered only by "Don't you even think of movin'. You haven't got what's comin' to you yet."

Sweating profousely, Blondie's air-borne words hissed as her threats seemed to be mocking the old dented aluminum teapot's counter whistle steaming away on the heated stove's surface.

More than sixty years can't erase the heart-wrenching sounds or expunge the burning flesh stench that filled that farm house kitchen that sunny Saturday morning.

Nor can more than sixty years of a grandfather clock's *tick-tocking* heal the memory of a petite freckle-nosed girl gently rolling her favorite dress into a small ball, and then walking gingerly with her scalding welted legs to toss that freshly tear-stained watermelon dress into that coal stove's inferno of flames.

Did the little girl pray for her mother's soul that July Sunday so very long ago?

A prayer can be meaningful to God if it is influenced by an innocent heart and two respectful hands folded in prayer, even if all that can be mustered in silent reverence is *1-2-3-4, 1-2-3-4, 1-2-3-4* repeatedly for the duration of the service. When the congregation knelt, when they stood or when they sat, J did likewise, but always looking upward with questioning eyes toward the Almighty Crucifix. Her youthful hands didn't unclasp until she was jolted out of her dazed concentration by the booming priest's words, "This Mass is ended. Go in peace."

It would be more than sixty years later before the child left stranded in the adult heart could still wonder in bewilderment *just who was the saint and who was the sinner* that rainy July morning so long ago?

Who could have ever guessed that a seven year old girl's birthday would have been filled with such mind-numbing horror?

How could a child cope with such an experience, when the adult mother didn't even comprehend the impact of her repugnant actions?

J often wonders *what ever became of her childish block-printed note that was so bravely left on her mother's pillow that evening?* She wonders, too, *what did Mom think as she read:*

Dear Mom, I hate you. Love, J

JAKE

Jake, Jake!
You rotten snake.
When it wasn't given,
you didn't hesitate to take.

Wreaking havoc,
Prince of uncouth,
stealing innocence
from many a youth.

Wrong or right,
at those he spat.
His own rules,
his Ma's favored brat.

One son of a bitch,
from cradle to the grave;
from youth to old age
never learned to behave.

Knowing what he knew,
never altered his plan.
He couldn't have cared less
to be less than a man.

So, rest easy, old boy,
now that you're dead.
I know you're still out there
dancin' in the devil's bed.

HOLY WHAT?

August 15, 1949 was going to be a grand day for J. She was so looking forward to Sunday's celebration. Tomorrow was Saturday, August 14, practice day. She was even excited about that.

Her anticipated summer vacation was such a big joke. Unlike other neighborhood kids who spent their days freely enjoying games, fishing or swimming, J's days were utilized doing garden chores and housework that filled what should have been child's play time. Her only respite was summer catechism and preparing for her First Holy Communion.

To a young Catholic girl, this awaited event was something special. This meant getting your hair curled, wearing a lacey white party dress with a wedding-type veil, and going to a celebratory party in the church's basement hall. "I'm gonna taste my very first communion host ever. I can't wait," J told her sister, Adela.

"My stomach feels so full of butterflies that I think I could fly all the way to Ramey tomorrow," J confided, causing them both to break out in giggles.

"You're so silly," Adela replied. "You'll be scared stiff when the Priest starts asking his questions. You just wait, you'll see. I know, 'cause I've already done my Communion."

J hadn't minded the two mile walk to and from the church on weekdays for the past four weeks. Adela did, though. "I'm so glad it's Friday and the last day of the summer catechism classes. You're such a big baby. You're old enough to walk alone, but nooooo, somebody has to go with you and be your protector. Protected from what, or who, I'll never know. Nobody would want you with your mamoona face. That's one ugly monkey face you're stuck with," Adela taunted.

J continued singing to the birds, to the sky, to the trees. Singing made the journey seem shorter and quieter. She'd learned to concentrate on the song's words and not on Adela's rude wise-acre remarks. Catechism classes would begin promptly at eight o'clock and end at noon. At that time, the kids were each handed a chocolate-chip cookie and promptly shooed on home. At one o'clock, J's cheap physical labor began again at #11 Lemon Lane.

It had been an intense summer for the family. It seemed that none of the kids could do enough work in the house or in the fields to satisfy their mother. Blondie's constant harping was an unavoidable annoyance.

"Get your ass out there and get those weeds pulled."

"Go help your dad rake that hay and get it thrown into the loft."

"Get those dishes washed and put away."

"Go upstairs and straighten the beds. Don't forget to air out the one your baby sister Marsha pissed in last night!"

Blondie allowed the kids very little playtime. She kept them occupied with chores, or so she thought. Blondie summoned task upon task upon task. "Everyone's gotta do Pet's share of the workload. Since she left for the city it seems there's double work for me. It's time that work got spread around a little," she'd whine mercilessly.

Blondie didn't seem angry because Pet was gone, but more so because she had left her share of the work load behind.

Blondie was constantly moaning and groaning about something, but mostly about money. More to the point, the lack of funds was the major source of her bitching.

"Damn it to Hell, Mihal, can't you go somewhere and find a decent job? Other men around here are goin' to the cities to find work in factories. They're bringin' big paychecks home. What's wrong with you? Are you too stupid, or too lazy? Maybe you're afraid to leave your mommy? Is that it?"

"Damn it to Hell, Blondie," an irritated Mihal would answer. "I'm goin' back to work Monday morning. Stop your belly-achin' already. It's not like I sit on my ass all day, or haven't you noticed how much work I do. It's not just you who works around this place, you know. Why Hell, these kids do more in one day than you do in a week."

Mihal was finally returning to his mining job in the Koxis coal mines after being laid off for the past four months. The miners seemed to work five or six months, or until coal demands were met, then the mines would shut down until new coal orders came through. The theory of supply and demand was alive and well in Gunther and the Koxis coal mines.

It wasn't as though Mihal didn't work when he was unemployed. During his lay-off period, Mihal farmed his acreage. His bronze-tanned skin was proof of the long hours he recorded in the burning sunshine. He faithfully registered for his unemployment funds every Thursday so that a check would come in the mail every Tuesday, much to Blondie's delight.

His large, low-income family qualified them to receive weekly rations of surplus government food, which was distributed from local offices. Once a week, he'd drive into the nearest town to collect their granted allotment.

Powdered milk in five pound boxes, cocoa in five pound tins, yellow American cheese in five pound blocks, white all-purpose flour in fifty pound sacks, large tins of canned beef with gravy and huge jars of chunky peanut butter culminated the list of welcomed freebies.

To save a few dollars, Mihal also spent many hours each night hauling wagon loads of loose coal back to their cellar. Scooped into burlap bags, the coal bits that were called sludge would be pilfered from the temporarily closed coal mine's tipple area. Walking the two miles from his home, he'd often be accompanied by a couple of his kids. Instead of helping to pull the coal-filled bags in their kiddie wagons, more often than not, the kids arrived home riding atop the sacks in the wagons that Mihal was pulling. Singing along with their father, Show Me the Way to go Home became their theme song.

Often he'd pass neighbors in the night, friends who were in a similar unemployed state. These folks would also be helping themselves to the sludge lying loosely scattered around the tipple. This area was where the coal would be poured from the railcars into dump trucks or train cars. When the truckbeds were filled and mounded, the excess would roll off the top and onto the ground leaving a bevy of loose coal chips for the taking. These *night robbers* held to the rationale that this coal was just going to waste lying there, so someone should get some benefit from it.

The season didn't matter. The reason for the scavenging did. With coal as the only source of furnace or kitchen-stove fuel, the fossilized mineral was as much a necessity to this depressed community as was air or water. When it came right down to it, an unemployed neighbor supported a needy neighbor's plight. No one ever had any knowledge about a little missing coal. It didn't matter if you were eight or eighty, "I don't know nothin' 'bout no missing coal, period!" was the official answer to the official question. That was, if any official was stupid enough to attempt eliciting information from this bunch of Gunther yahoots, the official name assigned by the coal company's managment to the coal miners in this town.

Despite knowing that Mihal would be returning to his mining job, Blondie kept up her verbal bashing and hammering. She was determined to get Mihal to seek employment in the big city, as she called it. Labor Day was nearing and that meant the return to the school year for the kids. Blondie was keenly aware of the rising costs for school necessities vying with their dwindling bank account.

She also knew J's First Communion was on the horizon and the kid would be doing without her own special outfit. Blondie felt that couldn't be helped. The choice was food on the table or a fancy dress for a day. "J, you'll have to wear Adela's dress and veil. So what if it's too big. Pull the ribboned belt a little tighter," Blondie advised on Saturday morning.

For reasons that she didn't care to discuss with Mihal, Blondie had decided not to attend J's Communion day. She was adamant and became braver with every word directed to Mihal anytime he broached the subject. "I am not goin' with that brat to her first communion. You go if it's such a damned important date on your big-shot calendar," she suggested to her husband.

"What's more important, her party or you gettin' off your behind to find a real payin' job? You could leave tomorrow mornin' to get a job in a factory. Big John said there's work at the car plant in Tonawanda where he works. He even said you could ride back and forth with him every weekend. How much more of an offer do you need?"

She was relentless. Mihal knew the harassment would continue until he finally agreed to go to Buffalo, "Okay, okay, I'll apply for a factory job if that will make you quit harpin', but I'm not goin' until I see our Joni receive her First Communion on Sunday," he answered.

"She's worked and studied so hard, mostly to try and please you. Why is it you don't pay any attention to that child? She's thrilled just to be goin' to a rehearsal tomorrow. It's the highlight of her summer. It's the only fun you'll let her have. Is that what's wrong with you, Blondie? She has a party to go to and you don't?" Mihal asked.

Mihal pounded his opinion home, and Blondie did not find it amusing.

"She's a kid, Mihal. Don't worry about what's wrong with me. It's my business if I don't want to go to this damned church celebration. You go. She'll have plenty of disappointments in her lifetime. This won't be the first, and it won't be the last," Blondie shouted directly into Mihal's face.

"She'll just have to get used to the facts of life, and so will you. You'll be going with Big John for that city job. That's one fact that you're gonna get straight into your noggin, Mister," Blondie's controlling tactics had reared again.

Mihal knew there was no further discussion, not with this Polack's attitude. He was destined to drive the kids to the communion ceremony on Sunday.

He knew work in a city factory was in his future, but he was in no hurry to leave his coal mining job. *Why should I hurry and jump into a factory job?* He was comfortable there with his friends. *I'll go when I'm good and ready, and not until then* was his thought, even if Blondie had spoken her last words to him, " . . . and that is the end of that decision!"

"Blondie," Mihal was shouting through the kitchen doorway, "you had better get Adela and Jake to walk J to the church this mornin'. The car won't start and I don't have any idea what's wrong with it. If they start walkin' now, they should get there in time for the practice."

"Dad, can't you walk with me? I don't want Jake to walk me there. Please, Dad, please?" J pleaded.

J was becoming frightened of Jake lately. Jake had been acting strangely toward her. He had been touching her butt and teasing her about kissing. She had slapped him a couple of times, but he'd cautioned her the last time she had hit him. He'd pushed his face directly in front of J's and sneered, "You're gonna get yours yet. You'll see. I'm not finished with you."

J had tried to tell her mother about Jake, but Blondie warned her, "Just shut your mouth. You're just tryin' to get my Jakey boy in trouble. If you say one more word, you won't be goin' to any big time Communion party on Sunday."

So, J stopped trying to talk to her mother about Jake. She told her Baba instead. "Get yourself a kitchen fork and carry it with you. If Jake does anything to you, scratch him with it. Then, let him explain the scratches to his Ma," was Baba's answer to J's dilemma.

"I'll do that, startin' right after I get my Communion on Sunday," J promised in as determined a tone as a seven year old could muster.

Mihal tried to explain why he couldn't walk his girl the two miles to the church. "I can't go with you, J. I need to fix the car today, so I'll be able to drive all of you to the Communion service tomorrow."

"You don't want to walk when you're all dressed up in that pretty white dress, do you? Do you understand? Can you be a good girl and start walkin' with Adela and Jake now?" Mihal asked as he gently patted the girl's shoulder.

Not totally satisfied with his remedy, J asked, "Well then, can Baba go with me instead?" Shuffling her feet, J indicated that she still wasn't comfortable with her dad's request or his reasoning.

"No kid, she's too old. You'd still be walkin' to church tomorrow at this time if she started out this mornin'. She walks at a snail's pace these days." Mihal was snickering lightly as he added, "so, just do what I'm tellin' you and go now so that you won't be late."

The day began as a beautifully clear and sunny August morning, but it would evolve into a dark stormy afternoon in more ways than anyone could possibly have imagined. It was only a matter of hours before the sweltering heat set in.

The three kids arrived just as the rehearsal line was forming outside on the church steps. "J, come up here to the front with the short kids. You'll be between Rita and Babs in line. Remember to genuflect as you are coming into the pew, and again when you're leaving. Don't forget, no talking during the service except to answer the Priest's questions," instructed Sister Mary Louise.

J nodded an understanding of the nun's words as she stood in obedience with the others. She listened attentively to the Nun's raised voice indicating it was time for the group to run through the procedure. "Okay everyone, once again for good measure," echoed through the empty church. No glitches in the second half hour practice meant the Communion class was free to leave.

"See you all tomorrow morning at seven thirty. Wear your white dress and veil. Don't forget to polish your shoes," teased Father Joe.

Shoes? A thought ran amuck through J's head, *Oh, no. I don't think I have any nice shoes to wear.*

"Adela, do you have any nice shoes I can wear tomorrow?" J asked her older sister as they started their long trek home in the August sunshine.

"Ask Ma whose shoes you can wear tomorrow. I'm wearin' my own, and no, you can't borrow them. They're too big for you anyway," answered Adela as they continued their stroll homeward.

"You're wearin' my dress and my veil as it is. Look in the old shoe box. You might find a pair in there you can wear," Adela suggested.

Adela seemed distracted as she and Jake and briskly walked ahead of J. They were whispering to one another and seemed to be arguing about something. J didn't want bothered with their squabbles. She had other things on her mind this day. She couldn't stop thinking about having no shoes to wear the next day.

J became a straggler, walking slower than her siblings. She lagged behind, deep in thought about a pair of long-forgotten sandals. *If only my shoe plant had grown, I'd be rich with shoes right now. Dad said shoes don't grow on trees and Ma said money doesn't either, but I wonder why not? Everybody's gonna look so pretty tomorrow. I want to look pretty for a change, too.*

J was pouting by the time they reached the short-cut path through the Terrier's fragrant evergreens. *It smells like Christmas in here.* J's mind sadly recalled a holiday when she'd learned not to rely on the fantasies of a Santa Claus.

"What's wrong with you?" Jake asked. "Are you gonna cry about something?"

"Maybe I am," J answered haughtily. "I just know there are no nice shoes for me to wear tomorrow. Ma's not gonna buy me any, neither. I'll have to wear a pair of somebody's old clown shows with that pretty dress. Everybody's gonna laugh at me, I just know it."

J was getting used to the other kids poking fun at the fashions their family wore. J's thoughts turned sullen. *It's not my fault we're poor and dress in hand-me-down clothes all the time.*

"Come on, Adela," said Jake as he handed Adela a dollar bill and then pointed to a clump of large dark evergreen trees indicating that they should go into them.

"This is our play house. Me and Adela come here and play mommy and daddy. Sometimes Steve and Paul come, too," Jake said as he stared straight ahead looking at nothing in particular.

Grabbing J's right arm, Jake began guiding her toward the darkened patch of evergreens. "You're gettin' to be a big girl now, J, so it's time you learn how to play mommy. Come on. Come over here and lay down on that patch of pine needles," Jake coldly instructed, as he forcibly pushed her down onto the flattened patch.

"That's our bed," Jake harshly informed J, "and today you're gonna learn what that's all about."

Pulling a small black stick-like object out of his pants pocket, Jake pressed a button revealing a knife protruding from the stick's handle. He quickly pushed the blade onto her right cheek making a small cut into her skin. "Ow! What are you doin'?" shrieked J.

Tears rolled freely from the corners of her eyes as she reached up and touched the painful bleeding spot on her face.

"You just shut up and do what I tell you, or your whole face is gonna get cut up. Tell her to shut up and do what she's told, Adela," Jake commanded.

"Do what he's tellin' you, J. He means business," Adela instructed her little sister. "You might as well learn now from Jake, instead of from the other boys. They won't be as easy on you, believe me. So shut up now and get this over with."

As Adela was talking, Jake had reached up under J's skirt and cut her panties up one side with his knife. With one quick jerk, he pulled them from under her.

"Hey, stop that. Get off me! Adela, tell him to leave me alone," J cried out angrily.

Becoming frightened, J tried to get up off the ground, but Jake applied all his weight onto her skinny body. He was sitting on her thighs and pushing her shoulders down with the palms of his hands. Forcing his knees between her legs, he brought the threatening knife up to her face again. She tried wriggling out from under him, but he yanked on her pony tail and slammed her head against the dry hardened ground. Instantly, she felt a weakness and a dizziness engulf her. It was at that moment she felt the pain between her spread legs.

Jake was smiling when J awakened from her fainting episode. "Get your ass up," Jake crudely told her. "You're mine now and I can do this to you anytime I want to. Do you hear me?"

He had a wild menacing look in his eyes, one that J didn't understand. "Adela, tell her what I call this," Jake shouted over his shoulder.

Jake was gloating. J was ashamed, not just for herself, but for all of them. She was ignorant and innocent, but she knew in her conscience *this just isn't right.*

Stumbling at first, she quietly arose from the pine scented bed. Rising slowly from the bed of pine needles, she watched as Jake handed Adela another dollar bill. He was saying, "You just keep bringin' me new ones and I'll keep payin' you in dollar bills."

She didn't understand what exactly had happened, but she would soon learn the ugly truth. She would come to learn that she had lost her virginity. Adela would eventually acknowledge that she had earned two dollars from Jake for arranging that to happen.

Trembling, J began the slow agonizing walk home. Adela and Jake lagged behind, but Jake called out to her, "Remember, keep your mouth shut or your monkey face will be one cut up mess. The only thing you'll look good in will be a zoo."

Jake sniggered every so often during the rest of his walk home. He seemed to think he'd cracked a pretty good joke. J never did think his joke was funny.

"What happened to your face? Is that a scratch? Where are Jake and Adela?" Blondie's rapid-paced questions filled the air.

J wasn't talking, at least not to Blondie. The shivering girl looked around the kitchen at the younger kid's faces. They were all gawking at her. "You look like you've seen a ghost. What's wrong with you?" Blondie persisted.

"Where's Baba or Dad?" J asked.

"Your dad's out in the garage, workin' on the car. I think Baba's where she always is, sittin' on that damn swing outside," Blondie informed her sarcastically. "What do you want them for?"

J didn't hesitate. She ran from the room. *This is one thing Jake's not gonna get away with,* her brain screamed as she ran toward the garage.

Nearly knocking the old woman over, J had bumped into her grandmother who was climbing the steps to the back porch. J instantly burst into tears. "What is it child?" Baba asked, hugging the sobbing girl.

Pulling away to see her Baba's face, J could only manage to utter, "Jake hurt me, and Adela helped him."

"Mihal, come here quick," the old raspy-grandma's voice bellowed. "Jake's at it again. This time it's with this child. I won't let him get away with his cruelty anymore. He needs punished Mihal, and you've got to be the one who handles it."

Admonishing her son, Baba continued, "You know Jake and Blondie will only twist everything and try to say his dirty work is this little one's fault. That's what they've done before, just as when the other girl's came crying. There he is now, Mihal. Take care of this before it goes any further. I tried to tell you he's no good. He's a bad, bad apple!"

"Jake, come over here," Mihal called to the whistling boy, who was skipping through the front gate.

"Whacha want, Dad? Do you need some help fixin' the car? I'll bet it's just run out of gas. Did you check the gas tank?" Jake asked with an air of cockiness.

"What's J crying about now?" Jake asked, with a renewed annoyance in his voice.

"Well, for one thing, she's crying about the cut on her face. How did you get that cut, J?" her father's eyes were begging for the truth.

"Jake did it with a knife. It has a black handle and the blade pops out," she answered.

"Where would I get a knife like that?" Jake argued with a snicker.

"Oh, probably from in my top dresser drawer," said an agitated Mihal. "It's been missin' from there for a few weeks now. Which pocket did he keep it in, J?" Mihal inquired.

"His pants pocket, on the right side," J answered.

"Well, looky here," Mihal frowned, "it's my missin' knife and it has some blood on the blade. How did it get in your pocket, Jake?"

"J probably put it there when I wasn't lookin'. She's trying to get me in trouble by tellin' you some sort of a story, right? Well, you know J. Once she gets to talkin', she can talk the feathers off a goose! I'm tellin' Ma you guys are all pickin' on me again," Jake grumbled.

Jake attempted to walk away, only to be grabbed at the scruff of his neck by a giant's hand attached to Mihal's large muscular arm.

Mihal's strength was never questioned, at least not by anyone who knew how he'd saved nine coal miners by bracing a mine's support pillar during a roof collapse. The miners had all escaped to safety before Mihal left his post, only seconds ahead of the crumbling ceiling.

Jake must have realized that struggling with Mihal's brute strength was futile because he quit trying to pull himself free of Mihal's grasp.

"No, I don't think that's the real story. You sit right there Jake, while J tells what really happened. Adela, you get over here, too," Mihal ordered.

"But I don't know anything," Adela said, contempt mixed with spittle as she spoke rapidly. She tried to walk past Mihal.

"I said sit down here and I meant it," Mihal commanded.

"We're gonna get to the bottom of this, if it takes all afternoon," Mihal said as he jerked Adela's arm forcing her to sit down on the grass near his feet.

Feeling defiled and dirty, yet not truly understanding the magnitude of what had happened in those evergreen trees, J couldn't control her trembling or sobbing. She told every sordid detail of her shocking ordeal.

Adela hung her head with embarrassment, and then cried huge gulping sobs that raked her trembling body. Haltling between words, she explained, "If I wouldn't have helped Jake today, he warned me that him, Steve and Paul would hold me down again and do the same things to me that they did last week. I'm afraid of them, Dad," Adela said.

Mihal nodded his head as an indication for Adela to continue her story. Adela trembled as she spoke. "You don't know what all they do when you're at work. Ma lets Jake do whatever he wants. She says he has to learn somewhere and it might as well be here at home or with the girls around here. All of my friends are afraid of him, too. He does bad things with them all the time. Maddy's dad even said he was gonna shoot Jake if he ever came near her again."

"So, Jake, what do you have to say to these two girls?" the father asked the son.

Jake's response was loudly delivered after several seconds of contemplation. "Go to Hell! That's what I say to all of you. Ma's my boss, nobody else. Ask her, she'll tell you. She'll tell you why, too, if you're interested."

Jake's angry outburst startled the group, especially Mihal.

Mihal hadn't realized how far Jake's antics had escalated. *Blondie's to blame for this, but I'm just as guilty. I trusted her to handle him, but she's let it go too far. It looks as if she's encouraging him to be a young rooster. I should have seen that by the way she's given him free reign over the hen house and this neighborhood. Good God, what is goin' on here?* Mihal's thoughts spoke only to his own ears, while his heart whispered in melancholy to his soul.

"Jake, how many neighbors have been to see me and how many have complained about you molestin' their daughters? Or about you screwin' them? Is that what you did to your sister today? Did you rape her? Did you?" Mihal shouted directly into Jake's face, after grabbing him by the shoulders and lifting him up off the ground.

Looking into Jake's clear blue eyes, Mihal asked again, "Did you put your penis inside your sister?"

Answer me now, you piece of shit!" Mihal yelled to the boy.

"So what if I did. She's gotta learn sometime. That's what Ma says. Ma don't care, so why should you?" Jake sassed back.

Two girls and their grandmother sat and watched in wide-eyed horror at the maniacal callousness of the young man. He was cold and unfeeling about their pain. He was glaring at them and sneering. The girls weren't aware of the magnitude of his monstrosity. How would these crude violations affect their lives or the lives of their younger siblings in the coming years? Only time would tell.

Mihal saw the grotesque face on this handsome boy. He was a hideous creature hiding behind a sculptured youthful mask. He had bright sea-blue eyes, much like his mother's. He was destined for a devious existence if someone didn't draw rein on his offensive behavior. "Jake, you will feel your sister's pain today. You will learn that punishment follows a crime."

Jake's fear was evident. His fright gleened an azure-blue in his frigid eyes as Mihal dragged him by the arm toward the barn. A coward's whimpering was clearly heard while Jake's heels dug deeply into the soil. His shoes were skidding small trenches as he was pulled against his will.

"Blondie, come down to the barn. Come keep your son company. He's gonna learn a painful lesson, and you're gonna know that you are the cause of it all. You and your warped teachings have brought disgrace to our home. This is your son, not mine."

Once Mihal began to unleash his fury toward the boy and Blondie, he couldn't bring himself to contain it any longer. Holding the boy tautly by the arm, Mihal shouted as he began the punish-ment. "You have shamed me for the last time, do you two hear me? You're both evil, but for now, Jake will get his due."

Mihal spat his tobacco chew out of his lower lip. He reached for the bull whip hanging from a nail on the barn's rafter. "This is where this sin started and this is where it ends. Today!" he roared.

Mihal's wrath flayed at Blondie as the cracks repeated a staccato tempo to the whipping being inflicted on Jake. Mihal hated using the short cropped riding whip. He'd used it before to settle a cow in heat when the bull wasn't available. A few sharp whacks to the rump of the cow were usually all it took to stop the crazed animal from flailing and kicking with her hind legs. Once she was calmed, she would allow the milking to continue. Mihal wondered if Jake's whipping would calm his sex cravings. Sadly, he doubted it.

Blondie reached to grab the whip from Mihal's hand, but he used his elbow to shove her aside and into the wall. "Mihal, look you've hurt me, too. You've scraped my elbow on the stone wall," she appealed to his common decency.

She tried reaching his empathetic nature. "Come on now, that's enough. You're gonna hurt the boy. He's a good kid. Let him go already. I'll punish him. I'll take care of whatever he did. I promise," Blondie begged while trying to stroke Mihal's arm.

She stepped closer and closer to the bull whip, but Mihal saw what she was attempting to do. With a stronger shove, he knocked her into the corner hay mound.

"Stay there, Blondie, if you know what's good for you. This is somethin' he should have gotten long ago from me, not you. Stay out of it this time," Mihal warned, still grasping the wriggling boy's arm tightly. "I'm not lettin' go of you boy, so you best be still and take your medicine," Mihal warned.

Mihal gave Blondie notice as he continued swinging the whip at the screaming boy's buttocks and legs. "Go apologize to your daughters for the crimes you've allowed your Jakey boy to inflict upon them. If you're smart, you'll get on your knees and beg for their forgiveness. I won't let you continue to protect this pig any longer."

"And another thing Blondie, I'm stayin' right here to work in the coal mines. I'm gonna keep watch over you and Jake. I can't trust either one of you any longer," Mihal gasped. Tears streamed down Mihal's cheeks as he grew tired and ashamed of lashing the boy.

J stood outside of the barn watching and listening as Jake begged and bartered for his release. She heard her mother bark back at Mihal, "Apologize? For what? For givin' them life and breath? I don't get on my knees for no one, especially whores!"

J thought she was alone, but she wasn't. Baba stood right behind her, a kitchen fork in her hand. "Here, keep this with you at all times. Use it as I told you. It works better than a knife. Someday, you'll remember what this old gypsy taught you," she said.

The old woman smiled and wrapped an arm around J before speaking again. "Come now," Baba said. "Let's get out of this pouring rain and get you a warm bath. We need to get your clothes ready for your First Holy Communion tomorrow."

"But I don't have any shoes to wear with my pretty dress," J whispered timidly. "I'll have to look in the old shoe box for something that fits."

"Oh, I think you might be surprised to see the pretty white sandals I found hanging on a small bush out in the garden this morning," winked Baba. For the first time this day, J had a reason to smile.

As a post script, J wasn't laughed at the next day. She looked "angelic" in Adela's white lacey outfit and her new white sandals that Baba had purchased that morning when she had gone shopping with a neighbor.

J even managed to impress her family and the congregation as the only communicant who knew every catechetical answer to every one of the religious questions.

"She's one smart little girl, that's for sure," Mihal whispered to Baba after the service.

Baba smiled knowingly.

FISHING FROM THE RAFT

"Come on! Hurry up before Old Man LeCroix sees us. He won't miss these old boards today, so let's get movin'," Jake whispered to his two buddies.

"Besides," added Paul, "it won't be long before it's dark out here. They always go to bed early. From their house, they can't even see over here behind their barn."

"Yeah, but won't they miss them tomorrow?" Steve wanted to know.

"Maybe, but how will they know who took them if they don't catch us," answered sneaky Jake. "Just keep your mouths shut and nobody will ever know."

Taking boards from the top of a high pile of scrap barn lumber, they managed to stack the pilfered loot onto their little red wagon and head for the path that took them through the Terrier's tall overgrown evergreens. Balancing the boards precariously and wheeling them over the uneven grassy pathway, they skillfully managed to get the boards behind Jake's garage without a mishap. Amazed at their own resourcefulness, they succeeded in arriving home before dusk settled into darkness.

"Whew! That was one heck of a job," Jake said following up on his comment with a short whistle.

"Okay, we got the boards. Tomorrow we'll meet in the mornin' and start buildin' our raft. It's gonna be great to take it out to the strippin' hole for fishin'," exclaimed Steve enthusiastically.

"If we get caught . . ." started Paul, but before he could finish his sentence, Jake held up his palmed hand indicating enough talking had been done.

With a one-eyed wink, Jake quietly said, "Like I said, just keep your mouth shut. See you in the mornin'."

"Okay," rang out harmoniously from the two twelve year olds, as they skipped away from Jake and headed down Lemon Lane toward their own homes.

Morning came with a large clap of thunder, awakening Jake with a start. "Aw nuts! Don't tell me it's gonna rain all day," he uttered aloud.

"I might as well get up and be ready in case it does stop rainin'."

Then almost as if he'd willed the dark clouds to stop their storming, the pouring rain ceased. It didn't take long for Jake to gobble a raisin and oatmeal breakfast and he was soon off and running to his dad's garage, eager to get started on their big project.

Steve and Paul were already waiting for him. Holding hammers, they demonstrated to Jake that they were serious about building the raft. They also brought a couple of wood saws, a plane and an old coffee can that contained a potpourri of nails. His friends were anxious to start the summer project. "Where've you been? We've been here waitin' for the past hour. Afraid of a little rain?" they teased Jake.

"Shut up," he grumped, but continued walking over to their work site.

"You wanna start now, or tomorrow? I say now. So shut up and let's get busy!" Jake shouted.

Working diligently, they managed to assemble the framework before becoming hungry. A noon lunch was quietly stolen from Jake's kitchen. It consisted of a few mustard-lathered bologna and home-made bread sandwiches that were eaten hurriedly, and then washed down with fresh buttermilk from the early morning's butter churning. "If anybody asks what we had for lunch, we didn't. Okay? If my old lady finds out that we ate the whole loaf of bread, she'll kill us!"

Jake knew his mother wouldn't do anything to him. She never punished him. He just wanted his buddies to know who the boss of this project was. "Now let's get goin' or we won't be able to try this out tomorrow at the old strippin' hole."

"We are goin' fishin' with our dads and the other kids in the mornin' for sure," ordered Jake.

"Tonight we have to dig for worms down by the barn. They grow big and juicy in the cow's manure. We can do that after supper. Agreed?" No one disagreed.

They just went back to work, sawing and nailing together the raft. The cacophony of the hammers ripped their jarring sounds into the neighborhood. The rap, rap, rap left everyone wondering just what mischief the three whippersnappers were up to this time.

Sunday morning came up brightly with plenty of sunshine to awaken the boys. For a change, they were eager to get their routine Massses and Sunday school out of the way. Not waiting for the customary Heaven and Hell brimstone lectures from their mothers, the boys dressed quicker than usual, and then literally ran to the early services. Going fishing this morning was the priority. Going fishing on their newly crafted raft was the real priority!

Getting the raft to the fishing hole was another adventure. Just hoisting it onto the red wagon was a taskmaster's feat. Lifting one side of the wooden monstrosity, they were able to push the wagon beneath it, but the raft toppled off with the first attempt to move it. "Oh! Fart!" said one of the boys, causing them all to start a giggling frenzy.

The second try was equally unbalanced and equally comical to the boys. "Think we'll ever get it there? Whose stupid idea was this anyway?" asked Paul, before he took a deep breath and started laughing again.

On the third attempt, with the raft on the wagon the boys managed to move it several yards. With one boy pulling and the other two holding onto each side of the raft, they eventually maneuvered it down the old dusty trail to the fishing hole. Stopping every time one of them got a case of the chuckles didn't seem to hamper their progress. Eventually they managed to catch up to the rest of the fishing troupe.

"I can't believe we got it down here through all those trees," Paul explained to everyone through heavy raspy breathing.

"I never laughed so hard in all my life!" added Jake, as another outburst caused the boys to double over with instinctive laughter.

"We had a tough time pullin' it here, but we're gonna put it in the water." Then as an after-thought, Jake added, "Sure hope it doesn't go straight to the bottom of this old strippin' hole."

"Hey look, it floats! The son of a gun floats," shouted one of the boys to no one in particular.

"Let's get the fishin' poles and the worms. We came here to catch us some fish, didn't we?" Steve squealed.

The dads were paying little attention to the boys' chattering, so they heard only portions of Jake's mutterings. "Let's take J out with us. She's past seven years old. She knows how to fish and she should know how to swim already. She's just a big chicken about goin' in the water. She's afraid she'll drown! You guys keep quiet and let me do all the talkin'. She's gonna get what's comin' to her for tattlin' on me all this summer."

After the boys' snickering died down, the next thing out of Jake's mouth was "Hey J! Why don't you come fishin' with us on our new raft? Bring your pole. We have the worms. It's gonna be fun."

"Sit right there," Jake said to J. He was wearing a sly smirk as he pointed to a corner of the raft.

"We'll paddle this raft out a ways with our hands, and then we'll start fishin'. Maybe we'll catch some catfish for dinner," he added excitedly.

Fearing J would catch on to their plot, the boys covered their mouths with their hands, Paul and Steve kept sputtering as they tried to suppress their giggles. "We'll throw our lines in once we get out in the middle of this here fishin' hole. Bet there are some big ones out there," Jake ventured.

J hadn't learned how to swim yet, so she sat frightfully quiet on the edge of the questionably safe raft and concentrated on keeping still. She didn't see the three boys reach out to shove her off that edge and into the water. She attempted to scream, but the sound came out as a long squawk. It was enough of a noise, though, to reach the wet clay pond bank where the fathers were sitting contentedly drinking a cold rootbeer. The other kids were busy chattering while enjoying their cool cherry drinks.

"What was that?" asked Mihal as he stood up to look around for the source of the loud squeal.

Looking forward to the raft, he counted, "One, two, three boys."

Turning to the other scampering children, Mihal called, "Where's J?"

Turning back toward the boys on the raft, he anxiously hollered, "Hey! Where's J?"

Laughing boisterously, the boys began pointing to the water. "She's either gonna sink or swim, Dad! She should be comin' back up any second now," exclaimed Jake, catching his breath between the triumphant bursts of horse laughter.

Without hesitation, J's dad jumped into the musty colored water. Long deliberate swimming strokes propelled him toward the raft. With a swooshing sound, he disappeared under the surface of the water.

Panic and fear quickly replaced the boy's outburst of amusement.

Panic, because the girl hadn't surfaced yet and neither had the dad.

Fear, because they were acutely aware of the punishment awaiting them no matter the outcome of their prank.

"Oh, shit! We're in for it now. All of this is your fault," said Steve, who had turned to face Jake.

"I told you before, just shut up," replied a paling Jake.

"It was your big idea, Jake," added Paul nervously. "We always get into trouble when we listen to you. You think everything's a big joke. You're such an asshole! Why do we think you're our friend?"

What was in reality only seconds seemed like a lifetime of minutes to J. She had tried kicking and flailing her arms, but that didn't move her from the bottom of the pond. She remembered instructions from earlier swimming attempts. She'd been told to hold her breath if she ever went under the surface in deep water, but that was all that whirled in her bran until she felt someone slapping her face from side to side.

"Come on girl. Open your eyes. Breathe! Breathe, damn it, breathe!"

J recognized her dad's voice coming from somewhere, but where? She could tell she was out from under the water, but her face felt as though it were still stuck in the stinking clay muck at the bottom of the rain-filled crater.

"Cough, girl. Get that gunk out of your throat. That's it, cough! Keep coughin'. That'll get air into your lungs," Mihal was shouting encouragingly.

Someone was wiping her face with a wet rag, cleaning off her eyes so that she was able to finally open them. The brightness of sunshine was blinding. She could feel the sun's warmth engulfing her body, but that didn't stop the shivering that set in, nor did it halt the screaming that came from deep within her soul. "Help, help, help," she cried out, loudly at first, but then her cries waned to whimpered sobs.

"Shhh, your Pappy's got you now. You're okay. It's startin' to sprinkle, so let's get you home and into some dry clothes, unless you want to stay here and try fishin' again," Mihal tried teasing J as he cradled her in his muscular arms.

With the girl's renewed shivering, Mihal deeply sensed the reality of the boy's irresponsible act. An air of fear and disappointment shook all who had witnessed the incident. "Leave it to Jake," Mihal chittered to himself.

"This isn't my idea of a good fishin' trip. How about you, kid?" Mihal asked his little girl as they began their slow trek home through the thickly wooded fields.

"Why did they do it, Dad?" she asked, looking directly into his heavy grey eyes. "I didn't do nothin' to them. I just wanted to go fishin'."

"I don't know, Joni, but I'm sure gonna find out," he answered earnestly.

As they neared their home, the girl's mother came running down the pathway. She was calling curiously, "What happened, Jakey boy? Are you hurt or somethin'?"

"No!" quickly responded an irritated Mihal, still carrying the quivering girl. "Your Jakey boy's not the hurt one. It's our Joni. She nearly drowned!"

"Give the child to me," a raspy voice came from the grandmother walking toward the group.

Mihal's mother, called *Baba* by the children, continued to live with the family after her husband had died several years ago. Baba had reared her own five children to be considerate and kind. A serene and gentle natured woman, she was not one to tolerate abuse to a defenseless child, and so found herself in the midst of conflict with Blondie quite frequently. Many years ago, Baba had vowed to protect this undesired child, and she meant to keep that promise. She hadn't realized what a chore she'd assigned herself.

"This tyke is cold! I'll take her up to the house and get her into some clean and warm clothes," Baba offered graciously.

The girl's mother didn't object. Blondie actually appeared relieved as she cooed, "Come on Jakey boy, I'll get you somethin' warm to drink. You're shakin' like a wet dog!"

"Stay right here, Jake," his dad warned.

Despite Blondie's protesting glare, Mihal placed one hand on the boy's shoulder. Jake wasn't going anywhere at this moment.

"Okay now, what's your story? Why'd you three big boys push that little girl off the raft and into that murky water?" Mihal quizzed the three boys. He had no intention of showing any mercy to the scoundrels.

"You know that fishin' hole is where the farmers throw their dead animal carcasses to rot. Do you realize how disgustin' that water is? Well! I'm waitin' for an answer," Mihal stood waiting resolutely.

Mihal displayed an edge of impatience as he waited for one of the boys to speak. Their defense was slow coming. Three sets of scuffed boots shuffled in the dry dirt. Leaning against a large oak trunk, Mihal patiently waited until the dust had settled.

"I think she must 'a jumped in after one of those big ole catfishes," stammered a coy Jake, his blue eyes darted away from his father's stare.

"Or maybe, Paul or Steve pushed her in, but I know I wouldn't 'a pushed her. She's my sister!" he sheepishly answered, lowering his chin to hide his sneer.

"You bum! You're a louse!" Paul shouted.

"Some buddy you are. That's the last straw," Steve bellowed.

Out of sheer anger, they began pummeling Jake's chest and back with their fists. Jake twisted and turned to avoid their blows. Mihal stood between Jake and Blondie. Jake deserved whatever these two boys were dishing out, and Mihal was determined not to allow Blondie any interference.

Tears streaming down his face, Paul wailed his remarks to Jake's dad. "He said she needed to learn how to swim already and we were not to tattle on his idea. He promised it would be a big joke to play on her and we wouldn't get into any trouble."

"Yeah, Jake said she'd finally swim. He said that she wouldn't have any choice. Now we're the ones in deep shit!" Steve said, waving his arm in a semi-circle to include Paul.

So this was a joke, Jake? Mihal's thoughts swirled, as did J's.

If life was going to be one big joke for Jake, would trouble follow him or would he follow trouble? The question was a life-long game of tag for Jake. This day was only one of many that ended in tears for someone, but never for Jake. He always walked into, and out of, trouble with a conviction that he was immune to the rules. The joy of learning to swim was just as stolen from J as the raft boards had been from Mr. LeCroix's lumber pile that late summer weekend. J learned distrust and dishonesty are easily established, but a destroyed innocent joy is a treasure gone forever. Mr. LeCroix shared that valuable lesson with J. Neither of them ever forgot Jake for teaching it to them.

Jake walked away Scot free from any punishment that day. His mother saw to that by commenting, "He's just a boy. That's what boys do. They learn from getting into mischief."

Blondie often told her lady friends, "My boys are not bad boys. Whatever they do, they're just experiencing life."

Blondie always seemed to find a new defense for her boys. "They're always giving me little presents or picking me wildflowers," she'd brag.

"Of all my kids, my boys are my favorites," she'd tout. She would prove that many times over in the years that followed. This day was no exception.

Reaching for the weeping willow switch that was hanging on a kitchen hook, Blondie called for J. "Girl, get over here. Tell me why you blamed Jake for pushing you into the water? You know you jumped in all by yourself. You knew you couldn't swim! All you did was made me ashamed of you for causing so much trouble."

The girl stood in disbelief! She didn't try to defend herself. Jake had already told his convincing version of the day's near mishap. No other story would be credible to the mother this day, or any other day for that matter. Numbed by her own strong will, J refused to shed a single tear as the switch snapped repeatedly on her calves. She'd survived another day in *this damned house*. That's all that mattered to her.

A somber father walked steadily toward his shabby leaning barn, his shoulders slumped. Blondie had said, "You go milk the cow, Mihal. I'll take care of what punishing needs done to Jake."

He realized how untrusting the boy and his own wife had become. He needed to think through the day's occurrences, so he walked slowly and he held tightly to the handle of the swinging galvanized milk pail. His gentle tears were kissed by God's soft raindrops that evening. In the mild mist, he silently grieved for lost hopes and expectations. He sensed no good would come of this troublesome lad he was raising as his own son. Of that, he was sure. It was just a matter of time before the lying boy and his mother would prove him right again.

Mihal didn't know it, but before he ever drained the cow's filled teats, Blondie's Jakey boy was busy enjoying a game of marbles with his buddies. A stick-drawn circle in the dirt road called Lemon Lane, a couple of steelies and three cat-eye marbles were all it took for him to forget the day's near tragedy.

For Jake, this day was already history, but it wasn't so for the grandmother. Mihal was her son. She had seen what a toll this day had taken on him. In her mind, this day would not easily be forgiven or forgotten.

She was certain she'd remember this day clearly through to eternity.

She was also certain that eternity was where Jake would realize his regret for this day.

As he hugged his girl good night, Mihal knew J would probably never learn how to swim after this day's near-drowning, so he decided to share some light humor with the girl. "You know J, I think if you ever get in water over your head, the best thing you can do is get to the bottom as quickly as possible, then run like Hell."

J would never test his theory!

SOFT BUNNIES

"He wants to *give* me a pair of bunnies, Dad. He says they're called New Zealand Reds. He and his dad raise them. They sell them, but they're gonna give us ours, 'cause he's my best friend. Can we get a couple?"

"Only if they're two females," Mihal consented.

J's second grade friend, Bill, had offered her the bunnies during a school field trip. While they were walking in pairs and holding hands to cross a road, Bill had whispered, "You're my girlfriend and I want to give you a present."

With Mihal's approval, the present arrived the next day via Bill and his mother's special delivery.

Mihal had never seen rabbits this burnished color. He instantly became excited and amused watching them chase one another in his newly crafted hutch. Mihal had built the protective cage between two trees for shade. He made sure the rabbits new home was high off the ground to fend off conniving animals.

"Grass and clover, that's what they eat, Joni. The two of us will have to keep a steady pile over here in the corner or they'll starve. Is that a deal?" he asked.

There was no doubt in Joni's answer, "It's a deal, Dad."

Grasses and clovers were readily available in the summer and early fall months, but soon winter came and it became necessary to continuously keep a tall mound of hay in the corner of the hutch. "Those sure are two hungry critters," Mihal laughed one day.

"The one is about twice the size of the other. I swear, if that woman hadn't said she was positive these were two girl rabbits, I'd think the bigger one was ready to have young ones."

Two days later, young ones it was. There seemed to be about eight little pink squirming critters nestled in that furry nest at the far corner of their meager box.

"Don't touch them." Mihal cautioned.

"If they get the human scent on their skin, the mother won't go near them and then they'll starve. Just stand back here and watch. Wait until their pink skin is covered in fur and they have their eyes open, then you can pick them up. In the meantime, keep giving them hay from in the barn in the morning, after school and before it gets dark. As long as we feed the mother, she'll be able to feed her babies. Are you okay with that?"

That was more than okay with J. She couldn't wait until Monday morning to tell her friend Bill the good news. *I'm so excited. I love little soft fluffy bunnies* J reminded herself.

On Saturday and Sunday J hovered over the rabbits as though they were her creations. Hay and water were plentiful in their respective corners. The grown rabbits seemed to appreciate all of the new found attention. They'd nuzzle J's hands when she'd reach into their compound with a few carrots or celery stalks that she'd pilfered from the refrigerator crisper.

Monday morning proved no exception. She piled extra hay in the corner and put an extra pan of water into the cage before running off to catch the school bus.

"Honest, they had babies," J explained to Bill. He laughed with delight, then said, "That goes to show you what kind of a farmer woman my mom is. She only knows how to play the piano and bake bread. She's gonna think this is really funny."

Every time the two youngsters stole a glance at one another during the school day, they'd break out in a fit of giggles, forcing the second grade teacher to finally ask, "What's wrong with you two today?"

Bill braved it and answered her. "I gave Joni two girl rabbits and now one had babies. Everyone knows two girls can't make babies!"

After the laughter died down, the blushing teacher embarrassingly sputtered and asked, "When they're old enough, Joni, will you bring one of those special bunnies in to show the class?"

Amid her chuckles, the teacher added, "I do believe we'd all like to see one of those history making bunnies."

Joni couldn't wait to get home to tell her dad about the excitement the bunny's story had created in the classroom that day. She just knew *he's gonna be as excited about showing off one of the bunnies as I am.*

Bypassing the kitchen, Joni ran all the way down to the rabbit hutch to feed and water her rabbits, but what she found was an empty cage, its door flapping with the cold November wind. Standing there, her mouth agape, she couldn't imagine what possibly could have happened to the pets.

Hearing footsteps on the frozen dirt and stone pathway, J peered through the cage's wire mesh to see Blondie stepping stealthily toward the hutch. Stepping away from the hutch and onto the path, J cautiously asked, "Where are the rabbits and their babies?"

"They've gone to rabbit Heaven. What did you think I was gonna do with those hares? They were raised for food and that's what you're gettin' for dinner tonight. Them babies wouldn't have survived without their mama, so they had to be done away with. They're in the bottom of the shit house. They're better off there than without a mama. You can see that much, can't you?" Blondie asked. She brazenly stood there gaping at J. Blondie's apron bottom was folded up and around her crossed arms. She seemed to have been hoping to ward off some of the cold blowing breezes.

Blondie may have been feeling the November cold wind, but stunned was what J felt. Shocked and violated, she didn't know the adult words to describe the gnawing hurt she was feeling in her chest, so she just stammered, "I hate you."

With the speed of a fleeing deer, Blondie was standing right in front of her. Her wild eyes confronted J. "What did you just say to me?"

J said it again, "I hate you," but this time she added, "and I'll bet Bill and his mother will too." Then she screamed directly into Blondie's face, "And my teacher will hate you, and so will the whole class."

J never saw the whack coming to the left side of her head, but she certainly felt it.

Blondie never saw the whack coming either. Hers stemmed from Mihal, as his open-hand swept across the back of her head causing her to topple forward.

"Who gave you permission to kill those beautiful animals? Just who? They weren't yours for the killin'," Mihal angrily shouted as he stood over Blondie's plump body, which was lying in a sprawled position on the frosty gravel pathway.

Tears ran down his face, dripping onto Blondie's polka-dotted housedress.

"Quit your bawlin'," she yelled up at him. "Your dinner's roastin' in the oven. Help me up, before them rabbits burn all to Hell in that hot oven."

"No, Blondie, you can go to Hell," Mihal calmly answered. He ignored her reaching arm and her plea for assistance. He turned his back to Blondie and reached for J's extended hand.

Hand in hand, they slowly strolled up the stony pathway to the house. "From now on, Joni, you and I come home through the front door. You'll remember that, won't you? There's no more back door for us in this damned house. From now on Blondie will treat us as guests, not hired help."

Mihal tore down the rabbit hutch the next day. He made a bonfire out of it, right over Blondie's rose and gooseberry patch. "Hey Blondie, come see what's cookin' in my fire today," Mihal beckoned to Blondie.

Blondie peered through the kitchen window. Wide-eyed and her mouth forming an O, Blondie stood staring in disbelief. She shivered while watching in horror as her beautifully pruned rose and gooseberry bushes went up in flames.

Mihal watched his wife framed in the window. With his right index finger, he pointed to his eye. "An eye for an eye," he mimed to her.

"That's written somewhere in that Bible of yours, isn't it, Blondie?" Mihal vengefully hankered to himself as he stoicly gazed at the rising flames.

HAPPY MOTHER'S DAY!

"What am I supposed to do with this? It's not a real flower. This is nothin' but stinky toilet paper. Why would your teacher think this would make me a nice Mother's Day present?" J's mother asked the third grader, who had just presented her mother with a hand-made, perfumed carnation created from a facial tissue.

"Everybody made one for their mother," J said while holding the fake flower and nervously twisting the bobbi pin stem back and forth, back and forth in her little fingers.

"Gimme that damn thing," an agitated Blondie said as she snatched the posy from the girl's fingers and tossed it into the open hole of the flaming coal stove.

"God damned teachers! They should stick to readin', writin' and 'rithmatic," Blondie deduced. "Get outa here. Go do somethin' useful," she grumpily addressed the insulted little girl.

J did. She went out to her mother's flower garden and began weeding around her rose and snowball bushes. She knelt, she scooted, she stretched and she reached until every weed was pulled and piled neatly on the grass away from the plot of promising shrubs. Then she took a gardening fork and scraped the soil until it had neat furrows creating a manicured appearance to the garden. Lastly, she used a knife to cut around the uneven edges of the flower bed to make the border perfectly rectangular.

J threw the weeds and edging waste into the trash barrel behind her father's garage. She rinsed and replaced the tools. She then gave a final inspection to her Mother's Day project. She took her dad by the hand and asked his opinion of her handiwork.

"That looks beautiful, Clementine," he told J. "I don't know what your Ma will say, but I'm sayin' that's the prettiest that spot's ever looked."

"Blondie, come out here. Your little girl has a special present for you," Mihal called to his wife.

Blondie did come outside and she did take a look. She didn't smile, she didn't frown. She remained stoic. She didn't utter a single word. She just nodded her head *yes* several times, turned around and returned to the shelter of her kitchen.

Later that evening, Blondie brought two pink wintergreen candies into J's bedroom and placed them on the pillow in front of J's face as she lay nearly asleep. "That's the nicest thing any of you kids ever did for me," her mother said, "but if you ever touch my flowers again, I'll blister your ass with the switch. Understand that," Blondie said before turning and leaving the room.

Her message was concise and J clearly understood.

In the morning, J searched, but the pink mint candies were gone. Their disappearance remained just another secret in *that damned house.*

THE FEED MAN

In a small town, many secrets lay dormant and coddled in the bosoms of tight knit families. The village of Gunther was no different. The families of Lemon Lane created their own neighborhood where children and memories grew, despite small town constraints.

Lemon Lane was only one of a dozen or so short macadam roads in Gunther. An antique-looking wooden street sign marked the beginning of this pot-holed dirt road. No one laughed at the leaning, rock anchored post supporting a hand-hewn sign indicating **Lemon Lane**. Why would they laugh? They were friends and neighbors, all in similar depressed situations. They lived in old homes, each wearing a coat of faded or peeling paint. The dilapidated houses decorated the two mile stretch of this Pennsylvania cow town.

Coal mining financially supported some three hundred residents in Gunther. One grocery store stood at the town's entrance from the north. Its wooden floor had become patinaed by years of mining families tramping through the sawdust and banana oil. More money was owed to this store than the miners ever hoped to earn.

The families all lived on short lanes off of one main highway that ran thru the center of the village. These were all macadam roads that were hand dug during the times of economic depression when empty hours were plentiful, but jobs and food were practically non-existent. Somehow, this town's visionary road blocks always gave way to promised paths of an outside world. Somewhere, an education promised hope to the young person who had learned what hard work was from the moment they could take their first steps.

In this small town, work came first and then pleasure if time allowed. Entertainment was dancing on the front porch with a brother or a sister. Friendships grew over a rare evening spent yakking with a neighbor or a short walk to the one and only general store for a nickel fudgesicle or creamsicle with friends and their kids. The short walks became the opportune time for Mihal to bond with his children, while promoting educational tutoring sessions. The father would pronounce the street name or the neighbor's surname, thereby encouraging a spelling lesson. Often Mihal threw in a math equation, just to see if they were up on their arithmetic studies. "Study hard in school," he'd repeat frequently to his children.

"Learnin' won't ever do you any harm. It will only get you further ahead in life," Mihal would stress.

On one such jaunt, he'd lectured yet again to his little girl, J. "An education will be your only train ticket out of here. There's nothin' here for young people. I had to leave school when I was nine years old to work beside my father in the coal mines. I helped support my family. I worked hard for that $1.25 pay that got turned over to my mother each week. Out of that pay, I got a nickel each payday to spend at the Ramey movie house," he detailed to the attentive girl.

"My own Dad died too young from the miner's lung disease. I don't want that kind of life for you, or any of my kids. It's already into the '50's. Soon all of the hard coal will be gone from these mountains and so will the jobs. This is a dyin' town, that's for sure. Don't die with it, Joni," he cautioned.

A gentle man, *Mihal* had chosen Lemon Lane as the name for their scenic country road. He loved this land that had a roadway bordered by meadows that were covered with colorful blooming wild-flowers from early spring well into the late fall. Picking bouquets of daisies, buttercups or violets to give to his Blondie made him smile as brightly as the summer sunshine. The open fields, studded with tall chokecherry trees and elderberry bushes in full bloom brought happy tears to his eyes during the spring showers. Later in the summer months, he'd help his kids pick ripened berries from these meadows, always encouraging their enterprising spirits to sell the produce to local markets for twenty five cents a bushel. Mihal was quick to remind the kids that during the winter months, someone in some distant city would be enjoying costly wines, jellies and jams made from their pickings. Then he would add that a lot of folks in Gunther would also be enjoying homemade berry goodies, but at a fraction of the factory's production costs.

It was almost a certainty that during the berry picking excursions, Mihal would retell his favorite story. "Yep, Kids, I think we got the biggest house on the best street with the prettiest fields of berries in this here whole town." Mihal's head would nod *yes* to re-enforce his theory.

"Those yellow buttercups and your ma's yellow hair pretty much cinched the name Lemon Lane," Mihal's story always began.

Then he'd continue on with his elaboration. "The first time I saw Blondie, she was standing with her back toward me. She had such wavy and soft flaxen colored hair. It hung down to her waist. I said to myself, if she looks as good from the front as she does from the rear, I'm gonna marry her! She did, and I did!" Then he'd laugh his easy going "Te, he, he."

He clung to his precious memory. His was a good story. Mihal frequently repeated it to his kids when discussing the Lemon Lane sign. For quite some time though, Mihal's tale has remained silent in the crevice of a young girl's cracked heart. This story's well-intentioned core was meant to be left at the end of a small mining town road, or across the street at the bottom of the old Koxis coal mine.

Lemon Lane was often compared to Tangerine Road. Though their entrances were directly across the main highway from one another, they were as different as two states separated by a wide and winding river. Tangerine Road began with the one gray coal-dusted Pasovsky house and ended at the ongoing strip mines, which were nestled back in the crook of the Koxis Mountains. Tangerine Road was mainly used for hauling coal from the strip mines. The Pasovsky family refused to move from their two acres of American soil. They had worked too long and too hard for this meager accomplishment. Yielding to the rumblings of the dump-trucks, which sped back and forth from the strip mines, their home eventually became corroded with coal dust forcing it to resemble a powdered-sugar Christmas cookie.

The beleaguered families of Gunther realized the huge mounds of bulldozed earth with their water filled craters, called stripping holes by the locals, would be all that remained once the coal had been ripped from the mountain's bowels. Still, the Pasovskys and the other families in this town had decided to stay until the mining jobs petered out, or their coal-eroded houses collapsed.

The matured trees along Tangerine Road had long ago been utilized for mine support pillars, so the open fields appeared barren compared to the peaceful cow filled meadows lining Lemon Lane. Deteriorating white-washed shanty houses dotted the perimeter of Lemon Lane and sheltered an influx of immigrant families. These transplanted immigrants had acquired an appreciation for Lemon Lane as a subdued country road. It seemed a good place to raise their first generation American children. Though rarely disrupted by automobile sputtering, children's raucous laughter was the main noise heard continuously throughout the day, every day.

Occasionally, tranquil Lemon Lane was disturbed by the discordant sounds of a delivery truck. Large enclosed southern fruit trucks loaded with nuts, bananas, oranges or tangerines often found their loyal customers awaiting them on these country roads, especially during the winter holiday season.

However, it was the local *feed man* in his bright red pickup truck who stirred up the most dust when he brazenly returned to his best customer on Lemon Lane this one particular summer.

Knowing that conditions of a summer's drought would alter the August hay crop, the *feed man* delivered his supplies to the farmers more frequently than usual. He was now making deliveries regularly to #11 Lemon Lane. Every Tuesday afternoon, at one o'clock, the kids sat waiting for his arrival. Usually the children could hear his pickup truck's engine as it came up the lane. This one particular day, however, they saw a dust cloud billowing from the dry dirt road before they heard the truck's engine revving as it neared their house.

It was him all right. He'd have treats for each of them. He always did. This was his trick to keep the children busy while he did his business with their mother. He would come through the gate energetically with a 50# sack of cow oats or chicken grain on his shoulder.

"Hi kids," he'd call, as they'd gather around him with outstretched hands The kids were always eager to get that penny lollipop, tootsie roll or double bubble gum.

As soon as each child had some treat to munch on, the *feed man* would announce, "Okay, now go and play so your mother and I can do our business."

That was the clue that he'd doled out all the treats that he was going to give. It was now time for the grownups to get on with their business.

Wearing a big-toothed smile as he worked, he'd whistle some silly diddy through his two front teeth. Yankee Doodle seemed to be his favorite. A tall thin fellow, his sandy colored hair and bright blue eyes topped a menacing scarecrow's frame of dirty baggy clothes. When he would finally set the large brown burlap bags of oats or barley onto the ground, he'd drop them with an "Ugh, these damn bags must weigh a hundred pounds," encouraging the kids' mother to laugh at his routine remark.

Usually the kids rolled their eyes and groaned in boredom at this anticipated dull-witted comment. When he had the bags all lined up and ready to go into the barn, he'd call out to the mother, "Are you ready to show me where you want these bags to go?"

"Skedaddle," Blondie would say to the children meandering about. "Go play now. You don't need to be around here when we're doin' our work."

Then off the kids would scatter to play tag or hopscotch, while Blondie led the way into the barn for her and the *feed man* to do their business. The tall slim man would follow Blondie with a burlap bag balanced on his muscular shoulder. Into the musty cow barn they'd both go. Only he would return to get the other bags lining the door frame. Once the bags were all taken inside, the heavy wooden barn door would hurriedly be closed leaving an echo for the children to hear, "We need to do our business in private now. You kids go play, ya hear."

On this one particular hot summer's day, the heavy-planked barn door didn't fully close the way it always had before. It remained slightly ajar allowing a string-bean girl to maneuver sideways a few steps into the darkened room and curiously wonder *why would someone do their business in this dank, shit-floored barn instead of out in the fresh air.* J listened intently to the whispers she heard from the far corner of the hay room. "Come on now, you know you want me," the man's voice teased.

Loose wide barn boards gave way to dusty filtered sun rays. J could barely make out the silhouettes of the couple, but she was certain they were kissing. The girl stood barefoot in the cow manure, silently watching as the feed man moved his hands down the mother's back and onto her ass, just before the mother began to giggle.

"Oh! Ho! No underpants! You were ready for me today, weren't you, Blondie?" the *feed man* laughed snidely.

A giggle sounded again as if from a playful young girl, not a seasoned mother.

Could it really be her, J wondered, *or is there someone else in here?*

Almost afraid to breathe, the girl pinched her nose hoping the mustiness wouldn't make her sneeze. If the couple knew she was in there, she realized what kind of trouble she'd be in. Motionless, J waited and watched. Her eyes were locked onto the spectacle in the hay.

J's eyes widened with surprise as she watched the twosome lay back against the hay mound. "I do love you," the man said gently as he lowered his body on top of the woman's. "You were all I could think about when I was fighting over there."

"I knew you'd come back to me," the woman responded tenderly, after which only the moans and slapping sounds filled the air.

You better get out of here, a voice inside the girl's brain shouted.

Her heart drummed a cadence as she stole quickly and quietly out of the barn. Trembling, she slowly side-slipped over to the cow's watering pond and sat down on the muddy bank. Letting her bare feet dangle into the water, J managed to rinse off the sour smelling dung before the grinning handsome couple came out of the barn. If she weren't so terrified of swimming under water, J would have put her whole head into the muddy pond to clear her mind of the show she'd just witnessed.

"Which two are mine" the man wanted to know. The flushed couple leisurely walked out of the barn's shadow, their skin beaded with glistening perspiration in the afternoon's sunshine.

Blondie pointed to the girl sitting on the muddy bank, "Her, that skinny blonde one with the freckles on her nose. That's J. She came after you had been sent to Germany. And that's your tow-headed Jakey boy over there on the other side of the pond. He's your first. He arrived just shortly after you left for boot camp in Georgia. He's a rascal, that one! I wanted to give you two boys, but you got one of each," the girl heard her smiling mother explaining to the *feed man*.

"Come over here," the tall man said to the little girl. "What's your name?"

"J," she sheepishly replied hoping that the shame of what she had just witnessed wasn't written all over her face.

"Is that your brother, Jake?" the man asked.

"I suppose so," J answered.

"Go, bring him here," he commanded.

With a strange amused smirk on his face, the *feed man* pressed a five dollar bill into J's hand. "I want to have a look at the two of you. I want you both to know my name. It's Mr. Ed Strang. I don't want either of you to forget it. Now go and fetch your brother to me."

The little girl looked at that bill in her hand. Five dollars could have been a hundred dollars that day, but she just let it drop to the ground as she stumbled away from Mr. Ed Strang. It took no longer than the blink of an eye for her mother to scoop up the bill and thrust it into her apron pocket. J continued walking the pathway, away from them. She ignored her mother's shouts, "Hey, you come back here and do as you were told. Do you hear me? Get back here, girl!"

The girl didn't stop her postured steady gait until she reached the shiny red pickup truck that was parked next to the swinging front gate. The little girl dressed in faded jeans and a torn shirt took one last look at that truck's newness before courageously spitting on the driver's window. She smiled slowly as she watched the spittle drool down the shiny glass pane.

Nothing further was said to J that evening, at least not until bedtime. With an air of arrogance, the mother entered the girl's small shared bedroom. Shaking a straight index finger twice at the little girl, she began her haranguing. "The only reason you're not gettin' a beatin' right now is 'cause I promised my Ed I wouldn't touch you. You better not say one word about today. Do you understand? I'll break your skinny little neck if you ever say one word about this to Mihal. You got that?" she vented vehemently, baring her teeth like an angry rabid dog.

That skinny little neck was throbbing uncontrollably. It didn't need to be told twice. J's head was bobbing nervously, but the skinny youngster managed a one-word answer, "Yes."

J knew how to keep a secret. She knew plenty of them. She wasn't the only one who knew about the secrets at #11 Lemon Lane though, and she wasn't the only one keeping them.

At least, for now!

THAT HURTS

"Pull your pants down," Jake said. "Pull your pants down and let me see what you have under there. Do it, I said. Ma said you have to do what I tell you. If you don't I'll put this diggin' fork right through your foot," Jake threatened.

"Go ahead, 'cause I'm not doin' anything you say. Dad said I don't have to listen to you, so there," J sassed back by sticking her tongue out at him.

"Well, then this is gonna hurt," Jake laughed eerily as he plunged the two long tines of the digging fork into J's foot.

"I'm tellin' Dad," J screamed. She continued one piercing scream after another until Adela ran down to the twosome who were standing in the furrows of the newly plowed spring garden site.

"What happened, J?" Adela was asking as J began to hear a buzzing noise in her head.

"Joni," Mihal was calling her name, but the sound seemed to be coming from a distance.

"Joni, what happened?" Mihal was talking to her through a dark tunnel somewhere. She could hear him, but she wasn't seeing him very clearly.

"This is gonna hurt, kid," Mihal was saying, but she wasn't quite grasping what he was telling her.

Holding J's ankle steady with his left hand, Mihal managed a swift right-handed yank to remove the digging-fork tines from her foot.

After several "Oh God" screams, J took a deep breath and began to swiftly relate what had occurred.

"Jake did it. He did this 'cause I wouldn't pull down my pants. God it hurts, Dad. Jake said Ma told him I have to listen to him. I don't, do I?" J asked between sobs.

Her whole body was trembling, almost uncontrollably until Mihal wrapped his arms around her and carried her out of the garden patch and over to the back porch.

"Blondie, get some water to wash out these holes. They go straight through her foot. There are two of them. Spread on some of that black salve you use on the cow's teats. We've got to get her to a doctor, so wrap a towel around that foot and I'll take her to Old Doc's," an angered Mihal said. He quikly picked up the shivering petite girl and started walking toward his car.

"And Blondie," he called frigidly over his shoulder, "that son of yours had better be sittin' right there on that step when we get back. There's gonna be one helluva serious discussion on this back porch later this afternoon, and I'm not in any mood to hear that same old bullshit he tends to spread around in that head of yours. You got that?"

Old Doc was appalled at what Mihal brought to his office that morning, and he said as much. "Mark my words, Mihal, that kid is only gonna bring you grief. He's trouble with a capital T. Now Joni, suppose you tell me what happened and don't be afraid to tell me the truth. I'm gonna clean your foot and that might hurt a bit," he cautioned. "Can you sit still for that?"

J told her story while the doctor kept her distracted with his antiseptic sponging and gauze bandaging. "Mihal, if she doesn't get an infection in here, the foot should heal pretty quickly. This bandage can't get dirty or wet though. This foot needs to be cleaned and the dressing changed in the morning and in the evening. Can Blondie do that?"

"She'll have to, that's all there is to it," Mihal responded.

Shaking his head back and forth in disgust, Mihal confessed, "I don't know what to do with that kid already. He's only thirteen years old. I'm afraid of what's ahead with his dirty shenanigans. He's Blondie's favorite, you know."

Arriving home a short while later, Mihal offered Blondie some advice. "Well, Blondie, I don't care if he's your favorite boy, he can't get away with this. He has to learn that there's a punishment for every crime. You'll need to punish him, or I will. I guarantee he won't like what I'm gonna dish out. Do you understand?"

Mihal argued his point. "I don't buy his story about helpin' her dig for worms. He didn't miss his spot. He deliberately jabbed that girl's foot with that filthy diggin' fork when she wouldn't do what he asked. He's not to touch her ever again, do you understand? You had better make him understand that, too."

Mihal shouted at his wife, while her Jakey boy looked on from his perch on the back porch swing and feigned a sense of innocence.

Using the tip of his toe, Jake pushed the swing into a swaying movement. Back and forth, back and forth went the old wooden slatted swing. With the rhythmic breeze blowing his thin blonde pompadour-styled hair up and down, Jake watched and enjoyed the ongoing feud between Blondie and Mihal. Jake's lips held a steady sneer as he witnessed Blondie slowly win the argument.

"I'll handle this. Jake will get his. He's not gettin' away with any of this. Go, get out of here and let me get to the bottom of this situation," Blondie pushed at Mihal's shoulder as she aimed him toward the kitchen door.

"Go get some fresh coffee off the stove. It should be ready for drinkin' by now," Blondie said, hoping to alleviate some of the current tension on the back porch.

As soon as Mihal was out of earshot, Blondie began a whispering session with her Jakey boy. "What's wrong with you? Didn't I tell you to stay out of trouble? Now look what you've done and I'm supposed to punish you, or else he will."

"I told you, I was tryin' to help her. She's too small to dig for worms with that old fork. It's pretty heavy you know. She did it to herself, I tell you. I was just tryin' to help," Jake said, attempting to convince his mother of his version of the story.

"Them girls are always makin' up stories about me. You better not punish me, or I'll tell a few stories of my own, Blondie," Jake said.

Winking at his Ma, Jake drawled her name to sound like a southern gentleman's request for a glass of sweet tea, all the while using his polished cunning to convince her of his wavering truths.

"Okay, okay, Jake. I get the picture. I'll smooth things over with Mihal, but you had better watch your ps and qs from now on. I can't protect you forever. I'm gonna be watchin' you myself. I'll watch every step you take, do you understand?" Blondie hoped that she had stated her decision clearly to her son.

Jakey boy just smiled and propelled the swing higher.

Blondie wasn't the only one watching Jake's ps and qs.

An old gypsy woman was sitting on her wooden bench, out of sight on the sunny side of the back steps. She had paused long enough to take an over-due piss and to redo her chignon, which had become loose after two hours of pulling weeds from the strawberry patch. Hearing Blondie and Jake's conversation couldn't be considered eavesdropping. After all, no matter what

Blondie thought, this was still the gypsy woman's home. She was the first to have lived in *this damned house*, and she wasn't dead yet. She was still very much alive and capable of watching Blondie and Jake's p's and q's.

Yep, Baba would definitely watch those p's and q's.

JUNK YARDS AND TREASURE HUNTS

"Who wants to go with me to the junk yard?" Mihal called out to the youngsters scattered about the yard.

"I'll go," nine year old J volunteered. Following their older sisters vote, five year old Vera, four year old Cindy and two year old Marsha were shouting, "Me, too. Me, too. I wanna go."

Tiny Marsha piped in, "Where me wanna go, J? Where?"

Mihal burst out laughing. He was moving his head back and forth in disbelief. "You kids are somethin' else. You don't know where you're goin', but you're ready to go anywhere with your Pappy."

"Well, come on then. Get yourself a basket or a bucket from over by the garage, and let's go see what we find in the Brownstone junk yard. We'll call it a treasure hunt, okay?"

Mihal was still swinging his head back and forth like a pendulum. His toothless smile was still in full bloom as he hopped into the driver's seat of his old car.

"Hop in the car. I told your Ma where we're off to. I don't want her havin' a conniption fit if she doesn't know where we've gone. You all have your shoes on, right?" he asked for safety's sake. "We don't want no one cuttin' their feet out there."

Anticipation fluttered, much as a moth around a flame. "You kids all have ants in your pants," Mihal said as he observed the nervous energy bouncing in the back seat of the old car.

"Naw, we don't have any bugs in our pants," Cindy giggled as she returned the joking good humor.

"We're just 'cited, that's all. "Do you 'member last time? We found dolls and pretty bottles. I hope there's good stuff there today, too," she said with a slight giggle.

"Well, it's four o'clock right now and the gate gets locked at five, so we have one whole hour to shop around. Come on kids, let's get started," Mihal indicated as he turned off the engine and opened his car door.

"Oh my God," Vera shouted after she had taken only a few short steps out of the car. "Look what I found."

"That's a whole box of popsicles, and they're still frozen! Somebody must have just dumped them here. What do you think, kids?" Mihal asked while trying to act astonished.

"Maybe you should eat them while we look for other stuff, 'cause in this heat they won't last long. Go ahead, eat up," their dad encouraged.

With three double popsicles in her left hand and eating a cherry one from in her right, J wandered over to the lower side of the toppling mound of debris. "Dad, come here quick," she called out within minutes of exploring the garbage heap.

"It's a whole pile of bread and cakes and pies and cinnamon buns. They're all still wrapped in cellophane. They don't even look moldy like the ones we get at the second hand bakery, Dad. Why would anyone throw this good stuff away?" J asked Mihal.

"Well, I don't know now, Joni. Rich people throw away a lot of stuff when they have too much for themselves. That's how the successful people in this world do things, you know." Mihal said as he attempted to impress his youngsters with his street knowledge.

"Go, get your baskets. Let's take this stuff home to your Ma. She'll be happy if she doesn't have to make bread for a couple of days, don't you think," Mihal stated more than asked.

Fully loaded baskets, toppling with bakery goods, seemed to step their way into the kitchen of #11 Lemon Lane just as Blondie was about to dish out a chicken noodle soup supper. With ladle in hand, she held the back door open and allowed the straining little arms to come through with their heaping stacks of breads and desserts. "Where in the Hell did all of this come from? Mihal, you'd better have a good story cooked up for this," Blondie whispered to her husband as he walked past her with the last load of goodies.

"I don't know where it came from. We happened to stumble across all of this in the junk yard. Somebody must have just dumped it, because we even found frozen popsicles. Didn't we kids?" Mihal called out, begging confirmation from the youngsters with a quick wink from his twinkling eyes.

"As a matter of fact, Joni was the one who stumbled across it. She's the one we should be grateful to. Am I right kids?" Mihal asked.

"I'm grateful," Blondie said, "but I'm sure as Hell not gonna kiss anybody's ass over stuff from a garbage heap. Sit down already and eat your soup."

Two days later, J went along with Mihal to the local garage. Mihal's car inspection tag was due for its annual state renewal. Sitting on a chair just inside the entrance, and out of the direct sunshine, was Old Man Eisenberg. "Hey, Mihal," he called out in his familiar gruff voice, "did I do a good thing? Did you get your kids there in time to eat the popsicles? Was your woman pleased with all those breads and pastries? I certainly hope so. You know that took quite a few pennies out of my cash register, but my wife said I had to do a really good deed for someone needy to make up for what I did to her."

"Yeah, you did a really good deed, Sol. Thank you. I owe you a favor now," Mihal spoke in response to the whiskered man with the funny little beanie perched on the top of his head.

"It was worth it, Mihal. You know, I had a good time romping in the hay with Verna. She puts out like a New York hooker. It's just too bad she can't keep a secret. Why couldn't she have just kept her mouth shut, like you did when she gave you the lowdown about our one hot night," Sol quipped. The frown on his forhead seemed to say more than the words spilling out of the corners of his mouth.

J couldn't help but notice how fast this Sol guy talked. He was old and portly, but he was still handsome. His smile was wide and he had a space between his two front teeth, just like Junior's. When he smiled, J couldn't resist returning his friendliness with a smile of her own.

"Thanks for warning me that Verna was going to my wife for a few dollars to keep her jibber closed. My wife hit the roof when I confessed my sin to her, but it was still worth the risk I took. I may repeat that sin sometime soon, while I still can," Sol winked and laughed heartily as he began to step away from Mihal.

"See you around, my friend." The old man smiled to Mihal as he tipped his funny little hat as a feint farewell wave to Mihal.

Stopping after taking a few short steps, the squat guy returned and stood beside J. "Here kid, here's a quarter. You keep your mouth shut, too," he said with a smirk, revealing dimples in his cheeks, "and you can keep the change!"

Sol was still laughing when he got into his car and drove away.

A DAY OF GIVING THANKS

Thanksgiving Day, a day set aside to give thanks for everything good in your life, whether it's in the past, the present or the future.
Who distinguishes what is good?
Who set the standards?
How high did they set the bar?
Who are *they*?
In the household at #11 Lemon Lane, the bar was set pretty high. Being grateful to see another morning and just staying alive were real goals. A switch, a belt or a rubber hose all kept fear and discipline hanging on a bar that was elevated to a ceiling of behaving and towing the line at all costs.

The judge and jury was also the CEO of this household. What decisions Blondie made were usually what occurred at #11 Lemon Lane.! Arguments were usually won by Blondie. Punishments were usually doled out by Blondie. All of the children were the recipients of some form of punishment at one time or another with one exception, Jake. Affectionately called Jakey boy by his mother, he was held high above the bar. All forms of penance were afforded him. At times, he was even rewarded by his mother for being clever.

To his siblings, he was *the brat.*
To his mother, he was *my favorite.*
To the man he called Dad, Jake was *the spoiled, sneaky son of a bitch who couldn't be trusted, not even within ear shot.*
To J, who was now in the fourth grade, Jake was *someone to fear.*
Jake liked the word shot. Shooting was one of his favorite pastimes. A loaded and cocked BB gun usually stood propped and ready at his side. No one could ever guess what creature would be seen next in the gun's sight, and then popped just for Jake's sleazy amusement. "Oh God, that felt great," he'd say after shooting his target and watching it quiver through its last breath

He relished the malice of that sensation. He embraced it. Many years later during combat in Vietnam, he would feel that same elation under the guise of serving his country. When visiting at home on leave, R & R he called it, he would boast of his many service related conquests to anyone within listening distance.

"You'd never believe how green and lush the swamps are in Nam. Huge, ugly, slimy snakes and bugs are crawling everywhere in that damp rancid Indochinese jungle rot. It's so thick in those rain forests that you can't seem to find your way out. You start to think you'll be lost forever swallowed up in some animal's belly! That constant and putrid, nauseating smell makes you want to puke constantly," he expounded.

Holding his abdomen with one hand and pinching his nose with the other, he was getting his point across to his captive audience. "We came across one small village of thatched roofed huts," he continued his story without skipping a syllable.

"The slant-eyed people there were filthy, malnourished and skinny. These yellow, belly-bloated runts were down to wearing rags and eating cooked worms. We just knew they couldn't be trusted, especially if they were suffering from starvation. So, kapow, kapow, kapow and some more goons were gone."

He looked upward, after mimicking the gun shots, and crazily laughed. His eyes glazed over with an evil gleam while reminiscing about those vicious acts. The words spewing from his narcissistic mouth were his method of spinning one hell of an attention-getting tale. It was a powerful moment. It was self-importance at its finest and he knew it. His attentive audience was enraptured. His words were powerful. He had captured the essence of a horror none of them ever hoped to experience. After all, wasn't this his intent?

His proud mother stood at his side, overjoyed that her Jakey boy had returned home safely. Beaming proudly, she listened to each word knowing she'd have some amazing stories to repeat to her neighbors for days to come.

"He's so handsome in his uniform. Look at all those medals on his chest. I knew he'd get one for sharp shooting. That was a feather in his cap, that's for sure," Blondie boasted with an air of superficial pride.

Her thoughts rekindled memories that were a little edgier though. *He looks just like his very own daddy when he came back from his war,* she sadly recalled.

The thought of Jake's father, the love of her life, released a flood of emotions. One early December morning many years ago, Blondie had learned of Ed's tragedy from a neighbor lady who had casually mentioned hearing a local news broadcast detailing an accident on the Tyrone Turnpike.

"Blondie, do you remember Ed Strang, the feed man? Well, his pickup truck hit a utility pole head on earlier this morning. He lost control of his vehicle on an icy mountain road," the neighbor stated as a matter of fact.

"Are you sure it was Ed Strang?" Blondie asked her neighbor.

"The feed man, Ed?" she nervously pushed.

The neighbor answered, "Yes," to both of Blondie's questions.

"It was on the radio this morning, on the seven o'clock news. He was from Fallen Timber, wasn't he? "Big Annie asked. "The announcer said he died instantly," she continued, "and probably didn't feel a thing. The police report said he was drunk."

Blondie's heart cracked a million times that day, but no one knew it. That was a day of reckoning silence for Blondie, but she hid her torment well. A day without quarreling was a rare day for Blondie, indeed. Her teary eyes glistened through her memories, but the tears did not flow. She smiled at her neighbor and choked back her secrets. After she lost her Ed, she'd decided not to let anyone ever unlock her heart again.

The first one to leave her was her Timmy, followed by her Ed. *Love just isn't worth all the grief that tags along.* She had whispered her mind-set sentiment to her own heart on that sorrowful day so long ago. She felt that same emotion again this day as she watched her and Ed's son putting on a show for his friends. In the years to come, she would repeat her pessimistic opinions to each of her children on their wedding mornings. Optimism and best wishes were never this mother's forte. "Love ain't all it's cracked up to be," she'd warn.

Remembering that her son Jake was home from the Air Force, she forced her expressions to become jovial again. She teasingly shouted, "Hey Jake, you've been home for a whole day and you haven't made yourself a slingshot yet. I thought you said you were going to stay a slingin', marble playin' kid forever. What gives? Don't tell me you're too old for marbles and slingshots."

Blondie was the only one who laughed at her humorous attempt. No one ever expected Blondie to be comical.

As a youngster, a slingshot was yet another of Jake's preferred toys. He became quite the proficient shot with his crafted twig Y and its affixed strip of old bicycle tire. He wasn't nicknamed Speedy just for the fun of it. He could whip up a new slingshot in just a few minutes, much to the delight of his pals. For some ungodly reason, the neighborhood boys all had to have one of these contraptions dangling out of their back pockets, or else it seemed they wouldn't be able to strut like a man. He was their teacher. "Spot the target, take aim and fire before the critter even blinks an eye," he effectively told his friends, his pupils.

Jake genuinely enjoyed his actions. He couldn't comprehend the cruelty of it all. To him, killing creatures was fun. To him it was a sport to be displayed, not suppressed.

Anyone who knew Jake knew his ultimate toy was the shotgun. "What cha got there, Jakey?" little three year old Vera asked one chilly winter afternoon.

"What cha gonna do with that thing?" She was curious about that object in his hands.

"It's a shotgun and I'm gonna shoot it tonight at midnight," he proudly told her, wiping the stock for more sheen.

"Oh!" was her only reply, oblivious to the real meaning behind his statement.

In the wonderment of a child's mind, a thought skittered. *What kind of it was gonna get shot tonight?*

This little girl had already seen many *its* get shot by Jake. She had seen him shoot critters before, but wasn't curious enough at this time to stick around for any further answers from Jake. Instead, she cheerfully ran off to play jump rope with the other kids.

Jake was the only sibling allowed to shoot off a round from the shotgun on New Year's Eve. He would be the *hot shot* in the neighborhood, ready to announce to the town of Gunther that a new year had begun. "That's one of my important jobs around this damn house," he'd say to anyone who questioned his authority, "and if you don't like that point, you can lump it."

None of his siblings argued his point. His arrogance was the point. He did as he and his mother pleased.

Jake's other job with the shotgun was killing a hog on Thanksgiving Day. This was the highlight of the year for Jake. This shot made his holiday a *thanks for giving me this job* celebration. With the gun's barrel resting on the side of the hog's head, just in front of the ear, Jake would smile as he pulled the trigger. The loud boom would reverberate around the walls of the ramshackle pig sty before one final loud elongated and painful squealing "Oiiiiiiiiiink" would escape the pig's throat. Jake would smile broadly as the helpless animal fell into the pen's smelly dung-laced mud. "Good bye, Mr. Pig," he'd sneer to the swine as it lay dying.

"I could do that all day, everyday, and feel more excited every time I pulled the trigger. Too bad that damned fat pig doesn't have the guts to get up and let me do that all over again," Jake would sardonically twitter.

It may have been a joyous occasion for Jake, but this was not a day of celebration for the other kids, or the pig for that matter. These were not Thanksgiving Days at #11 Lemon Lane. They were "it's time to butcher the hog days".

Once the hog was downed, there was work to be done. There was no age discrimination at this address. Everyone had a job assignment, everyone except Jake. His job was completed once he had shot and killed the animal. That was all his mother required of him that special day. Was he a favored sap? You can bet your ass he was, thanks to his doting mother. At least, he had his mother's favor to be thankful for. The other ten kids couldn't claim as much. "Oh, no, not this again," the kids would grumble and whine.

Thanksgiving Day brought a morning no kid in *this damned house* was eager to greet.

Thanksgiving Day at #11 Lemon Lane was traditionally the day of chopping apart a fat slaughtered swine in the earthen cellar. A child's pet yesterday became today and tomorrow's dinner. To try chewing and swallowing that pet's prime cuts every day for the next few months was an acting performance worthy of a Broadway star.

Mihal's favorite hog was Boomer, a truly gentle creature. He'd respond to "Here Boomer, here," by running to anyone who called him. Much to the children's delight, Boomer would then snort happily as he shadowed them around the barnyard. After Boomer was shot, the kids referred to Thanksgiving Day as Boomer's Day. They'd sing a little ditty as they jumped rope, paying some semblance of a tribute to their fallen ally:

> "Friendly old Boomer,
> with a little pink snout,
> wandered happily around the barnyard
> until mean ole Jakey rubbed him out!"

Butchering day was eight hours of fresh animal blood and guts that left odors lingering in the nostrils for an eternity. "Ew, gads," became the phrase of the day, heard from at least one of the workers on a minute to minute basis.

As each new section of the pig's carcass was attacked by the butchering tools, a new stench would engulf the surrounding area. It became a day of pulling and stretching, squeezing and washing, rinsing and hosing. Everybody was in on the action!

The fetoring porcine entrails were removed for cleansing. Later the intestines would be restored to their original plump intestinal state by being filled with ground meat, fresh from the slaughtered pig itself. How ironic!

The pig's urinary bladder usually emerged with a gentle tug, and was then rinsed with hot water and refilled with air to become a dried toy balloon that would later be tossed about by the youngsters.

All day long, it was chaotic orders. "Do this. Do that. That's not right, do it again," Blondie would shout. "For Christ sake, it's not like younse ain't never done this before!"

When J was in the fourth grade, she thought Blondie's orders mimicked their dog's frenzied barking. She began to chuckle to herself as she mimicked her mother's words in doggie language. Somehow, this tiny speck of humor in a humorless day eased her cognizance of the tragedy that was occurring.

"Get that bucket." "Ruf ruf ra ruf".
"Catch that blood." "Ruf ruf ruf."
"Don't spill a drop." "Ruf ruf a ruf."
"Higher, let it drain." "Rufruf, ruf ra ruffff."

J's barking renditions were contagious. Before too long, all of the kids were either barking or howling with laughter, but when Mihal joined in the joshing his was the best of the banter!

On this butchering session, their large drooling St. Bernard, who had been chained to his house for the day, smelled the fresh blood and came bounding toward the cellar door. Needless to say, his linked abode wasn't far behind. The comical spectacle momentarily gave some relief to the solemness of the day. Much to Blondie's chagrin, everyone stopped their tasks and burst into laughter. Mihal rubbed the top of Jingleberry's head and led him to the barn for safe keeping.

"Let's keep you in here and out of Blondie's way today. This is serious stuff to her. I'll bring you some leftovers in a while, Boy," Mihal spoke as though the dog could understand his words.

Meanwhile, in the cold dampness of an earthen-floored cellar, the porcine blood from the gaffed carcass was draining into a large bucket to be salvaged for blood pudding, or to be mixed with cornmeal and seasonings to become kieshka, a blood sausage. Both were considered delicacies in the Polish household and impassioned by the mother and her Jakey boy.

The orders were given randomly. "Baba, get the sausage filler ready. Get that cornmeal mush mixed," was always an expected command. "Move your fat ass, you sloven sow," Blondie would shout disrespectfully at Mihal's mother.

Anna tolerated this chore. Everyone else barfed at the sight and stink of the so called delicacies. The kids could be heard questioning, "Why should we be thankful for this? It's like shovin' crap down our throats."

Mihal knew who would be enjoying his portion of kieshka. He could hear the "thank you" barking through his mind. "Ruf ruf," was what Mihal was hearing in his ear.

The rest of the pork would be divided into sections, and then frozen in Helmsley's grocery store's storage freezer. Portions of meat would be removed from the meat locker as needed. It would be cooked and served for supper meals during the harsh winter months ahead. There would be many arguments between Blondie and Mihal about the meat disappearing quicker than anticipated from that freezer. "Sure Helmsley's take the best cuts. Why do you think they let us store that damned meat there in the first place," Blondie would sarcastically growl at Mihal.

"You're stupid to think otherwise. You think they're your friends? Think again, Mister," Blondie would ridicule Mihal's ignorance.

Hams were cherry-wood cured in Mihal's stone smoking shed. This insured preservation of the meat for the yuletide holidays. The hog's skin with the fatty lining would bring future palatable pleasures, to be sure. Heated in a large pot on the kitchen stove, the fatty tissue rendered lard for future cooking and baking. The toughened skin would curl and harden, serving as a delightful treat for Jingleberry's gnawing pleasure through the cold winter months.

No part of this butchered animal escaped Blondie's kitchen. The hooves and snout were flavored with garlic, and then were boiled down for studinina, a seasoned gelatinous dish. Sweetbreads were chopped with the brain matter, and then cooked with spices into a sandwich loaf called head cheese. More often than not, the servings of this mass would be dropped to the bottom of the outhouse. No kid in their right mind could steal more than a glance at the brain, let alone eat it!

Soup was concocted from the tail when boiled with vegetables and homemade noodles became a Sunday fare. No one fought Mihal for the tail. It was all his with their blessings and gratitude!

Even the rasped hog's hair wasn't wasted. It was spread around the late garden cabbages to discourage rabbits or rodents from nibbling the leaves.

The organ meats were set aside for special recipes such as kidney pies that would be baked the next day before the meat had a chance to decompose. Much of that recipe found itself decomposing at the bottom of the shit house, too. Oh, if Blondie only knew what her family did with her delicacies!

This was a poor man and his family; there was no doubt about that. The kids at this household knew why none of the neighbors ever asked to trade any fancy recipes for dishes cooked in their mother's kitchen.

Fresh liver was traditionally saved for the Thanksgiving Day supper meal at #11 Lemon Lane. "It's the most delicious part of the hog," Blondie's alto voice sang out.

Blondie hummed tunes while preparing the liver with fried bacon and onions, and then she served the fried meat with a few boiled potatoes and hot homemade yeast bread. The meal was set before the peasants as if it were food for the Gods.

"Happy Thanksgiving! Now sit down, shut up and eat," was the grace offered by this *Christian Catholic mother* as she passed scantily mounded plates to each of the kids.

"You'll eat what you're given and be grateful," she would scold those who turned their noses up at the foul smelling organ meat.

On each Thanksgiving Day, many servings of fried liver also found their way dropped into the outhouse shit pile at #11 Lemon Lane.

"Lord Almighty" was a frequent phrase heard loud and clear, if and when a piece of that liver or headcheese was discovered hidden in one of the kid's pants pocket on laundry day. Punishment (with a capital P) for that offense was dished out as if a mortal sin had been committed. That mother sure did love and cherish those pig organs! Blondie's love for the pig's liver at times seemed more vibrant than any affection she ever expressed to her children.

The hours in this holiday flew by as all of the carving and butchering chipped away the minutes that became hours. Neighbors and co-workers had been excited about their special holiday, but not this father or his offspring. They remembered the malodor that went along with the butchering day and they were definitely glad when the day ended.

Neither Mihal nor the kids were very excited to return to work or school the Friday after the holiday. They knew what comments and discussions awaited them. They'd been through other Thanksgiving holidays and the current one would prove to be no different than the last.

"Time to lie again," the kids would say as they discussed their holiday menu while walking down muddy Lemon Lane to catch the school bus.

There was no telling which friend would be nosey about their day, so they needed their answers to be cohesive. They would rehearse and then they would be ready for the usual barrage of post-Thanksgiving Day questions.

"Time to lie again," Mihal would utter to Blondie as he donned his coal mining garb in the early hours of the morning after the holiday. Mihal would reluctantly return to his coal mining job, only too well aware of the verbal jesting he was about to encounter. "How was your Thanksgiving, Mihal? Eat a lot of that turkey and dressing?" his teasing co-workers inquired.

His buddies all knew how his holiday had been spent. There may have been secrets in Gunther, but Mihal's Thanksgiving Day wasn't one of them.

The miners would brag on and on about stuffing themselves with all sorts of fancy holiday foods that their wives had prepared. Then they'd talk about their after-dinner laziness and long afternoon naps. He'd just nod and endure their annoying comments. His thoughts were busy reflecting his appreciation for the holiday. *Thank goodness for God's grace to provide, even if it did take a whole day of laboring before that damned old liver was cooked and served!*

Somewhere in the furrows of his mind, he was thinking, *let them show off today. Tomorrow, when I pull out those pork chops and sausages, I'll be the one laughing while they'll be complaining about having soup made from turkey bones.*

Mihal knew that in the evening he'd smile and repeat his thoughts to his children. He'd patiently watch as they rolled out dough made with the rendered lard. He knew they'd soon taste the wisdom of his words in a hot apple pie. *It's too bad you're not around to enjoy a meal of leftover scraps from our evening meal, Boomer. You would have enjoyed the slop,* Mihal thought sadly.

Upon returning to school, the kids also faced peers who were gathered waiting for the school bus at the entrance to Lemon Lane. Those kids had enjoyed a huge turkey meal with all the trimmings, including pumpkin pies. Too embarrassed to be truthful about their holiday, J, Adela and Jake reserved honesty and strength of character for future encounters. "We're not really lying. We did gather together. We just didn't celebrate the way the rest of the world does," they'd rationalize to one another. They too had learned to fabricate and embellish their November festivity.

After all, did it really matter to anyone but their family? Triggered by imaginations lurking in the recesses of their bright minds, they'd spin a tale or two of their own to brag about. The morning conversations would be something at which to titter later in the day as they walked home from school. After all, they had to find some comedy somewhere in this holiday, even if it was solicitous.

"Did you have a big turkey dinner at your house this year?" Peggy, a rude jeering school mate waiting at the bus stop began the barrage of superior sounding questions. She was one of Adela's sixth grade friends.

"Don't let her scare ya," Jake would say, "her shit stinks just like everybody else's."

"Oh, sure, did you? Ours was huge and looked just as nice and browned as a picture," J would answer while her head hung lower than a turkey's on Thanksgiving morning.

Neither J nor the turkey had much energy left the morning after the holiday, but she'd lift her chin just high enough to smile broadly causing Peggy to blush with embarrassment.

"Did you have cranberries and chestnut dressing?" Suzette would ask. She was another neighbor girl who acted hotsy-totsy. She'd boast and brag about her wardrobe on a daily basis.

"Wardrobe, my ass," Jake would ridicule her, too.

"She has hand-me-downs just like everybody else. Who does she think she's kidding?"

Jake would shake his head like a school bell and laugh at the joke of it. "We sure did. We had jellied cranberries. Boy was that ever tasty," he would answer.

Jake would wink at his sisters before answering Suzettes's seemingly condescending questions. "The chestnut dressing is my favorite. I can't get enough of it. We had homemade root beer, too. You ever had that?" Jake asked.

No one answered Jake's question. Why would they when the latest craze was Coca Cola, which was now served in other homes on special occasions. Homemade root beer had become old fashioned. Even the *hicks* down on the farm knew that.

"Did you have pumpkin pie?" Margie, another fourth grade friend of J's asked. She was as curious as the rest of the lot. She was one who would ask any question hoping for an answer that made the trio feel awkward. *Well, we'll fool her,* or so they thought.

"Yep, we had apple and chocolate pies and we made fudge, too. What else did you have?" Adela would answer contemptuously. Despite feeling guilty at her smart-alecky retort, Adela knew only too well that the can of cocoa at #11 Lemon Lane was as empty as the parent's bank account at that same address.

The phony banter would continue until the conversation became tedious for the kids from #11 Lemon Lane. They thought none of their other school friends would know about the liver and onion sandwiches in their lunch bags, all wrapped snugly in the shiny pages torn from a winter's mail-order catalog. The trio failed to realize that the pungent odor emanating from their brown bags permeated the air around them, much like the odor of a skunk's piss would have. Their nostrils were accustomed to the stench, but their friend's noses weren't.

The kids from #11 Lemon Lane thought no one was ever the wiser about their Thanksgiving Day holiday. How could they have realized their friends were asking questions out of sympathy, not malice? Were their friend's remarks misinterpreted? Was that even possible?

The kids assumed #11 Lemon Lane's secrets would remain hidden in the rafters of *that damned house* forever. As far as they were concerned, the whole damned town had been fooled. They assumed the challenge of this holiday charade had been met.

Worldly experiences would teach these youngsters what happens when one assumes. Lessons learned through out their lives would eventually educate them. One such lesson was to not have a pet on the farm again, or at least not one that could be cooked for a Thanksgiving Day dinner.

CINDY

Cindy,
short for Cinderella.
Another neglected child,
while all attention went to Adela.

Pigeon toed,
curly blonde hair;
could hold her breath longer
than a koala bear.

Lived your life meek and humble,
Soft hearted and tender.
Why, oh why, did you settle
for a lesser one of the other gender?

So you enjoy being caring?
Goody, goody for you.
Waiting for a return on your favors,
you're bound to turn blue.

Have you looked in the mirror lately?
I have and we're all getting older.
I hope you're enjoying your life greatly.
cause your days are getting colder.

You've earned joy and contentment,
So go, kick up your heels, by golly.
Don't let life pass you by,
like it did to your older sister, Polly.

WHAT'S INSULIN?

I don't have six dollars to spend on this bitch's medicine. I don't think she even needs it. Damn it to Hell! That money could be put toward the new kitchen table and chairs. Those were something we did need. Insulin, what is it anyway? It's a pile of bullshit, that's what it is. It's a waste of good money. She's old enough to die already. I hope that happens sooner than later. I'm so tired of seeing her ugly puss around here! Blondie stood looking at her cloudy reflection on the side of the old metal teapot as she considered her nagging irritation with her mother-in-law, Anna. Blondie was muttering bitterly in her thoughts while standing near the kitchen coal-stove waiting for the water to boil.

She knew she wasn't talking to any human. "Mihal is so stupid. He doesn't know anything about this medical stuff," she said aloud and directly to the spout of the old tea kettle, which began to hiss and whistle with the boiling water.

Blondie found she was talking to herself a lot lately. She reminded herself that this was better than talking to Mihal's mother, the old lady that the kids called Baba. For that matter, Blondie wasn't ready to start having conversations with any of the brats running around in *this damn house, either. At least I can come up with some reasonable answers to my own questions,* she decided.

Slowly, she poured some of the bubbling water into an old chipped cafeteria coffee mug. She set it down carefully on the new chrome and red Formica kitchen table. J quietly watched her mother's movements from a precarious position behind the dining room door. Looking through the door's crack, J assumed her mother was having a cup of afternoon tea. *I wish I could have a cup of hot tea, too,* she thought, getting ready to leave her perch. *If she sees me behind this door though, she'll say I'm sneakin' around, and then I'm gonna get in trouble again, I can just feel it.*

Something mysteriously held her there. Mesmerized, she watched her mother take Baba's Insulin syringe from inside the old wooden cupboard and dunk it into the cup of hot water several times. *What is she doing,* J wondered. No sooner did she think the thought, when her Mother began to demonstrate her intentions. Blondie walked over to the refrigerator and took out the nearly empty bottle of Insulin.

What in the world is she doing, J continued to wonder. Being very still, J remained in her position and watched as her mother pulled back the plunger of the syringe. This caused the syringe to suck up water from the coffee cup and into the barrel of the device. Then Blondie inserted the needle into the rubber stopper of the Insulin bottle. She paused a second, then pushed down the plunger, forcing the hot water into the Insulin bottle.

Oh, my God, J thought. Too horrified to move, she watched her mother repeat the act until the medicine bottle was filled with hot tap water!

It's no wonder Baba's not getting any better, or why the doctor can't figure out what's happening to her. Ah, if he only knew! J's thoughts rumbled through her brain as fast as a run-away locomotive.

Her mother was humming the tune to My Grandfather's Clock as she replaced the items. The medicine bottle was carefully placed onto the refrigerator shelf, while the syringe was gently returned to its special hinged silver box, and then the box was placed back onto the cupboard shelf.

Now it appeared that Blondie was ready for a cup of tea. Taking a tea bag from a colorful tin box atop the coal stove, she began pouring boiling water into a flowered tea cup. Just then a scream, along with some shouting, was heard from outside the kitchen's screened door. "Mom, help! Cindy fell and cut her hand. It's bleedin' pretty bad."

"Aw, shit! Ma, Ma, Ma, that's all I hear all day long. There's never any peace and quiet around here," Blondie whined.

"Well, thank goodness that pretty soon there won't be anymore naggin' or bitchin' from the old hag. That won't be any too soon, neither," she whispered her secret to the teapot again, setting it back onto the stove top.

Grabbing a berry stained dish towel from a sink hook, she headed out the back door to see what kind of an injury Cindy had gotten. She grumbled as she stepped through the doorway, "God damned piss ant kids. It's always somethin'. When will it ever end?"

J knew if she didn't move now, she'd be caught for sure. Once the troops came into the kitchen, there'd be no way to walk away from that hiding spot behind the door. *Go, legs, go,* J mumbled softly to a sane spot in her mind. *Now I'm talkin' to my legs. What's wrong with me?* She wondered. *I think I'm getting as daffy as my mother!*

Her mother talked to teapots, and coffee pots and flowers, but she was crazy! *Maybe it runs in the family?* J needed to clarify the question and satisfy her thoughts. Shaking her head in humorous disbelief, she slowly moved out of the corner and headed for the stairs. Climbing the black rubber-treaded steps two at a time, she hurried to tattle to Baba. Her lips couldn't wait to start babbling the whole story. Baba needed to know what Blondie was doing with her medicine.

Rapping gently on the bedroom door, she waited for some type of a response. There was none. Turning the door knob slowly, she pushed open the door. There was no Baba, but there was Jake and his right hand was reaching into Baba's black leather purse. "What are you doin'? Are you stealin' from your grandma? What kind of a low-life are you anyway?" J asked in a shrill accusing tone.

J waited for answers, but Jake wasn't ready to start speaking. He was too busy rifling through the purse's contents. *What was he searchin' for* J wondered. He didn't say a single word until he whispered, "A dollar, a dime and two quarters. I hit the jackpot!"

A smiling Jake finally looked upward, and then turned toward the window, "I'd better get out of here. The old lady's comin' back."

J slowly backed away from the door. She made her way down the stairs without being noticed by the crowd of harried kids who were now in the kitchen hovering around little Cindy. The toddler's piercing screams only affirmed their early suspicions. "She's bleedin' to death," shouted Vera who had glimpsed the bloody rag wrapped around Cindy's hand.

The shouted words only served to draw more attention to the tyke. Cindy was secretly relishing the rarely gotten attention, becoming calmer as she sucked on a peppermint candy Adela had given her. "Here, can this shut you up for a couple of minutes?" Adela had asked, smiling at each slurp coming from the toddler.

Jake took his time and began to amble down the stairway, only to be cornered by one angry grandmother. "What were you doin' in my room? From down on the path, I looked up and saw you standin' in the window frame. What are you hidin' in your hand, the one behind your back, not this one stickin' out here? Do you think I'm an idiot? There had better be one dollar and sixty cents in my purse, Jakey boy. If that's not in there, my Mihal will deal with you."

Grabbing him by his right ear, she tugged him along and into her bedroom. Shovinging him down into her wooden bedside rocking chair, she reached for her purse and began the search for her money. "It's not here. Let's see what's in that fist of yours," she said angrily, pulling on his reddened ear a little harder.

"Ow, that hurts," an ashen-faced Jake cried out in pain. He opened his fist and freed the money to roll onto the floor.

"Take it, you ignorant bitch. I'll tell Ma you tried to blame me for stealin' money that was under your bed all along. She'll take my side. Your Mihal can't do anything to me. She won't let him. Why can't you just die already and go straight to Hell?"

Jake directed his frustration at the old woman. He was as mad as the devil in a snow storm. He hadn't gotten away with his impudent scam.

J stood outside the doorway listening attentively. When Jake left the bedroom, he headed for the stairway again. Sidling past J, he boldly stared at her, "You had just better keep your mouth shut or I'll tell Mom it was all your idea and we were gonna split it. Try gettin' out of that, Miss Prissy," he brazenly mouthed as he bobbed down the stairs.

Baba stood in the doorway, "I know that's not true. He's a bad one. He's gonna bring trouble to us all, I just know it. I saw him goin' to my room before I went to the outhouse. I knew he was after somethin'. Now here, take this quarter and go get a bag of penny candy from the store. All of you kids will get a piece, but not him. He deserves a swift kick in the rear, and that's all he's gonna get from me. Go on. Go now, while your mother is busy takin' care of Cindy's cut hand."

Repressing the Insulin bottle incident for the moment, J ran all the way to the Andrew's store. Candy was a treat not to be refused, ever. Methodically, she quickly selected everyone's favorite penny-candies. Everyone's, that was, except Jake's. He wasn't getting a piece anyway. Rushing home, she handed over the bag of candy to Baba, who would take care of doling it out to the kids.

"I don't want any stupid candy," Jake timidly remarked before even being asked. "I think I have a stomach ache."

Baba slid back a bit further into the comfort of her favorite old wooden rocking chair, braved a toothless smile to no one in particular, and triumphantly began gumming a stick of black licorice.

Everything was quiet on the home front for the evening, so J decided she'd wait until the next day to have her discussion with Baba. Would it make a difference to tell her tonight? J doubted it. So, tomorrow morning it would be.

Tomorrow awakened with a clatter. The sounds of heavy metal being thrown around caused Mihal to run down the stairs and into the kitchen shouting, "What the Hell are you tryin' to do, woman? Awaken the dead?"

He had arrived just in time to see a flushed Blondie wail an old utensil out of the back door.

"No, I'm tryin' to find the money I had stashed in that old blue speckled kettle. It's been on top of that cupboard for months," she said, pointing to the one tall white painted cupboard in the kitchen.

"That kettle has a hole in the bottom. It leaks, so I keep my cash hidden in it. Except this mornin' I looked and the cash is gone. The whole $34 is gone! Wait until I get my hands on who ever took it. They'll sure be sorry, I can promise you that," Blondie was screeching like a caged canary being eyeballed by a hungry house cat.

For sure, Blondie was one helluva mad bird to be dealing with this morning. "Everybody, downstairs now," she hollered up the stairwell to the frightened and confused kids who had been awakened by her shouts at such an early hour.

Ten step-sized, wide-awake children arrived in a flutter. "What happened? What's goin' on? What's all the noise about?" they were asking.

Blondie sputtered, "Someone took all of my money from my secret hidin' place. It's all gone. That's our grocery money for the rest of the month. Now what are we gonna do, Mihal?"

"Line up. Every one of you get right over here and line up in a row," Blondie shouted. "Now you'll all stand there until whoever took that money fesses up. You got that?"

A row of droopy-eyed children began to form as Blondie's questions were shot into the cool kitchen air. The kids were only too aware that her interrogation was aimed directly at their hearts. They'd been in Blondie's courtroom before and they all knew the rules.

"Did you know what was in that kettle?"

"Did you take the money?"

"Do you know who did?"

"Did any of you see someone lookin' up there?"

On, and on, and on went the interrogator. For the better part of the next hour, Blondie continued her barrage until Mihal stepped in, "Let these kids eat already, Blondie. The money will show up and when it does, you'll have your culprit."

It wasn't until several days later that Jake approached his mother as she sat peeling potatoes for supper. "Did you find your $34 yet?" he inquired.

"I'll bet one of the girls took it to buy somethin' girlie. What do you think?" he asked.

"Polly was lookin' for money to pay for her class ring. She said she was so embarrassed that she was the only one who hadn't paid for hers at the school office. Do you think she found the money in that old kettle and borrowed it?" Jake asked.

He baited his mother for an answer to his questions, but she just sat unflinching on the chair and kept staring at the pot of peeled potatoes at her feet. She was weeping. She had her answer, and so did Jake. He knew he had said too much. He knew he had pushed his mother to the limit, so he took another approach. "I'm sorry. I was just foolin' with you. I hid it from everybody 'cause the kids and that old Baba have been lookin' for candy money. I'll go get it now. You can have it back and it will be our secret, just like the water in the Insulin bottle. I will get a reward, right? I didn't get no candy the other night, 'cause of that damned crazy old Baba. Can I get some licorice for just me today?" he asked, bending around her shoulder to smile sweetly at her perspiring pale face.

Her answer was bracketed with sobs. "Sure, Son, go get me the money and I'll give you some pocket change for your good deed. You sure did save my money. Hurry now, before the others see you."

Baba stood outside at the corner near the screen door. She couldn't believe her ears. *He's being rewarded for stealin'. He's a con artist. Is he blackmailin' her? What was that he said about water in the Insulin bottle? Was he talkin' about my medicine?* The thoughts ran amuck in her brain, making her dizzy. *I have to sit down,* she thought, but it was too late. She had already hit the ground.

"Dad, Dad, come quick. Baba's fainted," screamed Adela.

"Ma, Ma, are you okay?" asked Mihal, gently shaking his mother's limp figure.

"What happened? Did you take your sugar medicine this morning? Did Blondie give you your shot?"

"Yes," the awakening old woman answered in a soft raspy voice. "Blondie gave me a shot," but a question ran through her mind, *a shot of what?*

"Mihal, take the bottle of medicine to the doctor and ask him to check if it's the right medicine in that bottle. Don't tell Blondie I asked you to do this. She'll only get more pissed and be meaner to me. Please, Mihal, do this for me," the old woman pleaded.

"Okay, Ma. I'll do it." Mihal tried to comfort his mother, unaware that a crafty Blondie was standing directly behind him hiding from Baba's view.

"You'll do no such thing, Mihal," Blondie said as she stepped forward. "Your old lady is batty in the head. I won't have people thinkin' I'm not takin' good care of her. I'll call the doctor myself and ask him if she needs more of that Insulin stuff."

"Take her inside, out of the heat," Blondie continued. "She's been sittin' out here in the sun all mornin'. She probably had a heat stroke. Give her some cold water to drink. Go on; what are you waitin' for?" Blondie squawked at Mihal, while her brain scrambled to avoid exposing her deceitful scheme.

How in the Hell did the bitch know about the Insulin bottle? Is Jake playin' both of us? He's pretty good at this blackmail shit. Harrowing thoughts plowed swiftly through her mind.

"I wonder what he's really up to this time," Blondie wondered aloud out of sheer curiosity. She was standing at the kitchen stove holding an empty coffee mug. This time she was talking to the percolating coffee pot.

"Start giving her 12 units of the Lente Insulin every morning, one half hour before her breakfast," Doc Romon directed Blondie, who stood holding the phone's receiver close to her ear.

"If that doesn't take care of her dizzy spells, we'll give her a bit more. By the way, is she checking her urine with those dip sticks I gave you?"

"She won't do it. I told you, she pisses standin' up. She said she's not botherin' with any sticks in her urine. She's a stubborn gypsy. She can't be forced to do somethin' she's not wantin' to do," Blondie reported to Doc.

"Well, maybe then the Insulin is old and not doing its job. Is it still a little cloudy looking? Are you rolling the bottle in your hand to mix the solution the way I showed you?" Doc asked skeptically.

"It looks the same as it always did, and yes, I do roll the bottle the way you showed me. Do you think I'm stupid? Do you think I can't follow your orders?" Blondie questioned the professional man.

The doctor had no way of knowing what was taking place in Blondie's kitchen, but Blondie made obscene hand gestures to the phone's receiver the entire time she was speaking with him. J stood peering through the porch window, watching her mother's ugly facial and hand gestures while she conversed with Doc.

"Well, the next time you go into town, you can tell the druggist to give you a new bottle. I'll leave a prescription with him so you won't have to wait in line," Doc told Blondie as he hung up his receiver.

Mihal met Blondie at the door with the bottle of Insulin in his hand. "Is this her sugar medicine?" he asked.

"Yes," answered Blondie caustically while reaching for the Insulin bottle filled with clear liquid. She was surprised when Mihal gave it a huge toss out of the door and into the small frog pond near the barn path.

"Doc said to get a new bottle, didn't he? You'll get it today. I'll take you myself. Oh, and it better be cloudy," Mihal firmly informed his startled wife. She was certainly paying attention to her husband now.

Later that evening, after everyone had gone to sleep, Blondie returned to the kitchen. She had thought all day about the cloudy Insulin. By adding baking soda to a clear glass of cold water she saw that she could duplicate the cloudiness of the Insulin. "That will be the last time I buy that damn stuff. She'll get what I give her from now on and I'll feed her all the sweets she wants. I don't care if it is like poison to her." Blondie whispered to herself.

Blondie's softly spoken words were just loud enough for J to hear the comments through the air vent on Baba's bedroom floor that was directly above the kitchen.

Once again Blondie was talking to a kettle. Once again, J lay in wait. This time though, J was smart enough to wait for her mother to go back to bed before she chanced tiptoeing back to her own bed.

Baba remained stable for a few weeks, but then began having dizzy spells again. When Doc Romon was called, by Mihal this time, the doctor said he was going to be in the neighborhood that afternoon seeing Carl Mantos, a neighbor. He was willing to stop in and check on Baba. He had added, "I'll bring her a new bottle of Insulin from the drugstore. You can pay me when I'm there, Mihal. This will save you a trip into town."

"Give me the old bottle from the Insulin you've been giving Mihal's mother," Doc made the request directly to Blondie after he'd arrived at #11 Lemon Lane.

Blondie was quick to answer, "I threw it into the stove this morning after you said you were bringin' us a new bottle. That one didn't have but a tiny bit left in it. Why do you want it anyway?" Blondie asked.

"Well," Doc began his strategy of trying to foil Blondie's ruse, "the druggist can refill those bottles. That saves you money because he doesn't have to charge you for a new bottle every time. He just charges for the Insulin and a new bottle top. So instead of paying six dollars, you only pay three dollars. That makes it a lot easier on your pocketbook, but today you'll have to pay me six dollars for the Insulin and five dollars for the house call," he shrewdly concluded.

Waving to Mihal as he left, Doc shouted, "See you next week. I'll see your Ma when I see Carl again next Tuesday."

Blondie now had some serious thinking to do. It didn't take her long to formulate another plan. "Doc was smart, but I can beat him at this game," she mumbled to a glass pitcher filled to the brim with thick cow's cream.

She proceeded to pour the heavy cream over a pot of boiled new potatoes. "That's a good enough lunch for these piss ant kids today. I don't feel like cookin' again in this heat," she said, adding a sprinkle of salt and pepper to the mixture.

Summer became autumn. Autumn became winter. Holidays came and their celebrations passed.

Life went on as usual. Not normal, but as usual at #11 Lemon Lane until early one cold and snowy February morning. "Dad, come in here. Quick! I can't wake Baba up," J was shouting frantically.

"Are you sure she can't wake up?" Mihal asked J.

"Tell your Ma to call Doc. I can't believe this. She was alright last night. We even stayed up talkin' for a couple of hours tellin' each other secrets. She said there were things that went on in this house that I needed to know about. She said she was relieved to finally be tellin' me about those secrets. She was okay, I tell you."

"I even tried shakin' her," J shouted to her dad as she ran down the stairs to ask her mother to call Doc Romon.

"Something is wrong with Baba. She won't wake up. Hurry up, call Doc," J anxiously told her Ma.

"Don't you start givin' me orders, Miss Smarty Pants. I'll call when I'm good and ready, not when you or anybody else tells me to call."

She walked to the sink, drew cold water from the faucet and placed the percolator to brew coffee on top of the kitchen coal stove. She then filled a large pan of water and placed it onto the stove's back burner to boil for the morning oatmeal. Only then did she reach for the black rotary phone and dial for the doctor.

Doc called her condition a coma. "She's sleeping peacefully," he explained.

"She's not in any pain. The sugar diabetes did this to her. It's a killer disease and we don't have all the answers for it yet. There's a lot of research going on and in years to come more will be known about how to treat it. I'm sorry, Mihal."

Baba slept peacefully for two more days and then slept eternally with *her Saviour*, as she called her Lord.

"That baking soda and cold water worked good, didn't it, Ma?" Jake confronted his mother, who was sitting lazily and drinking a cup of coffee in the kitchen. "I told you it would look just like the real stuff."

"Yeah, but I was the one who figured how to take the dose of Insulin out everyday and squirt it into the coal bucket, so it looked like she was gettin' the medicine. Old Doc isn't as smart as he thinks he is. I outsmarted him and all of his college degrees," Blondie was boasting.

Blondie appeared proud of herself and she was feeling as gratified as a loose horny rooster in a fickle hen house.

"Now I have the problems of arrangin' a funeral and a wake. That's gonna tie up everything in *this damn house* for the next three days. Get out of here Jake, and keep your mouth shut."

Jake turned to leave the room, only to find he was facing Mihal and J who stood blocking the door frame.

"Ma, keepin' my mouth shut isn't your only problem this mornin'." Jake's worried words echoed in the empty kitchen as he turned and ran the other direction through the back door. Jake was no dummy. He left his Ma alone to face the two in the doorway.

Secrets do sometimes have an echo. Mihal would realize that more and more in years to come. This fateful morning, as he despairingly gazed at his newly pregnant wife, Mihal made a promise to his mother. The next child would be named Annamaria, so that Blondie would never forget his mother, Anna, or a Gypsy woman he had come to love, Marja.

Blondie would have echoes of her own as she watched her and Mihal's final child be born, live, play, grow, and then die in that damned house at #11 Lemon Lane

PUDDIN' FOR BREAKFAST

"I'm going fishin', that's where I'm goin'. Does that answer your question, Blondie?"

Mihal stood face to face with his wife. She was a tall woman, standing six feet tall in her bare feet and only two inches shorter than Mihal. He was more afraid of her than she was of him.

There were a lot of reasons for him to feel this way, but this April day, by golly he was standing rigid. "Take this God-damned paycheck and do what the Hell ever you want with it. You'll get it one way or another anyway. I don't know what the Hell you do with it all. We don't owe anybody anything, not one nickel, but you'll find some way to spend it," spewed Mihal.

He had become a fuming internal inferno and needed to get away from Blondie before he spilled what was really bothering him.

"This paycheck won't go too far," Blondie shot back heatedly.

All fired up and ready to give Mihal his due, Blondie angrily persisted, "We've got a doctor bill to pay in a few weeks when this baby needs deliverin'. Or do you think Doc Romon is gonna do you a favor and do his work for free?"

"Another thing you had better think about Mister is all the plowin' and seeds we'll be needin' for plantin'. Do you think a garden is gonna sprout up from nothin' just to please you? Without those crops who's gonna feed all these kids you got runnin' around here?"

Without taking a full breath, she continued shouting at him. Her loose spit went flying from her mouth as she got angrier. "Go ahead, go fishin' at that river in Curtain. You just want to see your Gypsy girlfriend, Marja. You think I don't know about her. She's tellin' everybody what a big man you are." She made certain that the word *big* was drawled out for inflection.

"What do you think that's supposed to mean? And what am I supposed to do while you're there, just sit here and wait for your speedy return, Lover Boy?" Blondie continued her screeching dissertation.

Cautiously controlling his temperament, Mihal simply walked away. "Didn't you ever think of savin' for a rainy day, Blondie? You've had nine months," he mumbled to himself as he started whistling and headed for his car.

He had taken a cold bath to rid himself of the itchy coal dust, and then had splashed on some cheap cologne. He felt good and he smelled good. *What more could a man want after a hard day's work,* he wondered. "A little peace and relaxation, that's what," he answered his own question, still mumbling to himself.

He was headed for some fishing at the peaceful Curtain River. He did indeed hope he'd see Marja this night. She was one helluva beauty. He felt the attraction to the short, shapely woman the minute he laid eyes on that smooth, olive-skinned face. He somehow felt at peace when he was with her. "We speak the same language without saying a word," he had told her many times.

Why couldn't I have met her before I saw Blondie? He thought about Marja a lot lately, but knew nothing could ever come of their meetings. He had ten growing kids to feed and another due any day soon. *For Christ sake, what's come over you Mihal,* his brain was asking his heart.

Marja wasn't much better off than Mihal, especially considering the way her life was evolving. She felt the same attraction that Mihal felt, but she'd felt love before and often reflectively asked herself *and just where did it get me?*

She had two boys from her first husband, an eight year old girl from her second marriage, and a six month old bump in her belly from Mihal. With no husband to help her, Marja took what she could get from any man, especially from her loving Mihal.

Mihal would save a few dollars here and there. He'd give it to Marja when he'd make a fishing trek to the small coal mining town called Curtain. He tried to visit with her at least once a month. He'd make any excuse to get out of *that damned house* to be with this woman.

"Blondie, you're getting' on my nerves with all of your arguin' and whinin'. I sure could use some fresh air," he would blurt out at times and then leave for a fishing trip to Curtain.

"I just need some time to think, without listenin' to all this harpin'. God, woman, you're becomin' a naggin' bitch," he'd occasionally harp using exasperated tones.

Still at other times, he'd even slap his hand on the table top just to get rid of the frustration. That was a definite signal for the kids to scatter or to just leave the room. Today's argument would only worsen before Mihal left. "It's only a fishin' trip for Christ's sake," he'd bellowed back at Blondie.

Traveling alone to Curtain wasn't a problem for Mihal. He actually preferred the silence to the alternative of taking one of his cronies with him. He didn't relish explaining to his card-playing pals the what, where or why of his weekend fishing trips. Blondie wouldn't allow any of the kids to go on these overnight trips with Mihal. "They're not sleepin' outside on the damp ground all night, and then gettin' sick for the next week. I've got enough work to do as it is without havin' to nurse kids with colds."

All of Mihal's fishing buddies had become aware of his secret trysts and were not about to horn in on his action. If anything, they would bolster Mihal's ego with complimentary remarks. "I wish I had the balls to do what you're doing, but I'd be without a pair if my wife ever found out," they'd snicker.

Often they'd ask, "Mihal, what will happen when Blondie finds out?"

For some odd reason, Mihal always grinned before answering. "Nothin's gonna happen. She also has secrets she doesn't want anyone to know about. She'll put up with whatever I dish out. Where is she gonna go with a brood of kids? Not back to her mother, that's for sure. She's as stuck as I am."

Mihal kept whistling as he drove slowly in the heavy rain. During the drive to Curtain he continually tapped his fingers. Click, click sounds echoed on the steering wheel in time with the windshield wipers as they swish-swashed, swish-swashed back and forth. He felt as free as a young man again. He would see his gypsy lover tonight. He would not feel guilty about the twenty dollars he'd managed to win at a poker game that remained hidden in his billfold. He planned to give the worn bill to Marja. Blondie got all of his paychecks, but she didn't get his poker winnings. Those were his to do with as he pleased, and it pleased him to give this twenty dollar bill to his new love this rainy night.

It was nearing midnight when he pulled into Marja's rutted, muddy driveway. It had taken him better than three hours to get here, but it was going to be worth it. He could feel the joy in his dampened bones before he even stepped out of his car and into the wet night.

Excited, he hopped out of his auto and slammed the door shut. Marja had told him many times, "Please, Mihal, be quiet when you come here late at night. Don't awaken the kids, or the neighbors who love to wag their tongues and gossip. I sleep light. I'll hear your car's motor when you pull up to the house."

She had a way of saying things to him in a sweet way, not nagging or demeaning. That was just another thing Mihal loved about her.

Tonight though, when Mihal slammed the door he not only awakened Marja's older children and her next door neighbors, but unknowingly he had also awakened a hidden passenger on the rear floor of his car.

He couldn't have known she was there, but J had decided she too had tolerated enough of Blondie's yapping. She had taken the liberty of hiding under the tarp Mihal always folded and placed on the back seat of his car when he left for a weekend fishing trip.

Mihal had repeatedly explained the tarp's usefulness to Blondie. He'd point to it lying on the back seat and reinforce his reason for the tarp's necessity. "I make a tent out of it. I tie clothes-line rope to two trees and hang the tarp over it. I stake down the four corners with pieces of tree branches to stabilize it during the heavy spring rains."

A suspicious Blondie questioned every article that Mihal took with him when he went fishing. Each and every time he went to Curtain she took stock of every item he put in his trunk. Mihal found this to be an annoyance, but would be cautious with his comments to avoid any further confrontations with Blondie. He was always in a hurry to get on the road and head for Marja. This night, he was more perturbed than usual and had just thrown the tarp haphazardly into the back seat. Mihal had no way of knowing what surprises his precious tarp had in store for him this one particular rainy night in Curtain.

Startled by the loud noise of the car door slamming shut, J sat straight up under the tarp causing a pyramid-like configuration in the back seat of Mihal's car. In the moonlight, Mihal had watched the rising of the tarp.

"What in the Hell is goin' on here? Don't tell me there's a ghost under there," he whispered under his breath, "or worse yet, Blondie!"

Slowly he opened the car door, reached over the seat and tapped the point of the tarp. He imagined it would be soft or maybe empty if it was a spook. Instead, it was hard when he thumped it with his knuckles. "Ow! Don't do that again," J cried out as she lifted the cover from her head.

A startled Mihal was quick to respond. "Joni? What in the hell are you doing under there? You scared the Jesus out of me! Does your Ma know where you are?"

Cocking his head to the side, he began to realize, "We're both in a pickle. You know that, don't you?"

His astonished head was shaking *no* while moving back and forth, but J could definitely hear the amusement tainting her Dad's voice.

J shook her head, too. She bobbed her chin up and down, nodding a *yes*. "I just wanted to go fishin' with you. I ain't never stayed out all night fishin' in a tent. It sounded like fun, so I hid back here. I didn't mean to fall asleep though. I was gonna tell you I was here once we got a little ways away from home. Don't be mad at me, Dad," her voice begged.

Before he could answer, a voice called out, "Mihal, is that you? Who are you talking to? Come in out of the rain before you get drenched."

Marja stood in her doorway, her arms wrapping a bright red chenille bathrobe closer to her body. She was shivering from the gusting April rain. "Come on in, Mihal. I'm cold," she pled, but Mihal just continued to stand at the car door unmoving from his muddy footing.

"Well, Marja, I have a travelin' companion tonight. Can she come in too?"

He was laughing lightly as he extended his hand to the stowaway. "Might as well come in, J. I'll use Marja's phone and call Blondie. I'll let her know we'll be comin' home sometime Sunday. We'll sleep in here tonight, 'cause it's rainin' cats and dogs and I don't want you catchin' a cold. We'll sleep out under the tent tomorrow night and do some fishin'. We'll both be better off if we can take home some big fish for Sunday dinner. It won't hurt a thing to get back on Blondie's good side, right?"

For J this was a real adventure, but for Mihal the stowaway was an unnecessary inconvenience. Walking through the sloshing ruts and heading for Marja's back door, Mihal had lifted the skinny girl off of the ground to keep her shoes out of the mud. "There's no sense for both of us to get our shoes ruined," he said.

In all of her young life, J couldn't remember ever being treated so special by her Dad. She had no way of knowing, but this was just the beginning of an unusual weekend.

A cup of warm tea and three oatmeal cookies later, J was shooed off to a makeshift quilt bed on the floor of a little girl's bedroom. "Be quiet, little one," Marja cautioned.

"Shhhhh," she added pleasantly, "don't wake up Rosie. She'll start her crying and then everybody will be awake. So good night, sleep tight. Don't let the bed bugs bite."

She's nice J decided. *I wish our mother talked that way to us.*

Tired and ready for a good night's sleep, J was torn between taking a chance on being bitten to death by bedbugs or eavesdropping on the adult conversation going on in the next bedroom. She chose the latter. Listening through paper thin-walls seemed the logical choice.

"I don't think this is going to work out for us, Mihal," Marja was saying.

"You have so many kids. Good God Mihal, don't you ever keep your zipper up? You're a young stallion loose in the barnyard, but I have to admit I can't resist you. It must be the hot-blooded Gypsy in us. Stop that, Mihal, and listen to me."

Was that a slap I heard? I don't think it could have been. They're still giggling J noted. Marja kept talking, "Joe is still my husband. He wants to come back to me. He has a good job building houses and he says he's settled down. He's a good guy. He says he wants to help me and the kids have a nice life. Heaven knows, I could use some help raising these kids. He doesn't know about us. He thinks the baby is his. I won't ever tell that this baby is yours, Mihal. He says nothing matters without me in his life and he wants to come back here. Will you stop that and listen to what I'm telling you?"

"Alright I'll listen to you, as soon as you satisfy me," Mihal interjected, "but that might take all night," to which they both laughed playfully.

"I don't bed down with Blondie anymore, not since my mother died," Mihal told Marja.

"The flames of my anger toward Blondie grow higher each day. I'm afraid one day the combustion in my head will make me explode. At times, I can't bear the thought of my mother's end. That's one of the reasons I need you even more these days, Marja. You are the joy in my darkness. You're all I think about in my empty bed."

She was laughing teasingly at his comments, "And what about me? What about my empty bed? Who's going to pleasure me?"

"I will. We call that *tit for tat*," Mihal laughed before the moaning and the banging noises began.

Maybe I should have fallen asleep. I'm wide awake now for sure. J's brain itched, just like the rest of her body bundled in the scratchy wool quilt.

So, this is what he does on his fishin' trips. Ma was right. God, he's in bigger trouble than I'll ever be. J's thoughts reeled as she pulled the quilt over her ears hoping to block out the sounds coming through those thin walls.

Make the noises stop. Make them stop already, J prayed from the depths of her heart.

She cried herself to a nightmarish sleep thinking *what have I stumbled onto this time? What kind of a family do I belong to?*

Morning sunshine pouring through a dirty window awakened J early in the morning. She cringed when she spotted the dead and dried houseflys littering the windowsill. The bright sunlight may have caused J to stir, but then again it might have been the ogling from three pairs of eyes staring down at her. She realized that she was a stranger, one who was curled into a mound and entangled in their scratchy quilt, in their little sister's bedroom.

"Boy, you sure are a mess. Why'd you sleep in your clothes? Don't you have any p j's? Who are you anyway? And, where'd you come from?" they were shouting their questions, one kid talking over the other.

This bunch didn't have any manners. J could see that straight out. They started again, "Ain't you gonna answer us? Moooooom, there's some dirty girl in Rosie's room. You better get up here or we're gonna throw her straight out the window."

Marja stood on her tip-toes, peering over her tall children's shoulders and looking down at the girl all bundled into a ball on the floor. She was right where Marja had left her the night before. "Alright you young 'uns, that's enough. You kids get downstairs and have some of those pancakes I left in the warming oven. Save a couple for this little one. Bet you're hungry, aren't you?" Knowing the girl would awaken hungry, Marja waited for J to slowly nod affirmatively.

Before falling asleep, Mihal had told Marja, "Neither of us had any supper. Blondie refused to have anything ready when I decided to leave for Curtain. I couldn't wait any longer to come see you. Pancakes for breakfast? Well that sounds nice."

After eating the third plate-sized pancake, J nodded her head with pleasure. "The pancakes were very good," she said.

Then she remembered to add, "Thank you," to set an example for the gawking batch of Marja's kids. They all seemed ready to mischieviously pounce on this intruder for the slightest infraction, but instead, the younger boy asked, "Hey, are you done eatin' yet? If you are, then let's go outside and play." J gazed in amazement. He was actually smiling at her!

Marja's three kids didn't seem to mind having J around for the day. The time flew by quickly as the foursome played tag, hopscotched, or jumped rope. J was a novelty to these ragtag kids and almost an oddity since she didn't argue about anything, unlike the three of them who argued about everything.

"You jumped ten times; it was supposed to be five."

"I want to turn the rope now."
"No, I want to."
"You're it."
"No, you're it."

Geez, they could get on my nerves. They never shut up. They're just as noisy as our kids at home. J's thoughts turned verbal, as she reprimanded Marja's kids, "You're a bunch of wild scrapping Indians, that's what you are."

The only thing Marja's kids all agreed on was food, and they sure let everyone know they were hungry when dusk became darkness and a wiener roast began. "Let's get some sticks to hold the weenies over the fire," called Ed, the older boy.

"We can use the same sticks for the marshmallows, too. Hurry up! We don't want those hot dogs to disappear before we have a grab at them," the girl shouted while running after her brother.

"Just wait 'til you see what my Mom's lettin' us eat tonight," she continued shouting as she ran. "She's got hot dogs with mustard in store-bought buns, marshmallows and then cherry Kool-Aid to wash it all down!"

"This sure is the life," J said as she side-stepped closer to her dad. Mihal's burst of responsive laughter was pure joy to any listener's ear. J had never seen him so lively.

He was truly enjoying the fun. He was so at ease while kidding around with everyone. "Yeah, kid, I think you might be right," he answered. With a wide friendly grin, anyone could see he was languishing in the moment.

Soon an air of melancholy seemed to slowly fade his wistful smile as Marja began to speak. "It's ten o'clock and time to hit the hay," Marja called out to her kids.

It was also time for Mihal to keep his word to J, "Let's go camp out, Joni. It's time to do some night fishing. We need to get us some big ones to take home to your Ma tomorrow. I won't be coming back to Curtain for a long while. Right, Marja?"

Marja's mouth formed a sad, but affectionate, down-turning grimace. The import was evident as Marja parted her Gypsy red lips conveying a loving farewell smile to her Mihal. Her large brown eyes grew misty as she glanced one last time over her shoulder at her lover. There was no mistaking the message she received as his searching gray eyes returned the soulful glance.

Mihal and J got the tarp strung up and tacked down at the corners. Fishing lines were cast into the gently flowing shallow Curtain River. Two old army blankets were spread on the dew-covered grass at the river's edge. "Are those our beds for the night, Dad?" J asked.

Mihal nodded as he stoked the small fire burning lazily on the river bank. They were camped out on the musky smelling river bank, just as Mihal had promised his little girl.

Getting sleepier by the minute, J knew that if she didn't soon ask her pent-up question in this peaceful darkness she might never know the truth. Courageously, she opened her mouth and the words fell out. "Dad, is Marja your girlfriend? I heard you two talking last night before I fell asleep. I didn't mean to listen, honest, but you can tell Marja she has mighty thin walls. She said the baby in her belly is yours. What did she mean?"

Mihal spoke honestly. "Marja was my girlfriend, but she still has a husband. He went away for awhile, but he's coming back to her and her children tomorrow. You shouldn't have heard about the baby the way you did. That's a mighty big secret for a young girl to carry around in her heart. Are you strong enough to do that?" Mihal asked pointedly.

J could see pain filling his eyes as he continued his elaboration. "We didn't mean for that to happen. Sometimes things just can't be helped. Do you understand? Can you keep that secret for me?" he asked.

J watched him turn and lower his head before wiping the tears from his cheeks. "Sure," she said to the only Dad she knew. "I can do that for you."

Nothing else needed saying. Stretching out on the old faded blanket, J comfortably placed her head on her Dad's knee. It was only a few moments before she dozed off to sleep clinging to his huge calloused hand.

"You were one tired little girl, weren't you, Joni?" Mihal whispered quietly to his angel of the night. Slowly he leaned back against the large oak tree and dozed.

J awakened in the early morning to the tap, tap, tapping of softly falling raindrops gently washing the sleep out of her eyes.

"Good mornin', Clementine. How did you sleep? Did you catch that whole bucket of suckers in your dreams?" a teasing Mihal asked, pointing to the large dented and rusty bucket filled to the brim with clear river water and large gray fish.

"Blondie sure will be glad to see how many suckers and catfish we've caught. We need to head home though, kid. Your Ma's ready to go to the hospital for a few days to have her baby. Doc told her that she's too old to have any more babies at home. She gave me the news when I called to let her know we'd be home before noon. Looks like you're gonna get to do some cookin', Joni," Mihal informed her. "Are you up to doin' that?"

"Sure am. The kids already asked me to cook for them. Junior and Jake want baked beans for lunch, but the girls want chocolate puddin' for breakfast the first morning Ma is gone," J jokingly told her Dad.

Her words sang out with a child's mischievous lilt as she continued, "Remember how Baba used to make chocolate puddin' for breakfast on the mornings after Ma had the babies? I think she did that just to get Ma's goat. What do you think?"

"Well, I think that sounds like it could be a fun idea," he answered, almost absent mindedly.

He didn't seem to be paying attention to the girl's words, but he must have been because he repeated, "Yeah, that sounds like fun for a change!"

J could feel that his thoughts seemed to be somewhere else, maybe out in the distant rising fog on the Curtain River.

What the Hell? Who will it hurt? Mihal's brain concluded. *Puddin' for breakfast sounds good to me, too!*

He sensed this moment as a turning point knowing that his marriage to Blondie was now on a new level. Speaking calmly, he said, "Just don't tell your Ma what you cook. Sometimes what she doesn't know won't hurt her."

"Come on, let's get our stuff gathered together, J. It's time to go home. We have a long drive ahead of us," Mihal monotoned as he began folding the blankets.

"Marja has breakfast waiting for us. What do you say we go eat," Mihal said, after they'd packed up all of their fishing gear.

Looking down at the small girl, he reached out and gently grasped her soft hand with his huge calloused one. That simple gesture alone would have sealed their secret, but her dad's right eye wink was the clincher.

She didn't need to hear the question. Looking straight into the gentle soul so visible in his eyes, she conveyed her silent promise. *Yes, Dad, I'll keep your secret for as long as you live.*

Hand in hand, they happily walked toward Marja's kitchen for some more of those delicious pancakes dripping with sweet maple syrup.

As they ambled toward the back door, an intuitive little girl's thoughts embraced the clarity of an old gypsy's wisdom. *Whoever said blood is thicker than water must have been a fool.*

THE LAST TRIP

The weather was calm this cool April morning, but in Blondie's kitchen a storm was brewing. She was still stewing about Mihal and his announced fishing trip.

While slamming cast iron frying pans onto the surface of the kitchen coal stove, her thoughts were doing a little tripping of their own. *Well, this will be the last one of those damn weekend trips for him, and for J, too. She's not gonna get away with all the fright and worry she's caused everybody. I don't give a shit who or what's in Curtain. Mihal's main duty is here with me, especially now that I'm ready to deliver this baby. I have to stop this frettin' and bitchin',* she commenced, *or I'm gonna bring on the bloody labor pains. I'll be in a real pickle if that happens. There's no one here to take me to the hospital and old Doc says I can't take any chances on havin' this baby at home. Damn it to Hell anyway, Mihal, when will you ever grow up?*

The older kids were expected home from Sunday morning Mass in a short while. Blondie had been grateful for the extra few minutes of quiet afforded her this morning. She'd been feeling uncomfortable since awakening. She'd been waddling around aimlessly. She kept on bumping into anything within a two foot range of her huge protruding belly. "If I keep rammin' into everything in this damned small kitchen, I'll be knockin' this kid into a coma before it's even born," she scoffed at her predicament.

Earlier, Blondie had sent the six older kids walking off together to the eight o'clock Catholic Church Mass in the neighboring town of Ramey. Since Mihal had taken another fishing trip and wasn't there to drive them, she didn't seem to have any other choice. Blondie figured she would have at least two hours alone before needing to prepare some sort of breakfast meal for the returning hooligans, as she called them.

Glancing at the two sleeping toddlers, peacefully dozing in their cribs, she muttered, "Thank God for a couple minutes of peace and quiet."

At least, that's what her mind had envisioned earlier. It had seemed only a few minutes since the older kids had gone off to Mass, and yet here they were back already. Perplexed, she asked, "How in the Hell did you get home so soon?"

"Oh, Mrs. LeCroix saw us walking. She said she felt sorry for us, so she stopped her car and gave us a ride to the church. She even told us to wait on the church steps after Mass, and then she gave us a ride home. Wasn't that nice of her," reported Polly.

As if good luck wasn't enough for these kids this Sunday morning, they also wanted fed. Polly hurriedly asked, "What are we havin' for breakfast? That one Holy Host didn't even fill a tooth cavity. We're starvin', aren't we?" She pointed to the other children who hadn't eaten this morning when she asked for their input.

Anyone, and everyone, who was a Catholic knew that it was a mortal sin to eat or drink after midnight if the communion wafer was to be received at the Sunday morning Mass. Those were the communion fasting rules. Those rules were to be complied by all. There was no questioning the guidelines, there was only a period or you were a Catholic living in sin. Who in their right mind wanted to walk around in a state of sin? "Heaven forbid you should have an accident with a mortal sin hanging over your soul," mothers told their kids. That BIG SIN was right up there at the top of the list with dirty underwear, for crying out loud!

There were a lot of *yes* nodding heads sitting at #11 Lemon Lane's kitchen table, and they were all eager to answer Polly's question and ready to dig in to anything edible. "We're damned hungry," sputtered Jake.

Blondie laughed at her Jakey boy and tousled his hair. "So you're hungry, are ya boy. Well, let's see what your sister can fix for the lot of you."

"Do you think we can have silver dollar pancakes this mornin'? We have fresh strawberry jelly we can spread on them. I'll make them. I know how," volunteered Polly, the oldest girl in the household now.

Scooping white flour out of the cupboard bin and into the large green porcelain bowl, Polly began making the batter. Attempting to be helpful, Adela began cracking eggs to add to the mixture, and then Jake began to pour buttermilk into the flour. "Hold it, you two. We have to do this slowly so it doesn't get too thin. You guys are always in such a rush to do things.

Go sit down. Learn to be patient," scolded Polly, who stood with one hand resting on her hip and the other hand shaking an index finger at the bunch of antsy kids meandering around the small kitchen.

Blondie was already harried, but now she was also hurting. Realizing that her labor had begun, she wanted this brood's hunger satisfied and the kids scooted away from the table as quickly as possible. Rudely shoving Polly aside, she overtook the task at hand. As she stirred the mixture, she added the baking soda. "Good God girl, get out of my way. I'll make the damned batter before you kids ruin it. Then what will you piss ants eat?"

"When's Dad comin' home?" little Vera curiously asked. She was perched on a catalog, boosting her seat at the kitchen table.

"Think he caught any fish? He caught a bunch of big ones last time he went. They were tasty, too," she sweetly chattered while turning a fork end over end. She patiently waited for her pancakes to be served.

Blondie took a long cross look at this little roly-poly girl before speaking sarcastically to her, "You're so chubby, Vera, you could go for a week without eatin' and you still wouldn't starve."

The girl took the insult in stride by gently patting Blondie's extended abdomen and adding her own inane insult, "It looks like you could too, Ma."

Once again the little cutie with a sense of humor innocently diffused some tension. All the kids began giggling to enjoy the moment. Born with an innate comedic timing, this six year old seemed to sense when a laugh was needed in *this damn house*. Once again, it worked! It worked for everyone except Blondie who managed to maintain a stoic face while concentrating on the flat pans of sizzling pancakes. The browning pancakes bubbled on their top surface. Blondie gurgled on her inside. She was suffering in silence as the pain in her gut intensified.

"Your Dad phoned awhile ago," Blondie glumly relayed to the children. "He should be here before too long, if he doesn't dawdle along the way."

Doubled over with the pain of a severe contraction, she informed the hungry troop awaiting their breakfast, "I think today is the day you're gonna get that last baby I told you about. So, when I'm done feedin' your hungry mouths, I'm gonna sit down and you're gonna clean up this kitchen. Understood?"

The kids were all nodding again. They understood. They'd been down this road before and had the routine down pat.

"Should somebody go to get Big Annie?" one of the kids bravely asked.

"No, just eat. I'll wait for awhile before I decide if she's needed or not," Blondie answered.

It seemed an eternity before Blondie heard Mihal's car sputtering up Lemon Lane. It seemed only seconds until she heard the kids shouting, "Dad, hurry. Ma's ready to have her baby. Hurry!"

Pulling the car near the front gate, Mihal reached over to pat J's knee as she sat next to him on the front passenger seat. Mihal only needed to look into the child's big green eyes to know that his secret was safe. "I guess I'll just turn this old car around and head for the Philipsburg Hospital with your Ma. Don't you worry about getting' into trouble for hidin' and comin' with me on my fishing trip. You just remember what you're cookin' for breakfast tomorrow mornin', okay? I'll smooth everything over with your Ma. She'll be in too much pain to think about anything right now anyway."

"Is that what you think, Mihal?" Blondie stated more than questioned as she opened the car door allowing J to exit the front seat.

"J's punishment will be here waitin' when I get back. She won't sit for a week when I get through with her. You'll all mind your p's and q's when I come home from the hospital. This runnin' around shit is comin' to a screechin' halt. Do you understand, Mister?" she blared at Mihal.

"Yeah, yeah, yeah, Blondie, but for now just get in the car before you deliver this last baby out on Lemon Lane. Even you don't want the neighbors to see that happen," Mihal laughed, angering Blondie even further.

Doling out instructions to her driver, Blondie's warnings seemed to bypass Mihal's ears. He heard her words, but he didn't listen. Unperturbed, Blondie continued her coaching:

"Don't drive too fast. Watch out for the other cars on the road."

"Watch out for Doman's dog and Lizzie's cows, they're always loose, and runnin' around on the road in front of their house," she squawked, sounding like the chickens when they laid their eggs.

Blondie couldn't seem to control her front seat driving, even though they had yet to move an inch. She was curious enough to ask Mihal though, "Just what in the Hell took you so long to get home anyway?"

Ignoring Blondie's tirade, "And we're off to the races," Mihal shouted out the car's window to the excited kids left standing and giggling at #11 Lemon Lane.

"To answer your question, Blondie, I've been fishin' and eatin' pancakes. If you don't like that, you can just keep your trap shut," he snapped at her.

Before she could answer, he warned in no uncertain terms, "You damn well had better leave J alone when you get back home. You will not whip her. Do you understand? It's a shame that kid has to hide from you because of your cruelty. My mother was right when she called you a bully. I just wish I'd have seen it sooner."

Blondie sat in silence, much like a lacquered mannequin. It wasn't because she didn't have anything to say, but it was because she was having doozy contractions that temporarily took her breath away. "Just keep this car movin' forward, you dumb bastard! After I have this baby, I'll have plenty to say to you. I just pray this is a boy, because I'm through havin' girls for your enjoyment."

"Oh, you're through alright!" ripped Mihal. "Your bed and mine are two separate places from now on. I know all about you and your true love. I have true love to give too, but not to you." Mihal's voice had increased an octave as he shouted.

"Well, for your information, when I found out I was pregnant this time, I tried to get rid of the kid," Blondie taunted in a vengeful tone.

"Old Doc Romon gave me some pills that were supposed to get rid of this kid, but they didn't work. I tried two different times, but the pills still didn't do their job. Doc couldn't figure it out. He told me they worked for all of the other women who used them. Why they didn't work for me is somethin' he couldn't figure out," Blondie spewed her ugly confession to Mihal.

"You'll be havin' a girl this time, I just know it," Mihal said softly.

"My mother put a curse on you," he continued. "Do you even remember my mother, Anna? The gypsies predestined this child as your favorite, but this baby will carry your curse on her shoulders. Do you remember what Baba told you? She said this little Angel will never find her own happiness with you, just as you won't find your real happiness on this baby's wings," Mihal reminded his bitchy wife.

With confidence, Blondie hissed a retort to her husband's comments. "Don't you even dare try to tell me your gypsy mother's curse is the reason I'll be gettin' a girl this time, for I don't believe in that bunk! That's why I think this one is a strong boy, even Doc thinks so. You'll see how wrong you and your damned gypsy mother are."

Mihal concentrated as he drove along the winding mountain roads, clinging tightly to the steering wheel. He was afraid to remove his ten stiffened fingers from the steering wheel. His hands were now frozen in place by anger. He knew full well that if he did take even one hand off of the wheel, he would reach over and slap Blondie. He'd never hit a woman and he wasn't about to start now. "I should smack your face, Blondie, but I won't stoop to your level of ignorance. I can't believe you have the audacity to brag about tryin' to kill an unborn baby," a disgusted Mihal raised his voice, "and for your information, the word is pregnant not pregrant. You're such an ignoramus."

They rode in silence for the rest of the lengthy drive to the hospital. Several times Blondie attempted to say something, but Mihal silenced her, "Just shush, Blondie. I don't want to hear anything else you have to say. Just be quiet and hope this baby doesn't decide to be born before I get you to the hospital."

Little Annamaria arrived within an hour after Blondie was admitted to the hospital. She was long, skinny and blue eyed. "She looks just the way you looked as a newborn. She even has your blonde peach-fuzz hair. Her long face is the spitting image of yours when you were born," Blondie's mother whispered into Blondie's ear. Josephine's thoughts caused her own deep memories to surface. She remembered her own past birthing experiences beginning with her first born, Blondie.

"The doctor said she's anemic the way you were. He told me that you can't have anymore children. You could die," she fearfully added, as she gently stroked Blondie's damp hair back off of her face.

"I might as well die," Blondie responded to her mother. "I wanted another boy. My boys are my favorites. That crazy old gypsy woman is out there somewhere, and she's laughin' her fool head off. Well, that's her last curse. Anna's as dead as dead can get. She can't protect anyone anymore," an exhausted and tattered Blondie managed to utter before drifting off to a flowering meadow filled with colorful gypsies dancing around a blazing bonfire.

In her dream, Blondie floated upward as the merry wanderers danced and sang praises to their gypsy Gods. They held Blondie's naked newborn high into the air. They were offering it to their heavens. While tethered by golden ropes to a wispy white cloud, Blondie helplessly watched the spectacle through a torrent of translucent tears.

A dream? A foretelling?

Did the crazy old gypsy woman have the last laugh after all?

JUNIOR

Junior, oh Junior!
Where did you roam
in the military service,
so far from home?

Quite the womanizer,
so I understand,
but you went thru life
with your head in the sand.

Tall and handsome,
clever and quick,
gentle and kind,
but never a prick!

You could be friendly,
at times you were even nice,
but you deserted your siblings
at such a hefty price.

You liked the divorcees
and they liked you.
Ma said they were 2nd hand garbage.
Their faux wedding vows proved Ma true.

All you said you ever wanted
was to come back home,
prop your feet up on the front porch,
enjoy fishing, a good cigar and to be left alone.

A SUMMER TO REMEMBER

"You're drunk," Blondie shouted into Junior's face. "What do you think you're doin' coming home smellin' of booze and tellin' me you wrecked the car? Your Dad's gonna hit the roof when he hears about this. Do you know how long we had to scrimp and save for that God damned automobile?"

"You better believe I smell like booze. I drank enough tonight to last me for a couple of years. I think I'm as drunk as a skunk." Junior snickered and then hiccupped

"That's why I went off the road; I was looking for a tree to take a pee!" Junior said. He was laughing as he staggered toward the stairway that led to his bedroom.

He looked up at his mother with his wide toothed grin. "That was a joke, Ma. I thought you might need a laugh."

"I'll give you a joke and I'll tell you when to laugh," Blondie answered with cynicism.

"Further more, just where do you think you're marchin' off to, Big Boy, and when will you be coughin' up the money to have that damned car fixed?" Junior's mother asked without sucking in any fresh air between her sylables.

"You should be on a debate team, Ma." Junior slurred, still smiling widely.

"I'm going off to fight a war, that's where I'm marching off to. When I get my first paycheck, I'll cough it up to Dad to have the car repaired. It's only the front bumper and anybody can tell you that a bumper isn't necessary to drive a car," reasoned the young man, who continued hiccupping as he spoke.

"What do you mean you're off to a war?" Blondie asked indignantly, cocking her head to one side to get a better view of her son's face.

"I joined the Air Force today. Rich joined the Navy and Sheldon joined the Marines. We three buddies are marching to different beats, but you can bet we'll be together and bouncing to a jitterbug come Christmas. Laugh, Ma, it's another joke," Junior said as he slumped over the stair railing.

His speech was becoming more irrational, causing his mother to have a bit more difficulty understanding his slurred words.

"You can't even stand up. Look at you. Just who in the Hell do you think you are comin' home in this condition? Who gave you permission to join anything anywhere? I didn't put my "Henry J" on any forms for you to go into the service," Blondie informed him as she grabbed hold of his arm and tried pulling him off the stairs.

"I don't need you to sign any forms for me. I'm nineteen years old and I graduated from high school. That's all that's necessary for me to join the military. I'm done here. No more listening to you bitch about everything. No more of your yelling and telling me what a lazy bum I am, just because I won't go to work in the coal mines or that filthy cigar factory. I want more out of life than that. Now, let go of me. If you can't send me off to college, the least you can do is send me off to bed," Junior scorned. It took a bit of effort, but he unsteadily pulled his arm loose from her grasp.

"So, that's what you think in that thick skull of yours, is it?" his mother shouted as she angrily pushed the wobbling drunkard down onto the bottom step.

Reaching for a long butcher's knife that was laying on the nearby kitchen table, Blondie brought it forward and then thrust it downward. Pushing the blade at Junior's chest, she barked, "You'll be takin' orders from me, not givin' them. Do you understand me, you stupid-assed fool? I should push this knife through your heart. That's what I should do, and then you wouldn't be goin' anywhere, ever." Blondie maintained her position and glared into the frightened young man's eyes. Blondie's anger was no stranger to Junior, so he was clearly relieved to hear Mihal's voice calling out from the staircase.

"Blondie," Mihal's voiced boomed out of the darkness at the top of the stairwell. "What's goin' on down there? Put that knife down. Put it down I said, before I come and rip it out of your hands."

The resonating timbre of Mihal's voice thrust his message straight through his wife's tantrum. Reluctantly, Blondie moved away from her son and replaced the knife onto the table top.

"He's drunk. He wrecked your car and he joined the Air Force. That's the thanks I get for all of my hard work to raise him and see to it that he graduated from high school. He was supposed to get a job around here and help us out," Blondie's screeching sounded a lot like a barn owl on an October prowl.

"You didn't do it alone, you know," Mihal spoke sternly to his wife.

As he slowly descended the stairs, Mihal presented quite a sight. Wearing only pajama bottoms, he allowed his sinewy torso to silently speak strength in volumes. "Now, son, tell me what the Hell is goin' on here," he demanded.

Junior's speech was becoming more indistinct with each syllable, but the young man managed a slurred explanation. "I'm celebrating. I leave in two days for California to start basic training at an Air Force base. You know there are no worthwhile jobs around here. I already registered for some of my monthly allotment to come to you, Dad. You'll need to sign the checks. That way I'll feel better knowing it's you who's getting the money, not her," he said. Lifting and pointing his chin in Blondie's direction, he seemed to be indicating that Blondie was the "her" he didn't want signing his monthly allotment check.

"That's nice of you, kid. The extra money will come in handy around here," Mihal told Junior as he wrapped one of his muscular arms around his son and helped him to stand.

Mihal cautiously began to maneuver the boy up the stairs. "Let's get you to bed. I was young once, so I understand this celebrating stuff. The military will be good for you. The training will help you become a young man with character," Mihal said as he struggled to maintain his balance on the stairs.

"I tried to join the Army when WWII broke out, but the recruiter told me I had too many kids. With all the noise around here, I was actually looking forward to the quiet of a war," Mihal joked. He quickly added a serious inflection to his voice, "Oh, and by the way, we will discuss that wrecked car tomorrow."

"We'll talk about it now." Standing at the foot of the stairs, Blondie had renewed her screeching.

She was beginning to sound like the jungle parrots in the Tarzan movie J had seen once at the Houtzdale movie theatre. "Squawk, squa squa squaaaaawk," was leaking from the corners of her down trodden mouth.

She began to bellow her own set of orders at Junior. "You'll turn around and send your whole first paycheck to me, so I can get the car repairs taken care of. Do you hear me, Junior? And another thing, you'll turn around and change that form so that your service check comes to me, not to your dad. I do the bankin' around here, not him. Understood?"

Blondie may have been relentless with her harassment, but she was wise enough to know that if she didn't take advantage of the young man's current inebriated state she may miss this night's window of opportunity.

There was always the possibility of new regulations arising with the eastern sun in the morning.

As though Blondie were invisible, Mihal ignored her while he half-dragged his son up the stairs to his bedroom. He stood in silence as the young brawny man toppled onto his unopened bed. Mihal watched as his son stretched out across the crudely-sewn quilt, and then grabbed a corner of the coverlet and enveloped himself cocoon-style for warmth. Slipping his son's shoes off and tossing them into a corner, Mihal's fatherly voice uttered softly, "This won't be the first and it won't be the last good time you'll have, Son. I hope you have many of them. Have a couple for me while you're at it."

As Mihal turned to leave the bedroom, he ran smack dab into a bunch of disheveled kids. They were all wide awake and asking a multitude of questions. The frightened quivering voices mostly wanted to know, "Is Junior alright? He didn't get hurt, did he? How bad was the car crash?" and finally, one frightened little mouth asked, "Ma didn't stab him, did she?"

"He's fine. He just drank one too many beers to celebrate joinin' the Air Force. Your brother is a decent boy and he's going to be a soldier. What do you think about that?" Mihal asked, attempting to dispel the youngster's fears.

"I know he'll do alright and he'll make us proud of him, you'll see. I have an idea," Mihal said enthusiastically.

"Let's make a picnic to celebrate his leavin'. We'll go to Black Moshannon Park on Sunday. We'll cook hotdogs and marshmallows. You kids can take your swimmin' suits and play in the water. We'll have a good time. Who knows, we may even teach J how to swim," Mihal teased, winking in J's direction.

Walking back into the kitchen, Mihal grabbed the large butcher's knife off of the kitchen table and threw it into an open cupboard drawer. "If I ever see a spectacle like that one, Blondie, I will turn around and hit you," he threatened.

"How could you attack him that way? That's our boy! All of those kids stood at the top of the stairs and watched you. They were horrified. Don't you wonder what they think of you? You heard me tell them, we're havin' a goin' away picnic for Junior on Sunday after church. You better make it a good one. Make some of that potato salad I like. Why don't you turn around and do that?" Mihal sniggered when he made the mocking request to Blondie.

Mihal smiled to no one but himself as he lightly smacked Blondie across her butt with the palm of his hand before heading up the stairs leading to his bedroom. He left Blondie standing cross-armed in the middle of the kitchen. She was fuming. She had just been shot down and she knew it. That did not diminish Blondie's level of gloom. If anything, she was a tornado in the writhing stage and Mihal had just placed his body in the storm's eye.

Saturday morning's dawning found Blondie asleep and bent over the kitchen table. She was still wearing her Friday housedress. Her head was reeling as she awakened from sleeping on her forearms. She had been too angry to climb the stairs to her bed. She had awakened to an icy cold kitchen. The fire in the coal stove had died out sometime during the night, causing another reason for Blondie's temper to flare and her skin to flush. In a way, those were good things. They would keep her flesh warm until the stove fire blazed again and the coffee perked non-stop.

Recalling the events of the previous evening, Blondie's temper raged again. She had begun to rely on Junior's extra weekly paycheck coming into the household. Now, she'd be lucky if she ever saw any of her son's checks. She knew that once he flew the coop there'd be no returning for that rooster.

Well okay, she thought, *Polly's almost eighteen. She'll have to get a part-time job and start bringin' home some of the bacon. I'll speak to Old Man Eisenberg about gettin' her a job in his butcher shop. He's always making eyes at our shapely girl and tellin' her how beautiful she is. You can bet he'll be glad to get her behind his meat counter.*

Those formulated thoughts lightened Blondie's mood. By the time the first of the youngsters came downstairs for their morning oatmeal, Blondie was humming, "She'll be comin' round the mountain, when she comes."

"After you eat your breakfast, J, you and Adela have the chore of cleanin' some potatoes for tomorrow's picnic salad. Jake, you'll need to gather some eggs from the chicken coop, but get out of there as quick as you can. I don't want you gettin' chicken lice in your hair. Vera, you and Cindy will look after the little ones while I bake some oatmeal and raisin cookies for the picnic."

This was the mother doling directives to her children, but in her mind she conceded *my job will be to convince Junior to sign over those Air Force checks to me and to make sure Polly takes a job at the meat market. It can't be soon enough for me to have some extra money comin' in. I am so damned tired of pinchin' pennies to make nickels. I'm ready for dimes and quarters to start rollin' through this back door.*

Saturday evening's sunset saw Blondie's brood taking baths, one at a time they soaked in the portable, galvanized laundry tub. The area was surrounded by blankets pinned to kitchen chairs to provide some semblance of privacy for the bathers. A pot of warm water, heated on the kitchen coal stove, was added between each child's washing. This served to not only warm the tub's cooling water, but to dilute the dirtying water from each previous bather. From the youngest to the oldest, no one escaped the Saturday night Fels Naptha bath in the house with no bathroom. The only good thing about this system was that by the time the final kid got to take a bath, he could actually put his head under water and blow bubbles. "Next," was heard ten times before Blondie or Mihal could even consider being part of the lineup.

After Sunday's church service, the family piled into the wrecked car that was now minus its front bumper. They then headed for the picnic in the park. Oh, boy, what anticipation rode along! If they could have only imagined what awaited their day, they might have been satisfied to stay home and play in the dirty bath water.

"Everybody, get out of the water. Now, out," an older rotund man was shouting from the far side of the park's small swimming lake.

"Every one, count your children. Make sure they're all nearby and accounted for. Mrs. Harris, are you sure you saw your Teddy diving into the deep end?"

"Yes, yes, yes. Right over there, near where you are standing," a sobbing Mrs. Harris answered the plump and balding man.

"He jumped in, but I haven't seen him come back up yet. Oh, God, someone jump in after him. Please, somebody, anybody help him. I'd do it myself, but God help me, I can't swim," Mrs. Harris screamed from her kneeling position on the sandy beach.

Several of the adult men, including Mihal and Junior, quickly slipped off their shoes and shirts and then jumped into the water. They began swimming toward the area where Mrs. Harris had indicated she had last seen her Teddy. Those left standing on the beach remained silently hopeful that the missing eight year old boy was just playing a joke. It would have been like Teddy to be off somewhere and hiding in the brush along the embankment. Teddy was a known prankster, full of vim and vigor, so no one would have been surprised if he were to jump out from behind a bush and yell, "Hey, everybody, here I am," and then laugh like a crazy buffoon.

It wasn't very long before the first call was heard, "I found him, he's over here!"

"Somebody help us, hurry," another of the men was shouting loudly and rapidly.

Then a frightened man's voice began screaming, "He's under the water. I think he's caught under a fallen tree and I can't break him loose. Oh God, hurry and get over here. I need help freeing him from the tree limbs. We need to get him on the ground and get the water out of his lungs."

"That's him. That's my Teddy. I recognize his swimming trunks. Oh my God, he's not moving! Someone help my little boy. He's not moving at all," an anguished Mrs. Harris was screaming, while wringing her hands and walking in half circles.

"Oh God no, this cannot be my Teddy! Oh, please no, not my little Teddy!" The boy's mother was sobbing franticly as she gasped for air. She nervously watched as two men pulled the boy onto the sandy beach.

"This cannot be happening! It just cannot be happening," Mrs. Harris languished, tears streaming down her cheeks.

Stepping forward, a female's authoritative voice disrupted the crowd. "My name's Louise. I'm a registered nurse. Mihal, tell everyone to stand back and let me try to help him. Someone drive to the park gate and use the phone to call an ambulance. He'll need to be taken to the hospital for care if he can be revived," she commanded.

There was no hesitancy to this woman's orders, nor to her actions.

Mihal and Louise had grown up in the same little town of Gunther. They had remained friends as adults, even though they only saw each other during the summer months. Louise and Mihal visited one another when Louise brought her daughters for lengthy country vacations to her mother's farm. Mihal knew Louise had become a teaching nurse at a hospital college in Long Island. He didn't doubt for one second that she was in the right place at the right time. There wasn't anyone there more qualified than Louise to attempt resuscitation on this child. Mihal knew his friend very well and he trusted her instincts implicitly.

With precision, Louise knelt beside the lifeless boy lying on the sand. She looked to see if he was breathing and then felt for a heart beat. Next, she turned him onto his side to do a finger sweep of his mouth checking for any obstruction. Quickly, she turned him onto his stomach and pressed his back, forcing some water to drool out of his mouth. She rolled him onto his back, tilted his head back, pinched his nose and breathed twice into his mouth.

She efficiently started pressing on his chest. Up and down, up and down her stiffened body bobbed with the counting. "One thousand one, one thousand two, one thousand three, one thousand four, one thousand five," she counted loudly until she reached one thousand ten, when she would breathe twice into his mouth again. She repeated the steps actively, but it was all to no avail.

The little boy didn't respond. He just lay there water-logged. He could have been a purple and green swollen rubber doll, if only everyone hadn't known better. One of the openly weeping women commented, "He seems so still, it's as if he's waiting to be picked up and rocked by his Mama."

Standing on the sideline, J thought cuttingly, *yeah, rocked all the way to Heaven.*

Louise was becoming fatigued, her breathing was labored. Her resuscitative attempts had been useless. The boy lay motionless. Even after the energetic ambulance personnel arrived and relieved Louise of her efforts, there was no change in the boys condition. The nurse helped the others to load the child onto a gurney and into the back of the ambulance. Shaking her head helplessly, and visibly trembling, she clasped Mrs. Harris's hands saying, "I'm so sorry. I did everything I possibly could have done for him. He was under the water too long."

Wrapping an arm around Mrs. Harris' shoulder, Louise began leading the woman, "Come with me, I'll see to it that you ride in the ambulance with your son."

Parents stood numbed beside their children unable to believe what they had just witnessed. A schoolmate, a friend, a young neighbor was dead. Only minutes before, he'd been happily playing and enjoying his life. Those on the beach slowly mingled without speaking. Heads hung heavily. Strangers hugged strangers. Old and young alike wept for this family's loss.

Shivering noticeably, J needed to allay her grief and sought to find some solace somewhere. She stumbled her way to the rear of Mihal's car and leaned onto the sun-warmed trunk. Though trembling, she felt the summer's heat soothing away her goose bumps. She recalled that long ago morning and her own near drowning. She relived every second of that incident, comparing and contemplating if Teddy had perhaps felt the same floating sensation that she had. *Was he as frightened as I was? It must have been so hard trying to free himself from those underwater branches.* She even wondered *did someone put a curse on Teddy? Well, I guess we'll never know, now will we?*

A wake was held the next day in the Harris' living room. Teddy Harris' funeral was to be held Tuesday morning at ten o'clock. "J, you and your sister go pick some flowers from the garden. Make sure you cut some of those red roses. Put them in a jar of water and take them when you go to pay your respects to the little Harris boy this afternoon. It's a nice sunny day, so you can walk over to their farm after you have something to eat for lunch," Blondie told the girls.

"Aren't you going?" J asked her mother. "I think it would be nice of you, since you're a mother, too."

"Why would I want to go? Mrs. Harris didn't even speak to me yesterday. She thinks she's too high falootin' to bother with the likes of me," Blondie explained from a twisted mouth.

J began to realize what Mrs. Wilkers, her fifth grade teacher, had meant when she described Blondie as "antisocial and insecure with a weak side to her character".

J had decided her mother was cold hearted and disinterested. Blondie always had an excuse to decline the many extended invitations she received to attend PTA meetings or school functions. J now realized that maybe it was a plain and simple fact that her mother was embarrassed and unhappy in her less than affluent marriage and lifestyle. *Could she just be ashamed of how she looks? Cooould that be it* J wondered. *I can't believe I'm feeling sorry for her* she thought plaintively.

"No, you girls knew him, so you can go and say your good byes to the little fella," Blondie stated, holding steadfast to her decision.

The girls couldn't help but notice that their mother looked pathetic. She was wearing a faded blue housedress and a raggedy paisley bandana to cover her unkempt hair. She had actually spoken in a soft sympathetic manner. *Was she being thoughtful and concerned because Teddy was a boy? Did she favor all boys, or just her own?* The girl's curious unspoken questions hung in their minds and mingled with their suspicious doubts. *What's the real reason Blondie was being so considerate* they wondered.

"That boy was cleaner than we ever saw him. He looked like he was ready to go to Heaven. He was wearing his first communion suit, white shirt and black tie," Adela told the anxious kids awaiting a report about the boy's wake.

"He was smiling, too. You know how he always had that half smile that made you wonder what he was up to next. Well, that's the one he was wearing. I'll bet he's takin' it to Heaven with him. He was one to have fun. I'm sure gonna miss him," J told the family gathered around their kitchen table.

Later that evening, J confided to her dad, "Mrs. Harris said the innocent ones smile when they meet God in Heaven. Is that right, Dad?"

J was always the inquisitive one. Her dad wasn't always so gracious with his answers, but he managed to satisfy her question. "I suppose we'll all have a chance to find that out for ourselves someday, kid."

Gently rubbing the top of her head, Mihal gave J the secure feeling she had unknowingly craved since coming home from the boy's viewing. Openly giving permission to the girls, he told them, "You better get cleaned up for bed now, and lay your clothes out tonight for the funeral tomorrow. J, you and Adela can go with Mrs. Harris like she asked."

J fell asleep that night thinking *there are kind people in the world. Dad and Mrs. Harris are two of them.*

The girls were awakened during the night by their older sister, Polly, as she shuffled around on their slick bedroom linoleum flooriing. Rubbing her eyes, while trying to awaken quicker than she felt capable of doing, J began hazily asking, "Polly, why are you getting us up this early? It isn't even daylight yet."

Becoming more curious by the second, J asked, "Why are you dressed up in your best blue suit and why do you have a suitcase?"

Hearing Polly and J's whispered chatter, a wide-awake Adela sat straight up in bed and asked, "I thought Ma said you were going to talk to Old Man Eisenberg in the mornin' about a job in his meat market. What in the world are you doin'?"

"Well, I'm not going to work for that dirty-minded old man. He tried kissing me when I asked him for a job last Saturday. Me and Tod are running away to get married. We're going to have a baby. We'll be having our own house and our own family when we get back from Virginia, but you can't tell Mom and Dad yet," she warned. Putting her index finger over her pursed lips Polly made a "shushing" sound.

Lifting her suitcase off the floor, Polly explained, "Tod will tell where we've been when we come back home. You have to help me though. Pretend you didn't see me with this suitcase. Just get up and get dressed to go to the funeral in the morning. Ma will think you're excited about going and she won't even think about anyone else until me and Tod are long gone over the Tyrone mountains."

"Well, Tod's gonna say that you sure do look pretty with your hair curled and your face all made up, Polly. Bring us a picture of you dressed up in your bride's gown, but don't give it to Ma. She'll just tear it into smithereens. She's really gonna be pissed," J whispered to her pretty big sister.

Climbing out of her warm bed coverings, J stepped onto the cold flooring. Wrapping her small arms around Polly's thickened waist, she stopped short as she kissed Polly's bump of a stomach. "Hi baby. Good luck getting married today," she whispered.

Closing her eyes for a moment, J could have sworn she felt the baby kiss her back.

When J opened her eyes, Polly and her suitcase were tiptoeing down the staircase. Soon they would disappear into the early morning fog that was rising on Lemon Lane.

"Come on you two, you had better get movin' if you're going to that funeral today," Blondie shouted up the stairwell to Adela and J.

"The rest of you sleepy heads might as well get up, too. There's plenty to do around here today. Polly, make up the beds this mornin' before you come down for your breakfast. You can get ready to go ask for that job at Eisenberg's later this mornin'. Maybe the old man will have changed his mind about you by now."

There was no response echoing down the stairway.

Blondie called out again, "Polly, did you hear me?"

There still was no answer from Polly. "Polly, you had better answer me if you know what's good for you," Blondie yelled.

Marching up the stairs, Blondie's boot stomping was probably heard by the deaf cows in the neighbor's barn. Those same heifers may have even heard Blondie's shrieks when she saw that Polly's bed hadn't been slept in.

"We're headin' off to the funeral. Mrs. Harris is outside waitin' for us in her car. Bye," the two girls hurriedly shouted as they ran out of the back screened-door before Blondie could corner them.

They had made a promise to Polly. "By damned, we're gonna keep our promise," they said, entwining their pinky fingers in a solemn vow. They were smiling to one another as they entered the waiting car.

"The next car door I want to hear slammin' had better be by Polly, and she had better have a good explanation of where she's been today," Blondie griped to Mihal when the girls arrived home from the funeral service.

"Well, you two certainly ran out of here pretty fast this mornin'," Blondie began her admonishment.

"I don't suppose you know anything about where Polly has gone off to, do you? She didn't say anything to either of you last night or this mornin' about what she's up to? Well, don't just stand there like a couple of mummies, speak!" she screamed at the two girls.

Blondie's reddened face was within two inches of the girl's grimacing small faces. Neither of them spoke. As far as they were concerned, there wasn't anything they wanted to say.

"Get upstairs and change into some old clothes. Hang those dresses up and wipe your shoes off," Blondie intimidated the girls as she shouted. She was attempting to strengthen her misplaced control over the two.

Mihal interrupted Blondie's latest outburst. Concerned about the girl's residual feelings, he studied their tear stained faces and asked, "Hey you two, how did everything go at the funeral today? Are you hungry or did they give you somethin' to eat afterward?"

"It was awful, Dad. There was a lot of cryin'," Adela answered.

"I cried, too," J said, "but I think I was cryin' for myself, because I'll miss havin' fun with him on the school bus."

"Even the priest cried when he tried to tell a story about Teddy throwin' a ball through one of the church windows. He said Teddy didn't lie about it and that was why he didn't make him pay for the new glass. Father Mike said Teddy was a good boy, but full of the devilment. Is that why God took him to Heaven, to get the devil out of him?" J asked.

"Will Teddy brighten the days for the kids who are up there? Father said that on the really sunny summer days we kids should wave to Teddy up in the clouds. I'll do that, 'cause I sure will miss his smile," J told Mihal between sobs.

"Well, you two are sure gonna miss somethin' else, maybe your dinner, if you don't start tellin' the truth about Polly," Blondie scolded with hopes of frightening the emotional girls into spilling some known detail.

Somebody had to know something, Blondie knew that much. These two sure weren't talking. Blondie was astute enough to see that.

It was nearly midnight when a car slowly rolled to a stop at #11 Lemon Lane's front gate. The hesitant young newlyweds kept their gait to a slow frightened pace as they walked the moonlit path to the kitchen door. Holding hands, the trembling couple peered through the kitchen-door window before attempting to turn the door knob. They were greeted by Blondie's wide and angry blue eyes staring back at them.

"Well, look at what the cat dragged in! What have you two been off and doin', or shouldn't I ask?" Blondie noted that she had already mindlessly asked, and it seemed they were about to tell her.

"First, get Dad and the kids down here. We want to give all of you our news at the same time," Polly said calmly.

"Blondie, you'd better put a pot of coffee on to perk. It might be a long night," Mihal calmly suggested to his wife.

"What kind of news do you have for us, Polly?" Mihal gently asked his daughter before adding, "I think I can guess, but go ahead Tod. You need to be a man and tell us your news. If it's what I think it is, then you did step up to do the decent thing."

The only words Blondie heard coming out of Tod's mouth were married and pregnant. It took only about three seconds for everything to register in her mind. That was the moment Blondie lifted the coffee pot off of the stove top and slammed it down onto the kitchen table, directly in front of Mihal. The pot banged down on the table top, but the boiling liquid and the hot grounds flew right up into Mihal's face!

Instantly, kids screamed as Mihal cried out in pain. "Somebody give me a cold cloth. God damn it to Hell, Blondie. Look at what you've done now. You've scalded my face. Let me run cold water on it and maybe it won't get too blistered," Mihal remanded as he ventured away from his deleterious wife.

J was two steps ahead of her dad. Reaching the sink ahead of him, she had the cold water faucet running full blast as Mihal stepped forward and bent his face into the sink bowl. After splashing water onto his hot skin for a few minutes, Mihal stood straight and tall before releasing his verbal reteleation to his wife. "Blondie, one of these days your temper is gonna get you in a Hell of a lot of trouble with me. You're cruisin' to get yourself in some hot water. Do you know that?"

"Go to Hell, Mihal. You've let your son go off to the military without so much as one raised word about his drunken stupor or the car accident, and now you're almost congratulatin' your daughter for getting' pregnant and elopin'. It's *this damned house* and your mother's gypsy curse," Blondie lamented.

A cayenne-faced Blondie wasn't about to lose any further ground to Mihal. "This was the summer I was supposed to start seein' the payoff for raisin' this bunch of monkeys. It's time for these piss ant kids to start payin' me back. I gave them life. I raised them. If I'd have been smart, I'd have drowned them when they were born, just like I do to any kittens I find around here. It only takes a few minutes to tie up a burlap bag and toss it into that old well over there!"

Blondie's angry arm shook as she pointed to the neglected plank-covered well at the end of the sidewalk. "That's what I shoulda done! If any more crap happens before Labor Day, I still might do that. I may not send any of you kids back to school. Younse could all end up at the bottom of that hole," she threatened.

Labor Day came and the first day of the new school term did, too. No kid had been drowned in that old well. At least not yet! That was a *thanks to Dad* kind of deal. Not only did Mihal nail one lid down on the top of that old well, but he sealed the opening with a non-yielding second covering.

The first was a makeshift wooden layer that was nailed in place, but the second was a sturdy metal plate held in place by long screws. "Try drowning somethin' in there now, Blondie," he said as he tightened the last of the anchors. "Just go ahead and try."

For a few minutes, Mihal stood admiring his handiwork. He gathered his tools in his hands. Only then did he slowly begin a steady gait toward his garage. He was laughing and crying at the same time. It was a strange sight to watch. "For the first time in a long time, Joni, I feel free again. It's a good feelin'," he said.

"This sure has been one summer to remember, don't you think, Dad?" J asked as she walked along side her father. Mihal nodded in agreement and winked his usual one-eyed blink.

They sauntered hand in hand. J matched Mihal step for step.

No verbalizing was necessary. Their unspoken words dangled in the dusky air until a gentle evening breeze blew them away.

GOIN' FISHIN'

"Hey, kids," Mihal shouted out the front door, "I just got off the phone with your big brother, Junior. He's comin' home for a few days. He's drivin' from California and should be here in about five days. He tells me he has a big surprise for us, so what do you think that could be?"

"Well, his last surprise didn't go over so big around here, Mihal," Blondie said, gasping to catch her breath.

"I ran all the way from the barn when I heard you shoutin' out about Junior. I though something happened to him. You never know what's waitin' for the men in the service. I oughta know. I lost three of my brothers in World War II."

"Nothing happened to him, Blondie, so just settle down. He sounded pretty chipper, as a matter of fact. He says he'll save all the talkin' for when he gets here," Mihal said as he pointed to the porch stoop and indicated that Blondie should take a seat to ease her heavy breathing.

"He says we can chit-chat and catch up on the neighborhood gossip while we're fishin'. He wants to go down to Curtain for a day and catch some of those big suckers and catfish. What do you say, Blondie, are you gonna give me and the kids a day off around here?"

Much to the delight of the snickering youngsters, Mihal dropped to one knee, folded his hands as if in prayer, and teasingly asked his wife, "Please, can we play hooky for one day?"

"Get your ass up off the ground, Mihal. Quit actin' like a fool," Blondie quipped. "We'll see when Junior gets here and find out just what his big surprise is this time."

"Ma, there's a strange car sittin' out by the front gate," little Vera noticed a few days later.

Vera was standing at the large parlor picture window, looking out over the front porch railing. "It's one of them new fangled cars we see in the Sunday newspaper," she declared in her usual husky voice.

"Move over, let me take a gander," Blondie said as she edged the girl aside. "Yep, you're right. Must be somebody lost off the main road. I'll go see what they want."

Holding onto the corner of her mother's apron, a shy Vera walked along to the gate. Approaching the shiny two-toned brown car, Blondie called out, "Hey, what do you want here? Are you lost?"

The driver, turning to see who was calling out to him, thought *have I changed so much that my own mother doesn't recognize me?*

"It's me, Ma. It's Junior."

"Oh, my God, what have you done to yourself? Where did you get that wavey hair? My God, you got so fat," she was exclaiming to the son she hadn't seen for almost three years.

"You're not so thin yourself," he answered indignantly as he gave her a tight bear hug. Picking Blondie up and off the ground, he caused her feet to shuffle in mid air. Chubby Vera stood at her mother's side and giggled at the sight.

"Which one are you?" he asked, tussling Vera's blonde curly hair, "and are you big enough to go fishing with me and Pa?"

"My name's Vera and yes, I can go fishin'," she replied tartly.

"I can even put on my own worms. I'm not a baby anymore. I'm six years old, I'll have you know," she politely, but precisely, informed this brother she didn't remember.

"Where are Dad and the rest of the kids?" Junior asked.

"They're down pitchin' hay into the barn. Vera, run and get everybody," she said as she shoved the little girl by the shoulder and pointed her in the direction of the barn. "Hurry now," she encouraged. "Tell them Junior's here."

Here, not home! Junior thought. *Some things never change.*

"Junior, my boy, welcome home," Mihal greeted his handsome son with a handshake at first, but then spontaneously grabbed him into a huge manly hug.

Patting Junior's shoulder, Mihal quickly said, "Come on into the house. Let's get out of the heat. Blondie get something cold for all of us to drink. We've been working hard, haven't we kids?"

"Before we go into the house, Dad, I want to empty out the car. There are a few boxes in the trunk filled with pencils, crayons and paper tablets for the kids. You shouldn't have to buy any of those supplies for the next school year. I'll carry my suitcase. I only have one. Traveling light these days sure does making getting around a whole lot easier on a soldier," he commented with an easy laugh, exposing the large space between his bright-white front teeth.

"Oh, and something else that will make my traveling lighter is to hand over the keys to this new '52 Chevy. You can try her out in the morning when we go fishing in Curtain. It's yours, free and clear. The title's already in your name and it's completely paid for," Junior was rapidly detailing.

"I just hope you like the color. Not too many people do and that's why I got a better price for it." Junior was almost apologizing to his father.

"Here are your keys," he said, placing them in Mihal's open hand.

"It's a good running car. I ought to know. I drove it all the way from California and didn't have a lick of a problem."

Junior felt very proud of his generosity, so he allowed Mihal a few moments of quiet time that was necessary for the gift to register in the indebted fathers' heart and mind. Mihal stood in silence, his chin dipped. He slowly raised his head to look at his son. Mihal attempted to thank him for this huge gift, but the words seemed to stumble out of his mouth. One at a time, he finally managed to gather his words into one sincere sentence. "I can't thank you enough for this car, Son. I don't know what to say."

"You don't have to say anything, Dad. I'm just glad I can do this for you," Junior replied. "Did you notice, it has a front bumper," Junior teased.

The happy scene was temporarily interrupted by Blondie. She began scolding harshly, "Why did he bring this God damned thing here? That's not a car, that's a boat."

"I coulda used the money for the taxes, or some new wallpaper, or even a few new house dresses. You had better at least give him a dollar for this, Mihal, so he can't come back at you and say you stole this contraption from him. He could even say you crooked it from him with some pitiful story," Blondie bellowed, took a deep breath and then began shouting again.

"My God, what are the neighbors gonna think? I'll tell you what they'll think. They'll say we're puttin' on airs, that's what." Blondie always was good at answering her own questions.

"You know, for once, just once, Blondie, I wish you'd learn to keep your mouth shut and just say thank you," Mihal hissed in her ear as he pulled her away from the gaggle of kids, Mihal couldn't help but notice how excited they'd become. They were opening doors widely and examining the newness of the extravagant automobile.

Mihal glanced toward Junior and noted that his son seemed to be enjoying his reunion with the children. Smiling, Junior was busy handing out candy and gum by the handfuls to all the chirping youngsters. Mihal wasn't ready to make bets on who was the happiest of the lot. Mihal could only hope that Junior hadn't overheard his Ma's hateful remark.

"I heard what she said, Dad. I let it roll off my back. I won't let her get under my skin," Junior confided to his dad later that evening.

Junior had learned patience and understanding in the service, so he wasn't about to express his true opinion. "I really don't care what she thinks. This is my gift to you and the family to enjoy. It comes from my heart, so what do you say we ignore her hostility and go dig some worms for tomorrow's fishing expedition. I can't wait to pan fry some of those tasty Pennsylvania catfish," he remarked sprightly.

"And I can't wait to get up early and make you some puddin' for breakfast and pork and beans for lunch," J unselfishly announced. She was wearing a big a silly ear to ear grin, and it was aimed directly at her generous big brother.

WHAT'S NEXT, JAKE

"Mihal, the property taxes are comin' due. We need another supply of coal for the winter months ahead. Christmas is comin' and we don't have a pot to piss in. You haven't worked in the mines for the past four months, so where am I supposed to get money from? Tell me already; when in the Hell are you goin' to take Big John's offer to get a job in the factory over in Buffalo?"

It seemed to Blondie that this conversation was long overdue, so she broached the topic of their financial status to her husband while picking the few rusty-coat apples remaining on the old bent tree. Not wanting the kids to overhear their money woes, she had sent several of the younger children inside to tidy up the kitchen and set the table for their mid-day meal. The older ones had been sent to gather the winter cabbages from the remnant garden greens. A heavy autumn rainfall was expected later in the afternoon, so it would be a perfect day for the indoor chore of making crocked sauerkraut and apples for winter eating.

A lull in the conversation allowed Mihal the time to chew his Red Man tobacco while contemplating the correct way in which to deliver some necessary news to his wife. He decided honesty was the best route. "Well, Blondie, I just may have to do that now. The mines are closed, shut down permanently," he informed Blondie. "The coal's been all stripped out of Koxis."

"When did you find that out? You never said a word about it, Mihal," Blondie asked.

Blondie's facial expression was revealing a slow boil. It wouldn't be long before her pale Polish face would be flushed. She did not relish being kept in the dark about any news, especially anything of such importance. "So, when did you find that out, Mihal? Today? Yesterday? Last week? Just when? Answer me already, God damn you."

"What does it matter when I learned about the shut down? It was a rumor, but now it's a fact. I'll just have to look for some minin' jobs in Clearfield," Mihal said, turning his head and spitting some of his brown, mucousy tobacco juice to the ground.

"There's bound to be something I can get, but for now, drop it. Here comes Dick Helmsley. He doesn't need to hear our business. He probably wants some more of those pork chops from our butchered pig he's been storin' for us in his freezer. I was surprised he was so up front the last time he wanted a few cuts. Usually he just takes them and lets us find out on our own when some of our meat's missin'."

Dick quickly sized up the pair he was fast approaching. Mihal's wrinkled and grey-dusted dungarees appeared to have been worn for the entire week. Dick wondered if the stiff-looking filthy pants stood in a corner over night so Mihal could avoid bending in the morning to put them back on to wear for another day of farming in the fields.

Dick tilted his head slightly to give Blondie a gander. She wasn't any cleaner. Her housedress was soiled with everything from beets to blackberries. A tad of manure edged the hemline. *That must be just for good measure,* he imagined. He finally deduced that this must be canning week, so why soil two dresses. *Hell, that wouldn't make any sense at all.* His brain cringed, then did a u-turn to take a quick furtive glance at the great shock of wavy silver hair Mihal still sported. It was parted and combed neatly. Dick could see that Mihal's face was clean and shaven.

Blondie, on the other hand, had a mass of unkempt dull yellow frizz that appeared to have been shocked onto her head this early morning. The breeze kept blowing strands into her eyes, but she just brushed them aside instead of pinning them into some sort of a hairdo.

Dick's eyes narrowed as he peered at the mouths on these two hicks standing at attention. Mihal had no teeth. *Do I call that a toothless-smile or a smiling set of gums,* Dick wondered. *And how am I going talk to Blondie with her flopping upper dentures and those four rotting lower front teeth. Everything sounds like a whistle coming out of her mouth. I wonder what those two think when they see themselves in the mirror. Do they see what every one else does? How could they have allowed themselves to fall into such neglect? Don't they realize what kind of an example they're setting for their kids? If this situation wasn't so serious, I'd be laughing right now, but by damned, this is no laughing matter. They're going to have to deal with me right here . . . and right now!*

Dick was determined to see his mission through to its culmination, or live with self-damnation for eternity.

"Hello there, Mihal."

"Blondie, how are you?" came a semi-friendly greeting from a nodding head with a clenched jaw.

After a brief and weak handshake, Dick Helmsley began speaking. "I think you can tell by my face that I come with some disturbing news. I'm just going to come right out with it. I won't beat around the bush. It's about your son, Jake," he began.

"This small town has had enough of his shenanigans. Did you know that he's out running around and racing through the coal strippings with that old rusty pickup truck of yours? First he convinced my nine year old daughter to go for a short ride with him, and then he takes advantage of her!" Dick had begun his conversation in a mellow tone, but ended it as a tearful soprano.

A stunned and confused Mihal sputtered, "What? What are you talkin' about? When was this? And what do you mean he took advantage of your girl?"

"You heard me, Mihal. He raped my little girl! She's being examined at the doctor's office right now, as we speak," he shouted.

"I'm seriously considering filing charges with the state police, but I wanted to sort this all out with you and Blondie first. That's just the beginning of your bad news this morning though. You'll soon be hearing from the Kosko brothers, too," Dick added.

"Why the Kosko brothers and what about them? What else has Jake done today?" Mihal asked.

Feeling flustered, Mihal had to take a deep breath to inhale what had just been said by his friend and neighbor. "Oh, good God, Blondie, that boy of yours is gonna be the death of me yet," Mihal said as he turned to face his wife.

Dick Helmsley continued his dissertation with a speedy vengance. "About an hour ago, Jake tried to pass the Kosko's truck. This took place over on Hwy 9 near Ramey. There was an oncoming car, but your boy must not have seen it." Dick raised his hand, indicating to Mihal that he didn't want his interesting story interrupted.

"Your Jake forced the Kosko brothers' truck to veer off the highway and ram into a large tree. The vehicle hit into the tree, bounced back and rolled onto its side. Jake stopped, backed up and sat there watching as the Kosko boys crawled out of the wreckage, but then he took off driving on the dusty back road toward Ferndale. The Kosko's farm truck burst into flames and exploded. It's totally destroyed. Just wait until you get a look at it for yourself. You'll see, there's nothing left but the burnt frame. It's a good thing Andy Hiller came along and saw the whole thing as it happened. Andy was good enough to take those poor scared boys home. Those boys just got some minor bumps and bruises, but they're gonna come after your Jake to pay for their truck. You know, Mihal, they can't earn a living without a truck. Farming's how they make their bread and butter."

"Just who was this Andy Hiller person who witnessed this so called accident?" Blondie caustically interrupted Dick's story.

"Maybe he's the one who ran the Koskos off the road. Who told you Jake raped your girl? Was there a witness to that too? Everybody's always quick to jump the gun and blame Jake for every fartin' thing that goes wrong in this damn town. I, for one, am sick and tired of all of you blamin' him for everything that happens around here," a paled Blondie was shouting defensively.

Residents in the next three towns must have heard her wailing. The kids surely had. The smaller ones in the kitchen pulled the large wooden door ajar, just a teensy crack, so they could eavesdrop on the rising voices. The older kids, returning from the cabbage garden, overheard the loud arguing that stemmed from the back yard. Planting their bodies flat against the shingled side-wall near the back door, they too stood motionless and silent appearing much like a row of soldiers lined up for the firing squad. Well within earshot, they attentively listened as the morning events were being described to their distraught parents. Every child's breathing had slowed to a minimum. Fear in this household was known to do that!

This wasn't just a calamity, it was a double calamity. "What's next, Jake?" Mihal asked to the gust of wind that had just blown across his trembling body.

"Well, Dick, I do thank you for comin' here first. Right off, I can tell you that the young man will be punished severely for what he did to your daughter," Mihal promised, calming Dick momentarily.

Everyone knew Mihal's word was as good as his trusted handshake. "There is no way I can ask you to forgive what's been done. I've known for some time now that he's a bad seed." Mihal said.

"His Ma has protected him at every turn, but the tide has to turn sometime and it might as well be now. Blondie will not interfere with what has to be done to salvage some human element in this kid. If he's to survive out in the world, he has to grow up and accept his lot," Mihal reasoned.

"What's gotta be done, Mihal? You're not gonna lay a hand on him, do you hear me? Any punishment goes to that boy comes from me, and only me, and you damned well know why," Blondie stated emphatically.

"There are other ways to punish him, Blondie, besides with a whippin'," Mihal began.

"That's your way of punishment, not mine. I did that once to the boy and it did no good, none at all. He just repeats his errors. It's as though he can't learn right from wrong. There's something missin' in him," Mihal concluded.

Dick Helmsley stood agape. He couldn't believe his ears. They were only concerned about this wayward son of theirs. They were showing no real compassion for his damaged daughter. Didn't they realize this was a permanent scar, one she'd carry with her for the rest of her life? Dick was beginning to comprehend what some of the other neighbors had tried to explain to him.

Mihal and Blondie weren't seeing the true ugliness of the aftermath suffered by other daughters who had been attacked by Jake. Mihal and Blondie weren't seeing this son of theirs the way the neighborhood did. He was a menace! He would be going away from this community, far away, one way or another. Dick Helmsley vowed to see that would happen. He had made a firm decision and a definite commitment.

"Mihal," Dick directed his attention to the man before him, "there were witnesses to both of today's incidents. Jake's friend, Paul, was riding with him in your truck. Paul ran away when Jake started to rape my girl. He tried to tell your boy he was doing wrong, but your son wouldn't listen. Paul came and got me. He took me back to where Jake had just finished with my little girl. Jesus H Christ man, your son is a pedophile!"

"Your son cannot live in this town. He's a danger to the girls here, maybe even to your own daughters. Did you ever consider that?"

Dick was jolted into reality when he took a staunch look at the two terrified faces before him. "Mihal, don't tell me you have allowed incest to go on in your own home? What kind of parents are you?"

Mihal attempted to open his mouth in his own defense, but he couldn't bring himself to be a hypocrite. He had to take the blame for this monster Blondie called a son. Somehow, someway, he had to make amends to anyone Jake had ever assulted.

Dick stepped a couple of inches closer to Mihal and continued his verbal attack. "The people of this place want him to go to prison. I'm inclined to agree with them, unless you can come up with something that will rid his stink from our peaceful little community. He will be gone soon, one way or another! I'll personally see to it, if it comes down to that. So, do you understand what I'm saying to you, Mihal?"

"How about you, Blondie," Dick asked. "Can you accept the fact that your son is a juvenile delinquent and a social misfit? You've enabled him to continue his horrendous acts against the girls here? If we press charges against him, the law will attach those charges to you and Mihal. What will happen to the rest of your children? They'll go to the state home, that's what will happen. Is that what either of you want?"

Blondie had to sit down. Her knees had just turned to melting rubber. With a drooping posture, she collapsed onto the porch stoop. "What's gonna become of my boy? You can't send him to a prison. He won't survive that. He can be such a good boy at times. I don't know what comes over him at those other times. He just turned sixteen. He has his whole life ahead of him. Oh, if he could only understand what he's doing to himself! I still don't believe it," Blondie said, before adding staunchly, "I think your fancy little girl is makin' up a story!"

"Well, you and he had better begin to understand because this is no fabricated story. There are some consequences to be dealt with here, not just with my girl, but with the Kosko's truck as well. The Kosko's are not going to let him get away with his irresponsible actions. That old truck of yours, the one he's out there fooling around in, doesn't even have a plate on it," Dick sarcastically pointed out to Mihal and Blondie.

"These are not mischievous acts or pranks anymore. His actions are alarming and these dirty deeds of his need to be considered criminal in nature," Dick fumed to the boy's parents.

Dick Helmsley was not letting go. He had tried reasoning to get Blondie and Mihal to comprehend the severity of the situation, but he wasn't getting through to them. He could see and sense that fact. This time, this boy was going to be sent away. Dick didn't care where this kid Jake went, just so he was out of all of their lives . . . for good. The angered neighbor was not leaving #11 Lemon Lane until a decision had been made and an outcome had been resolved.

"Well, Blondie, it looks like you're gonna get your wish for me to go work in a factory," a highly agitated Mihal told his wife after comprehending the situation set before him.

"Dick, I have a chance to go to Buffalo to work. I could take Jake with me. He's sixteen now; he can quit high school and get a factory job workin' beside me. I'll keep a close watch on him and he won't step foot in Gunther until he's straightened himself out. Is that agreeable to you?"

"Well, that's one thing you can do. The other thing that needs done is that someday your son has to face all of these girls he's raped or molested, and he should sincerely apologize to each of them and their families. Each and every one of them needs to hear Jake say that what he did to the girls wasn't their faults," Dick insisted.

"He has a sickness and I hope somehow he gets some kind of treatment for it. As his parents, that's on your heads. How you can live with the knowledge of what your son has done to all of those innocents is beyond my understanding or forgiveness. Do the right thing now, for God's sake. Make him own up to what he's done," Dick begged as the tears flooded his tormented face.

"I don't understand how you can face your neighbors knowing what your son has done to this peaceful town. I don't know how I'm going to face my daughter knowing I didn't kill this kid of yours," Dick told the two adults as he turned his back on them defining his disgust for them and their boy.

Mihal and Blondie had plenty of problems to cope with. Dick thanked God they weren't his problems. He had enough to deal with under his own roof.

From the corner of his eye, Mihal saw two strapping young men coming toward him. The Kosko brothers had walked across the farm fields to confront Jake.

"He's not here," Mihal informed them. Leaning against the old curved apple tree, Mihal attempted to appear less nervous than his inner trembling would allow.

"Dick told me about your truck. I do apologize to you boys. I know how hard workin' you two farm fellas are. I'll see to it that you get paid every penny that's due you. I'll take you to the bank myself, right now, before it closes at noon. I'll take out a loan so that you can replace your truck. I just ask that you be fair with me. I've been out of work and just gettin' by for the past four months. Now, I know that's no problem of yours, but I have a brood here to look after. I think you boys understand what I mean, don't you?"

"Oh, yeah, we understand alright. That doesn't make matters any better. That kid of yours could have killed us, do you know that? He needs punished and he needs to be the one to pay for all the damages," the taller of the two spoke disgruntedly.

The other angered Kosko boy asked, "Where is that asshole kid of yours anyway? I want to slam that son of a bitch's head into a tree, so he can see what it feels like. From what I understand, he's a disgusting piece of shit! Some fathers around here are saying that he's slime and deserves to be strung up from a tall tree. If I were you, Mister, I'd get that kid far, far away from here, and I'd do it right quick."

Although he was disheartened and shamed, Mihal still had a reserve of pride to draw from. "Don't you come to my home and threaten me, young man. Now I've told you, I'll do right by you. You'll get the money today so you can get yourselves another truck. I'll decide what kind of punishment will be given to Jake, not you. So go, get in my car while I get my keys, and then we'll be on our way into town."

"There's no problem giving you the loan, Mihal, but are you sure you want to mortgage your home?" Tom Martin, Mihal's friend who was also the local bank manager asked out of curiosity.

"Wouldn't you rather just put some of your land on the block? This must be a very important matter. Are you in some kind of trouble?" Tom was being hospitable, but he sure as Hell was a nosey bastard.

Mihal didn't want to give out anymore information than he thought necessary. It was bad enough Gunther would be buzzing by the next morning. He certainly didn't want his problems discussed in the neighboring towns with the rest of their gossip.

"No, no trouble, Tom. I just want to have a few dollars handy for my family until I get my first paycheck from the factory. I'm going to Buffalo to work and I hear there's no pay for the first month. Most of us men have to go away from home to find jobs now that the mines have closed down for good. We knew the day would come. We just didn't see it comin' so soon," Mihal explained simply.

"You know you can trust me to pay back this entire loan as quick as I can. I'd certainly thank you for any help you can give me, my friend," Mihal asked earnestly as he reached out to shake Tom's hand as a genuine trustworthy gesture.

Dropping the two farm boys off at the one and only local car dealer's lot, Mihal handed them the stack of bills he had received from the bank manager. Mihal wasn't so sure that eight hundred dollars was a fair price for their rusty heap of a manure-laden truck. It seemed to him these two had taken advantage of the situation. He knew the Kosko boys had him over a barrel, and they also knew it. It was either pay their price or they'd call the state police and file charges against Jake, or maybe even Mihal and Blondie as well.

"Both of you fellas sign here on the dotted line," Mihal said, handing them a pencil to seal the transaction. "This says I gave you eight hundred dollars for full payment of your wrecked truck. We're all fair and square now, so I don't want you comin' 'round and botherin' me for more money. You got that?" he warned.

Speaking through his open car window, Mihal verbally affronted the young men as he slowly pulled away from the curb. "I thought you two were decent guys, but you're just a couple of hoodlums yourselves. I can't believe you'd take advantage of your own poor neighbor. You're both lucky nobody's strung you up yet."

Mihal drove slowly away from the brothers. When he could no longer see the car lot in his rear view mirror, he pulled over to the side of the road. He turned the key, shutting off the car's motor. Tightly gripping the steering wheel, he just sat and stared straight ahead. He was numbed by all that had taken place this day. "Good God, what have I done to deserve this? Help me!" he implored.

There was no one there to comfort or console him. He was as alone as only alone could get. "Ma," he sobbed, "you were right. You said her bastard son would only bring me pain and disgust."

His whole body shuddered in a convulsive torrent of gut wrenching tears. His anguish was his own. Blondie would never appreciate his plaintive cry to his God for guidance, at least not where her Jake was concerned.

Blondie had been intuitive enough to have Jake's clothes packed by the time Mihal returned from his trip to the bank. She did not wish to face another confrontation with her husband, not on this day anyway. Nor did she want to wreak any more havoc involving Jake, but she couldn't manage to restrain her inconsiderate self for more than a few seconds. "What the Hell happened to you?" she asked her husband.

"Your face is all red and swollen. Don't tell me the bank wouldn't give you a loan and you cried about it? Well, answer me. Did they give you a loan or not?" Blondie bellowed.

"Yeah, Blondie, I got the damn loan. Those two yahoots took eight hundred dollars in repayment for their damned old truck. Well, you can bet your sweet ass that son of yours is gonna pay back every cent of that loan. Where is he, anyway?" Mihal asked.

"He's in his bedroom. He's sound asleep. He came home a short while ago, ate some lunch, and then I sent him off to bed. He said he was tired from playin' in the strippin' mines today. He didn't let on that he'd done anything wrong, so I didn't ask him any questions. He acted perfectly normal. You can talk to him tomorrow mornin' and straighten this all out. He still doesn't know he's not goin' back to school on Monday, or that he's goin' to Buffalo with you to work in a factory. Telling him can wait until mornin'. Nothin's gonna change what's gonna be," Blondie said smugly.

Once again, Blondie was arrogantly manipulating the situation as only she could. She wasn't quite finished talking to Mihal though. "Maybe he wasn't the one who did all the stuff Dick told us about. There are other boys in this town, you know. There's a chance it could have been one of them. You should be getting'to bed yourself. You'll need to get up early to pack some clothes for your new job. You're still gonna leave with Big John at six o'clock tomorrow mornin', aren't you?"

Sunday morning rolled in, but Blondie didn't' roll out, of her bed that is. She couldn't believe that Mihal was actually taking her Jake along to Buffalo this morning. "He's my baby boy, my favorite. Why do you have to take him away from me, Mihal, why?" Blondie had cried out to Mihal as he and Jake drove off with Big John.

Jake sat in the back seat of the moving car. He was smiling as he waved out the rear window to his mother. *That's odd,* thought Blondie, *he's smilin'. I thought he'd be cryin'.*

"They could have both worked in the cigar factory right here in Philipsburg, but Mihal took the coward's way out. He wouldn't even stick up for Jake. He said he'd defended Jake too many times in the past already." Blondie was speaking in disbelief to her long-time friend and neighbor, Big Annie.

"Thank goodness we were busy cuttin' up the cabbages and makin' sauerkraut yesterday afternoon. That kept all of our minds from rehashin' what happened. Even so, I'm so discouraged. It was difficult to even get out of bed this mornin'. Adela and J made breakfast. They think I don't know what they cooked. Chocolate puddin', that's what they made and that's what they all ate. Not a one of them kids saved me even a thimble full."

"Blondie sounded so pathetic this afternoon," Big Annie told her husband later that day.

"She makes it sound like the neighbors have accosted her precious Jake, instead of the other way around." The neighbor twosome laughed as they ridiculed the thought of poor, pitiful Blondie and her predicament.

"Serves her right," Big John said. Annie agreed with him.

Two months, and two jobs, was time enough for Jake to earn the entire eight hundred dollars to pay off the bank loan. Two months and one day was time enough for Mihal to march the young man down to the Air Force recruiter's office for a "voluntary" enlistment.

"If it's good enough for your brother, the Air Force is good enough for you. Maybe the military will dole out the discipline you need to straighten out," Mihal sternly told Jake.

Mihal never truly understood the complexities of Jake's mind, but he hoped the military would. Mihal would realize one day that the Air Force never cared about Jake's mind, let alone the complexities lying hidden there.

Jake wasn't so sure he'd have called his a voluntary enlistment.

He'd been given another ultimatum by another distraught father, who had discovered Jake in his fourteen year old daughter's bed two days earlier.

How voluntary did that make his enlistment? Only Jake could honestly answer that question, if he had a mind to.

POLLY

Polly, by golly,
a singing, dancing girl.
Not always so jolly,
but through life she did twirl.

Polly was pretty, popular too.
Eloped with a six foot soldier,
with blonde hair, a big smile,
and icy-cold eyes of blue.

Never a good housekeeper,
and not a good cook;
that's how I'll portray her
in my chapter filled book.

I'll have her be warm
and forgiving, too.
Eventually doing
what she had to do.

She lived life to her fullest
in this little scrap town.
Never reaching potential,
just living became her crown.

So, gather ye rosebuds
and live your life in accord.
Enter the gentle Heavens, Polly,
as your final reward.

CRY, BABY, CRY

"Polly, I can't believe how big and beautiful that little girl of yours has gotten. How old is she now, about eighteen months?" asked Aunt Eve.

"When is your next one due? Are you hoping for another girl? It sure does cut down on the expenses when the clothes can be reused. I know all about that with the three girls we have," Polly's aunt said as she tried to make light conversation with Polly. Polly obviously was not feeling well and did not attempt to conceal her discomfort.

Polly was pale and would frequently rub her protruding belly. Occasionally she would moan, as though she were feeling uncomfortable. The aunt couldn't help but notice the sorry shape Polly's maternity clothes and shoes were in. They were clearly outdated and shabby. The shoes were badly scuffed and their heels were worn down to almost equal flatness with the soles. Her blouse was at least two sizes too large for her tiny frame and it was definitely faded three shades lighter than its original Kelly green color. The arm pits were badly stained with wide graduated perspiration marks. *She used to be such a beauty and always took pride in how she dressed. She almost seems to not care,* the aunt thought.

"Your Mom tells me you're taking J home with you for the week to help with some of your housework. Maybe she can baby sit little Tina while you catch up on your rest. That's the smart thing to do, especially if you're not feeling well, Polly," Aunt Eve had said as she reached forward to pat Polly on the shoulder.

"Yes, I don't quite feel like myself this week, so it'll be nice to have someone around to give me a hand with some of the housework," Polly answered.

"She can help with washing the laundry, then hanging it out on the clothes line to dry. She'll be a big help with the ironing too, but she can't call playing with this little one work. She's a lot of fun, but she does keep me busy. She doesn't sit still very long, that's for sure," Polly explained to her visiting aunt. *With three girls under the age of six, I know active when I see it,* Eve thought. *I don't need children explained to me.*

"How was your drive from Illinois? Did your girls enjoy the ride and how are they enjoying their visit to the farm?" Polly asked.

Polly realized that she was being obvious and solicitous, but at the moment she couldn't have cared less. She didn't feel well and only wanted to get off of her feet and into bed.

"Talk about getting bigger and cuter, your three sure are sweetie pies. Speaking of sweets, thanks for the all the cookies you send to the kids at Christmas time. On that note, Tod, we need to be going home," she said with urgency to her voice.

J couldn't help but notice that on the entire drive to Polly's house, neither Polly nor Tod said a word to each other. There was only stone-cold silence in the car. Tod was in another pissy mood, J instinctively understand that much.

Even as Tod entered his and Polly's sparsely furnished kitchen, Tod entered first leaving his wife to trail behind. He didn't even bother to hold the door open for anyone coming in behind him. He just let the rickety screened door slam shut in Polly's face. J entered last. She was toting her wriggling, chubby little niece in one skinny arm and a diaper bag in the other. Trying to balance both, and hold the door ajar at the same time became a dueling feat. Eventually J became the victor by using her one foot to prop open the door, while she snaked through the narrow opening.

"What's for dinner, Polly?" Tod asked with a rather contemptuous attitude.

Polly didn't respond to her husband's question. She gave him a glance as if to say *can you wait a minute. We barely got through the door.*

"It's a simple question. One that doesn't require a college degree to answer, or are you thinking I'm a stupid jackass and can't understand your answer? Say something. Don't just stand there looking like an idiot with an ugly sour puss! Get something started for my dinner. I'm hungry, woman," he shouted.

In an intimidating gesture, he bent his head closely toward Polly causing his flushed nose to touch the tip of hers.

"Phew! You smell like beer," Polly snapped. "You're drunk again, Tod. You shouldn't have even been driving the car. Now move back and stop this shouting. It's nonsense, and besides, you're scaring Tina and J. Get away from me. I told you, I don't feel well today."

Polly didn't back down from this six foot two, eyes of blue, husband of hers. He'd returned from the Korean War a changed man. He had been a POW for a short period of time. He had been threatened and tortured many times before being freed to return home. He was now an alcoholic, she was certain of that. He didn't talk about his traumatic experiences while in the Korean prison camp, but he had taken to keeping a pistol tucked under his pillow while sleeping. When asked, he'd explain, "I need it for protection in case the North Koreans invade our good old U S of A."

He had begun to lash out at the slightest irritation from Polly. He was quick to strike her with his fist at the slightest hint of indignation. Sometimes it took only one word to set his arm into motion, especially if that one word was *no*.

"What do you mean you don't feel well? Christ, you're pregnant, you don't have some illness. You always have some excuse to get out of doing any work. You can't even keep up with this little bit of housework in this shack. What are you going to do when you have a second baby to look after? Don't tell me, I know. You'll just add another of your little sisters to the helpers' list. Well, you can bring how ever many of your family you want into this house, but I'm not giving up my beer money to feed them. Understand that, Bitch," Tod yelled.

With a cocky attitude, Tod rudely smacked his lips as he swaggered over to stand behind Polly, who had begun cooking hamburgers in a frying pan. Grabbing her right elbow, he spun her around just as he swung out a tight fist that connected with her chin.

In an instant, she was on the floor with the frying pan following close behind. Her sweater sleeve had caught on the pan's handle, causing hot grease and the meat patties to spill down the back of her head and neck. Polly screamed, crying out in pain as she fell to the floor.

When she attempted to stand, the slippery grease on the linoleum flooring wouldn't allow her to get a footing to raise herself up. She slipped again, falling forward onto her swollen pregnant belly. "Look what you've done. Help me up, that's the least you can do," she appealed to Tod. Sobbing, she extended her hand to him.

"Get yourself up, just like you got yourself knocked up, you pathetic slut," he answered crudely.

He kicked her derriere, shoving her whole body a few feet to the opposite side of the slick floor. Greasy contempt seemed to ooze from the sole of his size thirteen shoe.

"So, you're just gonna sit there crying now? Get your fat ass up and start cooking something worthwhile to eat, and it better not be hamburgers and French fries again."

J couldn't help but think, *I agree with the guy. That's all she ever cooks, plain burgers between two slices of butter bread. I'm pretty sick of them myself. Maybe I'll just have a French fry sandwich for my dinner.*

"God, I hate to smell that stinking, frying, pig grease," Tod remarked.

His mouth formed an ugly distorted smile as he continued his verbal assault. "It reminds me of Korea and that's the last place I want to remember. The only good thing in that disgusting hole of a country was the mamason with her rear in the air. At least I knew I'd get a good piece of ass whenever I wanted it. Too bad I can't say the same about you, you ding bat whore!"

J had been standing in the living room archway holding little Tina's hand. They were both too frozen to move. Two little girls stood staring at the angry man, who just kept hitting his right fist into his left palm. When it became evident to J that Tod wasn't going to help her sister up off the floor, she began to slowly walk toward her. Still holding the toddler's hand, she knelt on one knee to whisper to her sister, "Polly, are you okay? Let me help you up. You can sit on this chair and catch your breath, okay?"

Tina wrapped an arm around her mother's neck and hugged her. Polly bit her lip to avoid sobbing any harder. The last thing she wanted was to frighten and upset her little one any further.

"She's fine. Get away from her. She can get up by herself, unless she's too lazy to do that too," Tod yelled.

"Here, you fancy those God damned hamburgers so much, eat one. Here's a good one. Too bad it's not cooked yet, or you'd really enjoy it," Tod said with melodramatic disdained tone.

Reaching out to deliberately push a round ball of the raw ground meat mixture into Polly's mouth, he squished and smeared the bloody meat around her mouth and onto her face.

Polly clenched her jaw tightly, abhorring his abuse. "Stop this. Please, stop," her voice and her eyes begged.

For some odd reason, Tod's face relaxed and he backed away from Polly. Wiping his bloody hands in a dish towel, he walked toward the kitchen door.

Pulling the door open, Tod grimaced at their wedding photo hanging on the entrance wall. Pointing with an index finger to Polly's face, he seemed to snarl as he spoke. "You won't have to cook me any dinner, so there. I'm going to the Moose Lodge for a decent meal and a few brewskies. How's that for gettin' out of cooking dinner?" he asked the framed photo.

"You can lick the floor and eat those God damned turd ball burgers laying there. And you can have one, too, since that's all she knows how to cook," he said to J as he nodded his face in her direction.

"Or you can both starve. That's your choice, Polly Baby!"

Tod sneered as he made a quick exit leaving three females behind. They were all seated on the cold kitchen floor clinging together. Frightened, they sat trembling and weeping for what seemed an eternity, but in essence was only a few minutes.

"Come on, Polly. I'll help you up. Sit here for awhile and I'll try to calm Tina for you," J said, attempting to act assured.

It didn't take but a few minutes before little Tina was perfectly satisfied eating a bowl of rice crispy cereal that had been topped with banana slices and a maraschino cherry. She had been easily calmed with a little knee bouncing and a nursery rhyme. The only noises coming from this toddler were "Yum" and "Nummy" much to the delight of her smiling mommy, who was sitting at the table watching her little beauty enjoying her treat.

Polly was grateful the child wasn't old enough to be cognizant of the earlier scuffle between her parents. Squealing with delight when she bit into the cherry, little Tina lit up the room with her wide smile of new pearly-white teeth.

It wasn't very long before a different type of noise was heard at the kitchen table. Polly was trying to eat a bowl of cereal with hopes that the mild food would sooth her unsettled stomach rumblings. Grasping her abdomen, Polly began a frightening moan.

"J, something is happening to me. I think I may have gotten hurt during that ruckus before. I'm having a lot of stomach pain. Help me to the sofa and let me lie down," she said as she leaned on the kitchen chair for support, she arose and propelled her body toward the living room couch.

"Go to the phone and call Dad to come drive me to the hospital. Something is terribly wrong. Tell Dad to hurry and get here," Polly pleaded.

"What's goin' on here, Polly?" Mihal asked the minute he saw his trembling daughter. "Don't tell me Tod beat you again. I can tell by the look on your face, that's what happened. It is, isn't it? Well, he's done here. I won't stand by any longer and watch him slug you around. It will be your kids he's poundin' on next, or maybe mine when they're in your house."

Smiling down at Tina, he said to J, "I'll drop you both off at home before takin' Polly to the hospital."

Trying to keep his thinking clear, Mihal added an after thought, "J, get some diapers and fill a bottle with milk for this cutie."

"It's too late for the hospital, Dad," Polly gasped, "I think the baby is coming now."

"J, you better run to the Calvin's house. Tell the missus we need her help over here. Before you go, dial up your Ma so she can tell me what to do until you get back," Mihal told the young frightened face staring back at him.

"You need to call the Doc before you call Ma. He'll need to get over here quicker, even I know that much," an anxious J was advising her dad.

Being sure fingered when it came to using the rotary phone, J had managed to quickly dial into the doctor's office declaring an emergency and then called her mother. "Polly's having her baby right now, on her couch," was the only message necessary to convey the urgency in her voice to the doctor's office and to Blondie.

"Doc is on his way, and here's Ma on the line. Just keep the phone next to you, but don't hang up, Dad. You're gonna have to learn how to work a telephone for yourself one of these days. It's not hard, you know. Kids use phones everyday!"

Calling out over her shoulder, J was already two steps out of the door and on her way to fetch Polly's neighbor. "I'll be right back with Mrs. Calvin, I hope."

Blondie wasn't one to be shy about giving orders. She was just glad she wasn't there to help with this delivery. She had delivered so many of her own babies that she wasn't keen on aiding her daughter's early delivery. *She made her bed, now she can lie in it* was Blondie's silent sentiment. She did, however, understand the harsh realities of birthing. She knew some deliveries were easy and some were unforgiving. She also understood the dangers of giving birth too early. She'd been down that road with a set of twin girls who were delivered as still born. Even Blondie didn't relish the thought of Polly experiencing a stillbirth.

"Keep Polly quiet, Mihal," Blondie began.

"Put one of the baby's rubber sheets under her and then cover her with a warm blanket. Try not to let little Tina see her gettin' upset. That will only frighten the kid and make matters worse. Have J keep Tina busy, or better yet, put her to sleep for the night."

Wondering aloud, she asked, "Where's Tod. Why isn't he there? He didn't get drunk and do somethin' to Polly, did he?" Blondie asked the questions, but as intuitive as she was, she already knew the answers. Besides, Mihal's silence confirmed her suspicions.

Mihal took a deep breath and then set about to do as he'd been instructed by Blondie. "Try to stay quiet, Polly. Your little one sittin' over there in her high chair is watchin' everything that's going on. You don't want to scare her, now do you?" he whispered to her.

"Doc will be here soon. Everything will be alright," he added.

Mihal had never felt so helpless in his whole life. He was a big guy, but at this moment his body felt the size of a midget's. This was one of his babies in trouble, and all he could do was hold her hand and wait for Doc to arrive.

I don't believe this. Wait till I see that husband of hers. He'll be wishing he was back in Korea. Mihal's mind would not stop reeling. It flung around and around like a broken film at the movie theatre.

Repositioning one of the straight back kitchen chairs, Mihal placed it next to Polly. She lay shaking and whimpering on the sofa in their scantily furnished living room. "Here, squeeze my hand if the pains start. That's' what your Ma always did and it seemed to help her. Of course, it didn't do much good for my hand," he joked as he sat down next to her.

Mihal hoped to see a glimmer of a smile cross Polly's face. That didn't happen.

"Doc will be here any minute now. He'll be the guy to help you," Mihal told her, trying to reduce some of her anxiety

"This baby's almost out," Polly said to Mrs. Calvin, who had just arrived. "Don't let anything happen to it, please?"

Hearing a car pull into the driveway, a relieved Mihal stood to look out a side window. "Thank God, Doc's here."

Mrs. Calvin was smart enough to intervene at this point by asking, "J, can you take little Tina upstairs and play with her. Just keep her busy, okay? If you do that, you'll be helping your sister. That will be one less thing Polly has to worry about. Go on now, scoot," shooed the nervous neighbor.

Polly knew that her shivering would stop when the baby emerged into the world, while an excited Mrs. Calvin's shaking only seemed to gradually increase. Nervously, she spurted to Doc, "Oh, my God! I can't believe this is happening."

Thankfully, she covered her mouth in time to keep her loose dentures from flying across the living room. Embarrassed, and at a loss for any further words, Mrs. Calvin quickly pushed her falsies back in place and stepped aside to let Doc enter the room. This was definitely a nerve wracking experience for her and one she wanted to cease as quickly as possible.

"Oh, Doc, the baby's coming," Polly was sobbing. "It's at least six weeks early. I'm afraid to move."

"What brought this on, young lady," the old general practitioner asked. "How long have you been in labor? How long has it been since your water broke?"

They were all questions Polly would have liked to answer, but she was becoming nauseated and suffering a renewed strong contraction. The only response she was able to muster was, "Just help me, Doc. I can feel the baby's head between my legs."

Placing a folded sheet under Polly, Mrs. Calvin followed the doctor's directions to hold the tiny head upward, allowing Doc to get a better view of the baby's positioning. "The umbilical cord is wrapped around the infant's neck," he said. There was a definite alarm in every syllable that escaped his mouth.

"I'll try my best, but honestly, Polly, we're in a bit of trouble here. Mihal, you had better dial the operator, that's an O, and tell her we need the ambulance for an emergency here," Doc said before continuing.

"I don't have any choice here, girlie. I'm gonna have to cut the cord and try to give this baby some air. Its little face is blue already. Get ready to push when I tell you. Are you okay with helping me?"

"As soon as the cord is cut, we need to get this baby out of your uterus. Do you understand what I'm telling you?" Doc asked.

Although breathing heavily, Polly was able to hear the snip of the scissors and feel a surge of warmth between her legs.

"Push now, Polly. Push harder! Push! Push once more! Good girl. The baby's out. I got her," Doc began speaking in a calm manner, but loud enough for Polly to understand his directions.

"Mrs. Calvin, massage Polly's lower abdomen. That's so she doesn't hemorrhage. Do it now, not tomorrow, for Christ's sake. I said massage, not rub. Knead it like bread dough!" Doc was frantic and genuinely needed cooperation from Mrs. Calvin. He had one catastrophe on his hands, and he didn't need a second.

Polly tried to peek around Mrs. Calvin's rotund body, but she had to strain to see the tiny baby the doctor was holding up by its feet. The baby's coloring was dusky and it had no movement. Doc slapped the baby's bottom, not once, but two, and then three times. There was still no movement from the baby. Doc brought the unclothed baby into the crook of his arm and breathed into its tiny mouth. He slapped its bare chest and breathed into its mouth again, but that still didn't bring any response. "Get me something to wrap her in. Something warm to get the blood flowing," he called out to Mrs. Calvin.

Mrs. Calvin wrapped the baby in a soft fluffy towel and handed her back to the doctor. He again tried compressing the baby's chest and breathing into its mouth repeatedly.

Polly laid on the old sofa, whimpering softly, "Cry, my baby, cry. Please, breathe for your mommy."

Polly prayed a beggar's prayer, "I'll do anything, just cry, my baby, cry. Please, God, help my child."

An uncontrollable trembling set in to Polly's body, while her sobbing grew louder. Somehow the mother in her heart sensed that there was no hope for her baby girl.

"I'm sorry, Polly. I can't do anymore. Your baby didn't make it. It was just too soon for her to leave your womb. Her lungs must not have been properly formed yet. Sometimes there's nothing anyone can do in these situations. Do you want to see her?" Doc gently asked, his tone reflecting his heart-felt sympathy.

"I want to see her, and I want to hold her," Polly answered unabashedly.

She didn't realize what was happening at that precise moment, but later she would tell her husband how she'd bathed their baby girl with her heart-wrenching tears.

After the infant's swaddling towel was unwrapped, the distraught mother looked and longed for a child's life that was never to be. When counting the ten tiny fingers and then the ten tiny toes, both complete with soft nails, she thought *I'll never have the chance to polish these for your high school prom.*

She wiped her finger across the miniscule eyebrows and touched the tiny nose. She brushed back the wispy little blonde curls that covered the still crown, and she thought *these curls will never bounce to the beat of a jitterbug.*

Polly had to take a deep breath to avoid choking on the sinus drainage in the back of her throat, but she just couldn't stop the huge teardrops that stormed from her burning eyes. "What a beautiful baby. I'm going to miss watching you grow up with your sister," she whispered, as she tenderly clutched the tiny babe lying still on her bosom. The angelic infant was so close to her mother's heavy heart.

Vengeful thoughts entered this grieving mother's soul. *It's too bad your father will never lay eyes on you. He doesn't deserve to see you, but he does need to know what he's done here today. Somehow, someway, he will pay. Something like this doesn't go unnoticed by a good and loving God.*

Tears continued barreling down Polly's cheeks as she reached upward to grasp her father's hand. "Thanks for staying with me, Dad. I don't know what I would have done without you here."

The two hands trembled together. This seemed to be the only source of solace Mihal could offer his daughter at this moment. Polly sobbed inconsolably as her father whispered, "Cry, my baby, cry. Let the tears come out. That will help mend your feelin's. Your baby knows you loved her. She won't ever doubt that."

Oh, Ma did you and your curse have anything to do with this tragedy? As he lay in his cold bed that night, Mihal's thoughts traversed to his Mother in her gypsy Heaven. He prayed; *take care of this tiny baby. Wrap her in your arms and love her. Protect her. Do that for me, Ma.* Before succumbing to a night of fitful dozing, Mihal hoped that his pleas would not go unheeded.

J also slept an unsettled sleep. She worried about little Tina dozing beside her. Their bed that night was a small mattress on the floor of a chilly unused bedroom. Sharing an itchy woolen coverlet with Tina, J scratched more than she slept. Her only peaceful moment came during one notion she considered. It had certainly pulled the children at #11 Lemon Lane through many traumatic mornings. J made a decision. She would make Baba's recipe of chocolate puddin' for their breakfast. Maybe, just maybe, that would make them all feel a tad better.

Tod wasn't seen for a week. When he returned the following Saturday evening, he was in a drunken stupor again.

Having just returned from her baby's funeral service, Polly wasn't ready to face another battle, but Mihal was. He had been waiting for a face off with his handsome son-in-law. Greeting Tod as he stepped out of his car, Mihal stood tall and firmly chastised the man, "You will give up this bender you're on, young man. Do you hear me? This type of behavior will cease as of this moment. Do you know what happened in your absence? Do you realize what you caused to happen?" Mihal asked, his breath so close to Tod's face that he wondered if he and Tod were breathing the same oxygen.

"You will understand the seriousness of your brutality before I'm through talking to you. Your wife and your child will come before the bottle. Is that clear?" Mihal's stance was enough to threaten the unsteady man and Mihal's somber voice seemed to encourage a speedy sobering process.

At Mihal's towering insistence, and despite Tod's initial resistance, the two came to a mutual understanding, but only after Mihal informed Tod of the tragic loss of their infant daughter.

Tod's behavior and habits quickly changed after that bender. Life does have a way of altering circumstances, as Tod would quickly learn.

His life changed drastically a few months later when he learned of his diagnosed stage four renal and bladder cancer.

Coincidence or curse?

Good question!

Tod didn't believe in curses. He bet his life it was only a coincidence. He lost.

HE'S COMING BACK

Blondie sat on the old porch swing; she pushed the cradle with her toes, sending it into rhythmic motion. She swung freely as she remembered the many times she'd sat with her Jakey boy on this very swing. This was where the two of them could be found after Jake had gotten caught up in some type of mischief. She recalled that the last time was on the Saturday evening before Jake left with Mihal to get a job in a New York factory.

She remembered awakening that ominous Sunday morning and feeling exhausted. There was no way she could have gone down to that kitchen and cooked the daily pot of oatmeal. She recalled how she'd called out to the kids to fix their own breakfast.

"You kids are gonna have to get yourselves up this mornin'. You'll need to get dressed for Mass. Big John said he can drop you off at the church, but you'll have to walk back." Blondie had called out to the sleeping youngsters as she lay in her bed, too anguished to even consider going down to the kitchen to put a pot of coffee on to percolate.

I don't want to get out of bed this morning. I feel so miserable, but somebody's gotta milk them two damn cows and feed those stinkin' chickens was what Blondie remembered thinking. She also recalled that her mind was at a slow idle that fateful morning.

"I still can't believe you're takin' my Jake out of school to go work in a factory, Mihal," Blondie had groveled. "You'll pay for this stunt, just you wait and see." Blondie remembered that she had uttered those words quietly under the sheet that she'd pulled up over her face.

Staring vindictively, she had watched Mihal across the hall in his bedroom getting dressed to leave for Buffalo. She didn't care if he heard her utterances or not.

"Jake, are you awake? Get up and get dressed," Mihal had called out to the boy lying lazily in the bed next to his.

"Come on now, you knew this was comin'. As soon as you get a job, you're gonna be gettin' up a lot earlier than this. You better learn to get used to it, 'cause it's gonna happen. Come on, I said get up. Do it before I pick you up by your ears. You don't want that to happen, believe me," Mihal had cautioned.

Jake should have known better than to ire Mihal, especially with the anticipated long drive ahead. He had thought about the length of time it would take before he'd be free to get an apartment and be on his own in Buffalo.

Blondie knew how Jake's mind worked, and she remembered how he'd told her what he'd been thinking while he was being reprimanded by Mihal. *I know one thing for sure, once I get that damned loan paid off, I'm outta his sights. I'll be gone for good and he won't know where to start lookin' for me,* Jake had told Blondie that those were his precise thoughts.

Blondie didn't know it, but Jake was silently sulking to himself and thinking *I'll be free of both of them. Her constant naggin' and his forever eyeballin' me will be done and over with. They'll both be outa' my picture for good!*

"Yeah, I'm gettin' up, and I'll bet I'll be ready before you, Old Man," Jake had spoken brazenly to Mihal.

Jake couldn't seem to help himself. *I'm gonna piss off the old geezer yet,* he had thought with a hidden smirk.

"You're still cocky, eh Jake?" Mihal had asked.

"Well, we'll see how long that lasts when you get in with those street smart factory workers. They won't take any of your lip, you'll see," a wisened Mihal had told him.

"You'll learn a lesson or two pretty quick. You'll learn, and mark my words, you'll soon be chokin' on your own smart mouthed remarks," Mihal had warned the kid a second time.

"Blondie," Mihal had called out, "get yourself up and get me and this boy of yours somethin' to eat before we head out for New York."

Blondie recalled complacently arising from her toasty warm bed covers. Clomping noisily down the stairs, she knew she'd grumbled, "Shit, no peace for me this mornin' either. Maybe it'll be a quiet two weeks without his yappin' back at me all the time. The only good thing about his comin' back will be a fat paycheck, the kind Big Annie told me about. It's about time he started takin' care of this family the right way, not his Ma's old ways."

Blondie remembered that it was a long two weeks of waiting to feast her eyes on Mihal's first paycheck. She smiled while reading what was written after the dollar sign.

"Well that's more like it, Mihal," she had exclaimed after taking a lengthy gander at the slip of paper Mihal had handed over to her.

Tonawanda Plant, Buffalo, New York was the heading in the upper left corner. Her thought about how her sullen eyes had quickly scanned down the slip of paper to the amount stamped on a dotted line that read $825.00. Blondie remembered how her somber eyes rapidly became happy eyes.

"I'm workin' in the foundry. Me and two other guys shovel coal into the furnace for eight hours, Monday through Friday, 4 a.m. to 2.p.m. On four of those days, I work two extra hours to make some overtime. At time and a half, I'd be a fool to pass it up. Nobody seems to want this job, except for a few of us guys. The boss says heat from the furnace fire is hard on the eyes. Even with the thick goggles they gave us to wear that strong heat comes right through the glass. Pay's good, though. Better'n I ever thought I'd see. They didn't seem to care about me not havin' an education or a high school diploma. They were only lookin' at the muscles in my arms to see if I could handle the work. Shit, Blondie, this is a piece of cake compared to diggin' in the mines."

Mihal had given her a blow by blow job description. That had been more than she cared to hear.

Blondie had stood patiently waiting for Mihal to complete his dissertation. She didn't remember all that he'd told her. She had only been interested in calculating the $825 on her brain's cash register. She had been so excited that her eyes twitched.

In a few sentences, Mihal had slowly explained his new position in the foundry. He was genuinely excited to have found gainful employment in the city factory on his first interview. He knew the lengthy car trips would be wearisome. He convinced himself that the riding back and forth every two weeks just to spend the weekends at home would be worth the gas money he'd be paying Big John. He had also told himself, "It will be good not to have to scrape pennies and eat crumbs."

Blondie thought about Mihal's first return trip home. He described how it felt exciting to be chauffeured by Big John, but then after a few more trips he began to realize just how tedious these wasted hours had become.

Hell, I could just mail Blondie the check. That's all she's interested in anyway, he had considered on one such trip home.

Mihal would eventually tell Blondie about one nagging thought that had given way to a second idea. *I could cut back and travel home only once a month. That would give me time to get a part-time job in that corner restaurant next to the boardin' house. I could earn some pocket money that Blondie wouldn't even need to know about* became almost an obsession on that one long drive home from Buffalo.

Blondie knew Mihal thought about his kids and how he missed the rascals. "Those kids are the reason I work my ass off," he would tell Big John during their long trips back to Pennsylvania one weekend.

"If I save the twenty dollars I pay you for gas by skippin' one trip home, and if I work second shift and three weekends a month, I'll be able to get those kids some real toys for Christmas. Santa's bag could bust at the seams this year. For once I'd be proud of what I deliver to those kids on Christmas Eve, instead of feelin' embarrassed."

"I see what you mean," Big John had replied. "Plain and simple, I know exactly what you mean."

"For years me and Annie have scrimped and saved for every little thing we've given our kids, too. For once, it will make me happy to see my wife and kids smile when they open their gifts on Christmas morning. Don't get me wrong, they never say anything bitchy about their gifts, but deep down I know they're disappointed with what little they get. I'm looking forward to a real excited smile from each of them, not the forced ones they usually flash. I'm with you on this idea, Mihal," Big John had said as he flashed a huge smile in Mihal's direction.

"Well, John, you're lucky you only have four kids to raise. I still have seven at home, and I'm a grandpa to one of Polly's. Boy that Tina sure is a cutie and she's as smart as a French cookie. She'll be lookin' forward to Santa's visit this year, right along with all of mine."

Later that evening, Mihal would tell Blondie how he'd grinned ear to ear when he bragged about his granddaughter to Big John.

During the drive home, Mihal found himself in deep thought before he continued his conversation with Big John. "I sometimes wish me and Blondie would have had better sense and not had so many kids, but then again, I wouldn't give a one back. Well, maybe one. That Jake's a real pistol. Thank God he's in the military and I don't have to worry about him anymore. I let the Air Force do the worryin' now."

Big John had told Mihal that he was glad Jake was out of their lives. He had gone on to tell of his own trials with Jake. "You know, Mihal, I never did tell you, but a while back your Jake told my Maddy that he loved her, just to get in her pants. Can you imagine the gall that kid had? It happened just once, though. She came to me and told what he'd done to her. She was so ashamed of herself. For the longest time, she didn't want to go anywhere with her friends. She was afraid she'd run into him and he'd try something again. I took care of it though. I hope you don't mind, but I warned him that

I'd shoot him dead if he even so much as looked her way again. It seemed to do the trick, because he's never bothered her since."

Big John had paused long enough to let out a heavy sigh before continuing, "I'm sorry that it had to come to that, Mihal, but you have girls of your own and I knew you'd understand my worries."

"You don't have to apologize to me, John," Mihal had said to his friend.

"You have no idea what grief that kid of Blondie's has brought to my home. I hope he doesn't return to Gunther for a long, long time. That's one smart ass I don't miss," Mihal had admitted to his long valued pal.

Mihal noted how gentle snow flakes had begun to swiftly drift across the windshield. The confinement of the car had encouraged conducive and friendly conversations between the two long-time friends. The overall drive from Buffalo to Gunther took at least twelve hours, so they had time to touch on a variety of subjects. This snowy-night's topic seemed to stray toward Jake's antics in their small town. This town was so small that everyone knew everyone else's secrets. Everyone knew Jake and everyone knew there were no secrets when it came to him. Everyone, it seemed, except Mihal as he had just learned. He knew Jake's havoc had reached every Gunther family with a young girl in their household, but he hadn't known of Maddy's molestation, so he bravely asked, "Did you or Annie ever tell Blondie about this?"

"Oh sure, Mihal, Annie told Blondie about it as soon as it happened. Blondie said Jake would be punished severely for his actions. She assured Annie the very next day that he'd gotten a whippin' from her and that she had taken away some of his privileges. She said he wasn't allowed to go to any of his friend's homes for a month. Didn't she tell you?" John had asked.

"No, I didn't know anything about it," Mihal had uttered, almost inaudibly because he had been so embarrassed.

It was during this trip that Mihal had confided Blondie's secret to Big John. He began by saying, "Well, John, maybe I should tell you the truth about Jake. First of all, he's not my son. He's Blondie's and some guy she got mixed up with when I was workin' long hours in the mines. He's a lot like his real daddy. He's the spittin' image of him and he's a horny bastard just like him. My Ma told me all about Blondie's love affairs in the hay barn with Ed Strang, the feed man. Ma used to watch them through the holes in the barn boards. My Ma told me the whole story the night before she died. Sometimes, I think she held off dyin' until she could tell me the truth about Blondie. No, John, Blondie's not the woman you think she is. If it wasn't for all those kids that need cared for, I'd have left her a long time ago, believe me."

"Second," Mihal continued, "he's done somethin' to just about every girl in this town, includin' my own. Don't think for one minute that I don't feel ashamed and embarrassed about that. I've tried to teach him good, but he's a sick person. He's sick in the head. He can't grasp what's right or wrong. He thinks and does what ever he pleases. He doesn't care about anyone or their feelin's. Blondie has let him get away with so much. You have no idea of the amount of damage he's caused to some families around here, includin' mine."

The driving time on each of these return trips seemed to get more tedious for Mihal. Blondie realized that when finally he'd decided to tell her about his latest decision. "I'll be coming home on a monthly basis, instead of every other week."

"Well Hell's bells, you'd have thought I dropped the atomic bomb into the kitchen at #11 Lemon Lane," Mihal confided to Big John.

"What do you mean you'll be comin' home once a month? Why? What brought this on? Maybe you found yourself another girlfriend, this time in the Tonawanda Plant? What am I supposed to live on if you don't bring home the paycheck every two weeks, thin air?" Blondie remembered the day her mind boomed. Something had snapped and she'd allowed her tirade to explode!

When Mihal had dropped the bomb, Blondie realized that she'd certainly pushed the detonator that caused the explosion! *He deserves what ever I dish out to him for takin' my Jake away* was her rationale as she remembered that day Mihal took Jake to work in the factory with him.

"You can wait until I bring the checks home," Mihal was now saying dryly.

"You should have plenty of money left over from the checks I give you. You shouldn't even need one full check to live on for a month, let alone two. Are you savin' any money at all? Are you puttin' money in the bank for the rainy day that's gonna come when the property taxes are due? Answer me, Blondie. What are you doin' with all my hard-earned money?" Mihal asked.

Mihal had felt his questions were legitimate, since he was now making more money in a month than he'd ever made in six, but Blondie didn't seem to think his questions made any sense at all. She couldn't help herself. She'd just shrugged her shoulders and walked away from him. *He hasn't answered my questions, so why should I answer his* was Blondie's inconsiderate sentiment.

Mihal decided to stand a few feet away from his wife and take an honest look at her. She had changed dramatically. She was now sporting a new short curly-permed hairdo. She looked like a New York hussy draped in a new slinky blue dress, nylon stockings and black velvet house slippers. "Why are you all gussied up to do housework, Blondie? How much did that permanent wave cost? How many new clothes have you gotten for yourself lately?" Mihal blatantly asked.

He could see the change in his wife's appearance, but the kids were all dressed in the same damned old hand-me-downs. He noted that each one of his kids needed a hair trim. "Have you spent any money on clothes or anything for these kids, or have you just spent every cent on yourself?" he asked.

"They don't need for nothin'," Blondie snapped. "If they need somethin', then I'll think about gettin' it for them, but not until then. I'm the one who's gone without all these years. It's my turn now and don't think for one second you're gonna turn that clock back around, Mister!"

Mihal persisted, "Have you saved any money? Any money at all? Get me the bank book right now. I want to check for myself."

Blondie laughed in his face, then moved about two inches closer and answered spitefully, "No, I'm not worried about savin' any money and I'm not goin' to until I get everything I want for myself. You took my Jake away from me, so consider this my repayment."

"Well, Blondie," Mihal began, "it's about time we get the savings book straight around here. You will make a list of everything that's needed for the next two week's spending money, and then that's all the money you're gettin'. You'll go to the bank with me tomorrow and I'll give you that amount after I cash my own check. I plan to open a new account, one that only I can draw from. I don't plan on stayin' in Buffalo for the rest of my life, just long enough to get ahead in the money department."

Saturday morning found Blondie still in a foul mood. Neither had Mihal's attitude changed from the evening before. The kids walked around on tiptoes, not knowing what to say or what they were even permitted to think. Oatmeal was the usual breakfast staple, and as usual it was eaten hurriedly so that a quick get-away could be accomplished before the Saturday morning squabbling began. This morning's battle of words was certain to be a dilly.

A determined Mihal asked politely, "Well, Blondie, are you ready to go into town and get this bankin' business done? That's the only way you're gonna get any money from this paycheck, so you'd better get off of your high horse and saddle up."

Blondie must have considered the alternative, because she saddled up in a hurry and was sitting in the passenger seat before Mihal had ever reached for his car keys.

"Silence, ah sweet silence," Mihal chimed as they rode.

Blondie was loathed at his smart-mouthed remark, but she kept quiet. She'd decided to speak to him if and only when necessary, and she'd further decided that a "thank you" was not a necessity when he handed her the household money.

Mihal had noted the items written on Blondie's list. He could spot where the amounts were padded and where they weren't. He'd attend to that when he gave her a set amount of money for her expected expenditures. He planned on letting her know he was the one earning the dollars and he'd be the one deciding where it was spent, or saved.

"I may not have an education past the third grade, but I've learned how to use my noodle to get ahead in life," he reminded Blondie as he folded the list and slid it into his jacket pocket, "so you can quit Lordin' your high and mighty eighth grade education over my head."

"Good morning, Mihal," Tom Martin greeted him as he and Blondie walked through the bank's front door. "You know, Mihal, I've been meaning to come out to your house to talk to you. It's kind of awkward out here in the lobby, so come on into my office. Blondie you can come too, since this concerns the both of you."

When they had settled into soft brown leather chairs and were facing Tom, who was sitting in a larger black leather chair on the opposite side of his desk, Mihal casually asked, "What did you want to talk to me about, Tom? I just needed to come in this mornin' and open a new savin's account for myself. Can you help me with that?"

"Well, of course I can," Tom answered, "but first I'd like to know when you plan on paying off the loan you got from the bank. You remember the money you borrowed before going to work in New York? Now I know what you told me, that lame reason for requesting the money, but the Kosko brothers told me a different story when they came in here and made a loan of their own."

Ignoring Tom's intrusive comments, Mihal began to put Tom to the task. "Geez, Tom, my boy was sendin' almost his whole paycheck to his Ma here every two weeks, and she was supposed to be makin' the payments right along. I had it figured out almost to the penny. How much has been paid on that loan?" Mihal asked Tom the question, but when seeking the answer, he turned his body to aim a glare straight into Blondie's Polish blue eyes.

"Well, let me pull that file and I can tell you exactly," Tom said, as he bent to pull some forms from a low desk drawer. "Two hundred sixty eight dollars, all total. That's it. You do know this loan comes due in two weeks, don't you?"

"Well now, Tom, I know you helped me out when I needed the funds and I promised to pay you back in full in a reasonable time. So it looks as if that bank account will have to be opened the next time I'm back from Buffalo, but this time $532 from this paycheck will go to pay off that loan. I'd prefer to keep my record clean in your bank."

Mihal, the gentleman, thanked the bank manager for his patience regarding the loan repayment. Mihal, the angry husband, grabbed Blondie's upper arm tightly and led her out of the office. Although Blondie was wearing a heavy winter coat, she felt the smarting grasp of each of Mihal's fingers as they squeezed tightly. "Stop it," Blondie hissed at him, "you'll leave a bruise on my arm and then what will the neighbors think?"

"Who gives a shit what the neighbors think," Mihal hissed back. "Tell them how you swindled your own son out of $532 dollars and spent every penny on yourself. Then tell them how your husband had to bail you out. You and that yahoot son of yours are gonna drive me to drinkin' yet!"

"You got it all wrong," Blondie stammered.

"I did not spend all that money on myself. Jake needed some money to pay for some girl in Buffalo who had an abortion. You were supposed to be watchin' him, but just where in the Hell were you?"

Almost choking on her jealousy, Blondie paused and then asked, "Have you found yourself a girlfriend, too? Is that what was occupying your time?"

She didn't give her husband a moment to answer her questions. She felt certain that she already knew what his response would be. It was her time to shed a few secrets of her own. She was not about to take the blame for missing funds.

"Jake got every penny back that he sent me. He said he needed it for that girl, or her parents were gonna send him to jail. What was I supposed to do? He's my son!"

Blondie had become indignant and she didn't seem to care what opinion Mihal had of her when it came down to protecting her Jakey boy.

"For your information, Blondie, I've been workin' a part-time job in the evenin's and on those weekends when I don't come home. I'm savin' money to buy our kids some nice Christmas presents. For once, I'd enjoy seein' real smiles on their faces when Santa hands out the presents."

Simply stated, Mihal hoped Blondie would comprehend his true intentions.

She didn't. "And what about me?" she asked.

"Where do I fall on that gift list? If anybody deserves presents, it ought to be me, not these snot nosed kids. Damn it to Hell, where is all of this extra money anyway? Why haven't you been givin' it to me to buy these presents? I could have already sent out something for Junior and Jake. They should be getting' something nice from us, if anybody should. They're the ones protectin' your sorry ass, Mihal."

"What in Satan's Hell are you talkin' about Blondie? We're not sendin' your Jake a pissin' penny, do you understand? And speakin' of Junior, just what are you doing with the money from the allotment checks he sends us every month? Please, don't tell me you're sendin' that to your precious Jake, too?"

Mihal was so angered at this point that he was afraid of what his own response would be if she answered as he was suspecting.

"Well, what am I to do? He calls and tells me he needs money for different things and he doesn't have anywhere else to turn. I'm his mother, so what do you expect me to do? He didn't even have the five dollars to pay for a marriage license last week. At least he didn't until I mailed him a money order."

"A marriage license?" A wide-eyed Mihal repeated, "A marriage license?"

Mihal's enraged fist hit the kitchen table, knocking over a cream pitcher. "Who's he marryin'? He just turned eighteen years old, for Christ's sake. He's still wet behind the ears. Did he get some English girl in trouble? Is that it, Blondie?"

Mihal was rodeo red angry and pushing for answers, but Blondie was not very quick about lassoing a response for her husband. She hesitated for a few minutes before relating the news she'd known for several weeks.

"Yeah, he got some *Johnny Bull* girl pregnant. Just havin' that word pregnant come out of my mouth is the same as havin' shit come out of my ass. When I think about my son havin' a baby with a *Johhny Bull* bitch, I could scream. I'll never understand how he could have been so stupid. Doesn't he see that all the English are worthless trash? Well, he'll be welcome in my home when they come here this Christmas, but not her. She didn't even have money for a plane ticket. I had to send Jake that $350 as well. Well, she may be comin' here, but I don't plan on kissin' her ass just because she's comin' all the way from England. She's not the queen, for Christ's sake!"

Mihal had determined Blondie was on another rampage. He'd seen enough of her rages through the years to know when Mt. Blondie's volcano was about to erupt. He felt ready to lash out at the lava that was about to start flowing.

Upon hearing the argument ongoing in the kitchen at #11 Lemon Lane, the kids all scampered upstairs to lie quietly around the air vent on their Baba's former bedroom floor. They were as still as vagabonds surrounding a campfire in a blizzard. They listened attentively to chilled and angered voices rising along with the smoky warmth from the kitchen coal stove's heat.

When the words "Sam's comin' home for Christmas" floated upward through the vented opening, four girls' eyes widened. Nothing further needed said. Four old table forks would quickly be retrieved from four secret hiding places. They'd be weapons in four girls' pants pockets until the day Sam and his new wife returned to England.

"What else haven't you been tellin' me, Blondie? What other dirty little secrets are you keepin' to yourself?" Mihal asked.

He was pushing her for answers, but he knew Blondie could be secretive when she had a mind to be.

"You had a letter from Junior, didn't you? The kids told me that he's comin' home for the holiday and he also has some news for us. You wouldn't know what that is, would you?" Mihal asked.

Mihal spat some of his brown tobacco saliva into the coal bucket sitting handy near the stove, but it may as well have been spit at his conniving wife. "God damn it Blondie! For once be honest and up front about what's goin' on around here," he yelled.

Blondie tipped her chin to accentuate her gloating. "Oh, you had better believe I know what Junior's news is all about," Blondie snapped as quickly as a rotten rubber band.

"Your special Junior is bringin' some bitch home. They'll be here two days before Christmas. She's a divorcee. She's been divorced twice! Her name's Christine. He gave her an engagement ring. Well, I'll spit on her, the damned bitch. She's not gonna take that allotment check away from me, no siree. She'll be leavin' the day she arrives, you'll see. I plan on seein' to that. No son of mine is marryin' someone else's damaged goods!"

Blondie was adamant about making this Christine miserable the day she and Junior arrived. "She'll be only too happy to return to one of her ex-husbands when I get through with her," Blondie yapped to Mihal.

On December 23rd, a tall, dark haired beauty arrived arm in arm with Junior. They were as handsome as a couple of fresh movie stars. Christine was treated miserably by Blondie the minute she walked through the door frame. Junior's mother greeted the stranger with, "I hear you've been married twice. That makes you something of a slut, doesn't it?"

Standing staunchly, Blondie fired off her caustic remark to the pretty woman on Junior's arm. "Well, you're not marryin' my son and that's final, so you can leave by the same door you just came through."

"The only thing you're gettin' from me is a good bye,' a resolute Blondie concluded her cutting greeting to the beauty Junior had hoped to make his wife. With that final remark to the newly arrived couple, Blondie turned and slammed the door in Junior and his Christine's face, leaving them standing outside on the cold porch.

Christine did leave the same way and the same day she arrived! Junior told the family a few months later that Christine had flown straight back into the arms of her waiting former husband. Christine managed to have the last word, though. She responded to Blondie's frontal attack by leaving Junior's engagement ring behind. An attached note addressed to Blondie read:

"You can have this, you fat bitch. The joke's on you! It came out of a box of Cracker Jack."

Jake and his bride arrived as scheduled, also. They had taken a plane from England to New York, then a train to the Tyrone rail station, where Mihal met and drove them home. Their visit was riddled with *Johnny Bull* insults from Blondie. Each snide insult delivered by Blondie was as sharp-tongued as the serrated blade of her pie server.

Blondie couldn't believe her misfortune. Her son had married into a nationality unlike her own Polish heritage. She couldn't believe that her grandchildren would be half English. To make matters worse, Jake's wife's name was Anne.

"I don't believe it," she complained to her friend, Big Annie. "I got another God damned Anne in my house! This damned place is still under that old gypsy's curse." How ironic that Jake's wife would bear the same name as her despised mother-in-law.

Well, Blondie was determined to make this bride as unwelcome as she had felt when she married Mihal and moved into *this damned house*. Blondie's hostility was a certainty after Anne had corrected Blondie's grammar. "It's pregnant, not pregnant," Anne brazenly informed Blondie after Jake had announced that they were expecting their first child.

That was a big mistake on Anne's part and from that sentence on, Blondie certainly made sure Anne felt the cramp in these crowded quarters. Blondie's level of hospitality dropped thirty degrees in less than a minute after her grammer had been corrected by Jake's highly educated bride.

The few days Jake and Junior had visited seemed an extremely long seventy two hours. "I'll be so glad to see them all go. This may have been a vacation for them, but it was only cleaning and cooking for me," Blondie told her friend, Big Annie.

"What a couple of bimbos my boys brought home. Well, one thing's for sure, one of them won't be coming back and the other knows she's not welcomed here. Some Merry Christmas this turned out to be," Blondie's stinging statement was anything but tacit.

Feigning interest in Big Annie's holiday, Blondie forced herself to ask, "So, how was your Christmas holiday?"

Blondie's mind didn't register a single word of Big Annie's recollections, although Big Annie had talked for almost ten minutes without interruption.

With their coffers filled, the newlyweds had hurriedly walked out of the front door at #11 Lemon Lane the morning of December 26th. Jake and Anne had endured enough of this insulting hospitality.

Jake's chubby, blonde-haired wife left with a few treats easily pilfered from the girl's hidden treasure chests. The girl's valuables had been tucked in shoe boxes and, they had thought, safely hidden under their beds. A gold trimmed rose china cup and saucer, several hand-crocheted doilies, an antique milk glass platter and a new pink angora sweater were all cleverly hidden between Anne's suit case belongings. The traveling items would wind their way to jolly old England, never to return to their owners at #11 Lemon Lane.

The four girls wouldn't miss the items until the couple was long gone, but Jake's wife would miss something. She'd missed the opportunity to gain the love, trust and respect of four lovely sisters-in-law. The young girls kept their disrespect for the couple boxed and wrapped as a memorable gift from Jake and Anne that holiday visit. The bow on that package was never to be undone.

Jake escaped his home that morning with a wad of newly found twenty dollar bills tucked into his front pants pocket. He also left with some long scratches on both of his forearms. Jake kept his left hand in his pants pocket to hide the bulging bills. His shirt sleeves remained pulled down over his wrists to hide the long scratches that mimed tracks from a set of defensive kitchen fork tines.

The four sisters held their heads proudly as they waved to the couple leaving for their return trip to England.

There were no hugs to say *good bye.*
There were no kisses to have a *smacking good trip.*
There were no tears crying *we'll miss you.*
There was no hospitable greeting entertaining a *return welcome.*

Kneeling beside their beds later that evening, they did pray a *thank you* to their Baba, who had given them some forkin' good advice so very long ago.

Blondie awakened from a fretful sleep. She had an unsettling feeling in the pit of her stomach. Unknowingly, her sons had left behind a set of unanswered questions. Questions that even Blondie couldn't answer.

What was she supposed to do with a Cracker Jack diamond ring? One that her first born son had explained was very much a real diamond and gold ring minutes before he resolutely said, "You can shove it up your ass, as far as I'm concerned!"

How would she explain to Mihal that she truly didn't know what happened to the $500 missing from the special compartment of his wallet? After all that had happened recently, Mihal didn't believe a word she uttered these days.

What was she to say to four girls who had their prized possessions stolen by an unaccepted newcomer to their family?

What would she say when she would learn of Jake's attempted aggrieved offenses against his sisters?

How would her life be without Jakey boy to confide in? After all, he'd been her favorite child, but now he belonged to the wiles of a loose *Johnny Bull* trollep?

The only answer she could conjure up to Mihal was, "I blame every second of the holiday ruckus on the gypsy's curse in *this damned house*."

Blondie had finally said something comical this Christmas holiday.

"Knowin' you're under the gypsy curse is worth losin' the $500," Mihal said to her as he burst out in hearty laughter. "Blondie, your performance these past few days has left Al Jolson's act in the dust, and he's the best around."

Blondie didn't have a clue what Mihal was referring to. She didn't have the slightest idea what Mihal was talking about!

It didn't matter. Mihal knew.

SLEEPING IN THE HAY

French toast? We call that old bread dipped in scrambled eggs, J laughed to herself at the notion of such a high-falutin' name for something so simple. *Who did these people think they were anyway?*

Okay, so they say they're French. So, what did that prove? Ma says we're Polish and that don't make us any better or any worse than the next guy. J's thoughts were scrambling as she stood in the kitchen door way and watched the short pretty woman cooking on a green enameled coal stove that was set in the middle of the cleanest kitchen she had ever seen.

The room was filled with sparkles. The sunshine coming through the windows brought brightness to everything in that one room. Every rag rug was straight. J had never seen a rug stay straight in their house. In their kitchen, when a rug was stepped on a ruffle would appear, but no one took the time to straighten it. In this French house everyone walked on the rugs, but no one seemed to leave a wrinkle. *Was there magic in their feet,* she wondered. *How can I get some of that magic for the kids in our house?*

The pretty woman was humming a strange tune as she cooked, quietly at first, but then she sang louder as her children joined in and added the words, "Fair a jock ah, fair a jock ah, do may voo, do may voo."

Was this French? Ohhh, so that's what French sounds like! J stood fascinated by the sounds of the French singing that was merrily encircling her brain.

The woman began laughing in amusement. Soon all of her kids joyously chimed in with the revelry. This was something new for J's thoughts to process. *Happy laughing! How about that.*

Most of the laughter in J's house was of a nervous kind. *We always have to look at our Ma to see if she's laughing before we start,* J was reminded.

This whole family is in their kitchen, singing and laughing. They're just happy to be together eating old bread and eggs for breakfast. Their mother even gave each child a good morning hug. J's brain was working overtime eavesdropping on this scene.

We eat in our kitchen every morning, but nobody sings or laughs. We'd get smacked upside the head if we made any noise first thing in the morning, she reminded herself.

"Get your eatin' done and get outa here," was their mother's sarcastic morning greeting, followed up with "go get your chores done, or go get ready for the school bus, or get yourselves dressed for church."

All orders from Blondie were punctuated with "Skedaddle, go on. What are you waitin' for, Christmas?"

If the skedaddle wasn't quick enough, then "Get the Hell outa here already," would be shouted by Blondie.

"J," Suzette's mother called out, "why don't you come over here and have some breakfast with us? You girls can be off to your Confirmation practice when you're done eating. There's plenty of this toast for everyone. Come on now, don't be bashful. I'll bet you haven't eaten yet this morning, have you, child?"

Mrs. LeCroix had glanced at her husband as she placed a large flowered plate on the kitchen table next to Suzette's. Scooting a chair over to the table so that J could sit right next to her friend, Mrs. LeCroix encouragingly said, "Come, sit here next to Suzette. You know you're always welcome here," as she smiled down at the pathetically skinny blonde-haired visitor.

Hesitating at first, but then with slight trepidation, J ambled over to her place at the kitchen table. She was hungry, with a capital H. The French toast looked picture-pretty arranged on a wide gold trimmed platter. The toppling stack of crispy-edged, golden triangles was dripping with brown maple syrup. Passing the toast, Suzette's mother nudged J with her elbow. "Take two more. I told you there's plenty for everyone. Don't they look and smell wonderful?"

God, that really does look and smell so good rattled through her thoughts and rumbled through her belly. "Dig in, girl. You ain't seen nothin' so purrty for breakfast before. I just know you haven't," Suzette's father teased with a chipper drawl. J didn't need to see if he was smiling, she heard it.

"Would you like a napkin, dear?" Mrs. LeCroix asked.

"I suppose so," she answered. Not knowing any correct French etiquette, she sat waiting until it was handed to her. "Thank you," was appropriate, that much she did know.

She observed the other children unfold their cloth piece and place it on their laps, so she did likewise. From then on, she followed their lead as they dug in and joyfully ate the delicious French toast triangles. J couldn't help but wonder *if it was the fancy name that made it taste better or if Suzette's mother had special cooking powers? From now on, I'll call it French toast too,* she decided.

When it was time to clear the dirty dishes off of the table, Mrs. LeCroix took over. "Run along, kids. You all have things of your own to do. Be good!" she called out to her three girls and J as they scattered in three directions.

"You don't have to wash the dishes or clean off the stove?" J asked in wonderment.

"Of course not," Suzette answered. "Our Mom does that. She says kids have their own job to do and it's called growing up."

"Who makes your beds or feeds your chickens? Don't you have barn work to do?" J asked.

"No, she does those, too. She says we'll have plenty of time for working when we're all grown up. The only chore I have is keeping my bedroom tidied up," Suzette said, popping a piece of bubble gum into her mouth.

"Want one?" she asked, handing a pink softball of rubbery sweetness to J.

"Let's see who can blow the biggest bubble while we're walking to church. Bet I win," Suzette challenged with a lilt to her voice.

If J could have frozen moments in time, this would be one of them. She felt *family* for the first time in her young life. Everyday before this had been day to say existing. *Someday I'll have a nice family like this one,* she promised herself, but today she had found a few more nice people to add to her growing list.

The morning passed by quickly as the girls each practiced for their own Confirmation celebrations. J's was in the Catholic faith and Suzette's was in the Methodist tradition. The religious ceremonies meant the young people of the congregations would be admitted to full membership of the church. Both girls attended special training sessions every Saturday morning for six months prior to these special ceremonies. It was time spent learning still more background information about one's Christian rites and rituals.

"Well, what did you learn this morning?" J asked Suzette when they began their trek back home.

"Borrrrring," exclaimed dramatic Suzette. "How about you? Don't tell me you actually enjoy learning this hocus pocus stuff?"

"We had a pretend Mass this morning," J said.

"We're supposed to know all about this ancient custom and what every part of the service means. The Mass is supposed to make all of the church's teachings meaningful. At least that's what the nun says. Well, I didn't mind going to catechism, but now I'm getting kind of scared. All of this talk about the Holy Ghost entering your soul has got me a little worried. What's he gonna look like and what's he gonna do?" *And, God Almighty, where is the soul anyway?* J couldn't help but wonder. She often spent hours wondering about all of life's mysteries.

Maybe, she thought, *I missed learning about the Holy Ghost's big entrance, too.* Being ill with the measles the prior Saturday should have allowed J to have a valid reason for being absent from the class which had explained the Holy Ghost and each increment of the Mass. She learned very quickly how important attendance at every catechetical lesson was to her religious education.

Earlier in the church basement, the faux Mass was rehearsed for the awaited big day. Just prior to the Gospel being read, the prayer to cleanse the heart was said. The priest prayed, "Pray, the Lord be in my mind, on my lips and in my heart," at which time the priest and the congregation were to make the Sign of the Cross on their forehead, lips and breast. J hadn't paid too much attention to this gesture before and she didn't recall anyone ever explaining its meaning, so she didn't partake of the practice.

That was a big mistake, according to Sister Mary Louise, the visiting nun who directed these special events. Upon witnessing J's weak attempt to imitate the other kid's signing gestures, the strict nun became irate. Intimidating in her long black flowing dress and veil, she had been pacing back and forth at the front of the room. In a mocking gesture, the nun swung her large black wooden Rosary beads in a swaying motion as she stepped.

When the nun saw J making signings that were unacceptable during the heart cleansing portion of the Mass, she reached over and backhanded J's left ear and head. This knocked J off of the wooden folded chair, and sent her sprawling across the concrete basement floor. Before the girl could pick herself up off the floor, the nun was standing over her with a ruler in her hand. She began chastising J and striking the top of her head. "Don't you dare insult my holiness or the reverence of the Mass by not doing the correct signing technique, you ignorant little shit. Who do you think you are? Do you think you're better than everybody else, including God?"

In one swooping motion, J reached up and grabbed the ruler. She pulled it from the surprised nun's hand. Holding the ends of the ruler, J smacked its middle against her now raised and bent knee, breaking it into two pieces. Politely, she handed the two pieces of the wooden ruler to the nun.

"Don't ever hit me again!" was all J said, as she calmly returned to her chair. She didn't cry. She didn't let it be known that her ear was ringing and her head felt like it was splitting into three pieces. She didn't apologize for her innocent ignorance. She just sat quietly collected in her chair until they were dismissed.

"What did you do in your class today?" Suzette asked as they were slowly walking on the roadway heading home.

She had noticed that J was awfully quiet, not her usual talkative self. "Did something happen? Did you finally meet the Holy Ghost? What's wrong with you?"

Alarmed, Suzette pressed further, "What happened in there? Come on, you can tell me."

And J did tell her. Still shaken by the trauma, she told her everything, not forgetting any of the harsh details regarding the religious nun's pummeling. "I'll be glad when this Confirmation is over and done with, and I don't ever have to see that woman again. I don't know who she thinks she is, but she's not so holy." J lashed out in anger, but she didn't cry. She deemed *that would have been a waste of good tears.*

Suzette followed her mothering instincts and began examining J's head and ear. "Well, you do have a little blood in your ear, but there's no bump on your hard head," she said in an attempt to improve J's attitude.

"Let me see your legs. Yep, you got some scrapes to both of your knees. Do they hurt? We'll put some mercurochrome on them when we get to my house. That will help."

"No mercurochrome," J quickly responded.

"If my Ma sees that orange stuff on my knees, she'll want to know the whole story and I don't want to tell her anything. I just wish the head hurting and the ringing in my ear would quit," J told her friend.

"Ma would just call me stupid again and I'd get another switching. I better stay smart and keep my mouth shut," J said with subtlty.

"Well, I know one thing that can cheer you up," Suzette said candidly.

"I'm gonna ask your mother if you can spend the night with me. We could sleep out in the barn on the hay. That's a lot of fun. Have you ever done that?"

No, J thought, *I haven't done that. I haven't done that or a lot of other things that other kids get to do, but someday . . .*

All of J's thoughts evaporated into an invisible mist when Blondie snapped, "All of your Saturday chores have to be done before you can go anywhere."

After a second of contemplation, Blondie spitefully questioned, "Why isn't Adela included in this pajama party? I thought the two of you were close friends, Suzette?

"We were," Suzette answered coldly, "until she told Daryl I was madly in love with him. Everybody on the bus laughed. I was so embarrassed."

"Well, you had better watch out, cause I'm gonna tell everybody on the bus you two got some queer thing going on," piped tattle-tale Adela as she came around the corner of the house toting a basket of dried laundry.

"Go ahead," Suzette warned right back at her. "I have a few things I can spill to the kids on the bus, too. We'll just see who gets even!"

Adela kept right on walking past both girls, vengefully sticking her tongue out at them when her back was to her mother.

The chores were done in record time for a change. J had just turned twelve and didn't realize it yet, but rebellion and independence were on the horizon. She was so looking forward to going back to Suzette's home. J would have been content spending time playing in the garage or barn, but the house was the best. Suzette's home was so clean and inviting, unlike her own home which was always messy and dirty from all of the kids motion, commotion, and locomotion.

Blondie relied on her children's manual labor. "Those piss ant kids make the messes around here, so they can clean up after themselves," Blondie would say as she presented her theory as justification for her lack of involvement with any of the housework.

"If you don't work, you don't eat," seemed to justify Blondie's lack of involvement with the barn and garden chores, also.

Blondie relegated the babysitting chores to the older girls when they weren't in school. Each toddler or infant had an assigned elder child who saw to all of their infantile needs. Little Marsha called J "Mama", Vera turned to Adela for her needs, and Cindy tailed Polly unmercifully. To Blondie this was an educational experience. No one dared to question Blondie about her laziness as the real motive for the pairings.

To her credit, Blondie did cook the meals and fill the wringer washer with water, but the girls did the meal cleanup, the laundry and almost all of the barnyard chores. Friday's were reserved for cleaning the house. Designated rooms were assigned to each of Blondie's daughters for weekly cleaning. Blondie's job was as the inspector. If a room wasn't cleaned to Blondie's expectations, that would be reason enough for her to start bitching about her girls' lassitude. "I see dust over in that corner. Clean this room again." Punishment was wrath from the angered Blondie.

Each of Blondie's girls would eventually realize this was their mother's ploy to justify her own laziness, while keeping her children reined in and under her thumb. Later in life, they'd learn that was called *intimidation*.

On this day, J hurriedly completed her chores. She hoped it would be satisfactory to Blondie's standards. "I did all of my house and barn work, now can I go to Suzette's?" J asked.

"Go," Mihal answered, beating Blondie's hesitant response.

"Have a good time, but be sure you're up and ready for your Confirmation in the morning," he called out as the two girls sped off down the path.

J's pink dress hung loosely draped over her forearm and flapped as she ran. Suzette was holding two ugly white shoes, one in each hand. "Are these the shoes you're wearing tomorrow? Good God, they're horrible. They look like the school cafeteria women's work shoes. They don't even have laces. They don't belong with an organdy dress. I'll have to loan you one of my slips to wear under this dress too, or everybody will see your old lady underpants. For crying out loud J, can't you do any better that this? No wonder my mother says she feels sorry for you," Suzette rattled her comments so rapidly that J wondered if her brain had registered them all.

"Shut up already, Suzette," J replied with a note of hostility.

J's tone sounded bitter. She realized the dress was transparent, but it was the dress her mother was forcing her to wear. She wasn't given an under slip of her own and Adela had refused to loan her one. Blondie laughed when J asked for an under slip. "Go without one. Who cares if everybody can see your skinny ass? Not me, that's for sure," was her mother's cruel and tasteless response.

J also knew the shoes were awful, but that's what her mother had found in their old shoe box. "This is what you'll wear, Missy. Who gives a shit what a mamoona face like you has on her big feet," Blondie had told her, tossing the shoes in her direction.

The old shoe box was kept behind the kitchen coal stove. The box kept the family's everyday shoes from gathering in a heap at the kitchen's entrance. The stove's heat worked well for drying wet shoes for the next day's wearing. These cloddy shoes that Suzette was carrying were plenty dried, anyone could see that. They were terribly worn, too. You'd have to be blind not to see the hideousness in these cracked and scuffed clumsy hand-me downs.

Gawd, I must really be ugly from my head to my feet was the only thought strumming through J's head after considering Blondie's cruel remarks.

"Well," Suzette began, "we'll just have to do a little magic on these shoes when we get to my house."

A can of white outdoor house paint provided the tough coat of shoe polish to cover all the graying and cracking on the old clodhoppers, while two pieces of pink ribbon cut and borrowed from the attic's Christmas wrappings became a pair of fancy shoe laces.

"See, I told you we could do magic with them. They'll dry overnight and be ready to wear in the morning. They'll look cute, you'll see," Suzette told her friend.

"You should try on that dress, too," Suzette said, holding up the dress in the window's sunlight. "It looks mighty big. What size is it? I can't tell. The tag's been cut off, but it looks big enough to fit me and I'm twice your size. Put it on, J, and let's have a peak at you in a tent."

"You're right. This is huge! Now what do I do?" J asked in desperation.

"Turn that dress inside out and put it back on," Mrs. LeCroix said softly.

"I'll hand stitch the seam and make it fit for the day. When you get home you can pull out the thread and no one will ever know what we did. We'll use a piece of that same pink ribbon for a belt and a ponytail tie. You can wear one of my girl's under slips. How does that sound? We'll have you looking as spiffy as Suzette in the morning, but right now let's get you girls some quilts, a bowl of popcorn and a jar of Kool Aid. It's time for your sleep-over in the hayloft."

Suzette was a magician! She had just turned a lousy day into a happy moon lit night. *I'm so glad to have such a good friend. Someday I hope I can do her a real favor.*

"Take two heavy quilts, Suzette," Mrs. LeCroix told the girls. She was chuckling as she chided the girls, "It gets cool during the night and you don't want to freeze to death, not with your big day coming up tomorrow."

Handing them the snacks and drinks, she added a flashlight, "This is in case you need to use the outhouse during the night. You don't want to run into any grizzly bears, do you?"

"You're enjoying all of this kidding, aren't you, Mom?" Suzette asked, now turning the teasing back onto her mother. *How nice it would be to be able to talk to my mother like that* J thought, but she doubted that type of bantering would ever happen between Blondie and any of her girls.

"Come on J, let's go before my mother invites herself along. She and my dad sometimes sleep out here on hot summer nights. Can you believe it? They're like a couple of teenagers."

J could believe it, but she doubted if she'd ever see her parents sleeping in the hay loft. Her Ma and Ed Strang had ruined that escapade for Blondie and Mihal.

Even the barn loft smelled clean. Albeit the hay was still slightly scratchy in the spots where it poked through the quilt, but that was tolerable. The girls were set to enjoy their night out without any adult supervision.

Between bites of popcorn and sips of Kool Aid, they yakked. Their chatter could have been by two little old ladies on a sunny Sunday afternoon on a back porch glider. After a frank discussion about what they were gonna be when they grew up, their thoughts turned to more serious subjects.

"Are you gonna get married when you grow up," Suzette asked her friend. "Oh, I suppose so," J answered. "Are you?"

"I'm not sure," Suzette answered seriously.

"I was in love with Jake. Did you know that? I promised him I'd wait for him to come back from working in Buffalo. Then we were going to elope, but something happened to change all that. Now he's in the Air Force and married already."

"What do you mean something happened? Do you want to tell me about it? I'm a pretty good listener and I can keep a secret," J coaxed.

Coaxing wasn't necessary. J should have noticed that.

"Do you remember the night my dad had his heart attack and had to go to the hospital in an ambulance?" Suzette asked without hesitation.

"I remember. How could I forget? You were so scared. You thought he was going to die."

J patiently lay on her quilt. She was propped partially upward on one elbow and waiting for Suzette to continue.

"Well, I lied to my mother that night. She didn't want me to go to the hospital with her. She wanted me to stay at your house. She was going to stop and get your mother's permission on her way to the hospital, but I told her I'd already phoned you. I told her that your mother said it was perfectly fine for me to come right over. Well, my mother still insisted on dropping me off at your house and walking me to the door to thank your mother for letting me spend the night. She was going to tell her about my dad."

Suzette paused, took a deep breath and cautiously proceeded. "This part is hard to tell you, J. We're almost like sisters and I really hate telling you what happened."

"Go ahead, tell me. I'm listening." *Now what did Jake do,* J suspiciously wondered.

"Well, we walked up your front porch steps and started to go past the big picture window but we saw some movement in the parlor. The room was dark, but the full moon gave off enough light for us to see inside. We both stooped down and watched through the corner of the glass. My mom said that was pure instinct, because we didn't want to get caught on your porch right then. I couldn't believe my eyes, and neither could my mom. Jake and your mom were on the couch, together."

"Are you sure you want to hear this?" Suzette asked.

J nodded and her friend eagerly began where she had left off.

"Jake was on top of your mother and bouncing up and down. Your mother called Jake 'Ed'. I knew right away what was happening. Me and Jake had done the same thing many times, so I knew. When the bouncing stopped, Jake kissed her, right on the mouth. He got up first, and then he held out his hand and helped her stand up. She buttoned the top of her nightgown right away. Jake pulled his p j bottoms up. She reached over and patted Jake on the shoulder before she left the room. He stayed there for a few minutes, and then he left. I thought I was gonna puke, but I didn't make a peep. My mom was so upset. She said she couldn't catch her breath for a few seconds."

"What did you do? Where did you go, 'cause you didn't stay with us?" a trembling J asked.

"We waited for a few minutes until I stopped shaking, then we crept off the porch. My mom let me go with her to the hospital. We spent the night sleeping in big waiting room chairs."

"God, Suzette, I don't know what to say. I think I'm gonna throw up the popcorn I just ate. I believe you, but I don't know what to say. That's the sickest thing I ever heard. I knew Jake was my ma's favorite, but I never thought anything like this. Did you or your mom ever tell my ma what you saw?" J wanted to know.

"Sure, my mom did. She told her all of it. She told your ma that was disgusting, but your ma only laughed at her and told her to grow up already. She said that goes on all over the world these days. She called us liars, and then told my mom to get the Hell out of her *damned house* and to never come back!"

"She's really evil, isn't' she?" J asked her friend.

"That's what my mom said. My mom said she could tell your ma had a guilty conscience. It was written all over her face. Your ma said I couldn't be your friend anymore, but my mom threatened to tell your dad what we saw if that happened. I think that's why she won't look at me when I'm at your house."

"Well, we'll be friends for ever. Does that make you feel better?" J asked Suzette.

"It sure does. That's why I told you the story. Friends don't keep secrets, especially big ones like this." Suzette answered.

"Good night," she called out in the darkness to J, before coiling herself into her quilt.

J watched her friend wrap herself in her coverlet and she thought *I probably should do the same thing. I need to get some sleep, too.* She curled *right up, just like a snake. She didn't really sound sad telling me about that night. She sounded glad to finally be telling me what they saw. If she was a true friend, would she need to tell me that story?* Those words stung, and they made me ashamed. *Is that what a real friend does? I don't think I would have hurt her like that. I would have kept everything to myself.*

The more J lay wrapped up in the hay loft, the more she began to realize what Suzette's real reason was for inviting her to a sleep over. It wasn't a pretty thought. *Suzette hates ma for finding out that she wasn't important to Jake and that Jake had just used her for the sex. Suzette realized Jake lied to her about eloping. Suzette said she hadn't heard word one from Jake since he left for Buffalo. Well, Suzette was getting even with Jake and our ma by telling me this story,* J surmised. *But was it a story or was it truth?* J realized she would have to find out for herself, one way or another.

The last thing J thought before falling asleep was *I wonder what ma would say if I asked her about this?*

The next morning found J withdrawn and quiet, "What's wrong with you?" Suzette asked.

"Nothing, I'm just thinking. I have a lot to think about this morning."

And indeed J did have a lot on her mamoona mind. Thoughts swirled through J's brain. *I have a fiery whirlwind in my head and it's painful in more ways than just hurting.*

"Do you think your mom will drive us to church today? I don't think I can walk the two miles. My head and ear hurt, and I feel sick to my stomach."

J spoke without so much as a glance at Suzette who was all gussied up in a new blue taffeta skirted dress, nylon stockings and black patent ballerina shoes.

"You look nice, Suzette," she mustered, but her thoughts festered something different. *I hope that dress makes you look as fat and as mean as you really are.*

"Oh, she's driving us. She told your dad she would after he said he can't be bothered taking the time. I guess he has too much work to do on the weekends. It must be hard for him to come home once a month and have all kinds of home jobs waiting for him. Besides, he told my mom he's disillusioned with your church since it hasn't done any good for Blondie."

Pulling her car to a standstill in front of the Catholic Church, Mrs. LeCroix turned to face J as she stepped out of the car. Showing concern, she asked the young girl, "Are you alright? You seem so pale and you didn't eat anything this morning."

J took a few steps away from the car before responding. The older woman appeared surprised when J stared directly into her eyes and asked, "Did you really see my mom and Jake together? Did you watch them through the window the night you were on your way to the hospital?"

A strange pitiful look crossed the mother's face. "I'm sorry, dear, but yes we did."

A very confused J received her Confirmation that morning. She didn't stay for the complimentary meal served in the church basement after the ceremony was completed.

She walked home instead, stopping at the LeCroix's mailbox to place the pink ribbon ties and shoe laces inside. *They'll get my message.* She knew they would. If not today, someday soon, once they realized she didn't visit their house anymore.

It took two days for J to feel well enough to build up some courage and face her mother with Suzette's story. They were in the vegetable garden together and picking some green beans for their evening meal. Without making direct eye contact with her mother, J began her quest. "Suzette told me a story. It's about you and Jake on the night before he left for New York with Dad. Is it true?"

Blondie didn't hesitate to answer. With a reddened face and wearing a frightened looking grimace, she gloated as she spewed her response. "Suzette made up that damned story about me and Jake. On the night of her dad's heart attack Suzette and her mother spent the night at the hospital, so how in the Hell could they have been on our front porch? Anyway, it was dark out, so even if they were on our porch what could they have seen," Blondie angrily growled.

"You'll just keep your bloody mouth shut about any of these God damned lies, do you hear me?" Blondie said.

"Your Dad don't need to have somebody's made up stories worryin' him. He needs to concentrate on bringin' home the money to keep us afloat, instead of sinkin' into debt again. Some friend you picked. She's nothin' but a slut. I made sure my Jakey boy found that out before he left."

With that outburst completed, Blondie threw down her basket and left the garden. As she ambled toward the house, she shouted back over her shoulder, "If you got the time to waste with your bitchin' girlfriend, you got the time to fill both those baskets for our dinner, whore!"

J had her answer. She had seen that vested lying scorn on Blondie's face before. Besides, J hadn't spilled any details about Suzette's story, so how could Blondie have known to what she was referring?

The dictionary defines respect as to feel or show honor or esteem for someone, such as a parent or a friend. Disappointed in both, J had decided to reserve her respect for someone worth while from here on out. As far as she was concerned, the green beans were more honorable than her friend or her mother ever would be.

With two heaping-full baskets of green beans, J had found solace and consolation when slowly picking the vegetables from the lush green rows of her dad's vegetable garden.

She had survived another secret in this *damned house,* and another day in Gunther.

J never spent another night at the LeCroix home. *I can live without their pity.* When Suzette would extend an invitation to come to their home for a visit or a sleep-over, J would remind the corners of her mind and the lacey edges of her heart exactly what friendship was.

One day, leaving Gunther would be a lot easier for another member of this crazy *damned house.*

EASTER MORNING COMING DOWN

April showers bring May flowers ran around and around in J's mind as she sat riding the rickety rusting school bus. Staring out the window, she watched as torrents of rain blew sideways. *It sure is wet and windy out there,* she thought, *and it's as cold as a December morning. I sure hope we don't get snow for Easter. Put that thought right out of your head,* she reprimanded her brain, but it seemed her gray matter wasn't listening to her commands. *If we have snow, how will Dad be able to drive over the curving mountain roads to bring Pet home from the Tyrone railroad station on Good Friday?*

It had been nearly a year since she had last seen her eldest sister. Pet was now working full-time as a Western Union operator and could afford her own apartment in Washington, D.C. She also had a part-time job at a large department store as a sales girl. Occasionally she was asked to do in-store modeling. Pet looked the role of an ideal model. She had perfect posture and was tall, slender and strikingly attractive. Everyone said she was statuesque and commanded presence when she entered a room. J knew for certain that her sister most definitely did light up their home with each one of her highly anticipated visits.

The kids at #11 Lemon Lane fought verbally and physically to ride with their dad when it was time to meet Pet at the train station. In addition to a cheery greeting, the kids knew Pet always bought a round of ice cream cones at the station's Hop Shop. What kid wouldn't want in on this treat?

In letters written home, Pet always requested that J be among those meeting her at the railway station. J liked to think that just maybe she was favored because she wrote short letters to Pet that got included with Blondie's response notes.

For writing those loving messages to her sister, J's reward was a squishing bear hug from Pet after she stepped down from the huge, hissing locomotive's steps. "You sure do keep me in stitches when I read your notes, J," Pet would tell her later in the privacy of their bedroom. "You're quite the character."

"I do enjoy hearing from you. You make everything sound comical and your notes cheer me up, especially if I'm tired from a long hard work day. Promise you'll never stop writing to me," Pet asked.

An intelligent child, J easily understood that Pet valued her promise. Every hug and every honest smile from Pet told J that she was her older sister's favorite.

"Let me show you all the goodies I brought for you kids," Pet said as she pulled a large shopping bag closer to the edge of the bed.

J sat in patient anticipation as Pet pulled one item after another out of the bag. "I brought each of you a chocolate bunny, a bag of jelly beans, a box of yellow marshmallow chicks and an egg filled with bubble gum. I brought this big chocolate Easter egg for everyone to enjoy. It's filled with whipped strawberry-pecan fluff. It is sooooooooo good that you'll want to lick the box it came in. We'll tell the kids it's from a giant Easter chicken. They'll think that's a funny joke," Pet teased.

Pet's giggle became contagious and before two seconds had passed, they were both hugging and laughing wildly. It was such a great reunion for the two sisters. It didn't last long, though. The bedroom door abruptly flew open banging the wall before swinging back and forth several times. "Just what in the Hell is going on in here?" Blondie demanded.

J stood when the door flew open unexpectedly, but then swiftly moved several steps away from the bedside before speaking. "Pet was just showing me what all she brought everyone for Easter, that's all."

"And who are you, the queen of Persia?" Blondie asked J.

J's body seemed to shudder with a sudden chill.

"Why are you showin' her this stuff and not me?" Blondie directed this question and her anger toward Pet.

"I'm the *Boss* in this God *damned house,* not you and definitely not her," Blondie griped, pointing her index finger at J.

"Show me what you brought. I want to see it right now and I'll decide if these piss ant kids get anything for Easter," she commanded.

Was Heil Hitler next, Pet wondered.

Pet slowly began removing the candies from her large paper sack. One piece at a time, she explained which candy went to whom. When she had shown the final large chocolate egg, explaining that it was for everyone, Blondie exploded. "Where in that bag is there anything for me? I didn't hear you say a single word about some special candy for me, just for these ungrateful piss ant monsters. Do you know who is run ragged around here everyday? Do you know who? Me, your hard working mother, that's who. So why should these brats get all this special treatment? What makes these turds so special?" Blondie, the tyrant, asked the two trembling girls.

J snapped back without thinking carefully, "Because us kids are special." *Oh, oh, too late,* J realized. *I think I opened my mouth a little too quickly.*

"How dare you sass me? What are you now, a kid expert? Get downstairs right now and you had better have that willow switch waitin' on the table for me. Your ass is gonna be blistered tonight," Blondie screamed at J.

"Now, get out of here. Get goin' and do what you've been told. I can't wait to show you just who's boss around here. You're gettin' too big for your britches these days, Missy. Get! How many times do I have to repeat myself?"

Blondie finally stopped yelling. She was done screeching from that blanched red face and that gaping false-toothed mouth.

"Please, Mom," Pet was pleading, "don't do this. Can't we just have a nice Easter weekend? I have to leave early Sunday afternoon and I'd like to go back with a few nice Easter photos and some happy memories."

"Well, you could have had some pretty memories if you had handled this properly. You should have shown me all this candy, not her. How many times did she ask you to see what was in the bag? She's always so damned curious. Did she tell you not to show me? Is that it? This was her idea?" Blondie hammered out her crazy questions faster than a blacksmith on a lame horse's shoe.

"No, it wasn't anything like that," Pet attempted to explain.

"I thought it would be a nice surprise for everyone, including you. I was able to get this whole big bag of candy at a real good price from where I work. The store manager knows I'm a good worker and he knew I was going home to see my large family this holiday. He offered to let me buy it at cost. He even gave me an employee discount. Wasn't that nice of him?"

"So you think that was nice of him?" Blondie smirked when she aimed her next barb at Pet, "And just what *nice* did you have to give him to get this at cost with a discount? Once a whore always a whore, that's what I always say."

"I brought this candy for the kids and I'll be the one giving it out to them on Sunday morning," Pet answered angrily.

Pet stood adrenalized and firm in her intentions. "I am not giving it over to you and that's final. I will tell Dad how you've unnecessarily treated me and J just now. I'd like to hear what he thinks of that."

"You'll tell him no such thing, do you hear me? I'll run this house and these kids how I see fit. You don't have nothin' to say about nothin' in this house. You don't live here anymore. You're a visitor these days, Miss City Slicker. You'll keep your mouth shut, understood?"

Blondie was in a cornered Commander's rage tonight, that's what Pet understood.

"Oh, I understand alright, but you are not my boss anymore. I'm old enough to be the boss of me, do you understand that? I paid for this stuff, not you, so I'll distribute it any way I see fit. Can you understand that?" Pet asked, now standing nose to nose with Blondie.

After a fleeting moment, Pet asked her mother the question that had come to mind on several occasions. This seemed the perfect moment to ask it. "Has anyone ever told you that you might be insane, because you certainly act like it?"

Pet had kept her feelings bottled up for years, but she unleashed them finally when she had decided *I'm tired of this crap. That felt good to let her have it for once! I wonder if she understood what I just said?*

"Insane?" Blondie repeated. "I'll show you insane," she spewed, as she reached for the handles of Pet's shopping bag filled with the Easter candy.

"I'll show you just where this candy's goin' and it's not to this bunch of bastards."

As rapidly as Blondie had reached for the bag, that's how deftly Pet's hand reached Blondie's wrist. Pet held on tightly, squeezing and twisting that arm even as Blondie began swinging her free left hand toward Pet's face. That left hand never reached its goal.

J hadn't gone downstairs as she'd been instructed to do. She remained at the top of the landing, just in case Pet needed some assistance. J knew her mother and didn't trust her for a second. She knew the woman was capable of a strong tongue lashing, but she was also physically strong. J had seen her in action before, plenty of times.

J witnessed her mother's hand swing to strike Pet. Telling herself *that's not gonna happen,* J reached her mother's arm in flash time to harness and hold it tightly. The astonished look on Blondie's face told a surprising story of its own. "What in the Hell are you doin' up here? I thought I sent you downstairs," Blondie admonished J in a grizzly bear tone.

Mihal seemed to appear out of nowhere. "What in Heaven's name are you doin' now, Blondie? I thought I warned you to keep your mouth shut and not cause any grief this weekend. I thought I told you we were gonna' have a nice Easter with Pet at home. Do you remember that conversation? Huh, Blondie, do you?" he asked with a definite resolve to his tone.

"Look at what you've done. You've awakened all of the kids. Some of them are so scared they're even cryin'. What in the Hell is wrong with you? Every weekend I come home I have to serve as referee to your arguments. Now you're startin' fights with your own children? Why do you have to do things this way? Why?"

Mihal's face wore the most perplexed question mark J had ever seen.

"Pet told her what's wrong with her, Dad. She's insane, period. That's what's wrong with her," J answered.

Mihal appeared stunned, but soon a calmness returned to this gentle man's wrinkled face. "You know, kid, Pet may have a point there," was all he said before turning and shaking his head in disgust as he exited the bedroom.

Blondie also exited the room. Passing by J, she uttered, "Get your ass down stairs, Missy. You're gonna get yours now."

J marched as straight as an arrow into the kitchen. She was expecting to get a lashing with the willow whip. While Blondie was cursing under her breath, her eyes eagerly searched the kitchen for her switch. "Where is that damned thing? Where did you put it?" she turned seeking J.

"She didn't do anything with it, Blondie. I did," answered Mihal.

A resolved Mihal approached Blondie. "It's in the stove's flames. I did some of my own soul searchin' and decided to use it for kindlin' wood. That is the last switch and the last beatin' any of these kids will get from you. Is that understood?"

As usual, Blondie didn't respond. Instead, she briskly left the kitchen, slammed the door and proceeded to the weeping willow tree where she promptly broke off another twig.

Mihal was awake early the next morning. His and Blondie's subdued voices could be heard through the upstairs bedroom floor vent. The only audible verbalizing was from Mihal's voice, "This will be a peaceful weekend. Pet is going back to D.C. on Sunday afternoon and then I'm leavin' with Big John at three o'clock for Buffalo. You just tend to gettin' that Easter basket ready to be blessed in church at noon. That should help your hissy-assed attitude stay busy enough to keep you out of trouble this mornin'."

The kids were also kept occupied that Saturday. There were Easter outfits to be organized and ironed for the girls. A small white shirt and a pair of suspenders had to be altered for little Vic. Every pair of shoes needed polishing. The summer hat box was retrieved from the attic and brims were pressed flat with the help of a little sugar water.

Pet supervised every aspect of every wardrobe item these kids would wear to the early Mass on Easter morning. She was the city slicker now and extremely admired by her siblings. Foremost, she wanted each child to be proud of themselves when they walked into the church. "Okay, Pet," or "What ever you say, Pet" was their only responses to her gentle natured directions or requests.

While the kids worked at their assignments, Pet filled their heads with stories about life in the big city and how kind her aunt and uncle were during the short while she had lived with them.

"If Uncle Tony hadn't gotten his military orders to be stationed in Alaska, I would still be living with them. I wouldn't have minded that one bit," she said placidly.

Tony was Blondie's younger brother and was a career Air Force Colonel. "Uncle Tony is so kind hearted and so is Aunt Betty. Too bad they didn't have any children of their own. They would have made wonderful parents. They taught me a lot about living in the city. I'll always love them for giving me a chance at a life away from Gunther. I'm just glad I got away from this small town and this *damned house*. If I had wanted to go with them, I could be living in *brrrrrr* cold Alaska right now," Pet told her attentive audience of smiling cherub faces.

Pet was enjoying the duty-filled afternoon with her siblings. She truly hadn't realized how very much she had missed the kiddos, until she was smack-dab in the middle of their playful chaos.

By the time night fall had arrived, the kids were so fatigued from their own chores and their wardrobe duty that a warm Saturday night bath pushed them over the edge and right into dreamland. The only sibling who lay awake for a short while was fifteen year old Adela. She was wondering if there was a chance that she might someday experience Pet's big city lifestyle. *I'll have to work on making that dream come true* she thought as she also fell prisoner to the sandman's magic.

Mihal and the five older girls went to the Sunday morning service. Blondie excused herself saying, "I'm too tired and I don't feel like wrestlin' with these three pip squeaks for the next hour. You know they can't sit still in church yet, so how about if you do the praying for all of us, Mihal. Isn't that what the man of the house is supposed to do?"

He didn't know if she was being sarcastic or just plain mean. He decided to let her comment hover with the spirits. *It's not worth another argument,* he thought.

After coming home from Mass, Blondie served a traditional Polish Easter breakfast of ham, kielbasa, hard boiled eggs, Paska bread, fresh ground horseradish (compliments of a teary-eyed J), potato salad and coconut cream pie. Once all tummies were filled and every one burped, the kids were dismissed from the table by their father. Blondie wasn't to be outdone as she quickly instructed everyone to proceed to the parlor.

Each wide-eyed child wasn't sure of what to expect in that rarely used room. None of them ever knew what to expect of Blondie's orders. As J watched her mother standing and leaning against the far parlor wall, her memory strayed to another event in this room. *I wonder if she remembers that's the wall where Baba's casket stood for three days before her funeral a few years ago.*

This morning, however, everyone breathed a bit easier as Mihal arrived with them and remained a sentry in the doorway. It didn't take long before Pet appeared with her large tan shopping bag filled to the rim with assorted Easter goodies.

There was no need for baskets this particular Easter morning.

Each child was handed a box containing a whole chocolate bunny, not just the face or the ears.

Each child was handed their own full bag of jelly beans, not just a small handful.

Each child was handed a box containing, not one, but six yellow-sugared marshmallow chicks.

Each child, also, was given an egg shaped container filled with bubble gum. For once this packet of gum didn't need to be shared.

With eyes as big as saucers, each child stood in wonderment. This kind of an Easter surprise had never happened before, at least not at #11 Lemon Lane.

Later that afternoon, J would open her bubble gum egg. Tucked deep inside was a roll of postage stamps. *I'll keep my promise, Pet. My letters will keep making you smile.* J cemented her thoughts as she blew a large pink bubble, and then laughed with delight when it popped leaving a wide pink film covering her lips.

Pet removed the final box from the bottom of the bag, a large chocolate strawberry cream filled egg. She turned and handed it to her dad. "This is a special treat for everyone. I hope you all enjoy it," Pet said.

The smile on Mihal's face was a grateful one. The tears on his cheeks were shed with pride. "Thank you, Pet. You did a good thing here and I'm proud of you," he was saying, when Pet became surrounded by a mauling gaggle of seven happy snot-nosed youngsters. They were all trying to get their own "thank you" heard over the next kid's. It was a joyous scene, and that was a picture Pet would carry in her heart when she returned to D.C.

"Blondie, don't you have somethin' to say to your daughter?" Mihal asked.

"Yeah, I got a lot to say, but she don't want to hear none of it. Ask her what she had to do to get all that candy. See if she'll tell you the truth," Blondie yapped back.

"I paid for it all with my Easter paycheck, Dad. I didn't do anything wrong," an insulted Pet remarked.

Pet's facial expression was filled with pain. This was a pain that Mihal understood only too well.

"Blondie, apologize to your girl. Do it, and do it right now," Mihal said through gritted teeth. "Do it, I said!"

Blondie chose to leave the room without uttering a single word. She headed for the willow tree again and broke off another switch. *Let one of them brats make a wrong move and they'll find out who's the boss around here after him and Pet are gone,* she thought. Blondie tore the excess leaves off of the twig while she hummed to the tune of She'll be Comin' "Round the Mountain.

Day after day, Blondie broke herself another switch, but day after day the switch disappeared. J giggled every time Blondie discovered that another one had escaped from the kitchen hook. One day Blondie gave up on the idea of keeping a switch handy. She'd decided to resort to other measures of punishment. *In time, they'll find out who's the big cheese around here.*

Nibble by nibble, each child learned just who the big cheese was.

Day by day, the realization grew greater that it was almost anyone but Blondie.

Minute by minute, each learned not to care if it was or if it wasn't Blondie.

The only one who did care was Blondie.

FINALLY A FRESHMAN

Thirteen! I'm finally thirteen years old J thought as she visually checked herself out in the old wavy dresser mirror. *It's strange, but I don't feel any different. Maybe that will happen in a day or two.* It was nine thirty in the evening and not one single person had wished her a Happy Birthday. *Oh, well,* she thought, *who cares. Happy Birthday new teenager,* her thoughts whispered to the image gazing back at her.

J was eager to be a teenager. She was excited about attending high school. She was anxious about getting her first menstrual period. *God, when would that happen* she wondered. She felt sure that every other girl in her ninth grade class had gotten their curse ages ago, or so it seemed. It also seemed no one was willing to discuss it or reveal any of its secrets. A million questions had run through her head about this big mystery. Adela told her, "Don't be such a nag. It will happen and when it does, you'll wish it never started. It's the worst thing that can happen to you, you'll see."

Why is it the worst thing? I thought Polly said the worst thing was getting pregnant. Ma says the worst thing is sleeping with a man every night, and you'll find out why the way everybody else has. How many worst things are there in this world an inquisitive voice beckoned from the laterals of her brain?

J would conjure up so many different questions while doing her housework, gardening chores or barn tasks, but there was no one willing to give any straight answers. Her best friend, Henya, didn't know, or so she said. Although, J did notice Henya's face turned beet-red anytime the subject was broached.

J definitely couldn't turn to Adela for questions or answers. Adela was a huge tattletale. Whatever anyone confided in her went directly to Blondie. J wondered about that, too. *Is that why everyone calls them the grapevine?* That was something else for J to figure out.

Monday was Labor Day and once again Blondie volunteered for J to spend the weekend babysitting Polly and Tod's two adorable girls. J had whiled away her summer days feeling resentful of the Monday through Friday work load she was forced to endure at home. Then every Friday at noon, she'd have to take the local public bus to Madera, where she'd spend the next two and a half days babysitting Polly's kids and helping Polly with her housework. She learned to hate her week days. She learned to despise her weekends. She learned to loathe her summer.

Tina was now a talkative toddler and was as active as a hamster on a spinning wheel. Tess, the three month old baby, was a whining tiny tadpole with a lot of health problems. The doctor had cautioned Polly that this wasn't a strong infant and she would require multiple surgeries in the next few years, if she was to survive. Needless to say, baby Tess required a lot of time-consuming attention. Every weekend, J was expected to take over those mothering chores while Polly took what Polly called "a much needed break".

"Honest J, you have no idea how much I need some free time for myself. Can you change Tess's diaper? There's a poop odor coming from that direction. I can't check her myself right now. I'm trying to fix my hair so I can go downtown shopping pretty soon."

I, I, I, that's all you think about, Polly. J's thoughts spun as she changed Tess's diaper.

This kid's butt is so red! How long has she been laying here with this wet shitty diaper, J curiously wondered. She was not surprised at the infant's condition. This wasn't the first time she'd found the baby this way. Polly was not the most attentive mother; that was a certainty.

Polly saved all of her marketing or errands for Friday and Saturday when J would be there. Polly and Tod saved all of their partying and visiting for the weekend, when J would be there. That allowed J to call the bus ride to and from Polly's house her weekly entertainment.

On this Saturday before Labor Day, Polly took a few minutes to sit in a large overstuffed living room chair and study J's overall appearance. J sat quietly feeding Tess her bottle of milk, like the good substitute mother that she was.

"You know, J," Polly began her orchestration of a carefully planned secret make-over for J, "this is going to be a special afternoon. You're beginning to get a shape and it's about time you started to look like a young lady. You'll have to stop wearing bangs and a ponytail. What kind of a hairdo is that for a freshman in high school? And your eyebrows are two bushes. They're just drawing attention to your high forehead. It's about time you learned how to wear lipstick and nail polish, too," Polly babbled.

"Geez, Polly, are you sure you haven't missed checkin' out any part of my body?" J blandly asked.

"As a matter of fact there is," Polly quipped.

It's time for you to dress like a young lady and to polish your shoes every night. That should cover it," Polly remarked as she extended and waved her hands in the air as though she were giving a Papal blessing.

And . . . and . . . and . . . and . . . and, Polly's list seemed to go on and on and on! Polly was on a roll. J envisioned Polly as a loose caboose going downhill on an ice covered arctic railroad track. Polly was down right determined to give J a total once over. So two days before J's first day of high school, Polly began performing her younger sister's make-over.

Once the babies were put down for their afternoon nap, Polly began the challenge at the top of the heap. "This long hair has got to go. Nobody wears a ponytail anymore. Short bob's are in, so that's what you're gonna get."

Polly began by cutting eight inches off of the rubber-banded ponytail with a straight edged razor blade, leaving a stub sticking out from the back of J's head. As soon as Polly removed the rubber band, J glanced sideways and could see the uneven edges framing her face. Dropping her chin, J knew instantly that this was a mistake. Polly assured her she knew what she was doing. After all, she had watched the local beautician give the latest bob haircut . . . once!

Her next step was to use Tod's electric razor to shave three inches from the nape of J's neck. *What's next? A crew cut?* J silently began doubting this hick stylist's capabilities.

"Let me see what that looks like before you do anything else," J demanded.

Grabbing the hand mirror from Polly, J took a glance and screamed! "What are you doing? I didn't want a boy's haircut, for crying out loud!"

"Just relax. I've just started," Polly said impatiently. "Give me a chance, would you?"

Like I have a choice now, J thought.

Polly reached over to her sewing box and fished out a pair of large material scissors. "What are you doing with those?" J asked nervously.

"What do you think I'm doing? You didn't think I was good enough to give you a razor cut, did you? I'll cut the rest of your hair with these. I just had them sharpened a few weeks ago. They'll work fine for what I need to do now," Polly mimicked J's squeaky nervous-edged inflection.

She began by sectioning off clumps of J's hair, pinning it up and out of the way with bobbi-pins. "That way I won't cut the wrong hairs," she explained.

After what felt like three thousand clip, clip, clips, Polly announced, "That's all I can do with your straight and stringy hair."

J became instantly frightened. Her armpits dripped. Her hands became clammy. *That didn't sound too promising. As a matter of fact, it sounded down right scary* J considered, before racing to the bathroom mirror to see her new hairdo.

"Oh my God! Polly, you've made me look like one of the stooges. Did you put a bowl on my head for a pattern? What did you do to my hair? I can't go anywhere looking this way!" J screamed at her sister.

"Well, all I can say is I tried, but it didn't turn out like the cut I watched Peggy give in her shop. I have a Toni perm I was saving for myself. I'll use it on your hair and at least it will be curly," Polly commented indignantly, as though she were doing J a favor.

"Let's shampoo your hair and then we'll do the perm. Come on, I don't have all day just for your hair. We have a lot to tackle this afternoon before me and Tod have to leave for the Moose Club's party this evening," Polly blurted.

While the perm solution was curling J's hair, Polly began her eyebrow tweezing. "Ow, that hurts," J cried out in discomfort.

What seemed like three hundred painful tweaks to J's eyebrows was Polly's futile mission to arch the bushy patches. Polly wasn't about to be deterred by J's whining. Inflicting pain on someone else didn't seem to ruffle Polly at all.

"There, that ought to do it," was repeated many times during the course of the tweezing, only to be followed by, "whoops, I missed one."

You missed one, J thought, *is there one left? That's what I'm curious to see.*

"Oh my, look at the clock. We're ten minutes over the time limit for the perm solution. We better get you rinsed off in a big hurry. Quick, put your head under the faucet," Polly instructed, practically shoving J's face into the sink bowl.

"Don't worry about the water's temperature. We just need to get you rinsed off in a hurry and put the neutralizer on really fast," Polly informed her. "We don't want your hair falling out, now do we?"

Instinctively, J raised her curler-covered head ramming it straight up and into the faucet. "Good God, the water's freezing," J yelped.

"Ouch!" *God, the only good thing I'm getting here is a Russian concussion,* J thought as she rubbed the sore spot on her head.

"What do you mean hair falling out? What do you mean? Answer me, Polly."

"Let's just wait until we unroll it. If it doesn't come out with the rollers, then I think you'll be alright. Calm down, and let me rinse out the perm solution," Polly scolded.

J glanced at her sister. *Is she ridiculing me? Is she serious or is she joking? What is that weird look on her face? Don't tell me that's panic? Some big time makeover this is,* a provoked J thought glumly. *She can't seriously be thinking she's doing me a favor, can she?*

"While we're waiting for the neutralizer to work, let's file your nails and polish them."

Make-over. Polly at work. J rolled her eyes and imagined a descriptive cartoon bubble above Polly's head as she buffed and polished away at the fingernails.

"Okay," J said, "but what time is the neutralizer supposed to be done? I'll watch the timer this time, if you don't mind?"

An hour later, a very currrrrrrrly headed J timidly observed herself in the tall mirror hanging behind Polly's bedroom door.

J spoke to the person looking back at her from the mirror. "What in the Hell happened? Who in the Hell are you?"

J asked, but her brain couldn't answer. J was too stunned by the reflection. She had begun her day with a full mane of long straight hair. She now had short, pale, red curls. Her head was capped with tons of tiny, itty-bitty frizzy curls!

Where she once had bushes for eyebrows, she now had three hairs above each eye and a reddish-brown penciled half-moon.

Her eyelashes were coated with black gunk, which showered tiny dark specks every time she blinked.

She was now sporting bright red lips and was being told to pucker up, because "they're not dark enough yet."

Her finger nails were red to match her lipstick. "You can't touch them on anything for another hour or they'll smudge, and then we'll have to start all over again!"

Good and Gracious God, please, don't make us start all over again. I don't think I could live through that, J mimed to the image looking back at her from the large mirror.

Aloud she moaned, "I think I'm gonna be sick," while making a bee-line down the short hallway to the bathroom.

She didn't vomit, but she nearly wet her panties. At least that's what she thought it was, until she looked at the crotch of her underwear.

That's blood! Am I dying? A conclusion she almost hoped was true.

"J," Polly, who waas standing on the other side of the bathroom door, was cooing, "are you alright? Do you like your make-over? I think you look so much more grown up. Sophisticated, that's the word to describe you now."

Polly had changed her cooing to down right lying and that was no lie.

"Shut up," J yelled back at her. "I look like a clown and you know it. It will take a year before my scalp will let any of my hair grow back. I'm just gonna tell everyone that I got caught in a fire, and do you know what? They'll believe it! Oh, what does it matter anyway? I think I'm dying."

"Dying?" Polly questioned. "What on earth makes you say that?"

"Because I'm bleeding from my bottom and I didn't even cut myself. That's what happened to old Mrs. Perron. She died from cancer shortly after that happened to her."

J was attempting to explain her newly-discovered fears to Polly, but her sister was holding her sides and laughing her fool head off.

"What's so funny?" J asked.

"You don't have cancer, you idiot. You just got your first period. Come with me. I'll get you a few peri-pads and I'll show you what to do with them," Polly continued talking as she led J to the bedroom.

"You'll need to tell Adela and Ma so they can get you a supply of these pads. Here, this is called a peri-belt. Pin your pads onto these tabs. Okay? Do you know what this means? Ah, I'd better let Ma tell you all about it, so she doesn't get mad at me for *spillin' her beans,* as she calls it."

On Sunday afternoon, J packed her few weekend items into a brown grocery bag and headed down the stairs. "I'm ready to go home now," she called out to Polly.

"Do you have any babysitting money for me this week? Can you make sure there's a quarter in the change? The bus driver gets mad if I don't have the quarter to drop into the box," J explained.

"What do you mean babysitting money? I just gave you a full scale make-over, including a permanent wave. That would have cost you fifty dollars at the beauty shop. I don't have any money to give you. Don't you even have a quarter? I'll look around. Maybe Tod has some change in his ash tray upstairs. Here hold the baby while I go check," Polly mumbled as she ran up the stairs, taking two steps at a time so that she could shuffle the girl off to catch the bus back home.

"Well, you better make it snappy. The bus will be down at the corner in about fifteen minutes," J called out, awakening the baby as she shouted.

Bouncing the bundle in her arms, J patiently waited while she listened to Polly scrambling around upstairs. *I can't believe she doesn't even have a measly twenty-five cents to give me for the bus fare*, J thought as she listened to Polly's footsteps hurriedly searching in the upstairs bedrooms.

I am not going through this anymore J decided. It was time for Polly to find herself another maid.

I've babysat every weekend this summer and it's always the same. They go out every Friday and Saturday night to the Moose Hall to play Bingo and get drunk. Then they stagger in and stumble up the stairs awakening me and the kids. That's when they call out for me to get the baby a bottle and to pat Tina back to sleep. What do they think I am, an octopus? And besides, I'm not the mother of these kids. That's her job!

Recalling upstairs noises she was forced to hear every weekend, J wondered if Polly and Tod were aware of how boisterous they were in their bedroom when they'd come home from their evenings of partying. *As soon as they go upstairs, I hear "Stop, Tod! No, don't stop!"*

"Make up your mind, Polly. Either you want it or you don't".

It's the same damn conversation between the two of them every, every weekend, and then that damned banging of the headboard starts. Next comes Sunday when there's always some excuse for not having any money to pay me. Well, I've had enough of this bull shit.

"J," Polly was shaking J's elbow. "What are you daydreaming about?"

"Give me the baby. Here's a quarter, now run to the bus stop. You have time to catch the five o'clock for home. Run, now. See you next Friday," Polly was practically singing as she gave J a shove out of the front door.

Polly sounded chipper as she called out a "See you" after J, who was already bouncing down the sidewalk on her way to the bus stop.

Over my dead body stumbled through J's mind as she ran to catch the bus already rounding the corner.

"Adela, Polly said to tell you and Ma that I got my first period and you should help me get some pads," J tactfully whispered her news to her older sister.

"What do you want me to do about it? Run to the bank, borrow some money, and then run out and get you some pads? Go tell Ma yourself.

You're a big girl now," Adela said with a crooked twist to the corners of her big mouth.

"Ma, Polly said to tell you I got my first period and you should get me a box of pads," J tried again.

"What do you want me to do about it? Didn't Polly pay you for babysittin'? Don't you have that money, or did you spend it already like you do every week after she pays you?" her mother asked with a definite modulation in her voice.

"What do you mean Polly pays me? I am so sick of her lies. She has only given me quarters for the return bus tickets. I usually have to beg for that! Those two spend their money drinking and playing Bingo, and then your sweet Polly finds excuses not to pay me. She always has a reason. Look at me. See the fancy make-over she gave me? This is the reason she didn't pay me today. She made me out to look like a circus clown, and then she had the nerve to call it a make-over. I'll have to go to school this way. I'll be the laugh of the whole freshman class," J said between sobs.

"Quit your bawlin'. Get upstairs and get yourself cleaned up," Blondie yelled.

Adela," Blondie called out, "show your sister where those rags are and show her how to make a blood pad. I'm not buyin' any store pads for this monkey face."

Blondie started to walk away, when J had the gumption to ask, "What does having a period mean, anyway? Polly said you'd tell me all about it."

"It means that you don't let a boy touch you anywhere or you'll get pregnant. Is that enough of an answer for you?" Blondie asked, as she turned and walked out of the front door laughing at what she must have thought was a hilarious summation to J's question.

Over her shoulder, Blondie was quick to add, "The last thing you want to do around here is walk through this door pregnant. You had better understand that, Missy. Polly was the last one from *this damned house* to get away with that trick."

J was so right about the first day of school jesting. She had expected it, but that didn't mean she appreciated it. "Who gave you the special hairdo?" was the topic of conversation among J's friends. "Bobo, the clown?" they'd quip.

It gave everyone a reason for some hearty snickering. Quite a few students poked fun at J's hairdo, except this one huge junior boy. Everyone called him Duck. He *seemed* very sympathetic when J explained the answer to his hairy question. *Seemed* was the key word to Duck's sympathy, but J didn't catch on to his deceit until after he confessed that his only interest in her was a freshman hazing. He would soon brag, "And I'm the one to give you your initiation into high school."

"Fooled you, didn't I kid?" he laughed mockishly.

"Yeah, you got a sad story alright," Duck consoled, "but you still look like a fluffy orange-headed clown. Sit down right there on that brick wall and open your mouth. Open it, I said or I'll ram this snuff down your throat. Are these your two friends?" Duck asked, pointing to Henya and Joan. J nodded an affirmative.

"All three of you, open your mouths. Do it. Nobody is gonna save you. This is your first day initiation. Just chew this tobacco for a second, then you can spit it out, and you'll be free to go into school."

The three frightened girls did as they were told. They bit down once, and then spit the bitter tasting crap out of their mouths. J vomited, right on this Duck's shoes. He was not at all pleased with J's volatile response to his practical joke. He reached out to grab J's shirt, but she was speedy and had already entered the school's door before he was able to stomp his foot on the ground to shake the spittle off his new shiny shoes.

As J looked backward out of the closed door's window, she watched in amazement as Adela handed Duck a dollar bill.

Where did Adela get a dollar bill?

J's memory jogged a scene from a forgotten day, *but that was years ago,* she reflected.

Could Adela really be that vengeful?

It would be a few years before J would get the answers to her intuitive questions.

A QUICK DATE

"You're a bright young girl. How much studying do you do, or don't you really have to study much to get those good grades?" The high school principal asked J as she stood at the bus stop. "You've been on the honor roll right along, haven't you?"

It was five o'clock on a sunny Labor Day Sunday afternoon. J just wanted to board the bus and relax for the next half hour. She was tired of nothing but working, but she was well aware of what awaited her at home. *What does this guy want with all these questions?* J was beginning to feel agitated at this short, bald-headed man's nosiness.

"I don't have much time to study at home, so I try to get my homework done on the school bus. I have quite a few chores to do at home during the week, and on the weekends my Ma makes me go to my sister Polly's house to baby sit. I have to help her with her housework, too," J politely told the man dressed impeccably in a gray suit with a matching blue and gray striped necktie and shined black shoes.

"Well, that's good that you can help your sister and make some spending money, as well," he said, smiling empathetically at the skinny girl before him.

"Oh, pardon me, but she doesn't pay me. She gives me a quarter for the bus ride home on Sunday. Did she tell you that she pays me?" J asked cautiously. Her head was tilted and looking slightly upward at his puzzled looking face.

"Yes, she has. I saw your sister Polly at the grocery store last week. She told me how she pays you fifteen dollars for helping her out on the weekends. Don't tell me that isn't correct?" he questioned, raising his bushy eyebrows as he stared at J. He seemed to be waiting for her version of what payment she receives.

"That definitely is not correct," J answered sharply.

"I'll tell you again, she gives me a quarter for the bus fare, that's it. She always has an excuse for not paying me and she always makes some comment that I was able to eat while I was there."

J wondered, *just how much can I tell this guy without getting into some kind of trouble?* She decided to be frank and honest, and continued her admission. It was almost a relief to give an accurate description of her babysitting and financial woes to an unbiased adult. Telling her sister, Adela, about her weekends at Polly's always had strings attached. Adela wouldn't tattle to Blondie, if J didn't tattle about Adela's flirtatious antics on the school grounds. J finally understood the meaning of a viciouos circle.

"If you can call French fries between two slices of buttered bread for my dinners and corn flakes with warm water for my breakfasts, then I guess I eat there. This is the last time I ever want to hear her lies. I'm finished there," J said with tear filled eyes. "I'm not her personal maid."

She stood trembling and expecting a reprimand from the principal, but instead, he turned sympathetic. "I can't say that I blame you for being angry. I certainly would be. That's so unfair of her not to pay you something and then to lie about it. Have you discussed this with your parents? What do they say about it, and why do they make you go there if you're not being paid or fed properly?"

"My Ma believes Polly pays me, but Dad doesn't. He says he believes me, so he gives me five dollars every time he comes home for the weekend. He works away in Buffalo at a car factory. He tells me to be patient. 'Your day's coming,' he says. So, I'll be patient and wait. He's a good guy and he's kind to me, so I'll listen to him," J tells this educated inquisitive gentleman.

"By the way, J," the principal asked, "who tweezed your eyebrows? Whoever styled them for you didn't do you any favor."

His eyes were studying her face. J could sense him concentrating. He was deciding what approach to take with his next opinion. "They made a mess out of your hair too, didn't they? That eyebrow pencil is the wrong color. I'm an art major and I know about these things. You should be using a dark brown pencil, because your hairs are dark brown, not reddish-brown," he said.

"It couldn't have been Polly who did this to you, could it? Don't bother answering. I know she did, because that's the color she wears. The next time I run into her, I'm going to have a few words with her. Would you mind?"

"Mind? No, I'd be glad," J responded, surprised with his quick and open response.

Well, I'll give him an A+ for bravery she thought. *I don't think I could have been that coy with someone I barely met.*

"Maybe if she learns people know what she's really like, she might start showing me some appreciation for all I do for her. That's not going to change my mind, though. I plan on telling her and Ma that I won't be going to her house on the weekends anymore. Does that sound mean?" J looked to Mr. Jones for his opinion.

"No, it's not mean. It's being honest. You're old enough to make that choice for yourself. She has to learn to care for her own family. You need to start taking part in your own high school activities. You're taking clarinet lessons, aren't you? Well, we're going to see to it that you get a spot in the marching band, and then you won't have time for babysitting. You'll be marching in parades, going to the football games, and staying after school for practices. I'll take care of informing your parents. It's about time someone took your side, don't you think?"

"I suppose, but if Ma thinks I'm blabbing to you about this, I'll probably get a good tongue lashing. She still whips some of the kids, you know. Oh, not when I'm around, but they tell me about it later. I burn any switches I find." J cuffed her hand around her mouth as she informed him of what she thought to be a family secret.

"No, no, you don't have to worry about anything. I'll just go visit my sister Eleanor in Gunther, and while I'm there I'll drive up to your house. I can tell your mother about the open spot in the band that Mr. Sokolman wants you to fill. How long have you been taking lessons and practicing? Hasn't it been a couple of years?"

"Two years already. I even walk to Ramey once a week during the summers for a lesson with Mr. Sokolman. It's something to do, besides work," J told him.

"While I'm at your house, I plan on asking your Ma if she still uses a switch or a belt on any of her kids, because I know she's done that in the past. That's no great secret in your neighborhood, you know. I'm going to tell her about some new laws that are coming about and that she'll have to quit her beatings. It's time your Ma starts living in this century and it's time you started having some fun. What do you think?"

J could have jumped for joy, but instead she just smiled at Mr. Jones and sincerely said, "Thank you."

One more nice person to add to the list, J thought. *I'll bet a lot of people won't agree with me, though. Our Ma will be one after he gets done talking to her. I just know she'll be angry at him,* J thought, *and she'll take out her spite on me.*

In the middle of September, Mr. Jones just happened to be walking in the school hall between classes. "Well J, how are things going in the marching band?" the principal inquired.

"It's been two weeks and Mr. Sokolman tells me you're doing just fine. Keep up the good work. How does the uniform fit? I'm betting it's baggy on you. By the way, I hear you keep the other band members in stitches. A good sense of humor is a good thing to carry in your back pocket and save for the tough times," he said, winking and reminding J of her father.

"I'm not sure if I carry humor in my back pocket, but I'm glad I can make the kids laugh," J said. "My dad says to keep your own sunshine in your front pocket on rainy days," she added with a bright smile.

"I think I'm even making some good friends there, and that makes me happy. I just laugh when they tease me about the uniform. You're right, it is a little big, but I don't mind."

For some unknown reason, J felt some sort of a kinship with this man. He was easy to talk to. He didn't make her nervous.

He's an understanding person, that's it J thought. *I wonder what kind of a life he had when he was growing up.*

"How are things going at home?" he pushed his questioning.

Mr. Jones sure did seem interested in her life. J wondered *why. What's in it for him? Why is he keeping tabs on me? What makes me so special?*

"Your mother almost seemed relieved that she didn't have to send you to Polly's anymore. Polly, on the other hand, told me to mind my own business when I cautioned her about using child labor and not paying for all of the hours you put in at her house." Mr. Jones seemed delighted to pass this tid-bit along to his young student.

"Has she sent you any money? She said she was going to."

Mr. Jones was becoming a bit too nosey to suit J. She silently questioned, *why is he so interested in me and my life? What brought on all of this nosiness anyway?* Her face must have registered her questions, because Mr. Jones began to express an answer.

"In case you're wondering why I've decided to mind some of your business, young lady, I think you deserve an explanation," Mr. Jones declared in a soft voice.

He went on to explain that some of J's friends had discussed life at #11 Lemon Lane and that they felt that she needed to break out of Blondie's stronghold. "I see a very bright student. You're energetic, you work hard, and you're a decent young lady. I take an interest in my promising pupils. If I can ever help you with anything, come and talk to me. In the meantime, enjoy high school. Let me know if Polly doesn't square up with the money she owes you, okay?"

"Well, if she said she would, then I guess I'll just have to wait and see if she does. Isn't that right?" an embarrassed J asked, changing her posture to turn away from the man.

"I gotta go or I'll be late for English class. Thanks again for all your help."

Making a three-quarter turn, she ran smack-dab into the tallest, cutest, curly red-headed boy she had ever seen. *He's covered with freckles!* His armload of books flew to the right. Hers flew to the left.

"Here, let me help you with those," he said, scrambling to gather her scattered books and papers. "I'm sorry. I wasn't watching where I was going."

J would later learn what he was watching. He was busy gawking at a pair of thirty-eights in a pale blue sweater. Those perky boobs belonged to the most popular blonde cutie of the senior class. As a skinny dating novice, J would learn this bit of information in a very interesting way.

"No, I'm sorry. I turned quickly and didn't see you there until it was too late." She found herself apologizing to him as she began scooping his books into a heap.

"Are you a freshman? I haven't seen you around. What's your name? It looks like your name is probably J, since that's what's written on the cover of all your books. Is that really your last name," he paused and glanced upward to face her.

After scrutinizing the last name written on her math text, he said, "Please, don't tell me you're Adela's sister? I wouldn't have guessed that. You're cute. On the other hand, your sister isn't. Don't tell her I said that. She'd probably beat me up. She has this reputation to uphold, you know!" he teased and J blushed.

"My name's Nelson. Are you going my way? Come on, I'll walk you to your class, okay?"

"Sure," was all tongue-tied J could spit out of her dry cotton-mouth.

They walked in attenuated silence until they reached J's classroom. "So," he startled her, "would you like to go to a movie or something this Saturday? I'm sure you'll have to ask your parents if that's okay. Am I right?"

"Yes," was all that rolled off of her parched tongue. It was only one word, but she almost stuttered saying it.

God, why am I so tongue tied all of a sudden. He's just a freckle-faced kid, for crying out loud. Calm down, J remanded herself.

"I'll call you on Saturday morning to see if it's a date. Does that sound good to you?" he asked nonchalantly.

His blasé attitude should have been J's first clue to his character. It was evident that this wasn't his first date, but it sure was going to be hers. She didn't have a single dating clue to call her own.

"Somebody answer that phone," Blondie was shouting on Saturday morning. "I'm waitin' for Doc to call. I need to talk to him about this stomach pain I'm havin'."

"It's for J," Adela announced rather loudly.

"J, you got a phone call. Get down here," Adela was yelling up the staircase.

Covering the mouthpiece, Adela whispered, "He says his name is Nelson and you're expecting him to call. This isn't Freckle-Face, is it? God, what's wrong with you? Can't you date somebody who's nice? Date anybody, but not the boob man."

"Why don't you mind your own bees wax? You sound jealous that he's asking me out on a date and not you," was all J would reveal to her smug sister.

Before taking the phone receiver from Adela's hand, J walked over to her dad who was sitting at the kichen table sipping a cup of strong black coffee. "Dad, I met this nice guy at school and he asked me to go to a movie later today. Can I go?"

"Well, I suppose, but I want him to come to the door for you. None of this beepin' the horn stuff. If he beeps the horn, that means he doesn't care about you or your reputation, Joni. And, you're to be home by ten o'clock, understand?" Mihal wasn't asking her, he had informed his girl.

She's growin' up, too. It sure doesn't take long, Mihal thought as he watched her nod *yes* and take the phone from Adela.

"My Dad gave me his permission, but I have to be home by ten," she told Nelson.

"Six thirty," she repeated into the mouthpiece. "Okay, I'll see you then. Bye."

J's first-date phone conversation had ended, and as she turned to leave the room she found an audience staring back at her.

"What? What's everybody looking at? You're just mad 'cause I snagged a date for tonight and you didn't, Adela."

With that little outpouring, J hurriedly ran to her bedroom before any one could ask any more of their thoughts or make any further insulting comments.

Blondie stood holding a dishcloth in her left hand, while her right hand was set on her hip as though she needed it there to keep her body balanced upright. "What in the Hell do you think you're doin', Mihal? Tonight is bath night. Excuse me, but how is she supposed to take a bath and have a hotsy-totsy date at the same time?" Blondie asked the question, but she wasn't done yapping just yet.

"Further more, since when do you make the damned decisions about the girl's dates? This is not gonna be an every Saturday thing, you do know that don't you, Mihal? She's too damn young to be startin' this horse shit anyway!"

Before Mihal could respond, Blondie headed for the stairway and began shouting, "Do you understand, Missy. This is not goin' to happen every Saturday. You're lucky you didn't ask for my Henry J, 'cause you wouldn't be gettin' it. Now, get down here and get your Saturday work done. Now!" she screeched, and then promptly slumped to the floor.

"Blondie! What the Hell happened here?" Mihal asked as he knelt beside the lump on the floor.

"I'm in pain. My stomach is on fire. You better get me to the hospital, Mihal," a frightened Blondie was attempting to stand, but couldn't get up off of the floor without Mihal's assistance.

Holding her by the elbows, Mihal lifted her off the floor and guided her straight out the front door. "Get my purse," Blondie called over her shoulder as she was being helped into the family car.

Mihal reprimanded Blondie. "You can do without your purse for once, Blondie. What's in there anyway? Fort Knox?"

"They won't even open the emergency room door if they don't see our insurance card," Blondie was quick to blast back at an impatient Mihal.

"Here, Ma'" Adela was racing to the car with the old black leather purse.

Good old Adela, da bella da balla. What a nickname, J thought as she watched Adela brown nosing her mother.

"Adela, you're in charge," Blondie ordered.

"Make sure the kids get their supper and a bath. J can take hers first, so she can get ready for this big date of hers. If we're not back in time, make sure that guy comes to the door and make sure he don't have any of his buddies in the back seat. She's ignorant about this datin' stuff, but she'll catch on quick. She'll soon find out what that's all about, won't she?" Blondie snickered, before turning to Mihal and wincing.

"Let's go. The pain is gettin' worse," she groaned. J noticed that her right hand was pressing on her right side. *Is that where she's feeling the pain,* J wondered.

Blondie had conversed with sixteen year old Adela as though she were an equal. J stood on the sidelines with the rest of the kids and observed their closeness. *Well, shit look at that. They're bosom buddies. That could have been me. If only I'd been named Edwina. How long does a gypsy curse last* J wondered.

Mihal had been right about a gigolo guy who beeps the car horn when he picks up his date. This red-headed, freckle-faced cutie would be no different from the rest of the horny male teen population. He had told himself he was going out on a date with an inexperienced freshman, and had promised himself this night would not end in disappointment.

Arriving punctually, he beeped the horn several times before Adela walked J out to his car. As promised, Adela made certain there weren't any extra passengers in the back seat. She then sidled over to the driver's side of Nelson's car and reminded him that J was to be home by ten. Noticing Nelson hadn't extended the courtesy of opening the passenger door for J, Adela watched as he reached across the front seat and pushed the passenger door outward. He didn't even greet his date. He was too busy flirting with Adela's chest. Adela noticed every one of Nelson's idiosyncrasies. He may have thought that he could bluff J, but he wasn't fooling her.

Thinking *I can't wait to tell Ma all about this clod and what he was like when he came to pick up J,* Adela's innards relished the thought of making a few brownie points by giving a full report to her mother.

"Adela," one of the youngsters was shouting, "Dad's on the phone. He wants to talk to you. He said for you to hurry."

"Yes, Dad, I understand. I'll wait up for you," Adela responded to her father's comments on the other end of the phone line.

"Everything is okay here," she answered his question.

"Yes, J went on her date, but I'm betting she'll be home long before ten. I'll tell you all about it when you get here. Tell Ma to feel better. She's probably gonna have a lot of pain after having that gallbladder surgery. Well, tell her Big Annie just happened to come by to visit and she's decided to stay until you get home. She's gonna stay, so we'll be okay till then." Adela had tried to reassure her father that all was well on the home front. By the time she hung up the phone, she felt confident that she'd succeeded.

It wasn't very long before J ambled through the kitchen door and directly into the muddle of bath night. "Sure, I knew you'd be home long before ten. Don't ask me how I knew, I just knew. I've been on some lousy dates myself," experienced Adela spoke as she towel-dried a freshly bathed toddler.

"Nelson has a reputation for being an octopus when he's out on a date. He stares at all the girl's boobs when they walk past him. I don't like him. He can be a creep. Go change out of your good clothes. You can help me with the rest of these kid's baths while I tell you about Ma."

"So, tell me J, why did you come back home in less than forty five minutes? What happened on this big first date?"

Adela could be relentless when she chose to be. *You can be a down right pain in the ass, Adela,* was the only windmill that kept spinning through J's mind once she was blind-sided by her sister's inquisition.

"Let me see, how can I tell you about it? It was a quick date, thank goodness. When he first asked me to go out, he said we could go to a movie or something. I'd forgotten all about the something part, but he didn't," J said, walking toward the warming oven of the coal stove.

"I was so excited about this stupid date, I forgot to eat any dinner and now my gut is growling. Whose meatloaf is this? It doesn't matter, I'm eating it," she said as she dug in, breaking it into pieces with her fingers.

"You're eating like you're starved. Slow down or you'll choke," Adela cautioned.

"He drove straight to the old Fernwood mining road," J continued, after swallowing quickly.

"He put the car in park and turned off the ignition. I don't know how dumb he thought I was, but I kinda figured what he had in mind. I asked him why we weren't going to a movie, but he reached over and grabbed the back of my neck with his hand, pulled my face over to his and started kissing me hard on the lips."

J's grimace was followed by a shiver at the memory of his crudeness, but she continued her narrative. "He tried to jam his tongue into my mouth. Yuk!"

J cringed at the memory of his brashness, just as a wave of nausea caused her to momentarily reel. She stopped chewing the meatloaf long enough to spit the mushy bolus into the old coal bucket sitting near the kitchen coal stove. "I pulled away from him really fast. I asked him what he thought he was doing. He just sat there staring out of the window for a few seconds, then he reached over, put his hand on my right breast and started squeezing. He started telling me how soft my boob was, can you imagine? What nerve!"

J stopped talking long enough to shake her head in astonishment. "I didn't even think, I just reached out and slugged him right in the face. His nose started to bleed and he wiped his sleeve across his face. When he saw the blood on his sleeve, he got really, really mad and called me a stupid bitch."

"He hollered," J said. "He wanted to know what the Hell was wrong with me? He said this was what other people do when they go out on a date. I told him I wasn't other people. By that time I was plenty mad, with a capital M, and I slammed out of the car."

"Then what did you do," Adela asked.

"I started to walk home, that's what. He started the car up and followed along beside me. When I was almost by the LeCroix's house, he begged me to get back in the car. He kept on promising that he'd bring me straight home if I wouldn't tell anyone what he did. I wasn't going to promise him anything. I ran into Suzette's house and asked Mr. LeCroix to drive me home. And that's the end of the story for my big date!"

J had told Adela all about her date, but one thing she wanted to make clear to her sister was "I will tell all of this to Dad myself. I'll explain what happened on this date. I didn't do anything that I'm ashamed of and besides, I want to tell him that he was right about a guy with no manners."

Adela sat and listened as J repeated the tale to Mihal, but J didn't win the race when it came down to the wire for Blondie to get the story from the horse's mouth. Adela was ecstatic as she tattle-taled all of the date details to Blondie.

J stood behind the kitchen door and eavesdropped. A large margin of fabrication was nothing new from Adela, but this story heightened her verbal creativity. *I wonder if she'll ever learn to control her forked-tongue embellishments.*

It was only two days ago when J had learned the word embellish from her new friend, Mr. Jones. Already she understood its true meaning.

ONE WEEK WAS ENOUGH

"J, come here," Blondie called.

"My sister's comin' from Florida and she's bringin' her daughter, Sharon. She's gonna need someone to play with, someone to keep her entertained while she's here. You're just about her age, so you can go stay with her for the two weeks she'll be visiting at your grandmother's house in Osceola," Blondie excitedly announced.

"What are they, big shots or something?" J asked nonchalantly, but Blondie perceived her question with a greater sarcasm than J had intended.

"Yeah, for your information, they are. He's a big wheel in the Navy. He's high up on the ladder, that guy. He commands a big warship. That means he's in charge of the whole shittin' caboodle, Miss Smartie Pants," Blondie shot back.

"You should feel honored to be the chosen one. If I were you, I wouldn't look a gift horse in the mouth, Missy," Blondie chastened.

"You're gonna go there and do what the Hell ever they tell you to do. Do you understand me?" Blondie continued her military-type commands dotted with cussing, as usual.

"You're gonna be on your damned best behavior every minute. You'll refer to them as aunt and uncle. You're to call Sharon cousin, and you'll call my parents Grandmother and Grandfather, not Baba and Gido. Those are gypsy names and my parents are not trashy Gypsies. Do you understand what I'm tellin' you?"

"Do you?" Blondie repeated, standing rigidly before the girl.

Blondie's face was flushed and her words were squawking in tune with the colorful caged parrot that one of her New York relatives had deposited in their kitchen several weeks ago.

The only thing missing on Ma is a bunch of tail feathers and then it would be hard to tell her and the parrot apart. J amused herself with that picture circling in her mind.

"If you play your cards right, they might even ask you to go to Florida with them some summer. I know I'd love to escape this damned place sometimes. Maybe I wouldn't come back," Blondie mumbled an admission to the coffee pot, as she poured herself a tall white cup of the dark java.

Accidentally filling the cup to the rim, Blondie swore, "Damn it to Hell. See what you made me do. I filled it too full worryin' about talkin' sense to you. I should know better than to try doin' that."

Two days later, the knock on the front door brought a barefooted Blondie running from the kitchen. Her Polish blue eyes were darting back and forth as she made her way through the dining room before reaching for the front door's knob.

"Marty and her family are here. Where in the Hell are my shoes? Who put them over here?' Blondie was hissing as she tripped on a pair of dirty scuffed house slippers.

"Pick those kids' shoes up and throw them behind the stove. Get those books up off the floor. Straighten out those carpets, then line up and mind your manners," a visibly irritated Blondie ordered the seven kids.

As each child rapidly side-stepped into a military formation, Blondie cautioned, "Remember, children should be seen and not heard," while her glaring eyes re-enforced the message.

It was not necessary for Blondie to relinquish any explanation of her command. These kids had heard this rule countless times before. If a clearer understanding became necessary, it would come as an updated version from the end of a willow switch, but only after the visiting company left the premises.

Stepping into her house shoes to conceal her dirty feet, Blondie instantly transformed into a smiling gushing sister as Marty entered the front door.

"Marty, let me look at my little sis. Oh, how I've missed you," she cried out.

Seven pairs of eyes were watching a spectacle they'd never encountered with Blondie before. "Amazing," J said softly under her breath.

Thank God she didn't hear that, was J's next thought.

After a fast-paced tour of the barnyard, where each animal was dutifully described by its foul odor and its job description, the city folk decidedly had seen, smelled and heard enough information about the good farm life and the fresh country air. They were ready to call it a day at the farm.

"Well, Blondie, it's time for us to get going," Marty said. "We've really had a long driving trip from Florida and we're all exhausted. Which girl is going with us to keep Sharon entertained?"

With a nod of Blondie's head, and a shove to J's back, the visitors made a hasty departure for Grandma and Grandpa's house, taking J and her brown paper bag of clothes with them.

"Good God, Mom," Blondie's sister Marty was emphatically informing her mother, "she didn't even have sense enough to have the girl bathe before coming here. Do you still use that square galvanized tub for bathing? Ted and I will bring it into the laundry room and both girls can bathe. Sharon takes her bath first though. I'm not having my girl sit in that girl's pissy water. Sharon's not used to living without a bathroom, but that one sure is. Here, I'll help you fill the pots with water to heat. Blondie's kid isn't climbing into your clean bed sheets as filthy as she is," Aunt Marty was telling her and Blondie's mother.

J continued to stand frozen in place right outside of the kitchen door frame, at least until she heard footsteps approaching. Jaunting to the far corner of the house, she sat on a creosoted railroad tie that bordered a patch of blooming pink phlox. She knew it wouldn't be long before someone would be calling her to come and bathe, so she patiently waited for the beckoning.

"J, where are you? Come take a bath. Sharon is done already. You girls can have a treat afterward," but Aunt Marty's jovial spirit quickly diminished and turned into a scowl as she watched J's backside walk toward the kitchen door.

"Good God, girl, what is that black stuff all over the seat of your pants? Why on earth did you sit in tar? You don't think you can enter this house with those filthy clothes, do you? You did bring other pants to wear, didn't you?"

This Aunt Marty had the same way of screeching as Blondie. *I sure can tell this woman and Ma are related. I hope the rest of the vacation goes better than this short nightmare,* J thought.

"Your Grandmother has some blueberry muffins and a glass of cold milk waiting for us, so hurry with your bath," the aunt chirped, cleverly feigning a hospitable pleasantness as she waited for J to remove all of her filthy clothes and climb into the make-shift bathtub.

"I'm just going to put these in some hot water to soak. Heaven only knows what kind of germs these garments are breeding," she said, holding the clothing out at arm's length by her thumb and index finger.

The square tub didn't quite accommodate J's fourteen year old gangly body. Sitting Indian style, J managed to wash all of her necessary appendages and to even give her hair a wistful shampoo. Feeling refreshed, she grabbed the threadbare towel and quickly dried off. While slipping into her pajamas, she could overhear the two women in the next room discussing the muffins.

"I'll give the old muffins to Blondie's girl. You, Ted and Sharon can have the fresh ones with me and Frank. Don't let on there's anything wrong with those two cakes, but they're bound to be stale. They're three days old, for crying out loud."

So, the two of them are scheming, J thought pensively.

"Blondie's kids are used to eating whatever is thrown their direction. I don't know what could have happened to Blondie. I can't understand why she's satisfied with such a worthless existence on that rat-trap farm." Marty shook her head back and forth, and then "tsked" several times disgustedly.

"Here J, you sit here. This is your plate of muffins and your glass of milk. Bon appetite," the aunt said cheerfully, guiding J by the shoulder to one of the old wooden chairs at the round kitchen table, which was invitingly covered with a bright-striped tablecloth.

"No thanks. I'm not that hungry. I don't like stale food and I'm not used to it, either," J answered cooly.

J had surprised all of the relatives gathered in the small kitchen. They were gaping at J as she asked, "Which bed am I sleeping in? I'm tired and I'm ready to hit the hay."

"Well, you are sleeping on a quilt," the grandmother replied snidely.

"It's on the floor next to Sharon's bed. She's the company," the grandmother quickly added with a frown. "Sharon, show her which room it's in."

A short while later, Sharon rejoined J in their bedroom and showed her a handful of candy the grandmother had given her. "Here, I'll share these with you. You can have the tootsie rolls and this jelly thing. I don't like those. I like the rest of these chocolates, so I'm keeping these yummy ones for myself."

Despite a hunger headache, J managed a "No thanks, I'm not hungry" again.

Rolling over to hide her face that had become awash with silent tears, J prayed to her long gone Baba.

"Angel of God, my guardian Dear, to whom God's love commits me here. Ever this day, be at my side to light and guard, to rule and guide. Amen."

It was a soothing verse that her Gypsy grandmother had taught her many years ago. After a few deep breaths, feeling physically exhausted and mentally fatigued, she calmly drifted off to sleep.

The rest of the week didn't fare much better. Sharon found ways of ridiculing and belittling J to her parents and to the grandparents.

"She walks like a duck flapping those webbed feet of hers."

"She talks like a country bumpkin. She even says ain't."

Her clothes look as if they were handed down from a beggar's daughter."

"She eats everything with a spoon. Hasn't she learned to use a knife or a fork yet?"

She doesn't speak when she says her prayers. She just moves her mouth.

"If your mouth isn't moving and no one can hear the words, then God can't hear you either. I'll bet you don't even know proper prayers. You probably only know those stupid Catholic ditties anyway, and who wants to hear those. Probably not even God," Sharon said at one evening meal.

J fooled her though. She knew Sharon was just goading her into saying or doing something stupid so that the lot of them could have a good laugh. J just sat there smiling while she finished her meal. When she'd eaten the last morsel off of her plate, she repeated what she'd heard the LeCroix children say after they'd finished eating, "May I be excused, please?"

Without waiting for an answer, she carried her plate to the sink, rinsed it and then went out to the back porch swing where she sat alone until it was dark enough to go to bed. No one looked for her. *Did anyone even miss her,* she wondered.

The next morning, J found herself assigned to weeding a flower bed while Sharon and her parents went for a car ride, destination unknown. Upon their return, Sharon hopped out of their fancy car, and quickly announced, "We had the biggest and creamiest ice cream cones at this cute little general store down the road a ways. It's too bad you had to stay here and help with the weeding. I'm glad I don't know how to weed," she haughtily smirked.

J was given a glass of cold water as a reward for her hard work in the hot morning sun. After a bologna sandwich lunch was eaten, J was handed a book to read and instructed by the grandmother, "You can sit on the porch and read while Sharon and her mother take the horses for a jaunt."

A day later, the uncle attempted a bit of comraderie. "Let's take a trip into town to see a movie."

He tried to smile as he said, "That's what's on tap for the afternoon treat."

"Do you know who Elvis is?" he asked J.

"Of course I know. Everybody knows who he is. Why do you want to know?" she asked.

"Well, his movie, Love Me Tender, is playing at the Osceola theatre this week, so we'll go to the matinee. You girls can share a box of popcorn, can't you?" the stingy man asked the girls.

J didn't answer. She knew the popcorn decision must have already been determined. She had surmised as much from the smart-alecky smirk on Sharon's face when she pronounced to her father, "I get to hold the box, Daddy."

"Come on, let's go upstairs and get dressed up," Sharon told J. "You did bring a dress, didn't you?"

"Well, no. No one said I would need one," J answered defensively.

"I'll bet we can find one small enough to fit you from in that box of old clothes we brought to take to your house," Sharon said, pulling a cardboard box from a bedroom corner, "and I bet I know just which one will do."

"Yep, this is the one. My mom made it for me because I love to eat watermelon slices. That's my very favorite food. She's made me the same dress every summer since I was three years old, can you imagine? Look J, it even has big pockets, so you can put your hands in them and nobody will see your dirty broken fingernails," Sharon said, a cunning grin parting her lips. She extended her hands to evaluate the condition of her pink polished and manicured fingernails, and then lifted J's hands to compare their nails.

"I just think of everything, don't I, Cuz?" Sharon mockingly glared at J's unkempt fingers as she handed the dress to J.

Once again, J refused the cousin's gesture. "No thanks. I'll wear a pair of my own shorts."

J would have liked to tell her what she could do with her *watermelon dress*, but that memory wasn't Sharon's doing. *A pair of shorts will be perfect on this hot day*, she had decided.

J did remember to keep her hands hidden in her pockets. She was now ashamed of the ragged condition of her nails, but there didn't seem to be any offers to help her trim or polish them.

Sharon did rule over the box of popcorn. She held it high in the middle of her chest making it difficult for J to reach across and into the box. When Sharon had eaten most of the fluffy popped corn, she handed J the box with the half-popped kernels at the bottom of the box. They remained uneaten.

J did remember to say "thank you" for her share of the treat. She had so desperately wanted to see the Elvis movie that she was willing to keep still and mind her manners. *I can bite my tongue,* she told herself.

"I think I'm in love," Sharon told her dad after they'd left the theatre. "Elvis is so handsome," she drooled, rolling her eyes upward.

Her dad laughed at her comedic antics, asking, "What about you, J. What did you think of the movie?"

"I liked it. I enjoyed the songs," she replied.

"Smart girl," the uncle responded with a wink.

J's last morning at the grandparent's house was a beautifully sunny and warm morning. It had been decided that they were all going swimming. J didn't have a bathing suit, so Sharon had been instructed to loan J one of hers. Resentfully, she handed J a bathing suit. It was at least three sizes too big for the skinny girl, "Here, you can wear this. It's the only one I don't like. You can keep it, because I won't wear it once it's been on your stinky body."

Once again, J responded, "No thanks."

"I don't enjoy swimming, so I won't need your big ugly swimsuit."

"Mommy," Sharon was screaming, "she won't get dressed to go swimming. I'll bet she doesn't know how to swim. I think we should throw her in and let her swim or drown," Sharon called down to her mother.

Without hesitation, J took her cue. *That's the last straw.* She grabbed her few meager clothes, jammed them into the brown bag that she had arrived with, and headed down the stairs. She didn't say a word to anyone until she reached the rail station a short distance from her grandparents house. There she asked the train master, who she knew as Mihal's friend, "Would it be okay if I hop the next train to the Brookwood Mine, Mr. Henshaw? I've been visiting with a cousin at my grandparents for a week, but I've had all I can stomach of this vacation. It's a real pain in the ass entertaining a city slicker brat. If I'm gonna be in the entertainment business, I want paid. And this bunch ain't payin'!"

The next day, Marty, Ted and Sharon arrived at #11 Lemon Lane to say good bye to Blondie's family. *They were here for fifteen minutes the day they arrived and they were here for twenty minutes the day they're leaving,* Blondie thought. *Are they acting like they're too good to visit with us. Are they pulling the big shot act here? And weren't they supposed to stay for two weeks?* Blondie posed the question to her memory. Her memory quickly gave her the answers. "Yes, yes and yes."

None of them voiced any concern regarding J's disappearance from the grandparent's home yesterday. J knew why. She knew that they really didn't give a hoot about her or where she'd gone. They only had room in their hearts for their Sharon. That was as plain to see as the noses on their faces.

Well, I don't care what they think of me, she thought. *I'm not the idiot they thought I was, so there!*

Ted carried in the large cardboard carton labeled OLD CLOTHES FOR BLONDIE'S POOR KIDS, and a gallon of Neapolitan ice cream. *They act like they just brought us a box of gold,* Mihal thought. *What gives, do they think we've never eaten ice cream before?*

Sharon's face grew pale as she watched J give her own share of the treat to the gray barn cat. "Why did you give that good ice cream to a cat?" Sharon asked as she displayed a wrinkled and horrified look on her face.

J smiled watching the cat lick the plate bone-clean. "I'll have fresh ice cream some other time. We make our own, you know. Besides, this looked stale," J said. J had decided that it was time to take advantage of the opportunity to mock the city girl.

"Maybe you could spend a week entertaining me in Florida next summer, J. I live on a beach. You could play in the sand, instead of in the manure." Sharon's condescending tone rallied to deliver her retaliatory insult which was a lot quicker than sending a seashore postcard.

"No thanks, *Cuz*. I've quit the entertainment business," J responded with her own quick and concise response to the impudent snotty relative. "You don't pay enough."

The residents of #11 Lemon Lane stood waving as the city relatives made a quick get away. Their speeding car kicked up the dryness of Lemon Lane as they quickly drove through the dust. Neither Blondie nor Mihal reprimanded J for her insulting remarks to her cousin. Silently, they concurred with their daughter's opinion for a change.

GOOD DEEDS

"What do you have there, Mihal?" Blondie inquired as her husband pulled out a rectangular grey metal box from the trunk of his car. The box was held closed with a padlock, which only Mihal could open with a small silver key.

"It's a box, Blondie. What does it look like to you, a bouncin' ball?" Mihal's shoulders bobbed as he laughed at his own joke.

"Don't you get wise-assed with me or I'll show you two bouncin' balls," Blondie smart-mouthed right back at him.

"Are you gonna tell me or not?" she asked.

"I got your curiosity up, didn't I?" he said teasingly.

"Well, Blondie, it's somethin' I've been hoardin' for the past few years. I've been savin' a few dollars out of every paycheck and puttin' those crisp green bills into this box. When I'd get enough together, I'd buy up a piece of property around here." He paused, wondering if he should come clean with his secret.

Making a hasty decision, he decided that the best thing to do was to just fess up. If he didn't, Blondie would only snoop until she learned all there was to find out. *Here goes,* Mihal said to himself.

"This box holds deeds to over two hundred or more acres of land that surround our house. I think there's coal under all of these fields. That's just a hunch, mind you, but I have a nose for sniffin' out coal. You know I do. You know coal minin's in my blood. This land is our future. Yep, this land will be our nest egg, Blondie. Now, what do you think of that?"

The brawny man sitting at the kitchen table leaned his chair back and smiled proudly at his vigilant family standing before him. He took a deep breath and inhaled the aroma of fresh bread baking in their outdated kitchen coal stove. Keeping up with the neighbors had never been one of Mihal's strong suits. The coal stove worked just fine, and besides, everything baked in a coal oven was as good as baked goods ever got. Any fool and every baker knew that!

"What do you mean, what do I think of that?" Blondie asked, mimicking his inflection.

Hesitantly, she formed a slow answer. "I don't know what to make of that," she said flatly.

"Let me look at those deeds. Whose property did you buy up, anyway? And, how much did all of this cost?" As usual, Blondie showed no patience and wanted her questions answered yesterday.

"I'll be honest with you, Blondie. I waited till the taxes were overdue on the parcels. Tom Martin would let me know when they went into the bank's foreclosure file, and then I'd pluck them up dirt cheap. A couple of these fields were steals," he stated so excitedly that his voice crackled as though he were entering puberty again.

Mihal turned to the wide-eyed kids gathered around the kitchen table and announced, "Kids, all of the fields you can see around our house now belong to us." He made the announcement as he gestured in a circular wave with his outstretched arm.

He elaborated, "If you want to play in the Logan field, that's ours, and so is Simmons' big field. We own the Terrance acreage, along with the Kitchner piece way back there in the woods. That big piece of land next to Lazlos' is my favorite though. Having all this land is the same as having money in the bank, Blondie. Can't you see how good that will be for us, especially if there's coal under the top few layers of soil," his fluid voice was pleading for his petulant wife's understanding.

Mihal's face was glowing. The more he elaborated, the brighter his eyes beamed and the more animated his words became.

"I'm just gonna sit on this land, pay the taxes and hold on tight. One of these days, I'll have enough saved to get it spot tested, and then we'll know exactly what we have in our back pockets," he said, flailing his arms excitably as though he were in the hay field free-swinging his scythe.

Blondie had stood cross-armed near the sink. She was inhaling every word Mihal had verbalized. "You mean to tell me while I've been scrimpin' and savin', you've been spendin' all our extra money? When I've been doin' without, you had money to throw away to the God damned tax collector?" she twittered.

"It's not thrown away. Didn't you hear me? It's our savin's account. Take a look at yourself in the mirror, Blondie. Anybody can see, you ain't starvin'," Mihal snapped at his wife whom he viewed as a plump pigeon at that very moment.

"Well, I may not be starvin', but I am doin' without. What's wrong with me wantin' to have some free spendin' money for myself? Other women get it from their husbands, why should I be any different?"

Blondie tried capitalizing on the situation. She wasn't about to give in so easily. "What kind of a damned idiot do you take me for, Mihal? What's in all of this for me, huh?"

"I'll tell you what's in it for you, a lot of money someday. It takes money to get coal out of the ground, so we'll have to be patient and wait for some coal company's offer to buy the land from us. Then, and only then, will we be rollin' in the dough. Do you think you can quit your whinin' and accept my decision? I knew I shouldn't have told you about this. I could feel it in my bones that tellin' you anything was a mistake," he said, lowering his head into his opened calloused hands.

Within seconds, he lifted his head and stared straight at Blondie's agitated eyes.

"I thought you'd be happy about this good news, but no, not you. You just have to turn it around to be somethin' against you. When in the Hell are you gonna learn to be a dependable wife?" A fuming Mihal bellowed, and then slapped the table with his open palm. The sharp noise caused a gaggle of mesmerized kids to be startled out of their stupor state.

Little Marsha ran a bee-line straight to J. Her tiny body was trembling. She was desperately in need of some comforting. Wrapping her petite arms around J's thigh, she wiped the tears rolling down her soft pink cheeks onto J's denim pant leg. Copying Marsha's antics as usual, one year old Annamaria waddled along behind Marsha, and swiftly attached herself to J's other calf.

Giggling at the two little clinging monkeys, J sat down on the floor and allowed the toddler girls to climb onto her lap. Mihal stared intently through glazed eyes at the scene sitting on the dirty rag-rug covered kitchen floor.

"Look at those kids, Blondie. Those are our kids and they deserve a chance at life. If this is the opportunity that God has given us, then we're gonna sit on these deeds and wait for the right time to make somethin' out of all this land I've been buyin' up. God damn it, Blondie, we're not gonna starve. I won't let that happen and you know it."

"So that's what you think, is it Mihal?" Blondie shrieked.

"Between now and then, what are we gonna do? Will you just pay the damn taxes when they come due and let the land just set there like a bunch of mountain boulders? Is that your plan? You want to just throw good money after bad to that rich asshole who calls himself a tax collector? Everybody else did that and you can see where it got every one of them. Nowhere, that's where!" she yelled across the room at him.

Her angry Polish face was beginning to flush. *One more shade of pink and she'd resemble a ripe plum,* Mihal considered with a disdained look on his face and a frown on his forehead.

"You and your pipe dreams, that's what worries me," she persisted. "You've talked big schemes before, but none of them bring a pan of gold or a pot of soup to our wobbly dinner table. You haven't heard the last of this, Mihal, not by a long shot."

And that wouldn't be the last time Mihal would hear about his stash of land. Every time Blondie was short of cash, she'd rehash her tax collector's fears.

"What do you want me to pay the bills with? Do you think the tax man will settle for a shovelful of your precious dirt?" she'd fling a resentment-filled question at Mihal.

Mihal had noted a change in his wife's demeanor lately. *Blondie doesn't always have the answers to her own questions these days. I wonder why that is? Maybe that's what they call the change of life. If that's what the big change is, then I'm one grateful man.*

He'd nod his head and chuckle before antagonistically flinging his earthy answer right back at her. "Yeah, Blondie, that will definitely do it." He had graciously learned to ignore her insolence even though he knew it only irked her all the more.

The warm sunny day would eventually arrive when Mihal would be given an offer for the coal veins under his deeded earth.

"I told you it would happen one day, Blondie" Mihal sarcastically stung his doubting wife.

It's been a long time comin'. I just hope it will be worth it, he thought.

Standing to clearly view the fields and meadows that bordered #11 Lemon Lane, he remembered each sale as it happened. *I knew it would pay off one day for our future and I was right. Thank you God,* he solemnly prayed in his heart.

"Oh Lord, how I love this place," he uttered to himself as he forced his gaze to seek solitude in his land and his decision to disrupt its beauty. His soulful grey eyes visualized heavenly reverence in the tree covered hills and the colorful flowering meadows that surrounded his home.

"This land will soon be stripped of all its beauty, Blondie," he thoughtfully commented.

Raising his hand above his brow to shade the sun from his eyes, he looked out upon their properties. His heart winced at his reflections of the many years spent as a son, husband, father and friend on this land. He realized that once those dozers came onto this property the scenery would be bullied into a memory. Mihal would wonder and second guess his decision at that precise moment. *Are those measly dollars finally gonna make Blondie happy,* he'd pondered after the coal company's contract was signed.

Mihal knew Blondie would finally smile and allow a youthful glow to dance across her aging face. Money had a way of doing that for her. That was the obligatory price Mihal was willing to pay for both of their sins. He was resigned to accept his unwavering decision. The resolution was long overdue anyway.

A PRIESTLY VISIT

Many events shape the character of a maturing child.

Many people influence a child's moral values.

People and events effectively secured a satirical environmental edge for the children at #11 Lemon Lane.

J was no exception. At a very early age, she learned to recoil quietly and quickly to observe and remember.

Much dust had been kicked up on the drought ridden macadam road one early Monday morning in June, but Lemon Lane's dust wouldn't settle again until early evening that particular day.

Blondie watched with trepidation as her man stepped from Big John's auto and ambled toward her. "What are you doin' home so early, Mihal?" she asked.

Blondie was searching the wayward look on Mihal's face while waiting for a response. "You weren't due for another three weeks. What's goin' on?"

"The plant's on strike. Nobody's sayin' how long we'll be out, but we were told to go home and not count on workin' at Tonawanda this summer. Some of the guys were told it's a three month contract negotiation period. The old timers say this isn't anything new. This goes on every couple of years. They told me and Big John to go home, sign up every week and enjoy our summer. There's nothin' I can do about the situation, so here I am," was Mihal's explanation to his non-negotiating wife.

"Well, what do you plan on doin' with yourself all summer?" she huffed.

"I certainly hope you don't plan on just sittin' around all day, cause that's not gonna fly with me. There's too much work to do on this farm and there's no reason you can't pitch in," Blondie forewarned him.

"Yeah, Blondie, I'm well aware of all the work that needs done around here. I don't need you to remind me that you're not about to do it all by yourself. You've never done it alone. You've always had help from me, my

Ma and my Pa when they were alive, and all of our kids. I'm not blind. I see what takes place around here," Mihal hesitated before adding, "in more ways than you know."

"Anyway," Mihal continued, attempting to detour her concerns, "the Brookwood coal mine has reopened and I plan on gettin' a job there this summer. From what I hear, they're only hirin' a few fellas. It's not a big mine, remember? Besides, I gotta keep my minin' skills sharp. You never know when they're gonna come in handy again," Mihal reminded his wife while watching her face and waiting for another dramatically gratuitous response.

"Well, if you're goin' back to the mine just who in the Hell is gonna help me around here? Are you countin' on the Father, the Son and the Holy Ghost?" Blondie reacted with defiance as only Blondie could do.

"No," Mihal laughingly countered, "only the Father and the Son. I never did get to see the Holy Ghost!"

"What kind of a wise crack is that, Mihal?" Blondie asked with a puzzled eye roll. "I'm worried about gettin' work done around here and you're makin' jokes."

"I'll tell you what Blondie, you let me worry about the farm work. I can do the work of two men, and keep you happy, too. That is, if I wanted to, but I don't think I want to go that far," Mihal said daringly. He picked up his well-traveled leather satchel and headed into the kitchen through the weather-beaten screened door.

"It's a hot day. You wouldn't have anything cold to drink would you?" he called out, looking back over his shoulder.

Waiting for some smart-assed retort from Blondie, he winked at the smiling and welcoming cluster of kids now following him into the kitchen.

Oh, I got something cold for you to drink alright. Let me mix it with a little arsenic Blondie's hard heart was reverberating to her head, but she answered Mihal calmly instead.

"Yeah, there's lemonade in the fridge. Get it yourself. I'm not waitin' on you hand and foot this summer the way your fancy-pants waitresses did in Buffalo. I heard enough about them last winter from Big Annie."

Blondie, you do have a way of challenging a good man's soul, Mihal thought as he headed toward the noisy old Philco refrigerator.

His beckoning, "Come on kids, let's all go get somethin' cold to drink," was met with a stampede of sure-footed future farmers, all ready to quench their thirst on this hot June day.

After pouring lemonade into several small glass jelly jars for the young ones gathered around him, Mihal poured himself a tall cold glass of the same pale tangy drink from the pitcher found in the fridge. He found the lemonade just where Blondie said it would be. Mihal decided he was thirsty enough to drink a gallon of the thirst quenching citrus drink. "Damn, this stuff is tasty. What do you kids think?" he asked.

The silent answer was right before him as he refilled jelly-jar after jelly-jar at the end of each extended child's thirsty arm. After chugging down one glassful, Mihal began pouring a second for himself, when he just happened to glance out of the kitchen window. His timing was perfect to catch a glimpse of a long black car speeding toward #11 Lemon Lane.

"What the Hell? Who would be crazy enough to come racin' up this dry dusty road? Don't they know there's a bunch of kids playin' out there?" Mihal asked as he watched the car come to an impacting halt at their front gate.

Hopping out of the car, and almost stepping on two little kittens sleeping on the grass near the gate, the priest from Ramey came bounding up the front porch steps. Knocking on the old wooden door, he announced his arrival in a booming voice.

"Hey, is there anybody in there? It's Father Joe. Blondie? Mihal?"

Before anyone responded to his knocking or his yelling, he walked straight into the house, promptly encountering Mihal in the kitchen.

"Well, Father, what brings you to our house this hot afternoon?" asked Mihal.

"Can I get you a glass of cold lemonade?"

"Lemonade?" an angry priest asked the one word question in a radical tone.

"That's what I said, lemonade," answered a surprisingly agitated Mihal.

"Do you want a glass or not? It's a simple question, requiring a simple answer. Think you can handle that?" Mihal asked.

While evil-eyeing the priest, Mihal sat down on a kitchen chair near the dining table.

Hospitably pointing to another chair, Mihal sparingly asked, "Seat, or not?"

"Let's say not times two," was the priest's annoying answer.

Shaking his head *no,* the mouth of this flabby-jowled, red-faced priest began to speak loudly in reaction to Mihal's attitude.

"You have money for lemons to make lemonade, but your kids turned in seven envelopes, five pennies in each, to the church's collection basket yesterday. What in the Hell kind of contribution do you call that? I'm trying to build a new church for this community and you contribute thirty five cents. All of the other church members signed a pledge for a thousand dollars. Everybody, do you hear me, everybody but you and Blondie. Every one is sacrificing, but are you? It doesn't appear that way. Is this a new table and chairs. They're pretty fancy. Shining chrome and red naughahyde, that makes them pretty spiffy. Where did you get the money for these?" he shouted at Mihal.

Just as Mihal began to rise from the kitchen chair, the irate priest threw the seven envelopes at him. Pennies flew across Mihal's chest and rolled around on the linoleum floor's surface.

The group of disheveled kids observing from the kitchen doorway reacted with the recoiling common sense to stay outside on the porch, and away from the massive storming man dressed in a black suit. They quickly noted the bulging of the priest's eyes and the swollen neck veins under his priestly collar. They had seen this preacher man raise his voice while delivering a sermon on the church alter, but this scene of hostility was something different. This ensuing argument was becoming down right frightening.

"Where I get the money for anything in my house is my business." Mihal stood, thinking *if he can dish it out, he can take it.*

"As for sacrificing for a new church, we don't need something big and fancy in this community. The original church was on a rock under God's open sky, wasn't it? The little white church we've been using for thirty years is just fine for these people around here."

Mihal realized he was strangely defying this man of the cloth. *Well, Mihal, this is a new experience for you,* he thought. He didn't even fear the Lord at this moment. *Where did you get the courage to speak your mind, to a priest no less? Well, boy don't quit now. It's about time this hypocrite gets a tongue lashin' and knows that someone around here isn't afraid to speak up to him and his high and mighty ideas.*

Not about to relinquish the controlling level he had achieved, Mihal persisted in presenting his case. "Do you really think you're goin' to Heaven just because you're takin' these hard workin' people's money and squanderin' it on some buildin' to make an impression on some big-wig Pope somewhere? Do you think that Pope cares about you or me? Where were you, or your Pope for that matter, when me and my family were eatin' potatoes five days a week? We didn't see you bringin' us an Easter basket of food like the one you took to some family who lives fifty miles away from here. Yeah, I saw that picture in the Gazette. Nice picture of you and some family that don't even belong to your parish. What was the title of your sermon in that story? Could it have been Publicity for Father Joe or for the Pope?"

Mihal had just begun to give this priest a mouthful of more than boiled potatoes.

"As for that pledge, you can shove it up your ass. I'm not starving my kids to fill your coffers. I earn my paycheck with hard labor. How do you earn yours? I see you drive a big new fancy car. You don't hear me askin' you how you could afford that, do you."

Mihal knew he was on a roll and he was not about to cease. Not at this moment, anyway.

"You don't look like you're starving. You and your housekeeper both look like you eat pretty good. A lot of people around here have noticed you're both getting to be a little on the stout side lately. By the way, how was your housekeeper's trip to that special doctor in New York City? Didn't think anyone knew about that, did you?"

The observant kids noticed that Mihal's verbal attack had certainly caused the priest's neck veins to start jumping faster and to set his feet in motion making him move closer to the front door.

"What do you think you know about me and my housekeeper?" asked the irritated priest. "Who told you to stick your nose where it don't belong?"

"I came here to return your thirty five cents. I don't want your ingrate money. I've treated your family just the way I treat everyone else in the congregation," the highly insulted God-Almighty man was shouting. "It's not my fault you and Blondie have so many kids. I didn't help create them. That wasn't my doing. It was all yours and Blondie's fornicating that done that."

Who was this guy to be ridiculing or criticizing our beautiful creations, Mihal wondered. *Who gave him that right?*

"If it wasn't for you and your lame-brained church rules, we could have used some sort of prophylaxis. Do you even know what that word means? I doubt it. You don't know nothin' about being married and havin' or not havin' a family, yet here you are tryin' to act like an experienced husband. Talk about somebody being dumb," Mihal was opining as Blondie entered the kitchen, allowing the warped screen door to bang shut and announce that she'd just arrived.

"What's goin' on here," Blondie interrupted. She had come through the doorway carrying a basket of folded laundry fresh from the clothes line.

"What are you doin' here, Father, and what is all this hollerin'? I can hear the both of you all the way down to the pond. It seems your nosey kids got a front row seat to a real show right out here on the porch, Mihal."

"So, what's all this commotion about?" she reiterated.

"It's about the five pennies you put in the kids collection envelopes yesterday," Mihal said.

"Your priest came here to throw it back in your face! He says we can keep the thirty five cents for ourselves. He would rather have a thousand dollars. He came to get a signed pledge for a new church. What do you have to say about that, Blondie?"

Mihal spoke to his conniving wife, who was putting on a show of her own by acting the part of a properly mannered wife and mother for the priest's benefit. "You didn't promise that I'd sign the damn thing, did you?"

"Well, I didn't promise, but I told him I'd ask you to think about it," Blondie answered, while waving her open right hand and indicating the possibility to the priest.

"He said he could wait for a few weeks until you came home for the weekend and I could talk to you," she said, now gesturing with that same hand toward Mihal.

"Well, surprise, surprise! Look, I'm home for the summer. The plant's on strike, so I'm goin' back to the mines," Mihal informed the priest, who was now standing near the front door and holding onto the door handle.

It was rather apparent their visitor was prepared for a quick get away if the conversation became any more heated. "Blondie, you half promised that thousand. You told me how much money Mihal was making in the factory. We're rollin' in the dough," you bragged.

"You even gave me two hundred dollars down payment on the pledge. Why did you do that if you weren't sure?" the annoyed priest asked.

"You did what, Blondie? I didn't give you permission to do that," an irate Mihal stood looking directly into his wife's eyes.

Turning to the priest, Mihal advanced forward until he was face to face with this questionably holy man.

"Didn't you just hear me say the plant is on strike and I'm gonna have to go back to work in the mines. You will give me back that money by the end of today. It's my money and I'm gonna need it to feed and clothe my brood this summer. Blondie had no business givin' that much money to you."

Distrusting his angered state, Mihal kept his hands tucked inside his front pants pockets as he continued his verbal barrage.

"You're the one who's low down and ignorant. You're stealin' from the poor. I don't think this is what the Good Lord intended when he started a church. I can't believe a true follower of Christ would take food out of a hungry child's mouth just to build an unnecessary building," Mihal concluded.

"Well, you better believe it. I've made a commitment to God and to the Pope. This is a shrine I'm creating, not a building. This will be a blessed tabernacle to house religious artifacts," the priest bellowed. His voice boomed in the sacristy of this lowly house. His singed words were loud enough to scare the hidden devil out of the wainscoting.

"This church will serve generations to come, not just you scum who are living and breathing now. Think about the future, for Christ's sake," the priest continued.

Every word coming out of his heated mouth was steaming with spittle. His hanging jowls bobbled up and down and around as he yelled, causing the observing brood to giggle at the priest's facial gyrations.

"Your kids are no better than the other kids in this town. Everybody needs to sacrifice, even the young. They should learn to appreciate what this good cause will come to mean to them later in their lives. Your two hundred dollars has already been sent to the Bishop, so I can't give it back. You want it bad enough, you ask the Bishop. I am not stealing your money, I'm putting it back for the Great One who allowed you to earn it," Father Joe said in a coarse demonic sounding voice.

The priest's inflecting tone began frightening the youngsters, who were standing frozen in place on the back porch. They had listened and monitored this harsh and cruel exchange of verbiage from its inception and were now wishing it would quickly cease.

"If you want your family to belong to my church, you'll keep your mouth shut and leave the money where it is," a loud threatening response exuded from the paunch-bellied priest's mouth.

"So far, I've let your kids take part in all the sacraments, but that could change in a moments notice. Is that what you want for your kids, to be ostracized in the community?"

"Don't you come into my home tryin' to intimidate me, you jack ass," Mihal defied him.

Having a fairly even temperament, Mihal didn't easily become enraged. It took a definite insult to rile his temper, but Mihal was certainly provoked at this point.

"You're no holier than that dog runnin' around out there," Mihal said, pointing out the window to old Jingleberry chasing a loose hen around the leaning chicken coop.

"Do you think we're so illiterate that we're gonna sit on our asses and take these threats from you? What do you think your Bishop is gonna say about all of this?" Mihal asked brazenly.

"Now, Mihal, you don't want to start nothin' with the Bishop. They'll think you're crazy or somethin'. Let him keep the two hundred and we'll call it even," Blondie suggested in a plebeian tone.

"Call it even? What the Hell is wrong with you, woman? That money is coming back to my pocket. You had no business startin' this. Can't you see what a heathen he is? What were you thinkin'?" Mihal vehemently asked Blondie.

"This will be so embarrassin' to me, can't you see that? Everybody in this town will despise me if they find out about any of this. Father, just leave and I'll straighten this out. You'll get your money," Blondie coyly directed her statements to the priest in an attempt to smooth over the disagreement.

"Oh, he'll go alright, Blondie, but he's not getting' any more of my money. I just may send you packin' with him. Maybe you can be his new playmate. What do you think your Bishop is gonna think when he checks out your bookkeepin' records for your housekeeper's New York trip? I have a feelin' he's gonna be mighty interested in what I have to tell him about your shenanigans and your clever bamboozlin' to extort money from the women in these towns. We're not all as stupid as you'd like to think we are," Mihal indignantly informed this red-faced, toe-tapping man.

Shocked at Mihal's verbal accusations, the perspiring defeated priest proceeded with a hasty exit. Slamming the front door, the furious man reached his car with just a few long strides.

Mihal followed the black-suit to its parked car. "Don't forget my money. It's to be here this evenin'. I mean every word I've said, and don't think for one second that me or my family can't attend your church. This is America. Freedom of religion, remember!" Mihal shouted at the priest driving his long shiny black car at record speed down the dusty road.

Clouds of dust muffled Mihal's last and loudest shout, "Oh, by the way, the lemons were free. They came in the mail from Blondie's sister in Florida."

The next morning, Mihal found two one hundred dollar bills in a plain unsigned white envelope stuck in the front door jam.

Mihal sniggered, "Well, looky here, Blondie. It musta' been the tooth fairy paid us a visit sometime durin' the night."

SO, YOU WANT A JOB!

"J, where's your Ma?" Mihal asked his teen-aged daughter.

Busy ironing her second basket of damp, tightly rolled bundles of clothing, J was deep in thought and almost didn't hear Mihal's question.

I have calluses on my right palm from doing so much ironing, If I didn't know better, I'd think I'd been working in the coal mines these past fifteen years, J crisply thought as she pushed the hot iron back and forth on the jean's pant leg pressing a perfectly straight crease. She had paid only half attention to her father's question. Her mind was on the task at hand and how unmeaningful the repetitious chore had become.

As a blossoming teenager, J was beginning to appreciate her own thoughts, and her long tedious hours of ironing basket loads of dampened balls of clothing. *If I was working in the coal mine, I'd at least be getting paid. Free labor, that's what Mr. Jones called it.*

"I think she went down to the barn. The brown cow, Dolly, is sick or something," she answered her father.

"Naw, she's not sick. She's about ready to deliver that calf of hers," Mihal explained.

"Go tell your Ma I'm goin' down to the Brookwood mines to ask for a job. I should be back in a little while."

"Can I go with you? I'd like to get a job there, too. I'll work hard, I promise." J had set the hot iron down onto its heel and began pleading with her dad. "You know I'm not afraid to work. I do a lot around here. You know I do."

"Why would you want to work in a coal mine, Joni?" Mihal asked, chuckling as he scratched his head under the band of his pin-striped railroader's cap.

I know she's a hard worker and she don't complain none about anything she's told to do. She's been made to work harder than any of the other girls before her.

It might be good for her to get a payin' job, but in the mine, Mihal paused. His thoughts deliberated, *I'm just not so sure about this idea of hers is a good one.*

"I want to earn some money for some store bought clothes. I'm going to be a junior in high school and I want to dress in nice clothes like the other girls. I'm ashamed and tired of wearing everybody else's used clothing and shoes. Nothing seems to fit. Ma said the only way I'm getting new clothes is if I earn my own money, so that's what I want to do," she politely answered.

Mihal could see a bucket of tears forming in the wells of her eyes.

"Well, kid, run and tell your Ma where we'll be for the next hour or so. I'm pretty sure I'll be gettin' a job, but I'm not so certain about you," Mihal cautioned his young daughter, "but let's go talk to the Boss Man. Now, I don't want you to be disappointed if he says *no*, okay?"

Blondie couldn't believe her ears when J talked of her plans to ask for a job in the coal mines working along side of her Dad. *What in the Hell does this idiot think she's doin'* Blondie wondered. *She can't be serious, but why is Mihal encouragin' such an idea? Oh, for Christ's sake! It's always somethin' around this damned house.*

"Mihal, what do you think you're doin'? You know they won't give her a job in the mine. It's bad luck for a woman to go into the mine," Blondie said defiantly.

As she sat down on the back porch stoop, Blondie acquiesced, "Oh, shit, there's no tellin' you or her anything. Why am I tryin' to talk any sense to either of you? You're both as stubborn as mules and as deaf as statues, so go already. Get it over with and hurry back to help me with this cow's birthin'. I'm gonna need help, especially if any problems pop up with the calf. God, I'm tired already and I haven't even made dinner yet."

"Oh, and Missy, you're gonna finish that ironin' when you get back. That's one job you're not gettin' out of," Blondie shrilled as an after thought.

Refusing to drive any faster than thirty five miles an hour, Mihal headed toward the Brookwood Mine hoping to land a summer job. J could tell he was feeling rather confident.

Why wouldn't he be sure of getting a job? These miner's are all old buddies of his, J surmised as she stared out of the car's window. Knowing that, she reasoned *maybe they'll feel sorry for me or maybe they'll give me a job just to pay back a favor to Dad for saving their lives way back when.*

Sitting quietly as she rode alongside Mihal, J watched for the sign that read Brookwood Coal Company. Finding the sign would indicate the correct curved macadam road that led off the main highway toward the coal works.

"Okay, Joni, this is what you do when we get to the minin' shack. You wait until I ask for a job and you wait until Tom tells me I'm hired. Then you can ask him if he has ever hired a woman to work in the tunnels. I'm sure he'll say he hasn't. Tell him it's about time that he did and that you're just the person who's ready to take it on. Tell him you'll work hard, right along side of your Old Daddy," Mihal advised the young girl.

"He already knows I'm a safe miner and he owes me a couple of favors, so we'll just have to wait for his answer. You got all that?" Mihal asked the eager young lady sitting beside him.

"Yep, I'm ready," J said. That was it. That's all she said to her anxious father. "Yep, I'm ready."

You wouldn't believe how very ready I am to get a job and earn my own spending money, J thought, as she gazed heavenward watching the big blue open sky with its huge suspended mallow-white clouds. *I'd better take a good long look up there, 'cause if I get a job down under, it'll be a whole summer gone before I can stare at the sky again.*

As a youngster, J had sold Wolverine salve and greeting cards door to door, but Blondie handled the finances with both of those money making attempts. J learned that she was a persuasive salesman. She had even heard Blondie boasting about how persuasive of a salesman her girl was. "She sold a box of sympathy cards to a ninety eight year old woman, an aging woman who didn't have a single living relative left," Blondie repeated to her lady friends.

J recalled how uproarious Blondie's laughter became when she detailed that sale to their neighbors. J didn't reap the rewards of her money making ventures, but Blondie sure did.

This day, however, in J's brain the unearned dollars were already spent on some new shoes. J didn't know it yet, but those were merely a dream that would not be realized. *I can hardly wait for my first pay day. I wonder how much I'll be getting,* she asked her itching palms.

"So, you want a job, do you? You're asking to work in a tunnel mine alongside your Pappy. Is that what you're actually asking, girlie?" this hugely rotund Boss was asking J as he desperately chomped up and down on an unlit fat brown cigar.

"Do you know how hard this type of work is? Do you realize how dirty of a job this will be? You'll be going home dressed in coal dust, did you think about that? Are you willing to put up with all that plus the ribbing from the other miners?" This Boss Man wasn't timid as he drilled his questions to the young girl before him.

He asked the questions openly as he extended his chest forward and allowed his chubby thumbs to tug his cherry red suspenders outward. *The Boss sure is equipped with a bunch of questions,* J perceived, but she was prepared for his rash of queries.

"I know about the work and how dirty I'll get. I've seen my Daddy come home from the mines looking like a black man and as tired as an old coon dog after a duck hunt. I want a job to earn some money this summer and this is the only way I can see to do that. Besides, you've never hired a woman in the mine, so how would you know if one can do the work or not," J challenged this coal mogul.

Oh, yeah, he's the Boss Man alright. Who else could work all day in this shack dressed in a suit and tie. He must be blind though, 'cause his dusty clothes sure could use a good wash and press, she silently observed.

"Let me try doing the work. I'll bet I'll surprise you, won't I, Dad?"

J had turned to her Dad for his approval. Mihal did not disappoint her. He tipped his head and nodded a firm affirmative.

"Okay, then. You show up tomorrow morning at six, Missy, and we'll put you to the test, but Mihal, she had better know what she's gettin' herself in for," the fat man suggested.

Writing J's name right below Mihal's on the curled and yellow edged employee roster, the round bellied Boss Man had assured her of a job. "It's a tough life in there. I'll bet Mihal will be mighty proud of you if you can cut the mustard. Am I right, Mihal?" he asked.

Mihal watched and heard in amazement. *Maybe I need a hearin' aide. Did I just hear him give Joni a job in the tunnel?*

His girl had asked for something very difficult and unheard of, but she had won the confidence of the man doing the hiring. "Well Hell's bells, Joni, this calls for a celebration," Mihal exclaimed.

Mihal was elated and the only way he could think of to express his admiration was with a request to his maturing girl. Smiling a rarely exposed happiness, Mihal bent and whispered to J, "Holy smoke, kid, you did it! Let's go get us a bottle of Coca Cola over at Andrew's. I think we should celebrate. You landed your very first job out in this big cruel world. Come on, what do you say?"

Mihal trailed behind J, but as he turned to step out of the shack the Boss Man tugged at Mihal's sleeve, halting his gait through the doorway. "I say she lasts about four hours, Mihal. If she walks out, I'll drive her home for you, okay?"

"I wouldn't count on that, Tom. She works all day long. She may not look it, but she's as strong as an ox. She's no slacker, you'll see. You'll more than likely hear J's singin' comin' out of the mine's mouth quicker than you'll hear her mouth singin' about quittin'." An elated Mihal cajoled with his old friend as the two men shook hands to seal the transaction.

"I have a feeling she's gonna surprise the both of us," Mihal winked as he summed up J's attitude to their summer boss.

Mihal's other summer boss was waiting at the front gate when he and J pulled up in their dark green, '39 grease-pack Chevy. This car, affectionately referred to as Bessie, was Mihal's one extravagance. He was comfortable with this car and knew every inch of its body and soul. He knew where every belt, gear or piston was, why it was there and how it worked. He dreaded the day when he knew the car would die for the last time. Breakdowns were happening more frequently recently and the parts were becoming too expensive to replace.

Mihal was more aware of the pending doom than he dared to mention to anyone, especially to Blondie. *I sure am dreadin' the day I have to announce to Blondie that I have to buy a new car. I can just imagine the noise that blue eyed tiger's gonna make on that mornin'. I'd better keep savin' my pennies so as I don't have to enter Blondie's cage for the down payment*, Mihal would think every time he had to tinker with Bessie.

Pensively leaning on the gate post, Blondie stood as stoic as a mature tree trunk while waiting to greet Mihal and J. "Where in the Hell have you two been? It's been two hours since you left. I cooked dinner, fed half a dozen kids and helped Dolly deliver her calf. What have you two gotten accomplished?"

"Well, me and our Joni went job huntin' and we both got hired on at Brookwood. What do you think of that? We start at six tomorrow mornin'," Mihal proudly announced to a joyous cluster of wide eyed piss ant kids and an astonished Blondie, who purposly leaned more forward on the post. Her drooping jaw didn't move for a second, but her eyes spoke volumes.

"So who's gonna be helping me around here all day? You both better know you'll still be workin' here everyday after you get home. There's gonna be the evenin's to catch up on the barn work and the gardenin'," Blondie said with a true tone of indignation.

"I figured as much. You never let up, do you? If the girl comes home tired, she should be able to get some rest. Do you understand?" Mihal pummeled, but then thought better of his statement and reiterated in an unapologetic tone. "She will get some rest everyday when she gets home, period."

With a sardonic glance toward Blondie, Mihal turned and walked away.

J looked on, delighted at the show of Mihal's inner strength when dealing with Blondie lately. J realized she was smiling in amusement as Mihal swaggered down the path. Mihal was already nearing the old barn where he'd welcome the new calf.

Ma didn't say if it was a boy or a girl. It had to be a boy, 'cause she sure was happy about it. J's memory had been jogged. There was no getting around Blondie's favorite gender of man or beast.

Five fifteen the next morning arrived quickly for J. Exhausted from the long hours of back-breaking weeding she had done in the vegetable garden yesterday afternoon after completing her ironing chore, she'd fallen sound asleep as soon as her head hit the pillow at nine o'clock.

"Up and at 'em, Joni," Mihal called. "It's your first day on the job, remember?"

Oh, she remembered alright, but now that this morning was a reality she began feeling a bit queasy and nervous. Still a mite drowsy, she thought, *well, I asked for it, indigestion and all. Okay, now I've gotta do it.*

"I'll be right there," she sleepily called back to her dad.

Woolen underwear, old jeans, a man's flannel shirt, wool socks, winter boots, a heavy coat, and a knit cap constituted her first day's work outfit. It seemed a strange outfit for June temperatures, but Mihal knew what he was doing when he had hand-selected her work clothing. He knew how it had to accommodate the cool temperature inside the mine.

"The only thing missin' is a hard hat and a carbide lamp," he said.

"Well, we'll fix you up with those when we reach the mine," he said.

"I got your lunch box. Your Ma made one up for each of us, but you'll have to fix them for tomorrow. Your Ma says if you want to work, then you've got to know all that goes along with it. There's coffee in the bottom half and a sandwich in the top. If we're lucky, there'll be a piece of that left over apple pie in there, too. Are you ready? Did you eat your oatmeal?" Mihal asked.

After a *yes* nod toward her Dad, Mihal understood the moment had finally arrived.

"Then let's go to work, Joni."

Still sleepy and bundled in enough clothes to appear as an overweight scarecrow, J was happy just to be able to mumble, "Okey dokey," and stumble out to the car for the short drive to the mine.

The closer they got to the mines, the more anxious and excited she got. *I can't believe I'm doing this. I wonder what the other kids are gonna say? I don't give a damn what they think or say. I'll just keep thinking of the nice clothes I'll be able to buy when it's time to go back to school. I'll hold on to those thoughts* was a promise she made to her nervous gut that morning. She climbed her way into one of the three coal cars that would each carry eight day-shift miners deep into the dark tunnel's belly.

The coal car was no more than a heavily black-dusted wooden rectangular box on tireless wheel rims that would glide along on the steel rails that led deep into the tunnel. One push from a couple of strong arms was all it took to get the car rolling along the tracks. The car stopped when the tracks did.

The car had two purposes. The first was to carry the workers to and from the depth of the mountain. The second was to carry coal out to a dumping tipple, so that the car could be angled and tipped, pouring its contents to an awaiting dump truck or a train car parked below. Usually the system worked, but on occasion it would accidentally not hit its target, much to the delight of the miners who would return in the dark to retrieve the loose black shiny anthracite. Many freezing winter nights were warmed with these accidental mishaps. After all, there was more where those scraps came from. Mihal and Joni were no strangers to the midnight rendezvous' with the local coal pickin's, but J certainly felt the newness of her first day as a coal miner.

Mihal found a small sized miners hard-hat and attached a carbide lamp to the front of it. The lamp had to be filled with the gray gravel-sized carbide compound, after which Mihal spit into the opening at the top. Once the cap was screwed into place, Mihal lit the wick sticking from the front of the lamp.

"That stinks," J giggled nervously to her Dad as the flame gave off a strange gaseous odor.

"It may stink, but that's your flashlight in there. Wearing it on your hat leaves your hands free to do your work," Mihal politely informed her as he clipped the metal lamp onto her hat.

"I know that, Dad. I'm a coal miner's daughter, remember?" she teased.

"Everybody out," came the order from Jack to exit their transporting car after it had glided the length of the track into the tunnel.

Mihal's brother, and lead miner, turned and took a hard, long look at J. Jack held out a pair of sturdy looking leather work gloves and gently said,

"Here put these on. We don't want you gettin' blisters on your first day, now do we?"

"Come on, Joni," called Mihal. "Stay close to me so I can tell you what's what down here."

I have to be smart about this job, J thought. *Keep my mouth shut, my ears open and listen to everybody's advice.*

"I'm right behind you, Dad. Go ahead, start telling me."

"Put your lunch box over there, beside everybody else's." Mihal was pointing to a crate at a far corner.

"The whistle will blow when it's lunch time. If you get thirsty, take a swig of water from the jug over by that pillar. Use that tin cup, but don't forget to put the cup back on top for a lid. If you don't, sometimes a lizard crawls in and then the water's no good for anything, 'cept another lizard," he laughed.

The other six men seemed to enjoy Mihal's banter and joined in the laughter.

J didn't need to be told she was in good company. All of the miners were Mihal's friends. Some were fishing buddies, some were mushroom picking pals. Still others were junk pile scavengers, led by Mihal and his expertise to research deserted homesteads for an occasional treasure or two. They had all grown up together in this small burg called Gunther. There wasn't a single secret among them, but they parlayed a ton of respect for one another's bravery of working in this dangerous occupation.

"There's your pick and shovel, Joni. Come with me and I'll show you where to start pecking at the coal seam. Don't get too close to anyone's territory. You don't want to get hit with a swingin' pick or shovel. That's been known to happen, you know," Mihal warned her.

"Stretch your arms out, that's it, way out," he demonstrated.

"If you touch the guy next to you, one of you is too close and needs to move. You'll get the hang of it. After a while, you'll just know how far to go down the line. Right now, the guys are all watchin' out for you. They know you're only here for the summer and they don't expect you to do the work the way they know how to do it," Mihal instructed her, "but you still have to show them respect and work as hard as you can."

J nodded. It was a reticent agreement, but a firm one no less.

"Okay," Mihal began, "you know how to use the pick. Remember when we dug out that old moud, that ugly section of a stone foundation from somebody's forgotten house? Well, you swing the pick in here the same way you did then. That broke the mortared stones apart. In here, though, start just above the floorin' to break away a chink to get your groove started. You keep doin' that and before you know it, you'll have a pile of coal chunks to shovel into the car. Once the car is filled, we'll give it a shove and send it out with Jack and Andy ridin' on the bumper. They'll do the dumpin' off the tipple."

Mihal quit talking. He was done explaining.

"Now it's time to get to work," was the last thing he uttered until the lunch break at ten thirty.

"Are you hungry, kid?" Mihal asked.

"Even cold coffee tastes good right about now, don't you think?" he asked, tipping up the bottom half of his round lunch bucket to sip the cream-tinted bitter drink.

J followed suit. All of the men sat on the earthen floor and leaned against the black stoned wall of the mine, so she did likewise. She initially was amazed at how quickly her eyesight had adjusted to the poor lighting in the tunnel, but she hadn't realized how humid the inner earth was. It wasn't until she had removed her gloves, touched the soil and smelled the mustiness that she became aware of the dark dankness surrounding her. She also became acutely aware of the stillness that engulfed her senses. Every movement, every breath or bite was magnified. *If I listen carefully,* she thought, *I'll bet I can hear my hair growing.*

Opening her lunch bucket, she found a thermos bottle filled with creamed coffee. *No sugar? I guess that would be expecting too much,* she convened her thoughts to include the wrapped package in the other side of the pail. Here she found a wax-paper wrapped sandwich consisting of one slice of bologna layered between two slices of homemade bread. Both slices were lathered with what must have been a half bottle of mustard.

There was also a piece of apple pie, only it wasn't the piece she'd envisioned. J's piece was the crust, tinted with a smidgeon of apple filling. Mihal got the inner workings of the slice, which he promptly traded. Even in the barely lit darkness, his telltale glance said Blondie would be catching a bit of Hell for that dirty trick.

J managed to down a few more swallows of the coffee, when it dawned on her that she needed to urinate. During the hours prior to lunch, the men would wander a little ways further into the tunnel and she could hear them pissing, but now that she had to go, where was she supposed to do her business?

By the perplexed facial expression J was wearing, Mihal must have surmised she was pondering a toileting question, because as she was about to ask, he spoke, "You'll need to walk slowly. The mud floorin's awfully slippery, but you can go back there, around the corner, and squat. Nobody will bother you. They all know that's why you're goin' there. It's an honor system down here. You honor them, they honor you." So she went back around the corner, and on this her first day as a coal miner, she was honored!

J surprised everyone that day. Everyone, that is, except Mihal. Walking away from the mine entrance that first work-day, he wrapped an arm around J's shoulder and told her how proud of her he was.

"I had my doubts about you staying in the mine, but I never doubted that you'd survive the work. You're a real trooper, kid," he told her, as he winked and nodded respectfully to his new co-worker.

"Well, J, go get cleaned up and get yourself a bite to eat. You still have some ironing to finish from yesterday." Blondie smirked. She knew the waiting half-basket of ironing was something she'd quickly put together that afternoon, just to test the girl's tenacity. Later in the evening, little Marsha would tell J all about helping Blondie sprinkle and roll the items for the big surprise. "It's not a nice surprise, is it, J," the little one asked soulfully.

Not one to contain her observations, Blondie laughed as she took a gander at the girl who had just entered the kitchen. "You look so comical. Your face is as black as the brick yard junkies," she blared for all to hear.

"Let her alone, Blondie," Mihal scolded.

"She worked her ass off today. Get Vera to do the ironin'. She's twelve and that's old enough to start learnin' the chores. You set J up on a bench when she was six years old and put an iron in her hand. As soon as she could recognize a strawberry leaf from a weed, you gave her a bucket and set her to weedin'. Why didn't you do that to Vera? Come to think of it, she don't do much around here. Why is that Blondie? Is she another favorite? Another snitch since your Adela went to that Philipsburg nurses school? You're always lookin' out for yourself, aren't you, Blondie?"

Mihal found it easy to question Blondie's motives. He'd seen plenty of her actions through the years of being married to this manipulative, scheming, selfish woman.

Day one became day ten and then day thirty, and soon it was the last day J worked at the mine. During these past weeks, the men had learned they could talk freely with J working along side of them. They didn't need to curb their cussing or hold back their dirty jokes. Nor did they need to refrain from poking fun at their wives. They came to learn that J could keep secrets. The comfortable camaraderie made the hours flee in a flurry and the days soar like a scooter ride.

When the final day arrived, the men took up a collection for J's clothing fund, and another for her to get a haircut and a manicure. They affectionately hugged her goodbye and Mihal presented her with seventy five dollars in loose bills. J couldn't have known what a bitter-sweet day this was to be, and neither would Mihal.

Every Saturday morning for the past ten weeks, Mihal had taken J to the Houtzdale bank to cash their checks. J had managed to save a little over two hundred and fifty dollars. With each addition of bills to her old Calumet baking soda can, she marveled at her own restraint. Faithfully, she gave her mother ten dollars every week. That was as Mihal had dictated and she had complied.

J handed Blondie the ten dollars from her last pay check. "This is my last ten dollars from my last check, Ma. The good news is I'll be buying my own school clothes this week. You and Dad won't have to spend any of your money on me. Isn't that good?" she asked her mother.

"Well now, I've gotten used to that ten dollars coming in every week, Missy. So you're either gonna get another job, or you're gonna pay me ten dollars a week out of that old can of yours," Blondie sternly informed an astounded J.

"And another thing, there's a dress I bought for myself, but it makes me look like a big cow, so you can have it. Who cares if you look like a heifer with that mamoona face of yours? I threw it up on your bed. It's red and white stripes, with a black patent leather belt. It's a cute dress, but that flared skirt is what makes me look fat. That dress cost sixteen dollars. It was on sale, so I can't return it. Don't worry about paying me back. I already took the money out of your can." Blondie said as she stood gaping at J with an annoyingly complacent and twisted smile.

"Why are you staring at me that way/" J asked Blondie. "You can't seriously be waiting for me to thank you for what you've done, can you?"

J didn't return the smile. Instead, she immediately went to Mihal with this story of Blondie's.

Mihal immediately went to Blondie with J's story.

The shit immediately hit the fan, sort of speaking!

"Blondie, give that kid back her money, *NOW,*" Mihal screamed to his incongruous wife.

"She earned it and she already shared it with you every week. You are such a damned bitch. I can't believe some of the cruel and inconsiderate things you do," a tearful, trembling Mihal stated in an almost muted voice that seemed to barely be escaping his larynx.

"I will not give her back the money. She got a new dress out of it. She can just shut up about it and wear it on the first day of school, because that's the last new thing she's getting. She's not going anywhere shopping, if I have anything to say about it," Blondie reared back at Mihal.

"You won't have anything to say about it. I'll take her shopping myself, and no, you're not coming along to supervise her spending. That's all there is to be said about it, now shut your mouth while you're ahead," Mihal snarled at Blondie.

Blondie turned her back toward Mihal and sneered to the coffee pot. "Hey, Mihal, care for another cup of coffee . . . in your face?"

She laughed caustically at what she considered a threatening joke. Concealing a conceited grimace, Blondie already knowingly had spiteful plans for J's saved funds.

Deliberately changing the subject, Blondie announced, "Your Adela flunked out of that nurses training. They called earlier and said to come get her this afternoon sometime. It's still afternoon, so go collect her and her belongings," Blondie said in a provoking manner.

"What do you mean she flunked out?" Mihal asked.

"Why? We paid the first six month's tuition and she's only been there three months. Are they gonna reimburse us for the other three months?"

A visibly disappointed Mihal asked again, "Are they gonna reimburse us, Blondie? Why didn't she take advantage of this opportunity? Why? Why? Why? Didn't she understand what a sacrifice this was for this whole family?" he asked, sitting down gingerly on the porch step.

"Well, it seems she's enjoyed the partyin' that goes on every night, but she doesn't like the bookwork or the hospital work they're supposed to be trained for. She hasn't turned in any homework that was assigned. As far as I'm concerned, she can go live with Pet in D.C. Pet's got her own apartment now, so Adela can stay with her. Pet's old enough to be responsible for her. I'm sick of all this jack-assin' that goes on around here anyways," Blondie snapped at Mihal.

"By the way, she's not gettin' any of that tuition money back. It seems she's done some damage to her room durin' her party shenanigans and the school's gonna keep the balance for repairs," Blondie said. Adding insult to injury seemed to give Blondie an inner glow that didn't go unnoticed by Mihal.

Adela came home that evening. She wasn't particularly embarrassed or regretful. She had a ready excuse for every question put before her. Before heading up the stairs to her former bedroom, her good night comment to her parents was, "Who wants to sling shit for the rest of their lives anyway? Maybe you don't mind, but it's not for me!"

"Tootles," she tooted as she reached the top of the stairs. "I'm leaving for the big city tomorrow. I won't miss any of you!"

Oh, Adela, J thought through her miserable silence the next afternoon, *I won't miss you either, but I will miss my three hundred twenty four dollars and my Calumet baking soda bank.*

Two days later, J found the Calumet can when she was putting some ironed clothing away. *It's empty. What's it doing in Blondie's apron drawer,* she wondered.

Blondie jeered when she answered, "I don't know how it got in there."

Accusingly, Blondie turned the guilt around and placed it squarely on J's shoulders. "What were you doing going through my dresser drawers anyway?" her mother asked.

Chuckling to herself, Blondie whispered to the old aluminum percolator, "Gotcha!"

Turning to face J, Blondie rasped, "That'll teach you not to give your Ma all of your paycheck. Thought you were smart, huh? Guess you just learned a lesson, didn't you, Miss Smarty Pants? Get the Hell outa here with them ugly starin' eyes before I teach you another lesson."

With a taunting look on her face, Blondie reached for a new willow switch near the sink.

A visibly angered sixteen year old beat her to it.

Blondie wasn't jeering any longer.

DRIVING BLONDIE

"I passed," J proclaimed as she ran into the kitchen. "I can't believe it. I passed my driving tests."

J was the first girl in her family to learn how to drive a car. She was the first girl from the driving class to pass the tests. J had opted for the Driver's Education classes instead of the Health class outings. "All the Phys Ed teacher does is run around in circles on the football field for thirty minutes. I already know how to run fast. I do that now to get away from stupid fartin' Martin," she had told the stoic guidance counselor, Mrs. Baranski.

Mrs. Baranski did not think that was comical. She deliberately didn't laugh at J's stinted attempt at humor.

"What other classes do you, or don't you, want?" the counselor asked in a stern unwavering voice. "What do you want to do after you've finished high school? Is there anything that interests you?"

"I was thinking of interior decorating," J replied.

Now, Mrs. Baranski did laugh, so hard that she began to cough. "Coming from that big white trash family of yours, what ever gave you such a notion?" she asked.

"I'm always changing my bedroom furniture around and all my friends think I do a good job with theirs when I help them with any of their rearranging," she brashly responded.

"That's it? That's the sum total of your creative ambitions? Well, I think you should take shorthand and typing. The best you can probably hope for in your lifetime is a secretarial job. Right now, be grateful I'm allowing you take the driving course. I'll be amazed if you can pass all the rigors of the driving sessions. I suppose that I should give you a chance, as you'll probably want to drive when you grow up, instead of walk to work in somebody's bedroom," the counselor said, again bursting out in arrogant laughter.

It was J's turn to ignore the cruel joke. It was her turn to sit and stare coldly. *I may be sixteen years old, but I'm not an idiot. I got it. I got your stupid joke. How would you know what kind of a job goes on in a bedroom,* she wondered. *Experience probably,* J told herself contentiously as she ambled from the counselor's office without so much as a Good Bye.

Now here it was, several months later. J called out to the counselor who happened to be walking a short distance ahead of her in the high school's hallway. "Hey, Mrs. Baranski, I passed the driving course with straight A's. How about that for passing those driving rigors?"

J was goading the counselor for a response.

"Well good for you, but I'm betting you don't pass when you go to Holidaysburg for the driving tests. There are written and a driving tests, you know. Good luck with those," the counselor smugly replied as she walked into her English classroom wearing a look of conceit and superiority.

"Oh, I know about the tests. I passed them both on Saturday," J said as she followed the counselor to her classroom.

Leaning against the classroom doorway, J began her boasting. "I even parallel parked on an icy street and the policeman said I did a really good job with the street driving. What smart-aleck remarks do you have about that?" she snapped a retort at Mrs. *Smart Ass* Baranski.

None, I guess, J thought as she watched a fey Mrs. Baranski make a complete turn on her heels and close the classroom door behind her.

Thinking about the many times the family had to rely on others to give them a ride into town or to some festivity, J anxiously approached her father with her ideas about driving the family car. *Now we don't have to walk to Mass or catechism anymore. I just have to show Dad that I can learn how to drive that old '39 Chevy.*

"I passed the driver's exams on Martin's car, Dad. Now I'd like to learn how to drive your car . . . the old one. I won't ask to drive the one Junior gave you, but at least I'll be able to drive the kids to catechism and church when you're at your job in Buffalo. What do you think?"

Mihal didn't take too long to make a decision. Within an hour, he and J were practicing shifting gears. Back and forth that old slow Chevy chugged along on Lemon Lane, causing Mihal to make several feisty comments. "Grind me a pound, would you?" Mihal finally asked when the old gear box made a labored grinding moan that brought them both to an escalated giggling outburst.

Once the tension was broken, the driving lessons became easier. A few hours later, Mihal declared J competent to drive Old Bessie.

The real driving test came the next day. Sunday would prove the real proving ground.

"Everybody up," Blondie was shouting up the stairwell. "J's driving all of us to Mass this morning. Kids, come on, get dressed. I'm goin' too. I gotta see this with my own eyes."

It didn't take long for Blondie to start her front seat coaching:

"Watch where you're goin'. These roads are gettin' slick from this fresh snow."

"Look out! You're too close to the berm!"

"Can't you get over more to the center?"

"Slow down, for cripes sake!"

Blondie's haranguing remarks were blowing faster than the God-driven blizzard snowflakes.

"I'm fine, just sit quietly and let me drive. Besides, there's a car coming, so I can't drive in the center of the road. How about leaving me alone to concentrate on my driving, please," J implored.

"You're goin' too fast. Slow down, for Christ's sake. Thirty is too fast on these wet roads," Blondie yapped belligerently. On and on and on and on she nagged for the duration of the short drive.

Two miles felt like twenty. J felt exhausted mentally, thanks mostly to Blondie's nearly constant harassment. Physically, her extremities were exerted from the effort it took to handle the stiff steering wheel and to operate the tight grease-pack gear mechanism.

Nearing the church, Blondie began to shout, "Don't you even think you're goin' down that steep hill. If it keeps snowin', we'll never be able to get this car back up to the top. Damn it to Hell, J, you'd better pull into the cemetery here. You park this God damned car right here and right now," she shrilled.

I swear she's a direct descendant of the Amazon parrots. There isn't this much screeching or squawking in a Tarzan movie! J's mind was becoming muddled with all of her mother's griping.

Needless to say, the kids in the back seat were becoming alarmed at this point and began begging J to park the car. "It's too cold to walk home. If you can't get the car back up the hill, how will we get back home?" Cindy cried out.

Vera started to bawl, causing another back seat commotion.

"Okay, settle down kids," J tried lowering the back seat volume. "I'll park up here. We'll make it home just fine, you'll see."

Totally ignoring Blondie's bitching, J allowed her siblings persistent whining pleas to convince her to park the car at the top of the hill on the cemetery's circular driveway.

The temperature dropped ten degrees in the hour and a half it took the Mass to conclude. The bad news was that the wintery gusts of wind were freezing cold. The good news was that the snowfall had ceased. Just walking in the crunching blanket of snow on the return jaunt back up the hill from the church to the parked car was enough to start the shivering little ones to howl again. Even before reaching the auto, their anxiety levels were rising as fast as the temperature was dropping.

"Pile in, quickly now," J shouted to the kids. "We'll be fine once we warm up the car."

"Hurry up and start this car. It's not gonna warm up in here if you don't get the engine started. Don't you even know that much? What are you anyway, an idiot?" Blondie cited.

"You answered your own question again, Ma," J chided.

Blondie didn't comprehend the comment. "Huh? What are you talkin' about?"

Getting the engine to turn over took several tries. J was heeding Mihal's advice. "What ever you do, Joni, don't flood the engine," he had cautioned the novice driver.

Okay, engine's running, so now to get the gears to shift. Dad said they sometimes freeze in the winter. Please, please, please car, just get us home safely. I'm talking to the car, J sat quietly smiling at her own questionable sanity.

"What the Hell are you sneerin' about," Blondie asked bringing J back to reality.

"The car won't go into gear. It's frozen in reverse. So I guess I'll take us home in reverse," J announced to a resounding, "Oh, shit!" from a panicked Blondie.

"Oh, sweet Jesus," Blondie proclaimed, "we're gonna crash for sure. Come on kids, we're walking home," she said, opening the front passenger door.

"Close that door right now," J barked. "We are all going home in this car, and on the same road that got us here. Just be quiet. Don't mess with my concentration and we'll be fine. Everybody, sit back and relax."

"Dad, you should have seen J. She drove us all the way home backwards! She wasn't even scared," Vera rip-roaringly recounted almost every inch of their unusual return journey.

"Give me those keys," Blondie demanded. She was holding out her open right hand.

"That's the last time you're drivin' me anywhere. Thought you were smart, didn't you? You got us home alright, but you scared the shit out of all of us. When you learn how to drive the right way, I'll think about givin' you these keys again, but not until then!" Blondie snarled, and then slammed the coffee pot down on the stove top to percolate.

"You did fine, Joni," Mihal whispered. "That was pretty smart," he tittered in amusement.

"I'd have never thought to do that. Next time I come home for the weekend, I'll teach you how to drive the other car. It's a lot easier to drive and since your Ma doesn't like the thing, she won't ever have to ride with you. That solves that problem, doesn't it?" he sat there bouncing with laughter.

Glancing up at his wife, Mihal forewarned his wife. "I can see that pot's not the only thing that's perking this morning, is it Blondie? Well, don't you even think of slamming it near my face again." The angry woman glared down at him. She didn't say a word.

De ja vu. Ah, I get it now, J thought as she gazed upon her parents and was reminded of a previous kitchen scene. That was one scene she didn't care to see repeated.

ADELA

Adela, da bella da ball.
You swore you knew it all.
You thought you knew everything,
but your brain was like a brick wall.

You'd tattletale to your Ma,
at the drop of a hat.
If anyone asked, you'd say,
"What's wrong with that?"

Short and stocky,
never lean,
but always and ever
you could be so mean.

You smeared on some lipstick,
you powdered your nose.
Went of to the big city
wearing high heels and hose.

Got a job,
And got a man!
You're right back in the kitchen,
scrubbing the old frying pan.

Now you're an old woman
and on Medicare.
So, you don't like me writing this?
Too bad. I'm too old to care!

YOU'RE GOIN' WHERE?

J sat drawing a pattern around her shoe. She was making new soles for the only pair of shoes that fit her long narrow feet. The throw away corn flakes box was a suitable thickness for cutting and then fitting the inserts into the shoes. J measured the holes in the soles of her black and white saddle shoes and determined she could get four new inserts from this one cereal box.

"There's no money for new shoes for you," her mother had said when J showed her the huge holes in the soles of her shoes.

"If you want new shoes, go get yourself a job somewhere. You want shoes to wear, look in the shoe box. There must be somethin' in there good enough for you, Miss Uppity Pants," Blondie chirped.

"I could use a new pair myself, but the little kids are always growin' out of theirs, so they come first. It wouldn't kill you to walk the two miles into Whiteside or Ramey to see if there's any work for you there. What about cleanin' somebody's house?"

"Well, I just may do that, but I'm not going to walk there. You know very well there's no job waiting for any teenager in these small towns. Besides, I already have a job cleaning house and that's right here, but I don't collect any pay," J stated curtly, with a twinge of insolence in her voice.

Judging by the brutal glance Blondie cast toward J, one would have thought Blondie had just been slapped. J resumed cutting out her new shoe inserts and ignored her mother's side glances. She knew that thin slice of cardboard would be all that came between her socks and the earth beneath her feet. She didn't stand a snowball's chance in Hell of getting a new pair of shoes after her last remark to Blondie.

"Don't you get sassy with me, Missy. You eat, don't you? You have a roof over your head, don't you?" Blondie was quick to retaliate and correct the girl's way of thinking, or so she thought. "Nobody yaps at me and gets away with it, just you remember that!"

Two more weeks of school and Pet will be home for a visit. When she goes back to the city, I'm going with her. I'll be smart about my money this time, though. Adela and Ma won't have a chance to get their fingers on it.

J wondered if she was wasting her time daydreaming or could this pipedream come true? *Please, two weeks pass by quickly. I think I'll explode if I have to spend one more summer listening to all of Ma's yelling and bitching.*

School let out for summer vacation on Friday, June 14th. On the following sunny Sunday afternoon, J rode to the Tyrone train station with Mihal. Little Vic and baby Annamaria dozed quietly on the back seat and dreamt of chocolate ice cream cone treats, while J and Mihal chattered away about nothing, and yet it seemed about everything.

Blondie had warned J as she and the excited toddlers had climbed into the old car for their slow trek over the curved mountain roads. "Don't you take your eyes off those kids for one minute, do you hear me, you stupid monkey face? If anything happens to either of them kids, you'll pay dearly," Blondie stressed to J.

"J ain't gonna let anything happen to those kids, so for Christ's sake Blondie, let the girl alone. You badger her more than a game warden. What's wrong with you?' Mihal had sourly asked his wife.

"Come on kids, let's go get Pet," Mihal had called out, happily waving his arm in a half circle indicating a roundup of his accompanying crew.

Turning to Blondie, he had cautioned, "And Blondie, you will not cause any bullshit while Pet is here, understand? She's comin' for a visit and it's gonna be a nice one. There's no if, ands or buts about it. Do you hear me?"

"Yeah, Mihal, I hear you," Blondie had snapped her reply. "Now get the Hell outa my sight, you stupid jackass."

Blondie was in no mood to tolerate any early morning orders, but she was in an irritated state and ready for an argument.

"Get goin' and leave me alone," she had shouted at Mihal as he slowly drove away from the gate at #11 Lemon Lane.

"I got a whole house to clean while you're gone. If this place isn't spic and span in here when younse get back, your Pet will come nibby-nosin' around and she'll start her own cleanin'. She does that every time she comes home. It drives me crazy. Nothin' is ever clean enough to suit her now that she's a fancy city slicker," Blondie mumbled to the gate knowing the gate wouldn't sass back. She didn't care. She had to vent to something or she'd go crazy for sure. Blondie sure did know Blondie!

Mihal could just see it. Old Blondie was on another rampage. He knew that by the time they'd return she'd be ready to fly off the handle at anyone or anything.

"Kids, when we get back home, don't do anything to rile your Ma. She's in a piss ant's mood again," Mihal toyfully teased the youngsters sitting in the rear.

The only response Mihal got from the three passengers was a gaggle of giggles. Mihal never tossed the words piss ants in their direction. They knew that was Blondie's reserved nickname for them.

"You're being goofy today, Dad," little Vic squeaked, creating a few more chuckles. This time, even Mihal joined in the giggling.

Mihal's speed limit centered around 35mph, no matter what the State Highway Department deemed suitable for the winding Pennsylvania mountain roads. "We'll get there when we get there," was his motto. It worked for an easy going trip to Tyrone and it worked the same way for the return trip home.

Pet wasn't home fifteen minutes, when she announced, "I'm going to start cleaning tomorrow morning. I'll start upstairs and work my way down to the kitchen. The kids can all help. There'll be a job for everyone and at the end of our chores, there'll be a big treat for everyone as well as a huge surprise from me," Pet announced joyfully.

Pet smiled at her captive audience. Blondie didn't.

"Dad, I'll give you some money for a couple cans of white paint. If you wouldn't mind, could you paint the front porch?" Pet asked.

"What's goin' on here, Pet?" Mihal asked. "You seem to be spiffin' up the old place for some reason. Care to tell us what your secret's all about?"

"Well, Dad, I was going to wait to tell you my good news, but I'm too excited to wait any longer. The truth is," she hesitated, and then took a deep breath before completing her sentence, "I got engaged and my guy, Phillip, is driving here to meet you, Ma and the kids. I'd like the house to look nice when he gets here. Do you mind?" Pet asked, or rather, her big silly grin posed the question.

"That's good news, Pet. I have this week off from work, so yeah, sure, we can clean up the old joint. Can't we Blondie?" Mihal asked.

"It's her news, not mine," Blondie "tsked" and smacked her lips several times before snapping back at the two of them.

"I don't give a shit what she does. She's gonna do it anyway, aren't you?" she deliberately aimed this response to Pet.

"I thought you'd be happy for me. Why are you so angry?" Pet asked her mother.

"Happy for you?" Blondie yelped.

"I can tell you somethin' that would make me happy. That's you payin' me back the money I loaned you to go to the city in the first place. I haven't seen a cent of that yet, Miss Big Shot," Blondie yapped, while hurling her face to within inches of Pet's.

"What do you mean, pay you back? I've sent you money anytime I've had a few extra dollars. I've sent presents and candy for the kids at the holidays. I took in Adela when you sent her to me, unannounced I might add. I'm only charging her twenty dollars a week, which doesn't go very far in the city. That's not nearly enough to pay for all of the food she consumes. I don't think you realize how expensive city living is, so consider yourself lucky that I send any money home to you at all. Do you even tell Dad when I do that?"

Pet had finished her retaliatory remarks with clearly visible racking sobs and large teardrops rolling off her cheeks and onto her starched white blouse.

"Blondie, I warned you about starting somethin'. Now look at what you've done," Mihal reprimanded.

"It's okay, Dad. Philip will be here tomorrow evening and I've decided I'll meet him at the gate and then go right back to D.C. There's no use for me to stay here any longer. This is Hell on earth. I don't know how you and the kids stand her," Pet said sadly, walking up the stairway to the bedroom where J was waiting.

Sitting on the edge of the bed that she and Pet would share as usual when Pet visited, J witnessed a sorry sight walking through the door frame. Pet was trembling. She was trying to wipe her red eyes and blow her runny nose at the same time. "I don't know why I even try," she whispered. "I can't stand all this bickering anymore. It's just not what normal people do in the real world."

"I can't stand it either, Pet," J adamantly told her older sister.

"I was going to ask you if I could spend the summer with you. I can get a job. I'll be a good worker. My teachers gave me reference letters telling that I'm an honor student and of good character. I wouldn't be any trouble, I promise. I'll beg, if I have to," J said as she pleadingly dropped to her knees.

"Get up, J. You can come. You don't have to beg. I see how life is in *this damned house*. Be ready to go tomorrow after we have our supper. I'm not kidding about having Philip help us to return to D.C. That's where my home is now. I'll tell Dad. There won't be any problem, I'm sure. You'll have to double up with Adela on the sleeper sofa, though. Is that okay with you?"

Pet had asked in such a considerate tone that J had no choice, even though she hesitated before answering, "Okay."

In her mind, J's thoughts traversed elsewhere to a past summer when Adela revealed her true character. Adela may have left home and gained her fredom, but she had left behind a huge gap in J's heart. *I haven't missed you Adela. I've missed what my money could have done for me, but I haven't missed you. Sleep with you? In the same bed? I'll sleep in the bathtub if I have to, but I won't sleep in the same bed with you,* J's all-consuming memory conceded.

Philip was tall, slender, good looking and well groomed. Pet had only said, "He's such a nice man." He was soft spoken and articulate. He was an attorney and had connections to the White House. Blondie's pupils dilated at the word "attorney", but they nearly popped out of their sockets when she heard the words "White House"!

"Why don't you come in and have some supper?" Blondie smiled sweetly when she politely asked the man to join their evening meal of *pigs in the blanket*, a Polish cabbage and ground meat dish.

"No thanks. That's very hospitable of you, though. Pet has already informed me she wants to leave before it gets too dark. The winding mountain roads scare her, you know. So, I'll take her and her little sister to the train station this evening and they can be in D.C. by morning. I have to go to New York on a case and won't be driving right back as I'd originally planned. Pet understands and I hope you all do, too," Philip said smoothly.

He's a crafty one, Blondie thought. *He's as smooth as butter. Yeah, I'll bet he's charmed the pants right off her already. He'll never marry her. He looks at her like she's a piece of shit now that he's seen where she comes from. He'll end up with one of them society babes, she'll see. I just may tell her that in the next letter that I send Miss City Slicker. Wait, what did he say about a little sister?*

That single thought seemed to awaken Blondie from her fugue.

"What did you say about a little sister? What little sister is goin' to the train station with Pet? I don't know nothin' about any of this, Mister. What's goin' on here, Mihal? What do you take me for, some God damned suckin' fool?"

A fuming Blondie wasn't worried any longer about being demure or impressing the suited man in his big white convertible. "I said, what in the

Hell is goin' on here?" Blondie repeated the question as though no one had heard the original.

"J is going to D.C. for the summer. She'll be with Pet and Adela. She can get a job in the city, quicker than she can around here. Even you can understand that much, Blondie," Mihal said.

"Besides, the experience away from here will be good for her. She can earn some money for her senior year clothes. She'll be fine. Go girl, get your suitcase. Have a wonderful summer with your sisters," Mihal commanded as he nudged the stupefied girl to run for her baggage.

The huffing and puffing steam-powered engine jerked continuously as it shuffled clickety-clack, clickety-clack along the many miles from the tiny Tyrone train station to the grand and glorious Union Station. J was awe struck when she stepped off the train in Washington, D.C. What a sight this was! She had never been in such a vast expanse in her whole life. She had never before encountered so many people in one building, and these all seemed to be scurrying in a variety of directions. "My gosh," she said to Pet. "So this is the city?"

"No, J," this isn't the city," Pet chuckled.

"This is just the train station. The city is out those golden revolving doors. Let's go out there and get some breakfast on the run. I'm hungry, how about you?" Pet asked enthusiastically.

Grab breakfast is exactly what they did. They sat at a counter after going through and making their selections from a cafeteria line. Pet had her usual scrambled eggs, bacon and toast, but J had the oatmeal. She wondered if old habits were hard to break, but after licking the glaze from two donuts off of her two fingers, she decided maybe they weren't after all.

"Well, now that our bellies are full, let's catch a trolley and head for my apartment," Pet suggested.

The words rolled off her tongue as though she'd been riding a trolley all of her life. *She really is a city slicker* rattled around in J's brain, just as the trolley's wheels rapidly rolled around and around on the track.

J was in awe of the whole city scenario. She had only seen trolleys in magazine pictures, yet here she was riding on one. Gazing out the open windows of the electric car, she was amazed to see so many huge bronze statues at the corner of Constitution Avenue. She couldn't believe that was the White House they were passing, or The Blair House where important people stayed when they visited this city. When the trolley stopped at the corner of 14th Street NW, J couldn't stop herself from thinking, *Oh, God, if I'm dreaming, don't anyone awaken me*!

Adela was at work when Pet and J arrived at the twelve story building. Startled when she entered her fourth floor apartment living room, Pet made a hasty assumption. "It looks like a cyclone hit this place,"

"What did Adela do? Don't tell me she had a party while I was gone. Please, don't let that be what caused all this mess," Pet wailed.

"Come on, Pet," J said, "I'll help you clean up. We'll surprise Adela when she comes home."

"Two people cleaning sure goes much faster than one," Pet said, giving her little sister a slight nuzzle.

"We'll have time to take a nap before Adela gets home. You must be tired from your long day. I'll throw some chicken and potatoes into the oven to roast and then our dinner will be ready when Adela gets home from work," Pet added.

"Dinner?" asked J. "Don't you mean supper?"

"No, I mean dinner," Pet corrected.

Etiquette lesson #1, J thought before she had a chance to doze off for what Pet called *forty winks. I wonder what else I'll learn before I go back to Gunther on Labor Day.*

"It's supper back on the farm. It's dinner everywhere else in the world," Pet answered, holding her index finger to her lips.

"Shhhhhh, I think I hear Adela coming home. Let's hide and surprise her," Pet was saying as Adela pushed open the apartment door.

"Hey, I didn't know we had a cleaning lady. If I'd known that, we would have really made a mess last night," Adela commented, laughing lightly.

"Well, let's really party tonight," she said, encouraging the snickering five people following her into the apartment.

Pet and J popped out of the bedroom like two helium party balloons. The words, "Surprise! We're home!" stopped the six entering young people short in their tracks.

Before anyone of the new arrivals could say a word of their own, Pet was asking a question, although she already the answer. "Who are these people and why are they here, Adela?"

Pet sought an immediate response from anyone of the group, but mostly from her sister. No answer was forthcoming from the six standing frozen in place.

"So, all of you were thinking of having another party tonight? Is that why there was such a mess when we walked in here this morning? This is my place; did you remember that, Adela? You are just a visitor here and you were warned about the rules, weren't you? You can tell these fine, beer-toting people they can go home now."

Speaking loudly, and with a tinge of arrogance, Pet pointed her index finger toward the open door.

"Besides, we only made dinner for three," J added sarcastically.

Adela stood in the foyer with a warped twist to her mouth and appeared stultified. *I guess Pet made her out to be an idiot in front of her friends. Somehow, someway, she'll make me and Pet pay for that. I just know it* J thought as she watched Adela bidding adieu to her co-workers.

J knelt at the bedside that night and silently prayed. For once, she actually felt as though there was something to be grateful for. *This was only day one and I can't wait to go exploring this big city. There's something interesting on every inch here. I hope I find a job. I don't want to go back for my senior year without money and clothes. Please, God, help me find a job. I won't be fussy, I promise.*

With four vacation days left and no boyfriend in sight, Pet agreed to take J job hunting the next day.

With only ten dollars that Mihal had slipped into her pocket, J had nothing else but well-worn, old fashioned shoes and outfits in her suitcase. Pet began examining the shape and style of J's country attire.

"There isn't a single thing you can wear here, J. Is this the best you have? And what gives with these shoes and the cornflake cutouts?" Pet asked, now bent over in laughter.

"Good gravy girl, we are going to have to do something about your clothes or they'll put you in a poor house before they give you a job in this town."

"Try these on, I'll bet they fit," Pet said as she handed J some skirts and blouses. Try these shoes on, too. If they're a tad too long, just stuff some tissues in the toes. That always works for me when I find a savvy pair on sale," Pet told her good naturedly.

J was astonished at Pet's willingness to share. She had experienced stinginess from Adela, so she wasn't quite sure how to respond to Pet's generosity.

Adela sat on the edge of Pet's bed, silently surmising her competition. Her rolling eyes told their own story. "How come you never let me try on those clothes? There's bound to be something in that box that would fit me, you know," were Adela's only remarks.

Needless to say, Adela's comments went unheard and unheeded. To say that Pet was angry with Adela's sneakiness would be like cheating the devil of his due. Pet's annoyance just wasn't going away that quickly and Adela knew it!

Wearing her very first pair of high heeled pumps and a tan light-weight suit, compliments of Pet, J got a job on her first application. She was hired as a waitress at the corner Dash's Delight Shoppe. She was taken into a fitting room and measured, then given a shape-revealing short black dress with a white half apron, which she was instructed to wear the next day. "Wear a pair of black pumps and nylons to complete this outfit. Pull your hair back in a bun and wear some make-up, for goodness sake. You look like a hick," the attractive large bosomed assistant manager said.

Treated to a congratulatory hot fudge sundae and the movie North by Northwest starring the handsome Cary Grant, J's second day in the city ended with a loving hug from Pet. J received only a grunt from Adela.

J awakened very early the next morning to find Pet sitting in her favorite living room chair, the one she'd relax in while talking to Phillip on their evening phone calls. This time she was just holding the phone's receiver, and trembling.

"What is it? What's wrong, Pet?" J asked tenderly.

"That was Phillip. He's called off our engagement. He says he can't marry someone who comes from such squalor. He called us white trash. He labeled Ma a freaky lunatic. He said there's no way his family could ever have anything to do with ours. He didn't even apologize for breaking up. He said I owed him an apology for deceiving him, and for making him think we were decent people. The word love didn't come out of his mouth one time, not once," Pet was choking on her sobs, trying to come to terms with Phillip's harshness.

A cup of warm tea later, Pet hadn't yet uncurled from the chair. Still clutching the phone and staring off into space, she said, "Remember that cute older guy I met the last time I was home? The one from Clearfield who was visiting at Henya's house? I guess I'll give him a call when we go home for Labor Day. We seemed to hit it off, and he did say to call him the next time I was in town. What do you think, should I do it? He's from our kind of people, a large Catholic Polish family. I'm twenty eight years old. I can't afford to be too choosey anymore, J."

Pet exhaled a heavy sigh, then her sobbing resumed.

Adela walked J to her new job at the restaurant that morning, but at five o'clock on J's third day in the city, it was a swollen-faced Pet who arrived to walk J back to their apartment.

"How was the job today?" she asked.

Her voice is still shaky and her eyes look blood shot. I'll bet she's cried all day. I feel so bad for her J thought, as she reached for Pet's hand and squeezed. Pet weakly returned the squeeze.

"It was good, but my feet are killing me. I'll have to get used to high heeled shoes, I guess. I have good news though. I made over two hundred dollars in tips," J responded.

"You made how much? How in the world did you do that?" A surprised Pet asked, not quite sure she'd heard correctly.

"Well, the manager said not to get upset if the guys touched or pinched your behind. He said that's how you make the big tips. I didn't much like that idea, but if that's how it's done in the big city, then I suppose I'll have to get used to that," J shyly confided to her sister as she gently rubbed her aching bum. "Boy, my butt sure is stinging from all those pinches."

"Well, that's not how it's done in my book," Pet said angrily.

A highly agitated older sister grabbed J's arm, turned her completely around, and then headed straight back to the restaurant. Huffing noticeably, Pet began to set the record straight. "You're going to turn in that tight uniform today, J. I don't like what it implies. Anyway, it makes you look as shameless as a slumlord's skank."

Pet's facial expression softened after she'd offered her unsolicited opinion. "We'll find you another job tomorrow morning, little sister, something more attuned to a young lady. How does that sound? But, as far as today goes, I'm going to give that manager a piece of my mind, don't you think for one second that I won't."

Pet did just that and the next morning the high-heeled sisters clip-clopped down Pennsylvania Avenue, hot to trot for a new type of employment more suitable to a sixteen year old country girl.

"Miss Tozan," Pet began J's introduction to the manager of a woman's clothing store a few blocks around the corner from the Pennsylvania Avenue hub-bub, "this is my sister, J. She's looking for a summer job. You wouldn't happen to have any openings, would you?"

"Good morning, Pet. It's nice to see you again. We miss having you grace our shoppe with your perky advice to our customers. Some of our best clients still come in seeking your fashion sense and expertise," the manager cheerfully acknowledged to Pet.

"To answer your question, we really don't have any openings, but for you I'll make an exception. We pay $1.25 an hour plus commission. How does that sound to you, young lady? Can you start in the morning?" Miss Tozan asked J.

"It sounds great and I'm ready to start today, if you'd like," J eagerly answered.

"Good enough, J is it? Come with me and we'll get your paperwork completed. Pet, do come back around five and I'm sure J will be ready to call it a day by then," the manager said smiling good naturedly.

"If she's your sister, I feel confident she'll be just fine. Nice to see you again, Pet," she said, reaching out to give Pet a warm embrace. "Don't stay away so long. I love seeing you."

Fine was how the job became. Magic was how the summer evolved. Everyday revealed a new adventure. J was enthralled with her new life, even though she knew it was only temporary. That didn't matter. She was learning to smile and to treasure this city life.

She enjoyed her daily journey to work with her sisters, whether it was riding on the trolley or walking the long city blocks. J chatted jokingly with the secret service men patroling the White Houses gates. Pet and Adela flirted with the uniformed gaurds. J enjoyed the city noises and the hustle-bustle of the conglomoraation of varied nationalities living in this wonderful place. She didn't mind the rain or the humid hot days, since the wonderful new invention called air conditioning made work and home comfortable. She remembered the hot and muggy sleepless nights on the farm and knew she never hoped to experience those again.

She enjoyed window shopping. Just walking around the block on her lunch break was pure pleasure. Eating a Kosher hot dog that dripped with over-flowing sweet mustard relish and sipping an ice cold bottle of Coca Cola from one of the corner vendors was the perfect lunch. This was a tasty meal, one that reminded her of her fishing trip with Mihal so long ago. By the end of the summer, all four corner vendors knew her name, and they sensed she loved this over-grown town. *I'll bet they'll miss me as much as I'll miss their cheerful chats when I have to go back home.* J's feelings were sated with melancholy.

J applied her enthusiastically ambitious work ethic to every minute of every working day. She was the highest commission earner in the history of the boutique. She worked twelve hours, if needed. She wasn't ashamed to wipe shelves and counters, nor did she hesitate to fold and restock items where necessary to make the sales floor spotless and interesting. She worked Sunday morning inventory when the opportunity arose. Sitting in the storeroom counting items, or tagging new ones was a breeze compared to the work she'd left behind in Gunther.

In return for her efforts, she was given hefty paychecks to stash away for her senior year's expenses. Miss Tozan rewarded her with a seventy five per cent discount on any of the sales items she purchased. This was the manager's token of appreciation for J's willingness to work any assignment. The discount allowed J to take advantage of purchasing clothes dirt cheap. J wasn't dressing in country bumpkin styles any longer. Pet was actually complementing her on the wise mix and match choices she made. "You're learning how to put colors and styles together, J. You can make a dozen outfits out of three skirts and three tops. Good girl!" Pet would just smile and hug her little sister.

With J and Adela in tow, Pet seemed to enjoy showing off her knowledgeable sightseeing skills. "Let's go sit on the steps of the Potomac gateway and listen to the Marine Band rehearse this Sunday evening, and then afterward we can stop for a sundae or a shake."

This became their routine Sunday outing. They'd sit and chat, reminiscing and kibitzing, oblivious to the variety of people around them. "They call this the melting pot city," Pet explained, "because people from so many diverse ethnic cultures make up the mix of this city's population."

It was then, and not until then, did J begin noticing the varied ethnic garb that dressed this wonderful city. Vibrant caftan colors seemed to radiate in the bright sunshine or the rain. Jewelry sparkled everywhere. Bright turbans and bowler hats topped so many heads. J noted the spiked heels and cordovan flats as they trampled the sidewalks. The tapping noises added to the rushing sounds of the crowds, prompting her to comment one morning as they hurried to their jobs. "I haven't seen one single pair of clodhoppers since I've been here, Pet, not even on my feet. This is a great town!"

J couldn't help but notice the variety of skin colors of these varied ethnic peoples. She had heard of segregation, but she'd never actually witnessed it back home. She had seen colored people in the Osceola brick yards where they worked. "They are just people trying to get by in the world, just like the rest of us," Mihal would say if anyone asked why they were so dark skinned.

"They're no different than the rest of us," he'd add. Mihal had a way of looking beyond skin color. He was more interested in a person's character. "Always remember, J, it's not what a person thinks that matters, it's how they think that counts," he'd advised many times.

In D.C., racism was mostly visible in the restaurants or the dime-store lunch counters, where actual signs delineated WHITES from COLORED. The first time J saw those signs, she naively thought *what does it truly matter what color my clothes are as to where I can sit and eat?*

Pet quickly and quietly educated her on the true meaning behind the words. "That's disgusting!" was J's prompt response to her sister's explanation.

The first time J went to lunch at a large drugstore's soda counter, she and Pet sat waiting for their order to be filled. A Negro man, who was sitting directly beneath a COLORED ONLY sign, asked for some ketchup. The waitress ignored his request. Thinking the server was being rude by making the paying man wait for the ketchup bottle, J carried the one that had been set at their place-setting over to him.

"Here you go, sir. My sister told me that they make the best French fries here, do they?" she asked.

Flashing a bright country smile, J handed him the ketchup bottle and walked back to her seat. He smiled back and nodded, but rapidly replaced his head in a hung position.

J and Pet were still eating their BLT sandwiches at the counter when the man slid off of his stool to leave. He paused for only a second, but he looked directly at them and tipped his hat. J waved a small wave, but Pet angrily pinched J's waist, saying "Don't you ever do that again. You could have gotten us in some real trouble."

"Naw, he looked like a gentle person," J answered.

J wasn't worldly enough to grasp the direct meaning or full implication of her sister's cautious words. She was still naive enough to believe that all men were created equal, and secretly hoped that she'd always feel that way.

This large city in 1959 seemed safer than the farm the sisters had left behind. Often, to save cab or trolley fares, the brave girls would find themselves strolling through Lafayette Park later in the evenings. At these times, taking the shortcut through the park seemed the most logical thing to do. Returning from a concert on the Potomac, from a late-night movie or from an after-work dinner date downtown, they often threw caution to the wind. After all, it wasn't as though they were walking alone. There were three of them.

The park, located directly across from the White House on Pennsylvania Avenue, was notoriously known as the queer people's hangout. Spearheaded by Pet, the sisters devised a plan to warrant acceptance, rather than to generate fear, from the groups that gathered in this park. "Just hold hands and they'll think we're like them," Pet suggested.

Confidence won out as the park people became protective of the sisters and would insist on walking them safely to their building. Generated by their many late evening conversations that summer, the sisters became acquainted with the parks inhabitants. They in turn became aware that Pet, J, and Adela were sisters, and not a threesome. During easy conversations, their names, their histories, their dreams and plans were discussed. Differences didn't seem to matter to either side; fleeting summer friendships did.

On some evenings, the three sisters would visit a museum or an art show. On some Sundays they'd walk to the Washington National Cathedral and attend Mass, then go on to have a leisurely breakfast or visit one of the many monuments that graced this large metropolis. Some free afternoons, they'd sit up on the rooftop and sunbathe. They'd drink ice-cold lemonade, read novels and pass the afternoon peacefully away. "You look like a red lobster, J," a tanned Pet would tease her sister. The next morning, Pet would awaken with a tanned blush. J would awaken with more freckles and a reindeer-red nose, but never a tan.

Some evenings, they'd sit in the bay window nook and watch bodies being delivered to the funeral home in the alley below them. The highest count they witnessed in one evening was seven. That called for a "Hip, hip, hooray," and a tip of the coke bottles. Everything was entertainment to J.

On occasion, Pet's part-time job called for her to do in-store evening gown modeling. Occasionally, skinny J was included to model the teen outfits or the Girl Scout uniforms. *More money for my savings account* she would think when she'd accept the offers. Over the summer months, the stash grew to almost eight hundred dollars causing a long sock to bulge at the bottom of her underwear drawer.

The safety-deposit sock became a ready repository for Adela, when she discovered the hidden money. It seemed that Adela considered it a joint account to be unabashedly shared. If she was short a few dollars, she just went to J's bank. If she needed a new outfit, she would just happen to find a lost twenty at the bottom of her purse. She'd justify her find by saying, "Well, I just can't imagine how that money got into my purse."

She always managed to scrounge a few extra dollars to go out with her friends on her free evenings. She never seemed to be at a loss for money, which struck J as odd one particular late August evening. While they sat slurping their hot fudge sundaes and milkshakes, a curious J asked, "How much pay do you earn, Adela? You must make a lot of money, because you always have cash to spend. Don't you save any?"

"That's none of your business, J," Adela answered. "Where I get my money, and how I spend it, is my business."

Something is telling me to count my money, J thought when they got back to the apartment. "Pet, can you come with me. I want to count my money again," J whispered to her sister.

"Look at this," J said aghast.

"There's newspaper clippings stuck in between my dollar bills. I had almost eight hundred dollars in here. Look, I marked down the amount I saved every week. I didn't bother to count it. I just kept wrapping the bills around the wad. There's only four hundred dollars left. Oh, no, not again," J began to wail.

"Adela, come into the bedroom, please. I have something to show you," Pet's pleasant request instantly echoed through the flat.

Adela responded quickly, "What do you want? I hope you have something good for me."

"Simply put, Adela, it really isn't anything good. I'm so disappointed in you," Pet began.

"You will return every dollar you've used from J's savings. Do you understand? You have a savings account of your own, don't you? You'll go to the bank in the morning and withdraw what ever you need to replace what you've stolen from J's sock. Is that understood?" Pet was shouting at Adela, who had listened and instantly had an an ashen gray colored face.

"You will do it, or you will find yourself another place to live tomorrow. I don't think anyone else is going to let you live with them, or do your laundry and feed you for twenty dollars a week."

Pet did more than mildly reprove her sister. A warning had been laid out that Adela would heed, or else. She had all night to consider Pet's words and in the morning she left the apartment earlier than usual.

Four hundred dollars was found setting at the center of the dining table when J and Pet arrived home from work later that afternoon. There was no note of apology, only eight fifty-dollar bills. J smiled.

Pet cried.

Two weeks later, the sisters accepted an offer from a hometown neighbor, who also worked in the city. "I'm driving back to Madera to see my mother for the Labor Day weekend. If you girls want to share the gas expenses rather than pay train fare, you're more than welcome to ride along."

"We'd be foolish not to ride with John." They agreed and were soon on their way to #11 Lemon Lane.

J knew three girls were returning to Gunther, but only two would be making the return trip to D.C. *It's a sad thought to be going back there, but it's my senior year and that should be exciting.*

What the girls didn't realize was just how excited Marsha, one of the younger siblings, was to have her sister J coming back home to stay.

Five year old Marsha was the first of the five kids to see the dust being kicked up by a strange car coming up Lemon Lane. "Here comes J," she shouted to the others as she ran to welcome her sister home.

Marsha had aimed for the handle of the new aluminum storm door, but her little hand squarely hit the glass panel, which shattered on impact.

Instead of cheers of delight, J was greeted with a piercing scream as she stepped out of John's car.

"My God, what happened?" shouted Blondie, as she raced to the echoing screams.

"What the Hell did you do to this kid, J?" Blondie asked, as she and J arrived at Marsha's side.

"You just got back and already you've caused trouble. Look at her thumb! It's almost cut off!" Blondie yelped.

J grabbed the dishtowel draped over Blondie's shoulder and wrapped the frail and nearly faint girl's thumb tightly.

"She needs to see a doctor. She's probably going to need stitches," J said to her mother, who had now raised herself to a standing position.

"Well, get your boyfriend over there to drive her to Doc Romon's office. See what he can do for her," Blondie bullied.

"How should I tell him to bill you for what ever he does for her?" J asked her mother, as she carried the whimpering pale tyke toward John's car.

"You're the big city slicker girl. You've been workin' all summer. You should have the bucks to pay for what ever needs done. You caused this to happen. If you hadn't gone in the first place this never would have happened. If younse wouldn't 'a made a big deal about comin' back today, she wouldn't have been so wound up. Get goin' before she bleeds to death," Blondie caustically ordered her.

That's nice, Ma. That's sure to make this kid more nervous than she already is. What's wrong with you anyway? Don't you have any feelings for anyone but yourself J wondered as she held the tiny girl tightly cradled on her lap. John didn't hesitate. He quickly drove back down Lemon Lane.

Hours later, John returned with J and Marsha. John was kind enough to carry Marsha into the house and lay her on to the parlor sofa. "Don't put her on that good couch, that's for company," Blondie screeched in that shrill voice of hers.

"She might get blood on it and then who's gonna clean it up? Me, that's who," she answered her own question. "Why's she sleepin', anyway? What did Doc do? Did he drug her up?"

Blondie kept right on with a barrage of asinine questions. "How much did he charge? You did pay him, right? I don't want to find no doctor's bill comin' in the mail. You better understand that, Missy."

"Yes, I paid him the twenty five dollars he charged," J answered.

"You are going to pay J back, aren't you?" John asked Blondie.

"Who in the Hell are you to be askin' me somethin' like that? Adela told me how much money she has. She can afford to pay for it, and you can bet your sweet ass she'll pay the five dollars for the glass that's gotta be replaced in that new storm door. It was all her God damned fault. Now get the Hell off of my property, and don't even think about coming back," she hollered at John.

"John, let me thank you for helping with Marsha and for the ride home. I didn't pay you for my share of the gas yet. Let me get that for you," J said. She felt so embarrassed at her mother's inane outburst.

She began to open her purse, but John reached over and pushed it closed. "No thanks necessary, J. I was glad to do it for you. You don't owe me anything. Enjoy your senior year, if you can," he added, while giving a hard cold glare toward Blondie.

While carrying Marsha up the stairs to her bedroom, J over heard Blondie asking Adela, "Why did she take her purse with her? Is she ashamed for me to see what's in it? What's she hidin' in there?"

J ignored them and continued into the bedroom. After laying Marsha onto the bed and covering her with a quilt, J was horrified at what she witnessed as she glanced around the bedroom. Her new suitcase had been emptied and all of her belongings had been strewn about. Her new clothes had been tossed, about. Some were thrown onto the beds and others were scattered on the floor. Several had even been torn. "Who did this?" J angrily shouted.

"Ma and Adela," said little Vera, standing cross-legged in the doorway. "Ma was mad when she didn't find your money. She said she'll find it when you're sleepin', so you better watch it real good. She's plenty mad about you not sendin' her anything all summer."

Adela cunningly admitted to tearing the clothing. "They ripped when I tried them on. Obviously, they don't fit. Well, you have lots of money, so you'll be able to buy new ones. Be glad I didn't try all of them on. Ma said I should have."

Before Adela returned to the city, she let J in on a secret plan of Blondie's. "After you graduate in June, Ma says you're going to work in Philipsburg's Cigar Factory and you'll bring home your paycheck to her every week. She's got it all planned out to give you five dollars a week and she'll keep the rest. She said you can't do anything about it because you're under her roof until you're twenty one. What do you think about that, Miss Ssmarty Pants," Adela laughed.

As Adela left the bedroom, she hauntingly called out, "She's on the look out for your money, too. And, when she finds it, I get half!"

Pet cried that Labor Day weekend when she described Phillip's cruel phone conversation canceling their engagement. "Honest, Dad, I thought he loved me, but he was in love with himself. I can see that now," Pet admitted, just as her mother walked into the kitchen.

"What happened to your lover boy, Phillip was it? He dumped you for a high society dame, didn't he?" Blondie callously asked. "I knew he would. Why in the Hell are you crying? He didn't get you pregnant, did he?" she shouted at Pet.

Before Pet could respond, Blondie answered her own question again. It was a regular habit of hers. "I could tell he needled his way into your underpants, I just knew it," she trilled.

Pet simply glanced at her father, smiled and shook her head *no*.

"I'm done here, Dad," she said loud enough for everyone and everything in that room to hear.

With that, she picked up the receiver, dialed the rotary phone and called the guy from Clearfield. They went on a date and had a nice evening. The rest is history, as they say. They were married a year later. After many years of being happily married, Pet admitted to J that she hadn't loved her husband when she married him, but she learned to not only love, but respect, the kind man who had rescued her from spinsterhood.

Adela got booted out of living with Pet soon after they returned to D.C. that Labor Day weekend. Adela had to move in with and sponge off of some high school friends in another state until she was able to land two jobs to make ends meet. Eventually, she saved the necessary money to move into a small apartment with a co-worker. They didn't become friends. They could barely tolerate one another. For some odd reason, Adela's roommate seemed to always be short of funds. For some odd reason, Adela never was.

Experience had taught J to hide her money. She kept her savings tightly rolled in a small tobacco pouch. She kept the little sack pinned to her bra and tucked in her cleavage. Blondie never did lay one finger on it. J did buy some new speckled linoleum for their kitchen floor, as well as new draperies for the dining and parlor rooms. Despite Blondie's orders, J bypassed Blondie's claws and paid for the items herself.

J bought a navy blue dress for her mother to wear to church. It was such a pretty dress that Blondie wore it to every dress-up occasion that occurred that next year, but she never did say, "Thank you." J could live with just knowing the best outfit her mother owned was purchased with money that Blondie never did get her hands on. This was some astonishing feat in *that damned house,* and it warranted daily satisfaction for J's ego.

The long-sleeved, blue dress-shirt that J bought for Mihal became his favorite. "Joni got me this from the city. Sharp, huh?" was his staunch proud reply to any compliments he received.

J saw John only once after that homecoming day. He was riding in his new Chevy Impala. He slowed down when he passed J as she walked across the bridge near the high school. He tooted his car's horn and blew her a kiss. J blew him one back. She watched a smile creep across his face and she couldn't help but laugh out loud as she waved what she knew was a final good bye to him.

On that Labor Day, J met her Prince Charming. They danced the night away at the local dance hall. They would continue dancing happily for many years to come.

Was the old Baba still out there dancing in the great somewhere? Was she still taking her Guardian Angel role seriously?

J thought she was. After all, she had taken a solemn oath before her unselfish Gypsy God to protect J, hadn't she?

A WEDDING OR A WAR

The brilliant yellow and orange hues of the sun setting in the western sky somehow seemed to sadden Mihal as he watched the young couple walk through the front gate. He'd observed them every weekend for the past eight months. *Every time I see those two, they're holding hands. I like that,* he thought. *If only they weren't so young.*

Mihal winced as he stood gazing out of the large window. He was aware that the radiant sunset would bring this evening to a very unusual closing. There wouldn't be the casual "Hi" from J's boyfriend on this nervous visit. Mihal could see that from the solemn face the young buck was wearing. A serious discussion and a well deliberated decision on Mihal's part were on tap this warm, balmy April eve. That was as certain as the ache in his aging bones that were currently resting discontentedly in the sturdy chrome chair at the kitchen table. A table, he couldn't help but notice, was still littered with the evening meal's dirty coffee mugs.

Yep, tonight will be the beginnin' of a new phase in our Joni's life. These are her final days of living with us. Mihal's pensive thoughts ran amuck as he watched the lovers walk through the kitchen doorway. *Letting her go at such an early age is not going to be easy, but this is her life and her chance at happiness. I only pray that she's prepared for what lies ahead.*

The heat in the confinement of the small kitchen was stifling. J and Ben sat at the kitchen table across from Mihal. Blondie had refused to sit. "I'll stand," she said coldly when Ben offered her one of the chrome kitchen chairs.

Blondie seemed satisfied to be standing and waving her dish towel at the air above her head. She was pretending to swat away the houseflies that were confidently buzzing around the cooling, freshly-jarred strawberry preserves. On such a warm evening, the short jars were patiently cooling on the sink drain board. Blondie smiled, as though amused each time one of the flies landed on the uncoiling tacky strip hanging from the ceiling. "Got cha, you damn bugger," she'd mumble.

"You kids go sit in the other room and watch the television for a few minutes while your dad talks to J and Ben. Skedaddle. Get in there and close the door. Younse don't need to be nosing into the grownup's business, so get goin' now." Blondie shouted as she shooed the lot of them with that same swishing rag she was waving at the buzzing flies.

"Mihal, I love your daughter and I want to marry her, if that's okay with you," Ben nervously asked. With a heavy sigh of relief, he waited. *There, I've done it. I've asked and now I'll just have to wait and see what Mihal answers.*

After presenting his request to his future father-in-law, Ben anxiously concluded, "We hoped July 16th would be okay with both of you as our wedding day." Ben intentionally turned his gaze to include Blondie in the conversation.

"Well now, young man, are you gonna take good care of my Joni? Are you gonna stay true to her? If you give me your word that you'll be an honest and kind husband, then I'll give you my blessing," Mihal responded.

As Mihal studied the young girl's glowing face, he thought *she's just a baby. She can't know what she's getting herself into. He seems to be a decent guy, though. He comes from a large family. They're our kind of people, and they know what rough times are all about in these coal minin' towns. I gotta believe he'll treat her well. He sure seems to love her.*

"Yes, I give you my word," Ben replied sincerely, but quickly. *Whew, I'm glad that's over with* was his true sentiment. *I don't think I have anymore sweat left!*

"Well Blondie, it looks like we're gonna have a wedding this summer," Mihal announced.

He wore a bittersweet smile as he stood to shake hands with the young man. *I like this young guy,* Mihal considered. *It took some guts to come and ask to marry Joni. He showed respect for the old custom. I wonder if I've made the right decision here tonight, though. I just want this girl to have a good life. Heaven only knows, she's had it rough from Blondie all these years.*

Mihal knew he would sleep well this night. Soothing hope rumbled through his heart while ambiguous thoughts spun as fast as windmills in his mind. The thought of losing another daughter set his eyes to glisten, but he knew that any tears shed tonight would only be wasteful. He felt resigned to having made the right decision for his Clementine.

Ben removed his right hand from its resting place on J's left shoulder. "You sure were nervous, Ben," Blondie remarked.

"Look at the big wet spot on J's fancy dress where your hand was sittin'," she smirked, attempting to belittle the young man. "What did you think you were asking for, the moon?" She laughed loudly as she returned to her duty of swishing the dish towel at the buzzing flies.

Listening to Blondie's loud gust of laughter, J attempted to thwart her irritation before responding to her mother's remark. "I don't mind, Ben. That damp spot will dry fast in this heat," she good naturedly quipped while gazing intently at her future husband.

"This is one of the dresses I bought in D.C., Ben. I've worn it a lot, so it's seen better days," J glibly uttered a solicitous reminder of her independence. She aimed the catty, yet subtle, remark directly to Blondie.

Ben didn't necessarily appreciate being ridiculed for perspiring during his coveted conversation with Mihal, especially by Blondie of all people. True to his gentle temperment, he remained nonchalant and ignored Blondie's abrasive remarks. *If J doesn't mind the spot on her dress, why should Blondie?* Ben silently asked himself the question as he reached for the comfort of J's thin hand. Ben knew his reserve would only serve to annoy Blondie. He had seen enough of the woman to know that she loved a good argument. *I'm not about to start something with this nut case,* he decided. Ben realized that he'd found a new appreciation for the restraint training that he'd learned while serving in the Army. He squeezed J's hand a bit tighter. He felt loved when he held her soft hand.

J, in return, loved Ben's hands. They were huge, paw-like, especially when she compared them to her own. They were calloused from hard work, yet had a gentleman's touch when his fingers were clasping hers. *I'm not going to mind anything his hands do to me,* she admitted freely to her newly unlocked heart.

On Good Friday, Ben had surprised J with a two pound box of holiday candy, cleverly wrapped in Easter lily cellophane. As they sat closely embracing in Ben's always polished '53 Ford 500, they listened to a soft romantic tune. With only the orange moonlight shining through the windshield, Ben had handed her the box and insisted nervously, "Open the box and have a piece. It's pretty smooth chocolate," he said enticingly.

"Come on, hurry up already! I'd like to try a couple of pieces myself," he said, tearing off the outer wrapper with the speed of a hypoglycemic man crashing into a coma.

With only the moon as a flashlight, he pointed, "Try that big piece in the middle."

He's too anxious. It's probably a hot pepper. J had reason to worry. *He's a practical joker* she thought cautiously. *I wonder what he has up his sleeve this time.*

In the near darkness, J reached for the square in the middle. Anticipating a chocolate, she became acutely aware of the soft texture. Her fingers were caressing velvet. "What is this?" she suspiciously asked.

"Open it and find out," he whispered closely into her ear.

Moonlight only added sparkle to the diamonds in the ring set. The brightest reflection came from Ben's eyes as he tenderly asked, "Will you marry me?"

I can't believe it, I'm tingling all over. I never dreamed I could be this happy. God, you know how much I love him, I don't want to live a day without him in it. I only pray he knows how I've come to adore him. I feel so certain that he feels the same way about me. J's thoughts materialized and became a resounding "Yes, yes, yes!" as she answered his tender question.

It became a special night as J excitedly accepted his proposal.

Taking two stairs at a time, J entered her mother's darkened bedroom. It was nearly midnight, so she spoke softly hoping to awaken only her mother, and not baby Annamaria who shared the bed. "Ma, I got engaged tonight. Look at the beautiful ring Ben gave me. Ben's going to talk to Dad tomorrow. He wants to ask properly for permission to get married," she whispered to Blondie.

Holding out her ringed hand, J allowed that glowing moon beam peeking through the ragged canvas window blind to capture the diamond's brilliance. She wanted her mother to see the ring's beauty, just as she had at the moment when Ben proposed. J quietly whispered, "I hope you'll be happy for me, Ma."

"Get the Hell out of here, you whore," Blondie hissed, pushing J's hand away.

"Don't you think I know how you got that piece of junk ring? He's turned you into his own personal whore, can't you see that? You're nothing more than a cheap slut." Her mother was whispering, but at the same time her voice was shouting.

"He'll get tired of you before you ever make it down the aisle, you stupid cheap-assed whore. You might be on the honor roll, but you're not even smart enough to charge for your tricks. You think he's done foolin' around with other girls and ready to settle down? Just wait, you'll see different. Get outa my sight. You make me sick," she scourged, before rolling over to face the wall of ferned wallpaper.

Insulted, but undaunted by her mother's rejection, J backed away from Blondie and sought comfort from her father. Going into his bedroom, she found him awake and sitting on the edge of his bed. "What's got Blondie all fired up?" he asked while rubbing the sleepiness out of his eyes with balled fingers.

"This," J said, holding out her hand to reveal her sparkling bauble. "It's an engagement ring. Ben wants to talk to you tomorrow evening. We want to get married. Is that okay with you?"

"Sure, turn the small dresser light on so you don't wake up Victor here," he said calmly, glancing back at the soundly sleeping little boy who shared his bed.

"Let me see that ring. That's sure a beauty, kid. Don't let your Ma's words get to you. She's jealous every time one of you girls get anything," Mihal exclaimed, reaching out to steady her trembling hand as he gazed at the white gold ring studded with diamonds.

"Are you sure you want to get married, especially after what you've seen around this house?" he asked with just the slightest hint of a snigger.

"I'm sure. We're in love! We'll be good for each other, you'll see," she answered, feeling a certainty unlike anything she'd ever felt in her short lifetime. J's heart felt lighter than she'd ever imagined possible. Her feet danced the two-step in every one of her happy dreams.

"You are gonna graduate from high school though. You have to promise me that. You'll need that diploma if you ever want to get a job," he advised.

"I plan on doing that, but we'd like to get married this summer. Then we'll move to Cleveland where Ben's working at a steel and iron mill. It will be a big change for me, but I really love this guy and I want to be his wife. The feeling is so hard to describe, Dad," J's unspoken words spoke incipiently to Mihal's own memory.

Mihal took his time before answering quietly. He was wearing the saddest face J had ever seen, "I felt that way once too, Joni," he sighed heavily.

"I hope your happiness grows along with your marriage and doesn't wither with time the way mine has. I'm happy for you. Go now, get some sleep. Your Ma will be on the warpath in the mornin'. You can bet on that," he forewarned.

Indeed the war began the next morning. The path began in the kitchen. "Are we having oatmeal for breakfast?" J asked politely as she entered the kitchen that smelled of fresh cinnamon.

J noted Blondie's heightened emotional state as Blondie jammed, and then bammed, the long black iron poker in and out of the stove's baffle to break up the hot burning coals. J sniffed the spicey aroma floating throughout the kitchen before asking in a subdued voice, "Is there any oatmeal left?"

"We're eating, but there's none left for you. You got yourself a man now, let him start feedin' you. I threw your share in the pig's slop. At least I'll get something in return for raisin' those sows," Blondie answered caustically.

"I was counting on you to repay me for all the hard work I've put in these eighteen years of raisin' you. If I'd have known you were gonna turn around and become a damned pig-whore, I'd have drowned you when you were born," an infuriated Blondie raged much like the blazing coals.

Barely stopping to catch her breath, Blondie continued haranguing, "You had better get a job to pay for this raffish weddin', because I'm certainly not puttin' out any of my money for a bunch of strangers to eat up. And another thing, you had better start bringin' some money into this house. I'm not gonna keep feedin' some man's whore. I don't give a shit how smart you think you are, you bitch! Every one of younse girls is turnin' out to be God damned whores. Why is that, Mihal?"

Blondie turned to seek an answer from her husband, who had just entered the kitchen for his morning cup of coffee. "Couldn't be because you spoiled every last one of them, could it, Mihal?"

"Stop it Blondie. I will not have you talkin' about our girls that way," he shot right back at Blondie. "So far, they're all turnin' out to be pretty good girls. They're just gettin' on with their own life, that's all. What'd you expect them to do when they grew up? Stay here and grease your fat ass?"

Eyeing his wife, Mihal contemplatively snapped. "You know, it's a puzzle to me how you know so much about what it takes to be a whore, Blondie. Why do you think I would say that, wife of mine? Huh?"

"You can shut your filthy mouth now and let the girl have some of that oatmeal," he continued his own barrage of words before Blondie could interrupt.

"She can have my share of your damned sticky gunk. I've lost my appetite!" Mihal yelped at Blondie.

All of the kids sitting at the breakfast table watched Mihal's face. None knew what to anticipate next. Wearing a sad-puppy look, he reached for the dented aluminum coffee pot perking on the hot coal stove. "I'll get my own coffee. I don't trust you to pour it," he said as Blondie's shocked face glared back at him.

J nervously watched Blondie's reaction and became acutely aware that indeed the war would precede the wedding. Her mother would make that a certainty.

With Ben as the bright light in her life, J knew the route to survival at #11 Lemon Lane was to stay out of Blondie's sight and complete her schooling. She wanted the two most important people in her life to be proud of her accomplishment. She vowed that Ben and Mihal would not be disappointed.

Girls married at a younger age in 1960. It came as no surprise to J's typing teacher when she was greeted by several newly engaged senior girls after any given holiday. "What's all this shouting? What's all of this excitement and noise? I can hear the frenzy way down the corridor?" she jokingly admonished when classes resumed after the Easter break.

"Come on now, let me see those beautiful rings so I can congratulate each of you," Mrs. Carr called out in her thick melodic voice. She carefully scrutinized each engagement ring on each extended youthful hand.

"I sincerely hope you girls will be as happy in your beds as Harry and I are in ours," Mrs. Carr said, tongue in cheek. The class broke out in gales of laughter. Everyone knew that happy twosome was married, just not to each other. *No pretense there,* J thought. *Too bad everyone can't be as honest.*

The next weekend, J's feelings turned ambiguous when she'd overheard too much honesty at Ben's home. She couldn't decide if she was disappointed or disgusted. Nearing the kitchen to get a class of water, she'd overheard Ben's mother and his sister-in-law discussing the pending nuptials. "I can't believe Ben's marrying into that trash family. I could slap him, I'm so angry," Ben's mother was voicing.

"Well, that family must have thought their girl hit the jackot by snagging Ben. I'll bet she's pregnant. That's got to be the only reason he'd be marrying her," the sister-in-law had responded, placing a great emphasis on the word *her*.

Upon entering the kitchen, J excused herself and did some responding of her own, "May I have a glass of water, please," and then she whispered a sincere "thank you" as she was handed an empty glass. Before turning on the cold water faucet, she looked Ben's mother straight in the eyes and said, "We are not a trashy family."

She then turned to the other woman in the room and politely added, "I am not pregnant and Ben does not have to marry me. Is that clear?"

She didn't wait for any argument. She just left the the two gaping women in the old-fashioned kitchen. Their mouths were still hanging open when she glanced back over her shoulder. She returned to Ben waiting in his mother's desperately out-dated living room. She sat down contentedly next to him on the sagging frieze sofa. She listened attentively to Ben's narration of the silent 8mm Korean movies that he'd filmed during his stint in the Army. She was viewing another side of the man she was about to commit her life to. She was genuinely enjoying her quiet time with him. "I love you, Ben," she whispered.

She knew by the twinkling in his eyes that he loved her in return. He didn't need to answer, but he did. "And I love you, too" he answered softly before pulling her closer and sealing his loving gesture with a concrete kiss.

School life was good for J. It was an escape from the daily harassment she was experiencing at #11 Lemon Lane. She studied and continued to be an honor student despite the daily turmoil at home.

Every weekday became a beleaguered battleground for Blondie. In her mind, J envisioned Blondie as *Custer at the last stand, unable to come to terms with losing again.*

"About the time I think I'm gonna start collecting from one of my kids, they're off and running, leavin' me in the dust without so much as even a nickel thanks," Blondie told Big Annie over a cup of tea one afternoon. "You're lucky you only have one girl left to betray you," she said askance.

Blondie remained as vengeful as only Blondie could be. Stemming from a feeling of betrayal, J wondered *does she have a list of daily chores written down somewhere. She doles out the same orders week after week. She wasn't kidding when she'd said she'd get even wth me for getting engaged.*

"Get this bitchin' laundry goin'," welcomed J home from school on Mondays.

"Get this God damned ironin' done," was Blondie's greeting every Tuesday. "Do both of those full bushel baskets of dampened laundry and get them done tonight!"

"It's your night to clean out the rancid barn manure," was Wednesday's order.

"Get this filthy downstairs cleaned. You might as well get it started for the weekend," was Thursday's chore.

"Get the upstairs cleaned, don't forget to change the sheets. Clean the kitchen, and scrub the floor this time," Blondie would shout the minute J's body appeared through the kitchen doorway on Fridays.

Saturdays would bring fresh orders. "Scrub down the shit out of the cow's stall and hose down the cow. Go, get it done this mornin'."

Sunday morning's greeting was usually, "Well, it looks like the queen whore is up and ready to go to church. Can you beat that?" Blondie would throw in the barb for good measure.

There was nothing Blondie could say or do to deter J's thoughts and dreams of a life with Ben. Absolutely nothing! Not even when she realized that her mother could be correct about some comments she'd made referencing her as Ben's property. It didn't matter what she thought. *It's too late to turn back now. I've committed my whole being to Ben and our love*, J happily thought.

Ben will be home for the weekend. When he calls, I'll be ready for our date. I'll get done whatever I can, but the other kids can pitch in with the chores. This is HER house, so let HER do some of the work. She'll just have to give up some of HER afternoon gossip sessions with the neighbors. I plan on spending my time with Ben when he's home for the weekend. No matter how angry or how irritated she became with her mother's wrath, J lived every waking moment thinking of Ben. She kept her happy thoughts to herself. She had to. There was no one in her home to share them with. *Independence* was beckoning as a new and exciting concept in her llife. It felt good to have this new word in her vocabulary.

Weekday dinner meals were often served to the other kids as soon as they arrived home on the early bus from elementary school. J arrived on the later bus and would be given an assigned chore as soon as she walked through the old weather-beaten door. Later, more often than not, J was offered skimpy leftovers that remained to wither or film-over in the uncovered pots setting on top of the hot coal stove. "You're the last one done, so you get to do the dishes and clean up the kitchen. Get your ass movin', girl," became a very familiar phrase to J after she'd eaten the table scraps.

Often Blondie's inane cruelty was blatantly evident as she'd laugh, "I threw the leftovers to the dog, so there's nothin' left for you."

On occasion, if the food was intolerable or unavailable, J ate pickles from a blue two-quart Mason jar retrieved from the dank cellar shelves. Many jars had been filled with the past summer's preserved foods, but the dilled cuccumbers were the only staple not on the "off limits" list. The dilled cucumbers filled the gullet and quenched the hungry intestinal rumblings, but only temporarily. The early morning's gut would have a different grumble to cope with in the outhouse.

"God, you're getting skinny," Ben commented to J one May Saturday evening as he encircled his fingers around her thin waist. "How much do you weigh now?" he asked.

"I'm just excited about graduation and about our upcoming wedding," she explalined away the weight loss, but she knew his observance was right on the money. She was five feet five inches tall and weighed ninty seven pounds. She had gone from a size ten to a size four. She could now fit into her thirteen year old sister's child-sized dresses, and she often resorted to wearing them for a comfortable fit.

She had also resorted to cutting corn flakes box templates to cover the large holes in the soles of the shoes she had purchased with her D.C. earnings last fall. J had learned that she could entertain the toddlers with a foot puppet. By flexing her foot upward, she'd expose the rooster character poking its beak through the large hole in the sole of her shoe. By imitating the bird's *pluck, pluck, plucking,* she'd exposed her own vulnerability. The price of humility was cheap in this household, but J soon learned that the outbursts of her sibling's laughter were priceless.

She had bravely asked Blondie once, and only once, for a new pair of shoes. "You got yourself a man now. Tell him you need shoes. He's the one who's gonna get from you, not me. You're lucky I didn't kick you out already, you bow-legged whore," Blondie growled, before crudely slapping J's cheek with the palm of her hand.

"Get out of my way, you ugly mamoona bitch," she said, and then roughly shoved J onto the floor.

From that moment on, J stayed out of Blondie's reach.

Unrequited love prevailed though as Ben began to realize the situation with Blondie. Extending two twenty dollar bills to J, Ben said, "Use this to buy what you need for your graduation clothes. I want my girl to look nice."

In 1960, forty dollars bought two pair of shoes, two dresses, and some new under garments at the Robert Hall Discount Store. With the few dollars left in change, J made an appointment for a permanent wave. Adela had convinced J that a perm would be necessary to control her long hair in Clevelalnd's summer's heat and humidity. J remembered D.C.'s humidity. Perhaps a perm was in order.

"I'd like a soft perm, but I don't want my hair cut," J told Margaret at the local Houtzdale Salon. "I don't want anything fuzzy, please," she insisted.

"I have graduation next week and in one month I'm getting married, so I want my hair to be only a little curly," J carefully explained to the beautician.

Margaret seemed agreeable to J's request, but she did make a sour-puss expression when J declined a hair cut. After a quick shampoo, the hairdresser began the hair sectioning, and then attacked the rods and rolling. Once the stinky ammonia perm solution was squirted on, Margaret sat J under the heating hood. Ten minutes into the curling process, a thunderous rainstorm caused a power outage.

"Gawd," Margaret stopped chewing her gum long enough to squeal. "Now what am I supposed to do. Guess I'll just take a chance and leave the rods in longer without the heat and hope your hair curls."

Thirty minutes later, she was rinsing J's hair with icy-cold water. "We have an electric hot water tank. No electricity, no hot water," she declared without so much as noticing that J's shivering was about to rock her out of the stylist's chair.

After applying the neutralizer and rinsing with cold water again, she held out her hand expecting payment. "I'll only charge you five dollars, since I'm not sure how your hair is going to turn out," she whined.

Taking J by the elbow, Margaret nudged her out of the salon. J's dripping wet ringlets and chattering teeth didn't deter the beautician's goal. Margaret quickly pocketed the five dollar bill before slamming the shoppe door and pulling down the roller blind. In the blink of an eye, the stylist had been sucked out of sight into her beauty shoppe vacuum.

Two days later, J still couldn't pull a comb through the mass of tangled tight curls. "Oh, shit, what am I going to do now?" she asked the girl in the mirror. *I look like a damn clown. Did Margaret and Polly graduate from the same circus.*

Turning to Adela, who was visiting for the weekend, she complained, "This is your fault. It was your big bright idea. Now look at the fuzz ball surrounding my face. I should have known better than to listen to you."

With Blondie's large sewing scissors in hand, Adela volunteered, "Quit your belly aching. I'll give you a *bob*. This is not a major catastrophe, you know. Your hair will grow, give it time. Shush and be grateful she didn't make your head go bald. It could be worse, you could be getting a hair cut from Polly," she scoffed.

J sat in silence watching the mound of fuzz grow higher on the kitchen floor. *It's only hair,* she sadly concluded. *It's ironic though, I started high school with a frizzy hairdo and I'm ending with the same fuzzy carnival do!*

Hugs meant to last a life time were exchanged on the last day of high school. Congratulations were expressed to long-time friends at their graduation ceremony. The term "bittersweet" came to hold a whole new meaning for J. Filled with hope, her senior classmates marched to different drummers. Off they went down a variety of highways, some never to be seen or heard from again. Such was life!

J's next big day was approaching quickly, and valuable time couldn't be wasted on sentimentality. Plans were quickly shaping into a celebratory event unlike any J's family had ever experienced. Thanks to Ben, incoming wedding bills were being paid as they arose.

"Tell that man of yours if he wants a wedding, he's to pay the bills. I told you before and I'll tell you again, I'm not givin' a nickel for any shit you two are plannin'. You got that? You better get it!" Blondie's rages boomed daily.

J couldn't help but notice, Blondie always seemed to answer her own question. *Well, that's certainly the one thing she's good at, besides driving her point straight through the heart.*

J was seeing situations and comments from a different viewpoint these days. She was already standing on the outside looking in at #11 Lemon Lane.

J had certainly gotten Blondie's ever intimidating messages. They came through loud and clear. "You are not having that Henya girl in your bridal party. You'll have your sisters Adela and Vera, and you'll be buying them a dress they can wear for other occasions, not just for your shindig. You got that? You'd better get that through that thick head of yours."

Still somewhat frightened of her mother's affronting hostility, J would timidly answer, "Yeah, I got that," and then quietly walk away to avoid any further confrontation.

Ben willingly picked up the tab for the dresses and matching dyed shoes. Ben paid for the meats and vegetables necessary to concoct the ethnic foods that were expected at a Slovakian wedding. A variety of soft drinks, the cooks, the polka band, the hall rental, the bride's rented outfit, and even the booze were all bought and paid for by Ben with his earnings from the iron mill.

"He wants a wedding, let him pay the price," Blondie reasoned vociferously on a daily basis. "Just remember, I'm not payin' a God damned penny," she would yap as she pompously jingled her worn, black-leather coin purse in front of J's face.

Ben's family had promised to contribute home-made breads and pastries for the wedding, so it was a pleasant surprise when it was thought that Blondie was also giving them a hand with expenses. She had instructed J and Ben, "Go to Sammy's farm for your eggs. He's savin' the cracked-shell ones for us at a cheaper price."

After Ben picked up the twelve dozen of eggs that had been set aside at Blondie's request, he headed for the door. Sammy, the egg man, quickly called out, "Hey, ain't younse gonna pay for them? I run a business here not a second-hand store. You owe me twelve dollars. Them's fresh, you know!"

Those twelve dollars just about broke the bank! That was the start of Thursday morning, July 14th.

Friday morning rolled in steaming, just like the freight train that delivered Adela to the Tyrone station. Once Adela arrived she became a whirlwind of questions and suggestions to control the wedding plans. "Don't worry about a thing. Ben and I have everything under control," J assured her.

Dejected and in a huff Adela climbed the stairs, all the while bitching under her breath. "I'm taking a retreat. I'm tired and I desperately need a short nap after that long trip. You think you know what you're doing, but I have news for you, you're nothing more than an idiot."

If only Adela had napped, a fiasco wouldn't have ensued. J had quietly tiptoed up the staircase to change her pedal pushers that had gotten dirty from carrying groceries to the expectant cooks in the reception hall. At the top of the stairs, J stopped long enough to figure out what was happening in her bedroom.

Sure enough, there was twenty year old Adela wearing J's bridal gown. She was whirling around the room, humming and singing Here Comes the Bride.

Thirteen year old Vera had the toile veil wrapped around her head and was wearing the headpiece upside down. "Look at me! I'm a bride, too," she sang out.

"What do you think you're doing? I just spent two hours pressing my gown and veil," J cried out in anguish. "How disrespectful can you be?" she asked her two sisters.

"Oh, pipe down. We didn't hurt anything. So your stupid gown got a few wrinkles in it. Who really gives a shit anyway?" Adela asked. "But since you're here, unbutton this damned thing. It's so tight I'm having trouble breathing and I may just start popping buttons," she said tediously.

Addressing her cohort in crime, Adela sarcastically diverted J's attention to Vera. "Quit wiping your runny nose in that veil, Vera. Someone in this room has to wear that crappy thing tomorrow!"

Adela obviously felt that her warped sense of humor was entertaining as she began to leak giggles. Vera followed suit and joined in the snickering.

J stood stone still as she glared at the two trouble makers. She was not amused by their childish antics. J hadn't felt such inconsideration and betrayal from Adela since last September. "Still the jealous one, aren't you Adela?" J asked. "How many dollars did you give Vera to wear my veil and crown?"

Without hesitation, Vera promptly answered, "Two," before absentmindedly resuming her twirling and singing.

The ceremony began promptly at ten o'clock on the morning of July 16th. As custom prevailed, J walked down the aisle escorted by Mihal. "I look spiffy, if I have to say so myself," he ribbed, before they took step one.

"See, I'm even wearing my favorite shirt in your honor with this new blue suit your Ma bought me. How about that?" He was smiling broadly as he reached to straighten his blue and charcoal striped tie.

Taking one step backward to get a better view of the bride, Mihal complimented her. "You look beautiful, Joni," Mihal addressed his little girl in her freshly pressed gown and veil.

Mihal had no idea J's entire bridal outfit was rented from a costume shop in Cleveland at a cost of thirty nine dollars. He had no way of knowing that the costume needed to be returned by eight o'clock Monday morning. "This must have set Ben back a few dollars," Mihal determined, as he closely viewed the flowing rice cloth gown with its lace and sequined inserts.

J didn't speak. She couldn't smile at the moment. After a heavy sigh, she managed, "We rented it for the weekend."

Mihal was dumbfounded, "I won't say a word to anyone," he promised, giving her hand a gentle assuring pat.

Mihal drifted his thoughts to earlier events where he and J had shared other secrets. *God, send me a sign that I'm doing the right thing here* he thought. Just then the sun began to shine through the stained glass church windows. *Well, I'll be a son of a gun, the rain's stopped. That's the best sign* he mused at the same time that the ceremonial music began.

J may have been naïve on her wedding morning, but she certainly wasn't stupid. She had given serious consideration to the wedding vows rehearsed the prior day.

Truthfully, she decided, *I don't think I can promise to love, honor and obey till death do we part. I'll give it my best shot every day, but forever is a long time when it comes to a promise.*

With a congregation full of observant eyes and attentive ears, the priest pronounced the faithful vows, "Do you, Joni, forsaking all others, promise to love, honor and obey Ben, till death do you part?"

"I'll try," J responded.

"No, my dear," the priest challenged, "you're supposed to say I will or I do."

"Look, I said I'll try," she repeated with indignation.

"No, no, my dear," the priest pled. "You're supposed to say I will or I do."

"Look, I've told you, I'll try," she stubbornly reiterated, "take it or leave it."

Exasperated, the priest turned to Ben and requested his agreement to the same vow. This time the groom just stared at the priest and didn't even elicit a response.

What in God's name is going on here? The rehearsal went so smoothly yesterday, the very visibly puzzled priest couldn't help but wonder, *so what's going on here now?* He began to repeat the vows. A few words into the verse, and after a nudge from the best man, the groom shouted, "I will."

In retrospect, the priest was later heard to humorously tell Ben's mother, "I sure was happy to get past the vows. I can't wait to see if that gal is still trying twenty five years from now."

It wasn't until the reception music was loud enough to drift into the hall's corners and make the dust bunnies boogie that Ben admitted he hadn't heard the priest's words. "My ears are plugged with heavy dust from the iron mill. We tried flushing them out this morning, but I guess that didn't work. I'm not hearing much of anything," he told his new bride, to which she laughingly replied, "Don't worry about it. You only promised the priest you'd buy me an expensive mink coat!"

That too, J would soon learn, fell on deaf ears.

The Ukrainian Hall was gaily decorated with pale blue crepe paper ribbons and tissue carnations to match the usher's pale blue tuxedos, the bridesmaids' lace dresses and the tinted daisy floral arrangements. The place looked what it was, a remnant 1930's beer hall sporting faded walls and bare floor boards. A flip of a switch turned off two of the side chandeliers. With the dimmed lighting, voila, no more visible flaws.

"Anything can look good if the room's dark enough" was a laugh inducing comment J remembered from a converstion she'd once overheard. Two eldely neighbors had wailed hysterically after discussing one of their earlier sexual conquests. *They were so right. This darkened room looks a lot better now* she had to admit.

The long tables were set with white paper tablecloths and blue plastic flower arrangements. The head table was picture perfect with low blue daisy arrangements that surrounded a three-tiered wedding cake. Many pennies had been pinched to pull off this party, but the festivity went gaily into the night without a hitch.

The seated guests applauded and banged spoons on their glassware when the newlyweds arrived. Finally the highlight of the guests' day and the real purpose for some of them being there, the buffet lines could begin.

The four piece polka band arrived in time to get in the dinner line, right behind the wedding party. "Food is food, but free is better," the accordionist remarked as he heaped his plate with the delicious Polish and Slovak foods. He'd played his music at many local weddings and easily recognized the expertise poured into these ethnic dishes. The cooking by these studda babas was pure manna from the Heavens.

Guests drifted in accompanied by clusters of children who were not always their own. Food was food, but free food was better as the musician had proclaimed. These coal mining and farming families took advantage of any invitation arriving at an address. Once accepted, the invite meant the entire household would attend any aspect of an occasion where a free meal was anticipated. They assumed a meal offered was theirs for the eating.

The giving was another story. Gifts poured in by the piles. Ah, and what notable gifts they were, indeed! A prime example was Blondie's mother's donation of two hand-made pot holders, sewn from four different scraps of old dress material. They were generously wrapped in yesterday's newspaper.

Mihal's sister, MaryAnne, brought her five children. "So they can eat and have a good time," she told the bride. MaryAnne's gift was one eighteen-inch ruffled doily, encased in a box that was labeled: contains six varied size doilies. It was delightfully wrapped in white blood-spotted butcher's paper and a brown string bow.

Two neighbors jointly accumulated the Jewel tea company's free promotional dishes. Each piece was wrapped in the Sunday newpaper comic pages.

Several sets of drinking glasses, a variety of small kitchen utensils including a rolling pin, and an ironing board found their way to the heap on the gift table.

A wrapped box topped with a large bow was an automatic admission into the small town wedding receptions. The town's residents didn't view the invitation as mandatory. Some questionable guests were brazen enough to grab a gift as they exited the reception. Callosity roamed freely and without shame in dire times.

Money envelopes were tossed into a basket at the entrance to the dance hall, mostly to save the guest any embarrassment, especially the cheapskates. A few cards from Ben's family and J's sister, Pet, contained twenty dollar bills, but mostly the cardless envelopes contained only a few dollars.

Blondie had tossed her yellowed five-cent congratulatory card into the basket. She made a big showing of her deposit, at least according to little Cindy. "Ma told everybody she gave you a hundred bucks in her card. That's a whole lot of money, ain't it, J?" Cindy seemed so pleased with herself for being the bearer of that good news to her sister, the bride.

After the wedding buffet dinner, the fifty-five dollar cake was cut into small pieces by Pet. The slices were quickly scarved down by the guests. It was like watching soup bones being tossed to a bunch of hungry mongrels in a crowded den. Luckily, J and Ben had hidden the top layer to be frozen and eaten on their first wedding anniversary. If they hadn't done that, the cake top surely would have been found and gobbled up with the rest of the desserts. The couple should have let it be eaten. They didn't yet know how disrespected their special cake would be a year later.

Slovakian music got the old beer joint jumpin'. The newlyweds started the dancing segment of the reception with a slow two step. That seemed to get the floor cleared of the folding tables, which set the evening in motion. Even the youngsters seemed to be enjoying the music, bopping around the dance floor to the happy tempo of the She's Too Fat For Me Polka. Ben polkaed with his mother and J hop-stepped with her Dad to The Pennsylvania Polka. Happy guessts made for a joyful scene!

As J and her dad whirled light-footed around the floor, Mihal spoke, "You know, Joni, I'm not your real father, don't you? Baba said you already knew who your real father was, do you?" Mihal asked as simply as he could muster.

"Yes, I know about Jake and me, and Ed Strang. I saw that man and Ma once in the barn. Then that man, Ed Strang, told me, but it doesn't matter. As far as I'm concerned, you're my only dad," she said reverently. Mihal nodded an agreeable understanding.

"Another thing, Joni," Mihal went on, "I don't want any repayment for the savings bonds your Ma cashed to pay for this weddin'. Consider it a gift from me, to you and Ben with my blessin's."

"Ma didn't give us one penny toward this wedding, Dad. I don't know what she did with the bond money, but neither I nor Ben got any of it," J strongly countered to Mihal, who stopped short his fancy footwork and asked, "Are you sure?"

"I'm positive, Dad," J said. "She didn't give us any money. She didn't contribute a single penny. Ben even paid for the fancy socks the little ones are wearing today. She said if we didn't get them new socks, they couldn't go. How could I tell those kids they weren't coming to my wedding after they've been so excited about everything? I couldn't do that to them?"

"What about Vera's outfit? She told me she gave you two hundred dollars to pay for Vera and Adela's dresses. And," Mihal stuttered, "she said she put a hundred dollars in your weddin' card. Let's go see if she did."

Holding the empty wedding card Cindy had handed him, Mihal stood looking stupefied as he blankly stared across the dance floor at Blondie. He listened to J's softly spoken response. He realized J wanted to clear the slate of any further allegations about this wedding. "Ben paid for those bridesmaids dresses and shoes, along with every other thing it took to have this party."

That was the last straw for Mihal. It took precisely three long strides for him to catch up with Blondie, who was headed for the restroom. Mihal steered Blondie by the elbow, straight out the back door. That was the last J saw of either of them until a while later at *that damned house*.

At ten o'clock, while the newlyweds were slowly dancing, Ben whispered to his new bride, "Let's go. Let's get started on our honeymoon."

The naïve eighteen year-old bride answered, "Why? I'm having fun!"

Taking a lesson from Mihal, he began guiding his bride toward the unattended side exit. "It's time to take my favorite gal on a honeymoon, that's why," Ben whispered.

Slipping out of the hall unnoticed, Ben and J headed for *that damned house* to collect her belongings. J also needed to change out of her gown and into something more comfortably suited for a driving trip to their weekend honeymoon in Niagara Falls.

"What the Hell do you think you're doin'? Are you slinkin' outa here, and are you stealin' them clothes," Blondie snarled at J, as a hearing-impaired Ben continued carrying J's belongings to his car.

"What the Hell were you two doin' upstairs anyway. You're not doin' your dirty stuff in my house, are you? Get the Hell out of here, you whore. Don't you ever think you can come back and sleep in this house, for I won't allow that to ever happen. What are you waitin' for? I told you to get the Hell out!"

Blondie shouted, even though she was only a foot away from J's face. "And you had better leave some of that God damned weddin' money right there on that table. I raised you and I expect to get paid for that," Blondie added while pointing her shaking index finger to the littered kitchen table.

Backing away from her mother, J peered over Blondie's shoulder and caught a glimpse of a long, white envelope that had been addressed to her Jakey boy, c/o the USAF. The word *CONFIDENTIAL* had been printed in bold letters and angled across the top of the envelope, J noted. "What's so confidential in that letter to Jake?" J asked. "It couldn't be the missing bond money, could it?"

Without so much as a fleeting second, Blondie reached out with the back of her hand and attempted to slap J. Her outstretched arm didn't quite reach her daughter's face. Instead, Blondie hit the back of her hand against the door frame when J had rapidly moved sideways to avoid the impact of her mother's swing.

"Why you skinny turd, I'll beat the shit out of you when I get a good hold of your neck. I don't care whose missus you are now, you're still standin' in my kitchen and I'm still the boss here," Blondie crazily ranted, all the while rubbing her reddened knuckles.

"What's the matter?" a wide-eyed Ben asked as he re-entered the kitchen.

"Nothing," J answered, "nothing at all."

Too embarrassed and ashamed to repeat her mother's words to her new husband, J uttered softly, "Let's just go. Where's Dad? Did he take your parents back to Osceola?"

J had asked the questions merely to avert Ben's attention. She didn't care if Blondie answered or not.

Slowly, J panned one last dour glance at the kitchen she'd grown to hate these past few months. Her eyes scoured over the meager furnishings.

The fifteen year old Philco refrigerator was scratched and yellowed from aging. The chrome handle had been replaced with a piece of lead plumbing pipe. J remembered the day the shiny appliance had been delivered. That had been a very exciting day for a five year old.

Sitting atop the fridge was the cream colored plastic radio that Junior had sent as a Christmas gift several years ago. That one lonely item had brought joy to this outdated room. J smiled remembering music that had poured from the webbed circle on the radio's front. There were songs to sing while washing dishes, and melodies for dancing while sweeping the floor with a well-worn broom. That was the last gift Junior sent home.

The one white cupboard bore traces of yesteryear's paint. Its doors wore stained patches from years of dirty hands reaching into its cubicles or pulling out the tiltable flour bin.

A corner white metal sink had been a Christmas gift from Pet years ago. Cold water had been pumped from a well until recently when the piping had finally been attached to the faucet. The sink still did not have running hot water. It was 1960 and *this damned house* still didn't have a hot water tank or an indoor bathroom.

The flecked linoleum was beginning to show signs of wear, especially around the coal and ash buckets setting near the outdated coal stove. Brown burnt spots dotted the flooring, marring the simplicity of the pattern. J couldn't help but notice that the rag rugs were ruffled as usual. The feet in this house had never found LeCroix magic.

How they can be satisfied to live in this squalor is a wonder. Maybe it doesn't bother them, but it sure makes me ashamed. I can't understand why they didn't keep up with the rest of the world. Whatever happened to all of the money Mihal earned in Buffalo? I'll bet Jake and Blondie know, J thought angrily.

J knew in her heart that she'd never have a chance to learn the real answers to the hypothetical questions racing through her thoughts. She just knew she was now a part of the past in *this damned house.*

J didn't want to linger in this kitchen any longer, so she turned and squarely stared into her mother's widened eyes. It was then she said, "Good bye, Ma."

It was time to leave. There was nothing further in this place for her. She would miss some of her siblings, and Mihal of course, but Blondie was already fading into a memory.

J and Ben walked stiffly away from the aging maddened woman with the straggly blonde hair. J noted Blondie's thickened waist pushing the limits of the blue dress seams. Blondie was wearing the dress J had purchased for her some months ago. *I've lost weight, Ma, but you've gained. How did that happen and neither of us noticed, did we?* J kept her thought to herself, as usual.

A year passed before J searched the depths of Blondie's blue Polish eyes again.

The following July, J and Ben returned for a brief visit with Ben's widowed mother. They shared their frozen cake between their two families by giving half to Ben's home and the other portion to J's.

At Ben's home, the familiarity of the kitchen encouraged light-hearted conversation around a merry kitchen table. There the cake was eaten leisurely and enjoyed heartily with steaming cups of aromatic coffee. It was good to the last drop!

At J's house, an emotional detachment formed as Adela and Vera took turns throwing handfuls of the frosted cake at the kitchen ceiling, laughing hysterically if a piece stuck to the wooden slats.

Blondie looked on and laughed the loudest.

J couldn't help but wonder, *how many dollars did Adela pay Vera on that day?*

TIME FLYS

Where did all those years go J wondered? *Sure I've been busy with my own life, but it doesn't seem possible that twenty eight years have flown by so quickly.*

Oh, but they have, J thought. *It took all of my time to be a wife and a mother to two sons, and then the years raced by as I completed my nursing degrees while holding down a full-time hospital position. Then there were Ben's job transfers every few years. He didn't dare take a pass or he'd have never gotten another management promotion. The retail business policy prevailed and "family came second"* as J remembered one of Ben's supervisor's comments. *How selfish we've been with our visiting back home, and now it's too late* J deduced.

The last time J saw Mihal was in the fall, October 16th, to be exact. She recalled that it was Sweetest Day when she and Ben had driven to Gunther for a day. The weather on that day couldn't have been more conducive to a long drive from Michigan to Pennsylvania. It was a beautifully bright, sunny trip. The sky was a sea of baby blue with large billowy-white clouds. The autumn's red and gold mountain colors illuminated the scenic drive. Route 80 was more vivid and picturesque than she remembered it ever being.

Today the temperature was ten degrees above zero. It was a typical frosty and snowy February drive through Ohio to Pennsylvania. Dull shades of mountain grey beckoned J and Ben on their long melancholy trek to #11 Lemon Lane. This was not a relished weekend away from home. A long-dreaded phone call had pulled J and Ben out of their secure city living. They were being forced to revisit the out-dated lifestyle of their youth in the small Pennsylvania rural areas where they'd grown up.

Mihal had appeared healthy last October. He had gained some weight and his skin coloring was tinted pink. He sounded happy. His voice was strong for a seventy eight year old man. He anticipated spring planting and pruning, while looking forward to his usual long summer walks in the shaded Tyrone Mountains that he so loved. He even remembered a favorite story and reminisced with J and Ben about that one particular mid-July mountain fishing trip he had taken as a young man.

"Yes siree Joni, me, Jack and Steve were all set to go trout fishin' up in the Tyrone Mountains," he began.

"We collected night crawlers the night before and packed them in tin cans. We lined our fishin' creels with damp moss. We strung new fishin' line on our reels and waxed our rods. We packed bologna and cheese sandwiches in wrinkled brown pokes and poured coffee into Mason jars. At four o'clock on a Saturday mornin' we were set to go, so we all hopped into my old dark green Ford and took off for Tipton. We drove until we saw a macadam road leadin' off the main highway and we pulled in . . . way, way into the trees," he indicated with a waving arm gesture.

"None of us had a fishin' license, so we didn't want anyone to see the car from the highway, especially the game warden who prowled the mountain streams."

Mihal paused to change his position from where his shoulder was leaning against the crooked apple tree. He rubbed his shoulders back and forth as if to scratch an itch on his shoulder blades. Snickering as he did this, he continued his story.

"Yeah, we pulled that car into the trees, broke off a few branches to hide the trunk and then headed off to find a stream with some trout in it. Well, the three of us buddies walked and walked until we heard the slow steady murmur of runnin' water. It was a beauty of a clear flowin' stream and there were these big rainbow trout swimmin' around and under the fallen mossy tree trunks. It didn't take us long at all to cast out and then reel in some big fish to take home for our dinners."

Mihal was now laughing and swinging his head pendulum style. "Well, the next thing we knew we were lost. Can you imagine, three grown men in the thicket of the mountains and we had no idea which way to go to get back to my car. We walked and walked, then walked some more. It felt like we spent most of the day tryin' to find our way out of that mountain range, until we came upon an old leanin' cabin with white smoke comin' out of its chimney. This old unshaven dusty codger was livin' in that one room shack. We couldn't believe it, but there he was standin' on that rickety porch waitin' to see what we were doin' in his neck of the woods. It took some talkin' to convince him that we really were lost. He finally caved in and gave us a ride out to the main highway in his rustin' jalopy of a pickup truck, but that's as far as he'd go. He dropped us off and pointed for us to head east."

Mihal was laughing quite loudly by this time, but he persisted between guffaws. In his own way, he was demonstrating the necessity for full attention to details when it came to telling a whopper of a fisherman's story.

"Well, Joni, we picked up a steady stride and made it home by sunset. We all had blisters from walkin' and sweatin' so much in our work boots. By the time we got to Lemon Lane, we were all limpin' like loose lobsters. The next mornin', we took Steve's truck and went lookin' for my car. We found the macadam road, but there was no car anywhere to be found. We tried to find the dirt road to the old guy's cabin, but we never did. The only thing we found was a rattlesnake and it took the three of us to kill it before we could rip off its tail rattles. We never could figure that one out, Joni. Nope, we never did find that car."

Pointing to the roof top of #11 Lemon Lane, he said, "See that patch up there near the chimney? That's where Blondie went through the roof when we came back home without the car." Mihal was laughing so hard, tears were running down his cheeks.

J and Ben laughed with him. Neither of them let on they'd heard the tale before. He was enjoying the memory too much to be interrupted. Besides, it was good to see him so jovial.

When Ben and J drove away that late afternoon, Mihal continued waving until their car went over the knoll at the end of Lemon Lane. J waved back, watching Mihal who was wearing his familiar brown plaid flannel shirt, a pair of well-worn dungarees and an old baseball cap covering his snow-white hair. He was standing with his usual one-legged forward stance. The further Ben drove, the smaller Mihal became.

I don't know why, but I have this strange feeling that will be the last memory I have of him, J's intuition whispered. Her innermost feelings wavered as her outstretched arm moved back and forth as though she were Elizabethan royalty. She waved until Mihal disappeared from her view of the quaint country setting she used to call home.

Blondie was no where in sight. She had waved her *good bye* from inside the house, not bothering to come outside when the visiting twosome were leaving. She hadn't been hospitable when they arrived, so it was no surprise when Mihal's suggestion to put a pot of coffee on to perc went unheeded. Her response had been, "I don't have any coffee grounds. We'll be gettin' some this afternoon when we go into town."

That announcement seemed a surprise to Mihal. "We're goin' to town, Blondie? This afternoon? When did you decide that? And since when did you let your coffee can go empty? That's a first, isn't it?"

Blondie only turned her head away from her visitors, smirked and asked "Are younse stayin' long? I got things to do today, and besides my soap show's on the television now."

Plopping herself down into an oversized recliner, she sat in front of the television set for over an hour ignoring the visitors, all the while watching an early afternoon soap opera. Mihal chatted almost non-stop. The hours flew by pleasantly and quickly. He was relaxed and content to see the happy couple seated with him at the kitchen table.

"Don't mind your Ma, kid. It seems she's got a new bug up her ass every day lately," Mihal said. He whispered the excuse for Blondie's rudeness, avoiding at all cost any riling of antagonism from her.

"I've been feeling pretty good. Some days are good, some aren't. When you get to be my age, you take what you get, Joni," he said, laughing lightly when they'd inquired about his health.

J remembered that it hadn't been that long ago that he'd hit a rough spot with his heart.

Well, then again, maybe it was longer than I thought. J realized it had been over five years since his near fatal heart attack. He had collapsed while varnishing the stairs leading down to the cellar.

As he would tell it, "I shoulda let those damn steps alone, but Blondie just wouldn't drop the subject. She kept naggin' that they needed a new coat of spar varnish, so as they'd look better when the basement door was opened. I tried to tell her nobody gave a damn about those old wood steps, but you know your Ma. When she gets a bug up her behind, nothin' short of a broom handled enema gets it out. Doc said the fumes brought on my heart attack. He said my lungs were ruined. I got black lung disease from workin' in the coal mines and the foundry furnace. Doc said I shoulda had more ventilation."

Then, with a renewed twinkle in those gray eyes of his, he'd added, "But I'm good now, good as new."

Everyone knew he wasn't as good as new. He'd refused to have the recommended bypass surgery, so how could he be as good as new?

"When it's my time to go, then I'll go the way the Good Lord intended. No surgery, and that's that. In the meantime, I'm gonna enjoy fishin' and junk pile scavengin' with my buddies as long as I'm able to walk those mountains," he insisted stubbornly. His eyes misted over as he pointed with a head gesture to the hills in the distance.

Ma wasn't the only one with an obstinate streak. That wasn't merely a whim of a thought; it was a sure fact, known to everyone who grew up in *that damned house.*

He often spoke of his hospitalization and his related experiences. "You know, people tell stories about floatin' above their beds and lookin' down on themselves while the doctors are bringin' them back to life. I used to think that was a bunch of bunk, but you know what, it's true," he proclaimed.

As though surprising himself, with every retelling of his near-death experience his eyes would open wide as if he'd just seen a shadowy apparition. "That happened to me. I saw and heard the docs and the nurses tellin' each other what to do to bring me back to life. They said my heart had stopped beatin'."

He continued to speak in an animated tone as though he was in awe of himself. "The next day, I repeated words to them that only they could know. They said words like "resuscitate and call code blue". I even told the one nurse where her syringe with something called Epi had rolled. It was under the dresser. I watched it fall on the floor after she uncapped it and tried to hand it to the doctor. She looked and sure enough, there it was. They sure treated me like a prince when I was in that hospital though," he'd tell anyone who'd listen to his story.

Upon his discharge from the hospital, Mihal was prescribed medication to ease the workload on his heart and kidneys. Blondie took over as his nurse, doling out his pills at the appropriately prescribed times, or so everyone thought.

Mihal had stayed in reasonably good health until last November, when he began to retain fluid in his legs and feet. He found he'd get winded easily. Even during phone conversations, he'd become short of breath. He described his symptoms to J. "She's my Registered Nurse daughter," he'd boast to his friends. Understanding the seriousness of edema and dyspnea in a patient with a cardiac history, J began delving deeper into his complaints of fluid retention and difficulty breathing.

"Yeah, I take the pills Blondie gives me. I don't know what they are or what they're for, but they don't seem to be workin' any more. Here, ask her yourself," he said as he handed the phone to his wife.

"What do you want to know?" a hostile Blondie asked J at the other end of the phone line many hundreds of miles away.

"Is Dad taking his pills? What is he taking? Can you read me the names off of the labels," J asked rapidly. She hoped that Blondie would realize the significance of her pertinent questions.

"No, I'm not goin' into the kitchen and draggin' the bottles in here. I give him the same pills everyday, just the way it says on the labels. You want to read the labels, drive home and check it out for yourself," Blondie barked into the phone's mouthpiece.

She makes me think of old Jingleberry barking at those gobbling turkeys we used to have running around the barnyard. Does she, or doesn't she, see the value of my quest for information? Or maybe, just maybe, she's playing more game. J recalled how tricky Blondie could be when she saw a need for deception

"Well, I'll have Cindy check with his doctor. He may need to have some adjustments made to the prescriptions. When was the last time the medicine bottles were refilled?" J asked, but she realized Blondie wasn't about to part with any useful info.

"I don't know. I don't remember, but there's still some left in all three bottles. He doesn't take them everyday when I put them out for him. He says he doesn't always see them over on the window sill. That's where I leave them, 'cause that's where he sits every mornin' lookin' out at his fruit trees. Don't you go thinkin' that I'm gonna start baby sittin' him and his medicine," Blondie snapped. "You get that right out of that crazy city head of yours!"

After a moment's contemplation, Blondie spoke into the phone again. Responding in a tone that let J know how insulted she was, Blondie hissed, "He's a grown man, for Christ's sake. He should be able to get his own God damned pills. I'm not gonna be his Gypsy mother lookin' out for him every minute of every day.

"Well, I'll call Cindy," J persisted. "She's a Licensed Practical Nurse and she should be able to determine what's going on. Maybe she can take him in to see his doctor in the next couple of days. She can check with the pharmacy to verify the medicines being filled at the correct intervals," J said in a mustered intimidating voice that was intended to frighten Blondie into giving Mihal his medicines correctly.

J did have reason to doubt Blondie's honesty and accuracy. Blondie had a history where family and medicines were concerned. This time J trusted her own instincts, and not Blondie's vague interpretations of Mihal's medicine instructions.

Cindy was amendable to J's suggestion and she did take Mihal to his doctor's office for a follow up appointment. She also took the outdated Rx bottles to the pharmacy for verification. They hadn't been refilled in over a year. Mihal was given a diagnosis of severe congestive heart failure by his physician and admitted to the Clearfield Hospital for corrective therapy. His weakened heart muscle necessitated medication adjustments. Several days after being declared stable, he was discharged and released into Blondie's care.

Within two days, Mihal was again in trouble. He was dizzy, nauseated and experiencing great weakness. This time, J insisted on Blondie reading the medication labels. "I can't read the labels so good. I have beginnin' cataracts, you know. That affects my vision. You should know that much, if you're a real nurse," Blondie stressed. Her tone was attempting her usual cunning to elicit sympathy, while subtly giving only insulting wrath. Blondie had honed her attitude aptly.

"If you're having trouble with your vision, Ma, you should ask someone for help. There's no shame in that," J retorted.

Just what is her problem? Why is she so defensive all of a sudden? Is she looking for pity, is that it, J wondered? *Or was that a deliberate sort of dig at my nursing skills? Or is something else going on here?*

Once Blondie was able to read the medication labels, J realized Blondie had been giving Mihal a triple dose of Lanoxin, his heart medication, instead of the Erythromycin, an antibiotic.

"So, I got the two mixed up. I'm not a God damned doctor, you know. He takes a water pill four times a day, too," she added.

At that point, J was furious and not restraining her feelings. "If you don't know what you're doing, why don't you have Annamaria help you? She just lives down the road from you and she could be there in less than five minutes."

"Why would I want someone up here interfering in our business? He can take his own medicines. Startin' tomorrow, I wash my hands of the whole God damned mess," Blondie positioned her defensiveness quite effectively. She was roaring like a B29 going into combat.

"No, that won't do, Ma. I'm calling Annamaria right now. Dad needs to be seen in the emergency room tonight, and you need to see to it that he goes as soon as possible," J ordered.

"He could be suffering from a toxic overdose of the heart pill. That's a dangerous situation," she tried to explain to Blondie without igniting her mother's fuse again.

Once again, Mihal was admitted for overnight tests and medication readjustment. Blondie was not a happy farmer when the ambulance had pulled into the driveway earlier that evening at #11 Lemon Lane. Nor was she hospitable when the EMS crew insisted on transporting a weak, vomiting and dyspneac Mihal to the hospital.

"I don't see why he has to go to the hospital again. He just needs to start takin' his medicines at the right times," she argued. "Younse are makin' me a nervous wreck. I'm the one who should be in the hospital for a few days. I need to get some rest from all of this hellabalou," Blondie said in a piping voice to Annamaria as Mihal was being rolled out of the house on a gurney.

As the ambulance drove away and headed for the hospital, Mihal's anxiety level appeared to be decreasing. His breathing became less labored with the oxygen he was inhaling through the nasal cannula.

Meanwhile, Blondie spewed her harbored hate for J to Annamaria. Speaking with vengeful animosity, Blondie's eyes glared while her face and neck flushed a roseola red. "That bitch is still stickin' her nose into my affairs. It's a good thing she's not here right now or I'd knock those perfectly straight teeth right out of that mouth of hers."

After resting comfortably through the night, Mihal was discharged the next morning. Once again, he was declared stable by his doctor.

"Did they give Dad any new pills to take?" Annamaria asked her mother.

"Yeah and don't worry, they wrote everything down on a sheet of paper so I could understand what to do. Now leave me alone about all of this medicine shit," Blondie snarled.

Annamaria noted that Blondie's cold inflection could have frozen a waterfall and caused her renewed worry.

The next day, an astute Annamaria noticed that Mihal's breathing was labored again. "Did you give him his pills," she asked Blondie.

"Don't you start that with me this mornin' already," Blondie answered her youngest daughter.

Annamaria decided to spend the night at her parents home. Somehow, something just didn't jive. *Maybe, if I spend the night, I can see what and how she's giving him his medicines. He should be getting better. He should be breathing easier and his feet shouldn't be swelling with water again. If he's like this in the morning, I'm calling his doctor again. I don't care what she thinks or says,* Annamaria thought before retiring for the night in her former upstairs bedroom.

This was the bedroom that four of the younger girls had shared after Baba had died. *I remember how scared I was the first few nights I slept in this bedroom. Adela kept scaring us with ghost stories. Adela said the floor creaks were Baba walking across the room. Oh, Adela, you always were the instigator,* Annamaria remembered before drifting into a deep slumber.

It's two o'clock. What's Ma doing calling someone on the phone at this time of the morning? Annamaria asked herself the question, as she stooped near the curlicued floor vent in Baba's old bedroom. She was unashamedly eavesdropping on the hushed and fragmented conversation Blondie was having with someone.

"Well, it's done. He's gone. Yeah, just now. Well, I'll have to call the ambulance, that's all. They won't need to do no autopsy, 'cause he was discharged from a hospital within the last forty eight hours. No, Vic, you can come in the morning. Annamaria is here tonight. I'm gonna go wake her up now," Blondie whispered just before hanging up the phone's receiver.

Annamaria had quickly reached the bottom stair and stood frozen there. *What in the Hell is going on here,* she wondered.

"What's happened? Why did you just call Vic?" the daughter asked the mother.

"Your Dad's gone. He took his last breath just a few minutes ago. I heard him moan and heard him gasp for air, but then it was over. The ambulance is on its way." Blondie said.

Blondie stood with her arms crossed in front of her breasts. She had a way of planting her whole body so as to stand as stoic as a mannequin. Her face didn't change its fixed expression as she handed Annamaria a pharmacy bag that was still stapled closed. The white paper bag contained three Rx bottles filled with pills.

"Here, throw these into the stove's fire. I'll go and unlock the front door," Blondie sternly muttered to Annamaria.

Blondie had stretched out her right arm and was pointing to the kitchen coal stove which was blazing fiercely on this cold windy February night. "Do it! Do it right now, I said," Blondie commanded.

Tearing the bag slowly across the top, Annamaria noted the three Rx bottles. "You didn't give him any of these? You didn't even open the bag, did you?" she asked.

Annamaria could see that bottles hadn't been opened. The cautionary sticker was still intact across the lid.

In retrospect, Annamaria didn't recall her Mother admit to having given Mihal his morning discharge medication.

Beginning to shiver, a distraught Annamaria began to realize what hadn't been done. "Oh, my God! What have I done? Why didn't I check his medicines?" Annamaria sobbed to her mother.

Blondie paid no heed to her daughter's misery. Instead, she screamed, "Here comes the ambulance. Hurry up and throw them into the damn fire. Just do it! What in the Hell are you waitin' for? You had better do it right now or I'll blame you for everything."

Annamaria was a grown woman, but she found that she could still be intimidated by Blondie. It was as though the old fear had never left her soul and was gripping her body in a spasm of shivers.

Grabbing Annamaria's arm, Blondie pulled the young shocked woman nearer to the hot stove. Lifting one of the stovetop's circular lids, Blondie shook Annamaria's arm jostling the bag of medicines out of her daughter's hand and into their kitchen Plegethon. "You just keep your mouth shut about those pills. As far as I'm concerned we didn't get no pills when they sent your dad home the other day. Who knows what his nurse could have done with them?" Blondie deceptively reasoned, eerily pushing Annamaria to the side and away from the hot iron coal stove with its river of Hade's fire.

Blondie was correct in her knowledge that an autopsy wouldn't be necessary. None was ordered and none was requested. To Blondie, the only necessity was a funeral and that she did manage to arrange.

During the wake, Blondie sat stiffly in a folding chair at the foot of the casket. Her disconcern caused some of her children to wonder just who was the real stiff in this viewing room. During the visitation hours she coyly greeted relatives, friends and neighbors, many of whom had lost their own spouses already. She feigned sympathy, but she didn't cry when condolences were expressed. She just sat there, appearing either complacent or preoccupied.

She later told her old neighbor, Big Annie, "After all these years, my tears for Mihal are down there in that old shit house."

When recapping Blondie's sentiments to her husband, Big John, later that evening, Big Annie sarcastically remarked, "What a legacy. She could have found something nice to say about that good old boy after being married to him for over fifty years."

The couple of old friends had been sitting on their front porch glider, swinging back and forth in a casual manner. "What a legacy," Big Annie repeated. They reached for each other's hand, clasped tightly, and then let the tears for their old friend roll down their faces. They'd mourn and comfort each other. There was no room for any sympathy for Blondie on that glider that day, or any day thereafter.

After fifty six years of marriage, not too many of the original conglomerate of friends, neighbors or relatives remained. However, Mihal and Blondie's children and grandchildren were visible in all corners of the funeral home. Mihal's children and their families, ranking in order from the Pet the eldest to Annamaria the youngest, had arrived with their youngsters. They were almost as strangers as they stood making small talk with their rarely seen siblings or cousins.

All eleven of Mihal and Blondie's surviving children had scattered to different lifestyles in different states. They had become a variety of personalities, each influenced by their chosen careers or lifestyles. Mihal had taught and stressed to his children that each had an obligation to themselves to be an individual. It seemed they'd taken heed.

Sister greeted sister as they arrived at the funeral home to pay respect to their father's remains. Even semi-hugs seemed strained for some of the siblings, but for others there were genuine warm embraces.

Two brothers arrived. Jake came alone, as everyone had predicted he would. He'd long been declared the black sheep, detached from his childhood family as well as separated from his wife and children. Still a selfish son-of-a-bitch, he waved off Pet when she attempted to tell him of her son's recent auto accident. "I have so many problems of my own that I don't want to hear anyone else's," he remarked coldly, before turning to walk away from her.

Jake was still short and svelte. He was wearing the same handlebar mustache that was his trademark. *Strange how he came to wear that kind of a mustache* J thought. *That's the same style of waxed bristles that Ed Strang wore when he brought the cow feed to our house. I do believe Jake is making some sort of a statement, but to whom?*

Victor had grown to be a huge man. He stood six feet six and weighed over three hundred pounds. He had matured slowly into a gentle soul, but his good-natured intentions were often misunderstood. He was easily taken advantage of by the wayward chums he had a tendency to miscalculate. Blondie referred to him as a big dummy. Ironically, why then was it Vic whom Blondie had initially called after Mihal died?

Junior was a no show for the wake. He chose instead to have a personal early funeral morning viewing, long before anyone else was expected to arrive. He was alone when he said a solemn good bye to his father in the comforting solace of an empty viewing room. He attended the church service, but left early to avoid a confrontation with Blondie.

It was during the church service that Annamaria had felt an unexpected burst of cold air that caused her to become briefly chilled. She glanced to the rear of the church and caught a glimpse of Junior exiting the partially opened large glass door.

Junior had disparate views with Blondie and her opinion of his new wife. As chance would have it, she was another divorcee. So different were these opinions that Junior moved to the west coast just to get away from his meddlesome mother. Junior's loose wife would eventually prove Blondie to be a proficient mantis. Perhaps she had a bit of Gypsy powers herself!

Months later, Annamaria had confided to J all of the perplexing happenings that led to Mihal's passing. The two sisters were baffled by Blondie's behavior during the last episodes of Mihal's illness. Neither woman could comprehend why Blondie had failed to properly administer Mihal's medications to him.

Annamaria said she had asked Blondie, "Why didn't you just give him his heart pills?"

"What I did was none of your business. It's for me, and only me, to know," an indignant Blondie had responded.

Annamaria continued telling J about her conversation with their mother. "She blasted me for having the audacity to ask her any questions. You should have heard her, J," Annamaria said. "She screamed at me, the way she used to when we were children."

Annamaria said that Blondie had coldly stated, "As far as I'm concerned, his doctor didn't treat him properly. He lived long enough anyway. I wasn't gonna get stuck takin' care of him, too. I took care of enough old people in *this God damned house*. First it was his sickly dad, then his bitchin' mother. Then I got stuck bein' a nurse to my own mother and my lazy, good for nothin' stepfather. When do I get taken care of? That's a good question now, isn't it?"

Annamaria had noted *Ma didn't answer her own question this time. What could that mean?*

As fate would have it, Annamaria would eventually get her answer.

"You made me toss the pills into the stove. You made me throw away evidence, didn't you?" Annamaria said she'd implicitly expressed her guilt to her mother.

But Blondie was a shrewd one and had countered defensively. "You can't make me admit I did anything wrong. Did you see the nurse give him the pill bag? I didn't. If you did, then why didn't you give your Dad his medicines?"

"My God, what kind of a person are you? Do you realize what you did?" Annamaria said she'd defiantly asked. "Are you saying that you'll have me take the blame for Dad not getting the medications you were handed when he was discharged?"

"Shut up, or you'll be the sorry one explaining things. Get out of here and keep that trap of yours shut," Blondie had warned her youngest daughter.

"I couldn't believe what I'd just heard," Annamaria said. "Blondie turned on her heel, left the kitchen to go sit and watch a television show. I couldn't belileve that either. She acted like it was just another day in a soap opera!"

Not another day in the soap opera, J's thoughts bantered. *It's another day in that damned house where lies, tensions and emotions have always hung heavy in the air, much like those sparkling dust particles Baba and I viewed through the weathered barn slats so long ago.*

Mihal was laid to rest three days after he died. The day of his death had begun with a frosty morning, but the early afternoon brought a balmy spring sort of mid-day, with a short mild shower in the evening.

The day of his wake was a sunny and clear, sixty-five degree, spring-like day, which was unusual for February.

The funeral morning arrived with squalling snow flakes and hard sluicing rain that intensified as the temperatures plummeted to the teens. Just as Mihal's casket was being lowered into the prepared earthen site, a huge gust of wind blew causing a whirlwind of dried brown leaves to spiral as though Heaven bound. The green protective canopy billowed upward at the same time, away from the newly dug grave.

The old Gypsy woman had told stories of the soul's destiny being written in the winds. She said loved ones would be reunited with their families in the great beyond if all four seasons presented themselves before the dead were placed in their final resting place. She said the myth was predetermined, and that a huge gust of wind would occur when the coffin was laid to rest. This was the Divine's way of propelling the deceased person's pure soul to the heavens.

J remembered Baba's ethereal words and paused. *Anna and Josef have taken their son home. All is right in their Gypsy heaven. I can only pray for as much.*

J also remembered Mihal's farewell words last October. Searching Mihal's sad grey eyes, J had hugged him for what would become the last time. "I love you, Dad," was whispered instead of a final sounding "good bye".

Mihal didn't waste a second of time as he spontaneously answered, "I love you too, Joni."

As she and Ben were strolling slowly to their car that warm October day when they had visited with their beloved Mihal, J turned to gaze at the only father she'd known. He was smiling as he reflectively said, "You're still holding hands after all these years. That's nice. I like that."

Gently holding Ben's strong hand as she now walked away from Mihal's gravesite this freezing cold February morning, J solemnly thought *that's the warm memory of my Dad that I want to hold onto.*

WHERE DOES THE TIME GO

When time flies, where does it go?

Does it wrap its sinewy arms around events and just take flight?

Does it courageously kidnap memories and bury them deep into the portals of the mind?

Does it just disappear and take heartfelt treasures with it?

Does it numb the spirit with a knock out punch leaving scattered bits of the soul to deal with what's left of one's world?

Is that what happened to Blondie, J wondered. *Did she leave the world behind to cope with her heartbreak and her frustrations, or did the world leave her behind never to catch up with its revolutions?*

Looking at the old woman sitting in a wheel chair at the middle of a nursing home dining room was a difficult sight for J, as her daughter, to comprehend. What used to be a feisty buxom blonde had been reduced to a slumped and pruned hag.

Is this the result of someone's revenge, J thought. *Is this the workings of an old gypsy woman's curse, or perhaps worse was this disparate end due to Blondie's own doings?*

The unkempt appearance of Blondie's disheveled and mismatched clothing would have been uncharacteristic of any self-righteous woman, even a lowly coal miner's wife. The stretched gray men's sweatshirt had breakfast egg yolk and black coffee dribbled down its front, while the non-matching dark green sports sweatpants revealed an odorous diaper leakage all the way down to the knees. In years past, the short frazzled hairdo would have been so unacceptable to Blondie. Ah, but if she could have only stood at a mirror to appraise what was once long honey colored waves, what would she have uttered?

A Polish tune played on the outdated portable record player that was setting on a chrome utility cart in the far corner of the dining room. Blondie's bare left foot had fallen off of the wheelchair's foot rest. Her shoed right foot clung to the other foot rest. Her slippers were soiled brown and the one lay on the floor. Her bare toes were tapping to the beat of the polka's 1-2-3 rhythm. Her lips were moving, singing along with the Polish words in a weak squeaky alto-voice. Her eyes were glazed over, lost in a yesteryear's memory. She wore a slight smile on her lips as she sat quietly singing, but that glint of contentedness quickly dissipated when her visitors said "Hello".

"Who's there? Who's saying hello?" Blondie quietly drawled from a barely opened mouth. "Is it time to eat yet, or did we eat already?" the barely audible voice asked her visitors.

Before they could answer, she repeated her original question with a little more vigor. "Who's there? Answer me. I don't see well anymore."

"It's J and Ben. Do you remember us?" J asked.

"Oh, yeah, I remember you two alright,' she snarled, her mouth twisted in a grimace. Under her breath, she added sarcastically, "You're Mihal's pets."

"We brought your two great granddaughters to see you. Do you want to visit with us for a while?" J asked, as her eyes surveyed the dining hall with the tables neatly set for the resident's luncheon.

"No, I don't want to visit with anyone," Blondie mumbled as though her mouth were full of marbles.

"It's almost lunch time. Where do you sit to eat, Ma?" J asked. Blondie didn't speak. She chose to ignore the rest of J's questions.

After a moment's hesitation though, she confided, "I'm not good enough to eat in here. I eat in my home. I just want to go back to my bedroom and sleep."

Blondie's verbalizing sounded strangely muffled. Noting the absence of Blondie's upper dentures, J asked, "Where are your false teeth, Ma? I don't think I've ever seen you without them."

"I don't know. Somebody said they got lost with my last load of laundry," she angrily quipped. "Somethin' is always getting' lost around here. They can't find my rosary beads, neither. It's hard to tell what will be next. Maybe it'll be me," she grumped.

Between several throat clearings, she managed, "I'm tired, so go away," before feigning fatigue. Closing her eyes, she allowed her head to droop forward.

"Do you want us to wait for a while or do you want us to go?" J asked Blondie, who appeared to have dozed off to sleep.

"Just go," she responded, her eyes still clamped shut. In an almost inaudible whisper, she managed, "You're a whore. Younse girls were all whores. My boys were my favorites."

After all these years, she's still trying to intimidate her grown child. Well, it doesn't work that way anymore, J decided. *How odd, Ma, you never took the time to encourage my strengths, but instead chose to prey on my weaknesses. On how many of your children did you use this ploy,* J wondered.

"How would it be if I pushed you back to your room? Maybe then you'll want to eat or visit for a short while," J suggested, while she aimed the wheelchair down the corridor to Blondie's castle.

As the rotating wheels of the rolling chair swoosh-swooshed with each rotation, J tried to engage her mother in some light conversation. "I saw the sign out front about Bingo this morning. Did you play?"

Blondie answered, again in a muffled voice, "They said I did."

"Did you win anything," J pursued.

"They told me I did," Blondie said. Her voice became less raspy after she coughed again.

"What did you win?" J quizzed.

"Who gives a rat's ass what I won. They just give out junk anyway," Blondie snapped in a sharp tone. She wasn't sleeping now, that was a certainty.

"Well, here we are. You're home," J stated matter of factly, as she pushed the wheelchair further into the room leaving Ben and the two girls standing near the doorway. "Which bed is yours, Ma?" J asked.

Blondie pointed to the one nearest the door. *She can't even gaze out of the window to watch the seasons change. How sad must that be?* J asked herself the question, knowing full well what the answer was.

One shared nursing home bedroom was all that remained to eclipse a woman who was a beauty in her youth and had married a handsome Hungarian gypsy-woman's son. Together they had owned hundreds of acres of farm and coal rich land. Now her domain was reduced to a room with plain ecru painted walls, not the colorful floral and fern wallpaper Blondie had so relished in her own home. Now when she lay in her bed, she had only the cheap, cream colored block ceiling to stare at, not the silver-shaded fleur-de-lis squares that she had installed in her old farm house bedroom. The plain tan tiled flooring bore no resemblance to the speckled linoleum that used to be favored in her kitchen or the fern pattern she so relished in her bedroom. There were no rag rugs to shield the cold morning floor when her bare feet touched the tiling. She had a difficult time maneuvering her edematous legs on the slick flooring, so it was no wonder she'd chosen to confine most of her waking hours to sitting in a wheelchair.

Blondie shared the solitary bathroom with one roommate. Blondie's visitors couldn't help but notice the strong urine odor emanating from that room's toilet. It was overwhelming, burning the mucosa of the nostrils with every inspiration. "Do we have to stay in here? It smells pretty bad," the two young girls asked. With their grandfather, Ben, in tow, the two little girls made a hasty retreat to the outer corridor.

Blondie had been wheeled into what was now her home. A tray of food had been set before her. She was served all of her meals in her room. The Head Nurse said Blondie was too sloppy with her food to be permitted to eat in the dining room. The nurse said Blondie's poor eyesight, combined with decreased eye-hand coordination made it difficult for Blondie to eat alone. So, one of the staff would stay and encourage her to eat, but usually the aide was paying more attention to the soap opera on the television screen than to what Blondie was doing with her food.

The alert and oriented residents frowned upon those who were not meticulous with their eating habits, and Blondie had certainly slipped backwards with her dining room etiquette. In her old age, as in her prime, Blondie was still shunned by those who claimed superiority. Even in a nursing home filled with aging peers, Blondie must have felt the intimidation of inferred inequality.

"I don't want any dinner. Besides, it smells like an old shit house in here. Who could be hungry in this hole?" Blondie asked as she moved the over-bed table away with a fairly brisk shove demonstrating a reserve of strength.

As an adroit evasion, she dropped her chin against her sternum and seemed to doze off again. *Seemed* was the proper word to describe her actions as she once again opened her eyes partially and spoke softly, but precisely, "Go, get out, you stupid whore. I don't need you standin' and watchin' over me."

"Do you know who we are, Ma," J asked patiently, as though she were talking to a long lost relative.

"Yeah, I know. I'm not as dumb as people think I am. I fooled younse all, now get out. Younse think I got that Alzheimer's. Keep thinkin' that, if you want to," she said with a sneer to convey her message.

"How many times do I have to tell younse all the answers to your questions before you turn around and get out?" Blondie had rallied, this time with a fairly secure voice.

Raising the cane she'd been clinging in her right hand, she shrieked, "Get out before I use this cane to give you the damn whippin' you deserve for pickin' on my Jakey boy."

"He's dead now, so's Junior. My boys, my poor boys are gone," she moaned.

"Get out, you God damn whore," was the very last mean-spirited utterance J would ever hear from her mother's mouth.

Kindness was never on of her strong suits, unless it came with a price tag, J remembered.

With a heavy sigh and a laden heart, J walked out of her mother's *home* without saying "good bye". The last memory Blondie gave her daughter was one of a cane held high in the air, ready for the striking.

I am so discouraged that I don't even have the strength to raise my hand and wave to my own mother. What a pity. What a waste of a human life J realized as she walked toward her waiting family.

"Let's go get you girls a creamsicle. How does that sound to you two sweetie pies?" J asked the precious little ones waiting in the corridor. They didn't speak, they didn't need to as their eyes sparkled when they smiled their answer and ran to hug their grandmother, JoJo.

Two months later, Blondie passed on to the great beyond. Her death wasn't really unexpected. She had outlived half of her children. She had reached the ripe old age of ninety three. Most of those years were spent as an overbearing tyrant. She'd always said her best friends were a weeping willow switch, a rubber hose or a hearty whack with whatever was within her reach. Fear was how she kept her family walking the straight and narrow. Her methods worked for some of her kids, but not all.

Even thunder and lightening had been useful tools to further the existential angst her children would endure under her tutelage. "If you don't behave, God will strike you down with a bolt of electricity. Now go hide under your bed if you want to be saved. If you have any sins to confess, you had better start praying while you're under there," she'd say, mocking their exposed fright. The kids would hear Blondie laughing as they ran up the stairs to hide and wait out the storm.

Many had witnessed her laughing when the kids shuddered at the first hint of a rain storm. Her verbal intimidation could be as effective as her switch lashings. Her cruel methods succeeded for some of her kids, but a few escaped unscathed, while a fewer still were simply allowed to escape undaunted.

J tried to remember any acts of kindness extended from Blondie during the eighteen years she had lived at #11 Lemon Lane. She thought of a few, but they were all ostentatious. Blondie's favored children or next-door neighbors reaped the rewards of her pretentious affection. She could act like a decent person if it was to her advantage, but Heaven help those who didn't live up to Blondie's expectations. The windows of the world would never see the real Blondie. There wasn't any sweetness in her smile. Her heart housed a framework of cruelty shingled with a spirit of meanness.

Hugs and kisses were extinct at #11 Lemon Lane. The closest extensions of affection came from Mihal, and those were a minimal hand holding or a tussle of the hair. Mostly, the inflection of his words conveyed tenderness, even when doling out punishments. After he had his heart attack, Mihal freely told his kids he loved them. He'd openly displayed his genuine affections for his kids in Blondie's presence.

"What the Hell are you goin' on like that for?" she'd ask rudely. "You look and sound like some old fool," she'd mock, expressing her sentiment with a her own belittling inflection.

The words "I love you" were not casually spoken by Blondie. If she felt the love, it was a secretive and a selective disclosure. Mihal had once confided to J that his wife hadn't ever said those three little words to him.

"That's somethin' this young generation started," Mihal had said to J and Ben during one of their visits with him.

He went on to explain, "In my day, we showed our love by bringin' home the bacon and keepin' a roof over the family's head. Anyway, that lovin' stuff is for the young. Blondie and me had our day in the hay, even if wasn't always with each other," he said, allowing an inadvertent chuckle to escape his throat.

His eyes had glazed over allowing his mind to temporarily drift back to a world afflicted with forgotten memories, where affectionate smiles tempered all woes. As was his life, his chuckle was also ambiguous; it was neither a laugh nor a sob. "Yeah, the lovin' stuff is for the young," he repeated dreamily.

Oh, Dad, what wonderful memories you've left me. Thank you for being a gentle man. You demonstrated to your children what kindness could bring to our little sheltered corner of the world. You let us take that away when we left. What a gift to build a dream on, she thought.

J stood quietly content within her own cerebral world when a thought finally dawned on her. *I see what's missing here.*

The sadness of Blondie's passing became apparent at her wake vigil as J realized that in a room full of friends and relatives, she was all alone with her bucolic thoughts. *There's no laughter or cheerful banter, no old comical memories being discussed. There are no tears being shed for a lost mother who could never call that damned house "home", despite all of the beauty within its walls. You chose to overlook all the love and goodness growing in your own country garden, Ma. Why? Will you receive a harsh tribute from your God after the life of cruelty you caused others to endure? If there are truly wandering spirits after death, Ma, what does yours think of your legacy? I know what I think of it. There's no Mother Matriarch to remember here, that's for certain. Your children never became the persons they could have been with a loving mother's guidance and encouragement. Can you spend eternity with that knowledge tucked into a crevice of your heart? Are you at peace and happy now . . . finally? I hope so.*

J prayed as she viewed her mother's body that was dressed in a pink negligee. Her remains were lying in her sky-blue satin lined casket. *If Blondie were able to speak, she'd ask for a flannel night gown. She would have hated this flimsy transparent nightdress,* J surmised in her humble mind.

J watched as her siblings took their turn saying "good bye". They seemed to be seeing the same empty shelled Mother she had just walked away from. No one cried as they passed the open casket.

J's thoughts tangled with intrusion on what should have been the family's precious final moments. Instead of listening to the preacher's words, J's soul harkened and spoke to her mother's.

You could have been a revered temple, if only you hadn't been such an angry person. No child deserves to be punished for the sins of a parent. Yet, that's what you encouraged to take place for so many years at #11 Lemon Lane in what you called that damned house.

You never did let go of your dream for a home of your own, did you, Ma? I understand. It was a deep regret of yours, and you made everyone suffer the consequences for that one miserable fact, didn't you? Even Jake, your Jakey boy, was a pawn in your revenge, wasn't he?

You once told me that dreams are for the ignorant and you said that was the reason you had given up any hope of having any dreams of your own. Why were you so afraid of them becoming a reality? If you could have only known that your ignorance and your failed dreams were of your own doing. If you would have allowed yourself to have an open mind, or an open heart, you would have found peace and joy within the walls of that beautiful house that you, and you alone, damned.

Your children and grandchildren could have been living proof of a lifetime of love. Instead, you chose to shun them, and as a result you ended your life existing in a nursing home, alone and withered like an old sea dog. The workers in the home said you were a feisty one, swinging your cane at anyone who got in your way. Did someone finally retaliate and swing back? Annamaria didn't. Maybe she should have, and maybe then she wouldn't have suffered so. We, all of your children, suffered at your hand though, didn't we? I wish I could understand why. I wish I could cry for you, but I can't. My heart only weeps and mourns for the mother I never had.

Many years ago, the grandchildren had tucked a pack of Black Jack chewing gum and a pack of Red Man tobacco as loving mementoes under the white satin blanket that cloaked their precious grandfather Mihal in his casket.

Today, for whatever their reason, the grandchildren chose not to leave anything as a memento for their grandmother Blondie.

J didn't agree with their sentiment, though. She chose to send Blondie off to her reward with a small orange ceramic kitten tucked and nestled under Blondie's blue coverlet.

Attached was a note:

> Dear Mom, I hate you, Love, J

JUST LET ME WALK

"Stop the car, Ben. Just let me walk Lemon Lane one last time," J insisted. She tugged at his sleeve inducing him to stop the car.

"I need to do this for closure. I know it's hard for you to understand, but something is telling me to walk, not ride, this quarter mile. I need to listen to the memories floating in the breezes that blow the length and breadth of this road."

J gazed out of the car's window. Oblivious to the world around them, J's mind raced with the many lingering memories of Gunther. "Just let me take my time and reminisce in my own way. My early life was shaped by so many events that occurred here. I just need to clear those cobwebs from my mind. Park the car and wait by the old gate at #11. I'll be there in a few minutes," she told her husband of nearly fifty years as she literally darted from the car for one last reflective stroll down Lemon Lane.

I feel as energetic as a child again. I feel like kicking a stone up this old road, she mimed in her psyche. *Boy, I wish I had a nickel for every time I did that when I was a kid.*

"Memories do have a way of slipping a spring into your steps, don't they kid?" A voice from overhead seemed to bellow softly.

Glancing upward, J could have sworn it was Mihal's voice whispering to her from the Heavens. She knew that voice. If she lived to be a hundred years old, she'd recognize his voice anywhere. She could picture his overalls and plaid flannel shirted image standing at the crest of Lemon Lane's knoll. She could have sworn she'd seen him take off his baseball cap and scratch his head. *Yeah, I'll bet you're still walking these hills, aren't you Dad? These acres will always belong to you, no matter who takes them over,* she decided.

It hardly seemed possible that almost fifty years had drifted away since she had moved from Gunther. Yet it was as though time had played another trick on someone. This time it was her. In the blink of an eye, J's clear memories began resurfacing. Recollections tugged at her heart strings from a multitude of directions.

A brisk breeze kicked up and she imagined *rag tails on homemade kites flapping in the strong autumn winds.* The images were so vivid that she could count the knots holding the bows in place. In the wee dark corners of her memory she recalled *yellowed newspapers, twigs, and flour paste as the only ingredients necessary to design a kite. Their drawing board was on the restricted space of the speckled-linoleum kitchen floor. How many of those hand-hewn kites became the next morning's kindling to start the kitchen coal-stove's fire needed for Blondie to cook the morning's oatmeal?* J wondered if on some days there would have even been hot oatmeal if it weren't for the kindling those kites provided.

Blondie's early morning mood was not one to be reckoned with and neither was the evenings gathered damp kindling. *If only that old kitchen coal stove could talk. What curious stories it would tell about the people who savored its heat.* Wrapping her arms across her chest, J tried to ward off some of the chill from the cool winds as she smiled in amusement at her meandering thoughts.

She remembered *so many homemade toys created in that meager kitchen.* She pictured *all of the kids gathered around those stove legs soaking up the fire's warmth on cold winter days or rainy spring evenings. How those engrossing originals fostered an unappreciated sense of creativity that had been honed in her childhood. There were hand drawn paper dolls wearing Sears catalog dresses, scrap wallpaper valentines, a barn door board whittled into a baseball bat, loose ball-bearing marble games, carbon paper pictures and mimeographed Christmas cards that were hand crayoned by every kid in a household.*

Each child's piece of art was truly an unappreciated masterpiece. Blondie was more apt than not to describe these mementoes with her own glowing critique, "What do you want me to do with that? Get that piece of junk outa here."

As J ambled up the familiar roadway, her emerging thoughts only intensified the growing pains that were experienced in *that damned house. None of us understood the necessity of chores or handiwork. We only realized the immediate gratification or the dour frustration that whiled away the misting spring dawns or the balmy summer sunsets.*

Thinking retrospectively, J remembered that Blondie often said, "There's a method to my madness."

As a child, J didn't comprehend that sentence. She still wasn't sure if she understood Blondie's inept motives or cruel methods. What she certainly did comprehend was that a clean home, good hygiene and earned self-respect had definitely been instilled in her brain while she was growing up. She was certain those virtues would continue with her for the rest of her living days.

As her mind reeled backward to the memory of flying kites, J raised her chin and tilted her head to get a better view of the clear blue sky overhead. The blueness remained dotted with billowy marshmallow clouds slowly drifting toward the east. *Boy, how many times we amused ourselves with those fanciful and imaginative formations. How naïve we were to think we were the only kids in the whole world to see whales or poodles or cupids in those vapors,* J mused. The renewed memories didn't impede the smile that broke out anew on her face.

It didn't take long before the wind swirled some misguided dust across the now asphalted street. *How many times had we wished this macadam road wasn't covered with those waist-high snow drifts in those harsh Pennsylvania winters? How we all had dreaded walking shoes-in-hand through the sloshing mud after the heavy spring downpours. Boy, do I remember those mud puddles, the ones that soon became cracked dust bowls after the summer's Heavenly oven worked its baking magic.*

Photos in her mind recalled how this macadam road was always laden with ruts. Pot holes were ever present and had to be dodged by the young hot rodder, or the slower paced Sunday driver. Weekly neighborhood dirt crews filled the holes, only to see them replaced by new ones within a few days. Often a mere wind or a rain storm would blow or wash away the loose dirt, and then the work would need repeated in a day or two. These early proving grounds provided a young road crew the opportunity to learn a whole new language, one not found in any Webster's dictionary.

"Just look at this smooth street now," J said aloud to the wind. "Oh Dad, you would have loved driving on this."

Stepping slowly along on the glorious smooth pavement, J happily noted *after all these years it's hard to imagine that there's still clusters of pussy willow bushes growing in that small marshy bog. How we loved picking those twigs for an Easter bouquet. Just knowing the buds were blossoming meant spring and warm weather were on their way. We kids knew that soon the roadway's borders would be blooming with clumps of wild violets amidst the wavering tall wild grasses.* She couldn't resist. She bent and picked a nosegay of violets. She'd press them in a book and frame them someday . . . maybe.

Walking further, astonishingly enough J found a patch of rusty-leafed trailing arbutus with its tiny pink-waxen lilies. *I don't even need to bend forward to smell that recognizable fragrance. How amazing that these gifts from God survived all these years. Oh goodness gracious, there are Ma's favorite wild red rose bushes. They're still thriving, and so are the wild black-cap berry vines. I wonder if anyone picks the berries for baking or preserving these days. A blackberry pie used to be such a summer treat!*

I see someone was smart enough to place a drain pipe for that ever-flowing stream still trickling toward the frog pond. Finally, the water goes under, instead of over, the roadway. Dad would have thought that a modern marvel, that's for sure.

Can that be tadpoles? I see a cluster of frog eggs and pollywogs floating in that bunch of cat-o-nine tails at the edge of the stream. No matter what happens in this great universe, life and nature just continue to thrive, don't they? J was enjoying her stroll down memory lane. Knowing what a struggle growing up on Lemon Lane was, who would have thought that she'd find some memories to rejoice in?

And just as life goes on, J walked on. Nearing #11 Lemon Lane, her imagination heard melodic polka music with its oom-pah-pah beat being played on the grandfather's Polish concertina. She could hear the children's silly laughter and their light-hearted singing. Someone was shouting, "Hey Dad, get your spoons and tap along." *I'd give anything to see our Dad play his silver soup spoons one more time,* she thought.

Another thing I remember about Lemon Lane was the time Dad tried to teach Ma to drive. She couldn't remember any instructions he'd told her, and he couldn't stop laughing at her feeble attempt to keep the car on the road. They ended up in a ditch and the neighbors had to help Dad push the car out. Ma never tried to drive again, but Dad sure would break out laughing anytime the subject was broached. He always found delight in ducking Blondie's retaliative attempt at swatting him with any object within her reach. Her favorite was the old canvas flyswatter.

Getting closer to the gate at #11, J could see Ben sitting in their car. His head was tilted back as though he were napping while waiting for her to complete her gaited journey to the old homestead. *Go ahead, rest for a few minutes, Honey. This has been a long day for you, too.* She smiled at the thought of the man waiting so patiently for her. Theirs had been a good marriage. *Reunited star-crossed lovers? Is that even in the realm of a possibility?* J's thoughts drifted, much like the billowing clouds overhead.

As she continued her stroll, J took a long hard stare at *that damned house*. Annamaria had tried to revamp the old structure, but it had begun as a four room log cabin and never did rise above that status. Even with the additional dining room, parlor and two more upstairs bedrooms added to the rear, the shape had retained its distinguishing features. Despite getting a new exterior shell of white aluminum siding with red shutters for decoration, the house held onto its cabin-like pretense. Although the front porch was eventually enclosed, the large picture windows allowed the new sunroom to maintain the ambience it always had. That improvement would have been to Anna's liking.

In the early years, any music from Anna and Josef's wide front porch was an open invitation for the neighbors to come on over and join in the singing and the dancing. There was a different disposition once the house became Blondie's. Any music played during Blondie's reign usually stayed indoors and in the kitchen, with only an occasional music fest held outside on the porch under Mihal's supervision. Once the house became Annamaria and Denny's, the music stopped all together.

As Annamaria's reign took hold, every room was redecorated. The kitchen became modernized and the pantry became the bathroom. Blondie had been displaced as Queen of #11 Lemon Lane. Blondie refused to discuss the modernizing going on in her kitchen, let alone the entire house. Bitter was a good word to describe Blondie's attitude in those noisy reconstructive days, when she realized her house had been staked and claimed by her youngest daughter. There was no doubt in Blondie's mind that Annamaria's slick take-over had been encouraged by her shifty husband, Denny the Yahoot. It was 1994 and finally *that damned house* had cabinetry galore, hot and cold running water, and indoor plumbing. Annamaria did the old house proud, but the Gypsy curse wasn't done yet. Not by a long shot! Even Blondie knew that!

As J walked the final yardage to the gate at #11, she recalled her very last visit with Mihal and Blondie. It was in the fall, a few months before Mihal died. "You two are my success story," he said proudly.

"I'm glad I saw the love you had for one another. It did my heart good to know you went out into the world with only your raw ambition and determination to make a good life, Joni. I feel proud when I think of you and Ben. I just want you both to know that." Mihal spoke with conviction, as he shared his sincere thoughts with them during that final visit.

J's steps now felt light and carefree in comparison to the heaviness that had occurred during her childhood mountain jaunts when she and Mihal went trout fishing on Sunday mornings after Mass. Her memories flowed freely. *I can smell the moss, and the beech nuts and the sassafras roots. I can hear the roar of the rolling stream. I can hear the "whap" as the baited hook hit the water after the long cast. The laurel, the dogwood, and the aroma of the honeysuckle . . . they're all there, cast in my mind forever.*

My spirit feels elevated by ridding my heart of the cruel realities that were inflicted upon us as children in that damned house. The letting go is a transforming and healing forgiveness. I can actually feel it draining from my subconscious and my heart.

I hope you can hear me, Ma. You need to hear my thoughts. You need to know I transcended above your anger and your hatred. It's time to let go of the ugly, and remember the beauty.

My whole being left this place and this house when I married Ben. I went on to college. You can't even begin to imagine how educated I've become. I've applied my knowledge to assist and to give compassionate expertise to anyone in need. Thirty-five years of graphic experiences in the nursing professions has taught and equipped me with fortitude unlike any you could have ever foreseen. If you could only see the images of a life well spent that dance in my peaceful mind, I think you would be proud of all of my accomplishments, especially my happy marriage with Ben. I doubt that you'd ever admit it though. No, I'm certain that you wouldn't acknowledge any of your girl's trophies the way you touted your son's military accomplishments.

You know that I admired and watched the way that Dad treated people. He didn't fear extending a gentle hand to those in need. Remember the time that a tall, muscular black man came to our house and said he was hungry? You told him to go away, but Dad went to the door, and soon after speaking to him Dad decided the man could join us at our dinner table. Dad let him sleep in the hay loft that night, and then gave him milk and food to take on his journey in the morning. Do you remember how surprised Dad was to get a kind letter from that stranger some time later, along with a one hundred dollar bill? That arrived when Dad had only one dollar left in his wallet. That was all he had to his name that day. His next payday was almost two weeks away.

After Dad passed away, Ma, you chose to stay in what you had always referred to as that damned house. You could have traveled with some of your neighbors, visited your sisters in California or Detroit. You could have spent some time with your own children's families. Why didn't you spend some time getting to know your grandchildren? They'd have loved you for it, but instead you became even more of a stranger to them by steering clear of their lives. You remained in your prison, physically and mentally. It was of your own choosing. Why was it that you allowed only Annamaria to enter into your secluded life after you fell and broke your hip?

I could comprehend your decision to enter the rehab unit, but I could never figure out why you signed yourself into the nursing home. You weren't that old and *you were still able to take care of yourself and your house. What was the reasoning behind your decisions? Did you just give up and beat God to the punch?*

What were you so frightened of that you avoided all of your children? Were you shielding yourself from the sorrow of watching your children growing old right along with you? Or maybe you didn't want to see your favorites die before you did. Was that it?

Well, if that was your plan, it didn't work, did it? Your first to leave this earth before you was your Jakey boy, followed by Junior, then Pet, your first born, and finally your baby, Annamaria. Did you understand their passing, or did you feign that too? I refuse to believe that the mother in you didn't weep and mourn in the wee hours of your solitude just knowing that they all were gone within a nine month period. You had no way of knowing that you would soon follow those of your children. There had to be an inkling of love tucked tightly somewhere in the cracks of your perceived cold heart. There just had to be.

There was one thing your children couldn't understand. They questioned what on earth possessed you to sign over the house to Annamaria and her husband? You knew how Dad felt about her husband. Dad always referred to him as a yahoo, a skinny drug head and a no good bastard. You knew how Dad always said, "Don't trust a person with dark beady eyes or a thin upper lip." Annamaria's Denny had both! Did you sign over everything out of spite or revenge to the rest of the family? You knew Dad wanted his parent's home to be a family retreat for the children and grandchildren, so why did you give the home to Annamaria and her cunning husband? You should have known they'd find some reason to get you out of that damned house, especially once it was deeded over to them.

Despite everything, I still think you were smart enough to realize the significance of that one clause in your Last Will and Testament. You know the one, the clause allowing you to live at #11 Lemon Lane until your death. That was a moot deal, but you didn't see it coming, did you? The curse continues? Annamaria and Denny had inherited that damned house, but they didn't see the curse coming either, did they?

And, I guess, I have to wonder what really caused your death. I know your death certificate listed multiple thrombi and emboli, but what caused the large area of bruising to your abdomen? How did you really meet your end? Some of the staff members mentioned that you were pretty handy with your cane. Did you strike out at them the way you did to Annamaria. Did someone strike you back? Had they endured enough of your insolent cruelty?

In retrospect, I can see that you lived your life in anger, but at whom, and why? Your children will probably never know the real answer to those questions. Communicating cruelly was your strong suit, but loving gently was never in our deck of cards. What and how you communicated was your way of expressing hostility to your family. Your mean spirit was truly trash that even the devil wouldn't be willing to accept.

Was Annamaria telling truths when she said you were being vengeful to your children by giving the homestead to her? She told me that you were angry that none of your children had volunteered to keep you in their fancy homes. You know that simply was not the truth. Was Annamaria telling the truth that you were deliberately incontinent of urine and feces, and then claimed you were too weak to complete your own hygiene? Did you really feign weakness and Alzheimer's, and then force Annamaria to cleanse your private areas so you wouldn't get a urinary tract infection? She said she watched you grin the entire time she was washing the crap off your ass. How humiliated and embarrassed she must have been, but she bathed your behind out of love for you, her mother.

What was the reason for your vindictiveness and wrangling cruelty to your attentive daughter? Why did you whack your cane across her back causing her to receive a cracked vertebra? Annamaria told me how you asked her to tie your shoes, and when she stooped to do your bidding you hit her with your cane. She said you laughed boisterously when she screamed.

Why would a mother do that to her child? I guess if anyone would understand your penchant for being cruel, it was me. I remember being forcefully pushed off the back porch by you because I'd asked if we could keep a couple of newly born kittens. You and your Jakey boy had drowned the blind and pink hairless-newborns in a brown burlap bag down in the old frog pond. Do you remember that? I do. I was reminded daily for the first six weeks of my second grade. I had to wear a cast and a sling for a broken wrist and a dislocated shoulder. Do you remember how hard you laughed when the doctor told you about the x-ray results? You called me a big baby for trembling from the pain, but I didn't cry. That really pissed you off, didn't it? Do you remember that I wouldn't cry when you beat me with a willow switch, or with a belt, or with a rubber hose? Even as a toddler I refused to succumb to your inhumane brutality. What pleasure could you have ever derived from your actions? What? I'd like to know.

How many of the other children suffered your wrath after I married Ben and moved away from your damned house? Who broke your switches and threw them into the coal stove's fire? I know Cindy did, so did Marsha and Annamaria. They would tell me how frustrated you'd get when you'd reach to the hook behind the stove and find it empty of your pliant twigs. Even Dad told me how he had to limit his belts to one, the one holding up his pants, because he couldn't trust you not to use the buckle end to punish one of the kids for some stupid little infraction. I remember the time he swore on his parent's graves that he thought you were certifiably insane, but he couldn't and didn't do anything to harm you. He stuck by you through thick and through thin, didn't he, Ma?

In our own way, we all protected you. Not a one of your family ever admitted or revealed to the outside world what a life we tolerated in your damned house. We pretended our holidays were happy. We pretended our home life was as normal as the next kid's. We learned to hold our heads high and to be content when we wore hand-me-downs, even when they came from the neighbor's rag bag. We tolerated your mother's intimidation when we'd visit her house and she'd refer to us as filthy little bastards or whores, while you stood by and cackled as we'd blush cherry-red with embarrassment.

Thank God we encountered some positive adults who graced our lives as we were maturing. You should be grateful most of us were intelligent enough to grasp and appreciate their benevolence. How could we ever forget Mrs. LeCroix's countless acts of kindness and rainy-day car rides? Then there were Mrs. Lazlo's hearty toe-tingling bursts of laughter at our lousy jokes, and her late-night salty French fries at sleepovers. She never once complained about the work involved in doing her girls that midnight favor. When she referred to her girls, she always included us.

How about Aunt Eve's huge boxes of heart-sent Christmas cookies that were so tasty, or Uncle Booney's visits when each kid got his own gallon of ice cream to eat with a wooden spoon? And there was always Mihal's reliable and gentle paternal nature to sooth the hurts. Even Old Man Eisenberg's cold popsicles and day-old coconut cakes were generous gestures for your kids. And who could forget Pet's generosity with holiday treats and her ever-present tenderness. These were all examples of amiable souls worthy of a child's emulation. I thank God everyday for those virtuous persons I was fortunate enough to encounter during my childhood.

Yes, I think I'll hold on to the good thoughts, Ma. I'll concentrate on the ones that made me smile as I was growing up.

I remember the little kids giggling at the stupid sunfish that swallowed the end of a string with no hook or bait, and still got caught.

Do you remember your birthday bouquet of stinky dandelions on the kitchen table? The posies Dad insisted remain right where they were placed in that old jelly jar? You had one big hissy fit, but Dad just ignored you. What a triumphant moment that was for us kids!

Do you remember me making my first marble cake with melt-in-your-mouth, creamy chocolate frosting that everyone proclaimed as the best cake ever created at #11 Lemon Lane. Everyone ate a piece, except you, Ma. It was delicious. You missed a good thing.

I can still visualize Cindy lathering gobs of freshly churned butter on Dad's thick bread, toasted in a wire contraption over the open coal-stove's glowing embers. Then she'd stand right in front of him waiting for the hug that was to come. She'd stare as he enjoyed each bite of her special treat.

I can still grin at the thought of the kids gathered around the early morning kitchen table enjoying thick crème puddin' for breakfast. Somehow, after a hearty bowl of the sweet concoction everyone left the table wearing a smile, whether they arrived with one or not. That one indulgence soothed many hurts through the years.

And which of us could ever forget getting those affectionate good night hugs from Baba. Those were warm squeezes from a toothless old lady with licorice breath that would send a kid off to dreamland with a fuzzy feeling in their heart.

I thank God everyday for these invaluable and treasured memories. I hope you were able to take a few with you, where ever you went, Ma. I've made my own happy memories and I still carry my sunshine in my pocket. I have treasures galore. I've given in to forgiveness graciously, and now I've learned to gracefully say "Good bye."

J chuckled as she watched Ben dozing peacefully. He had fallen asleep while sitting behind the steering wheel waiting for her to arrive at the gate of #11 Lemon Lane. "Wake up, Honey," she sing-songed. "I'm here."

Smiling gently, she added, "We can go now, Ben. I've made my peace with this place. Let's head for home. I think tomorrow morning I'll make puddin' for breakfast. How does that sound to you?"

BUD

"Rub a dub, dub, baby in a tub,"
was what we'd sing to you.
You were our joy,
a precious little boy;
you were our morning dew.
Though the years have flown,
who could have known,
how much our love grew.
You're still our joy;
now a man,
no longer a boy.
Our gift from God, that's you!

To my son, Bud, I send my deepest appreciation for his computer technology and expertise.
Without his assistance, I would have spent countless hours in complete frustration. He saved me from myself.